street hungry

Also by Bill Kent

*Street Money*

*Under the Boardwalk*
*Down by the Sea*
*On a Blanket with My Baby*

# BILL KENT
## street hungry

Thomas Dunne Books / St. Martin's Minotaur ⋈ New York

THOMAS DUNNE BOOKS
An imprint of St. Martin's Press.

www.minotaurbooks.com

Library of Congress Cataloging-in-Publication Data

Kent, Bill, 1954-
   Street hungry / Bill Kent—1st ed.
      p. cm.
   ISBN 0-312-30847-7
   1. Obituaries—Authorship—Fiction. 2. Food industry and trade—Fiction. 3. Philadelphia (Pa.)–Fiction. 4. Organized crime—Fiction. 5. Journalists—Fiction. I. Title.

PS3561.E516S86 2003
813'.54--dc21

                             2003046831

First Edition: October 2003

10  9  8  7  6  5  4  3  2  1

*This book is for Elaine and Stephen,
who supported this effort with love.*

## author's note

Philadelphia does not have a neighborhood called Brideshead. All characters, locations, businesses, and food items in this story are imaginary and not intended to be a depiction or description of actual people, places, and things. As far as I know, nobody in Philadelphia has ever put plums on a cheesesteak.

Or so they tell me. . . .

# acknowledgments

I thank, again, my family and friends, for so much enthusiasm, encouragement, and generosity. Ruth Cavin, my editor, deserves special thanks, for liking this enough to want it to be better. Jake Elwell rendered agenting services. I'm grateful, also, to others: police officers, chefs, garage mechanics, members of the pharmaceutical industry and the medical and mortuary professions, and yes, a few demolition derby drivers, who shared some of their lives with me.

It seems to this reporter that there is a widespread tendency on the part of all human beings to believe that because a thing happens to a stranger, or to someone far away, it doesn't happen at all.

—Edward R. Murrow

# dead weight

The name of the man with the vegetables was Wisnitz but everybody
who bought from him, and even a few that didn't, called him Weight.
He'd stop his truck in front of a bus stop, a fire hydrant, up on the curb,
maybe even in front of somebody's garage door, and he wouldn't care,
because he knew he was providing a service to the community, and, in
the city, if you're providing a service—if you're a cop, a plumber, a car-
penter, an ambulance driver, a tow truck operator, a delivery man—then
you put your vehicle where you have to and you don't care if the bus can
get to the corner or you back up traffic all the way into the next neighborhood.

If you provide a service in a neighborhood, the rules of decorum do
not apply.

On that morning, the rush hour had come and gone. The streets were
clear of the drivers who will kill you if they are a minute late to work.

The man known as Weight Wisnitz didn't shave that morning. He simply didn't feel like it, and, in his line of work, if you don't feel like doing
something, you don't do it. His father had been boss at the Philadelphia
Navy Yard and because of that, or, maybe, because Weight's father had

been born in Poland and was lucky enough to make it in the Land of the Free where you were free to shave every day of the week, Tadieuz Wisnitz shaved every day.

His son was self-employed and when you're self-employed you are free to shave whenever you want, unless you are meeting the public. The public, of course, has expectations and if you sell produce for cheap, the public doesn't expect you should be making so much money that you'd be dressing decent and shaving every day.

So, in the land of the free, even unto the second generation, the freedom had more to do with what people thought of you, than what you thought of yourself.

Wisnitz wore shorts and a GO PHILLIES! T-shirt that, long ago, might have been white. The shorts/shirt combo, while affecting a decidedly casual air, made him look scrawnier than a scarecrow. Stuck halfway down his twisted nose were a pair of glasses grimy enough to be portholes on an ocean liner that had already sunk.

Weight did not get out of the truck as much as he swung one leg out, and then another, like a Pony Express rider who has braved the elements and stared down, or outrun, all kinds of nasty types, to be here, at this corner, to perform his service for the four people who now stood on the sidewalk beside the truck.

He went to the open flatbed of his truck, gazed past the jumble of crates and boxes. Then he impulsively plucked a handful of supremely purple plums from a box and, to prove that they were exactly what they appeared to be, bit into one so the juice exploded all over his face. He put the plum in his mouth, holding it between his teeth, and then came around and popped a plum into the hand of the breathtakingly beautiful girl in the running shorts and the T-shirt with BUY ART printed across her chest. He gave her a wink that said, "I got what you want."

This did not please the old woman in black next to her. She was wearing the uniform of a professional widow: a shapeless black dress, black sweater, black shoes and shawl. The woman was a little bit miffed that she'd known Weight before this half-naked girl was even born. More than that, this widow had become something of a local celebrity, appearing as an extra in two movies and one TV show (or was it two TV shows and one movie?) shot in South Philly, so that, whenever anybody recognized her on the street, she had to say that fame was not what it was cracked up to be, and that she had to spring for the video upgrade for her alarm system, and that, fame being what it is, the one thing she wanted was to be treated just like a normal person, even if the truth was she was talked into the upgrade by a no-good rip-off artist, and she really and truly enjoyed being treated like a celebrity, that she could get used to being treated like a celebrity.

So instead of treating her as she deserved, Weight Wisnitz gave the plum to the half-naked girl *first!* This was a low blow.

Behind the widow was a dignified man in a dark sport coat, white shirt, dark tie and black jef cap. His brown brogans gleamed.

For the old man, a peach or a pear or a coconut from Weight Wisnitz was a reason to be on the street, and smell the air and feel the sunlight on your face, and see all the changes in the neighborhood. It was also a chance to talk about everything except what he did for a living.

Weight Wisnitz liked seeing him, but Weight Wisnitz liked seeing just about anyone who would take from him. Talking to the customers Weight Wisnitz met on his route was part of the service he provided. It was a way of keeping in touch.

The man in the jef cap would typically wait until Weight had sold whatever he was selling to the last person, and then they'd talk about people they knew, or once knew. The conversation would frequently turn to the professional types that were coming into some of the neighborhoods and buying all the properties and kicking out the widows and the widowers and then reselling the places to even more professional types who never said hello when you passed them on the street, like the one that was standing next to the girl, trying not to jump all over her.

The man in the cap did not appreciate the professional types moving in, like this fellow who was trying not to stare at the girl in the shorts and T-shirt. You'd think a self-respecting person would keep his eyes to himself, but this young fellow was absolutely entranced with the girl.

The professional type had moved in a few months ago, into the second floor of a subdivided Smartt Street rowhouse. He'd picked the Brideshead section of South Philly to live in because he'd heard that South Philly is the city where you can park a car—even the old, classic BMW that he owned—anywhere you damn well want to—in the middle of the street, on the sidewalk, even—and not get a ticket. Exactly why this was so was never explained to him, but he believed it probably had something to do with South Philly also being the home of The Mob.

He had heard all kinds of things about the neighborhood when he moved in, but when you're working sixteen-hour days you don't have time to so much as walk around, but now that he'd been laid off he was sleeping late, and this asshole with the megaphone had to *wake him up*, telling him that he should eat, like he wasn't doing enough of that already, and now that he was up, he just had to see who it was who was being such an asshole and that brought him to the window of his apartment where he saw this blonde goddess in the oversized T-shirt and the undersized running shorts and he threw on some clothes and hoped he could get a conversation going and do something other than drink espresso, cruise the net and play computer solitaire, and instead of dropping one of a half-dozen of the lines that had gotten conversations going at bars with high-end microbrews, he found himself standing in front of a dorky geezer with plum slime dripping down his mouth.

Weight winked at the professional type. He stuck the sticky plum in professional type's hand. Then he removed the plum that he had been holding in his mouth, breathed plum breath at the professional type, winked and said, "A plum this good'll put lead in your pencil."

Right then, right there, the professional type decided that there was no way he was buying a plum from this man.

Weight popped the half-eaten plum back into his mouth and was going back to the truck when he heard the widow say, "Feh!" which is what old women are supposed to say when the worst that can possibly happen, happens.

Weight turned around and saw that the professional type dropped the plum. He opened his hand and it fell right out, hit the side walk, bounced off the curb and fell into the sewer grate.

The professional type had made a big mistake and he knew it, and his instinct was to pull out some money and buy something, when he stopped. He smelled a scam. The produce seller had put that plum in the professional type's hand in such a way that it fell right out, and if the professional type was inclined to feel like it was his fault, why, he'd be more likely to buy one of those plums, wouldn't he?

Sure enough, the produce seller pulled a plastic bag off a rack in the back of his truck, loaded it up with plums, dropped it on the hanging scale so the little arrow spun around like a pressure valve about to blow and then handed the bag to the professional guy, took the plum out of his mouth, and proclaimed, "You got weight!"

The professional guy didn't take the bag. He just stood there and said, "How much for the tomatoes?"

At this point, it would have been convenient if somebody standing next to him would have mentioned why people called Weight Wisnitz "Weight" instead of whatever his first name was: because, when you bought from Wisnitz, the plum he gave you to taste may not have been even remotely similar to those that went into the bag, but when Weight Wisnitz handed you pocked, bruised, squishy-on-one-side plums that had been sitting in his truck a little too long, that came from cases marked DIT (damaged in transit) from the Food Distribution Center down in South Philadelphia, he'd tell you that you got weight, as if to say that a pound of squishy plums may not look great or taste great, but they weighed every bit as much as a pound of plums should, if not maybe a little bit more.

If you watched what went into your bag, and watched even more carefully what went into the bags of some of Weight's regulars, you'd see that the man not only played favorites, but he had a way of slipping in all kinds of things.

The one thing you're not supposed to do, though, was talk price. Weight told you his price on the megaphone, and it didn't matter that the echoing buildings had turned it all to a garbled, incomprehensible mess of words. Just by standing there, you indicated your need for the service he was providing. What the hell else would you be doing on a street corner at 10:16 A.M.?

Weight Wisnitz had a rule about comparison shoppers, and the rule was, you don't say a thing to them. You pretend you don't hear and you stick something in your mouth so you can't talk, and you start filling another bag and then you hand it to them, take their money and hope they go away.

So Wisnitz clamped down on the plum with the few teeth he had left, tossed the bag of plums back in the truck, swaggered around to the flat bed where the produce lay in open cases under the September sun. He winked at the girl, and nodded at the old man and the widow.

Then he put both hands on the wad of plastic bags hanging from the rack by the truck's scale. Weight Wisnitz ripped one of those bags off the rack like a real man, a man with experience, a man who knows how to do things right.

He began filling the bag with Jersey beefsteaks, tossing them in such a way the professional guy would not see the tomatoes with bruises, the cracks, the blotches and green spots.

The professional-type guy became nervous, and it didn't help that he was at a loss for a conversational opening with the brilliantly blond woman. Though only in his mid-20s, he had learned how to work those insanely long hours that indicate that you're on the fast track, even if you're not. And he became an expert at the kind of women who would have absolutely nothing to do with him. This female next to him could go either way. She clearly kept herself in top physical condition, with that thin elastic skin stretched tight over the muscles, and he knew that women who keep themselves in shape don't always go for guys who keep themselves in shape because women who keep themselves in shape spend a lot of time in gyms and the guys who spend a lot of time in gyms are gay or unemployed, usually both. While it wasn't yet obvious that he was unemployed, the last time he had been in a gym was to find a pay-phone because he forgot to charge the battery on his cell phone and it had died and he needed to find out if the work on his BMW was done.

He told himself he could at least *pretend* that she might nevertheless be intrigued by a single, highly educated, formerly well-paid professional who, as a relatively new resident of the neighborhood, had a passionate commitment to urban pleasures, used but still functional BMWs, and the various lifestyle upgrades to which he considered himself entitled. Even if he personally hated exercise, he knew his way around imported beers and was proud of his intuitive grasp of inventory control software, though he hadn't been keeping up with the latest developments since he'd been laid off.

As he watched Weight fill the flimsy plastic bag with tomatoes, he imagined—no, he prayed—that this female goddess see through his unremarkable exterior and would use, as a pretext, a rather large collection of vegetables to begin a relationship that might . . .

Then he saw that one of the tomatoes tumbling into the bag was bruised. "Those better not be for me," he said.

Weight Wisnitz wasn't stupid. He could tell a guy who wanted to buy tomatoes from a guy who was trying to prevent himself from getting wall-eyed over a girl. For a moment, Weight Wisnitz wished he had his flask with him, but, somehow, a swig of cheap bourbon wasn't fitting on a day like today, with that girl looking at him. Here he was, 62 years old, but a girl in teeny-tiny shorts would still look his way.

As for the guy, well, Weight Wisnitz sold to many like him on his route, most of them stumbling out of their rowhouses, blinking and yawning, some of them in their overpriced pajamas and none of them happy, but all of them with money in their hands, in their pockets, in those stupid zipper bags they wore on a belt.

They'd come out complaining about spending the whole night awake, working on this or that, and here they were, sleeping until Weight came by, blasting them out of bed with his megaphone. They'd ask him if he had a permit for that megaphone, but then they'd check out his prices and they'd spend money because everybody wants to get a deal, and if nobody gave them a deal in their entire lives, Weight would give them a deal.

Such deals, you wouldn't believe them: three heads of iceberg lettuce for the price of two (he tried to unload iceberg fast because it wilts in the sun and gets gray and dirty after a few hours in the back of the truck with all the crud and dust blowing around). And then, they got that look in their eyes and they were pulling out the money, *that's* when he'd jack up the prices on the asparagus and endive and those shit-ta-tacky mush-rooms because these professionals figured that the only stuff that's worth having is what costs too much.

"I'd still like to hear a price for those tomatoes," the professional guy said, glancing at the girl as if to show he was being reasonable. He had to show her that he was reasonable, that he had to make sure that he wasn't being ripped off. Because, when he wasn't laid off, he worked insanely long hours in air-conditioned buildings where the delivery boys would try to rip him off, when they brought up the lattes and the pannini sandwiches, by pretending not to understand English, or to not have enough change in their pockets, hoping that he'd just hand over a $20 and say, "Keep it."

He didn't let the delivery boys rip him off, and he wasn't going to let this human bean pole rip him off, either. The guy said, "Excuse me, but I didn't hear the price."

Weight kept loading up the tomatoes. Then he dropped them briefly on the scale, let the arm of the scale flap wildly about, then turned to the professional guy, and said, through the half-eaten plum between his teeth, "I old oo, oo cot ate."

The widow translated: "He's saying 'I told you, you got weight.'"

The widow pitied the professional guy because the professional guy was holding a $20 in his hand like he was trying to get the attention of a hot dog vendor at a Phillies game. You don't do that with Weight Wisnitz. Weight Wisnitz was no hot dog vendor, selling the same damn thing to the same damn people as fast as possible.

No, Weight had been a part of her life before she became a widow. For upwards of thirty years, she saw him twice a week, and maybe a third time if he came around on the Friday before a holiday. And though she didn't buy as much now that her husband was dead, she still watched every damned thing Weight put in a bag because, now that she was a little bit famous, you'd think Weight would give her the better selection but, no, he was sticking her more and more with the worst, as if she was just some no-name nobody. If she wanted the no-name nobody treatment, she could go to the Italian Market, which wasn't even Italian anymore, with all the Vietnamese taking it over, selling bags of mushrooms and eggplants and not even with a thank you.

The way she saw it, when you were getting charged the same price for good vegetables as bad, and there were only so many perfect vegetables to go around, you either had to demand perfection, which never worked with Weight (he'd just load up a bag with banged-up peppers and tell her, "You got perfect!"), or you had to let him turn his back and, while he was pretending not to notice, take what he should've given you in the first place.

So last week she took some corn and, what should happen, but she got it back to her kitchen and the ears were wormy. Now she was waiting for the guy with the $20 to finish his business so she could give Weight hell for the wormy corn.

"What's that mean, I got weight?" the professional guy growled, as if she was making a crack about how heavy he was.

Then Weight did something stupid. He reached for the $20.

The guy whipped the bill back, like he was teasing a dog, and you could tell that it made Weight very, very angry. His eyes got round, his sunburned skin became even redder and, with the plum in his mouth leaking juice down his chin, he snapped the money out of the guy's hand, stuffed the bill in his pocket where he kept his change.

Then, after one of those long pauses that is only a few seconds but might as well be forever, Weight Wisnitz keeled over and died.

The older man stepped forward, dropped into a crouch and touched the side of Wisnitz's neck. "There's no need to call an ambulance," he said, standing up again. He glared at the professional guy, as if to say that Weight died for his sins. "He's left us."

The widow went to the side of the truck and peered at the vegetables. She said, "They don't know how to drive, those ambulances. They honk their horns and they run you over. They're always coming through here with their sirens on, and, you want to know the truth, and they don't need the sirens on, but they put them on, because making a big noise, they think they're important."

The professional guy waited a few seconds. Then he squatted down, grabbed Weight's sweaty GO PHILLIES! T-shirt, and shook him.

Weight flopped around but his eyes stayed open and his mouth started to leak blood. He didn't make any move like he was going to get up. Worst than that, Weight let go with a torrent of beer-colored urine that ran rudely out Weight's sawed-off shorts and down his legs.

The guy jumped back. He looked at Weight's mouth, at the plum in Weight's mouth, and saw that there was plenty of room around Weight's lips for the blood to come out and the air to get through. He caught a whiff of Weight's breath, and it smelled pretty close to disgusting.

The guy decided right then that there was no way in hell he was going to pull that plum out and give artificial respiration, even if it might make him a hero with that girl in the running shorts. He didn't want to be a hero. Then he remembered what the older guy had said, how there was no need for an ambulance. There was something strange about the older guy, the way he touched Wisnitz's neck just so, as if that older guy knew his way around dead people.

So the professional guy made a professional decision: this was not his affair. His knees made a crunching sound as he wobbled back up. He turned around and looked at the other people who had been waiting on Weight, and said, "I don't think he's going to get up."

The widow craned her neck. "His tomatoes actually look decent, for a change."

The professional guy said, "Really?" but he was thinking about the $20 bill that was in Weight's pocket.

"Some days," the widow went on, pulling a plastic bag off the rack, "he comes out here, he's got nothing worth taking. Now today, some of those tomatoes, and that cabbage over there, if somebody don't watch this, those creeps'll come in and they'll just take it. Around here, anything decent, if it ain't nailed down, it walks away."

The girl said, "Eating cabbage burns calories."

The widow handed her one, and the professional guy glanced at the cabbages with new respect. He decided that she was the type that would appreciate openness, honesty, and a willingness to share. He said, "I've always had an urge to . . . to know vegetables. I saw this truck and I figured I'd try him out, so he's got my $20 and what am I going to do?"

The older man couldn't take his eyes off Weight's emaciated face. He said, "What's done this to you? Oh my God, what's made you into such a tragedy?" He scrutinized Weight's hands, paying specific attention to the knuckles that bulged out from under the skin. His eyes went back to the face, seeing what looked like collapsed blood vessels under the skin. The half-eaten plum, its pit visible in the pink fruit, was clamped tightly in place by the few teeth Weight had left. Was that blood or plum juice dripping down?

"Aren't we supposed to call the cops first?" the professional guy asked. "You're not going to believe this, but I was actually a Boy Scout once—I dropped out because I could never tie those knots and I hated camping out. It's like, it's dirty, you know? So we had to memorize this list of things to do in an emergency."

He pulled out his cell phone and saw that the battery had died.

The older man took off his jef cap and held it over his heart. "There's no emergency. There's no bringing him back. We should show some consideration for him before the police arrive."

"Feh! The only thing the cops are going to do is ask a lot of questions," the widow said. "They ask questions because it's how they boss you around and poke into your business. They keep asking questions until you say something they don't like, and then they take you in. What they don't know, they don't have to know."

Then, right out of the blue, the professional guy's most earnest prayer was answered. The woman in the exercise shorts, this fitness goddess, put her arm in his, pulled him toward the truck, positioned him so he was standing over a case of brussels sprouts. She stuck a claw-like hand into the case while saying in a tone that salespeople use to immediately put people at ease, "Do you think any of this is organic?"

Just as she pulled something out of the case that may or may not have been a brussel sprout she smiled at him and it was like the touch of a balmy breeze across his face.

"I don't think so," the guy said, only slightly annoyed that she would think that he was in the produce business. "I have no idea what half of this stuff is, or if it's good or whatever."

"You go by the feel," the widow told her. She reached into the open flatbed of the truck and pulled up a dark purple head of cabbage. "Then you look for where it's brown. This one has a few places but . . ." she put it under her arm. "It's not bad."

The widow reached for the roll of tear-off plastic bags that were mounted on a rack next to the scale. She pulled down a bag, put the cabbage in it, and began loading the bag with plums. "You feel the skin," she went on. "If it has a spring to it."

"I don't think those are yours," the professional guy said.

The widow jabbed her finger, hard, into the soft spot just under his rib cage. "Weight run out of change the last time he came through and he said he'd owe me."

The man with his hat over his heart sadly shook his head.

The widow said, "I'm taking nothing that he wouldn't've given me." She turned to the girl. "Some of this, what I'm taking, it looks bad so he couldn't sell it, so he'd eat it himself."

She pulled down a bag and handed it to the girl. Then she began loading up a bag. "I used to tell him," the widow said, "it was bad for people to see him eating all the time, and I should know because appearances matter in my line of work. Yours, too, right, Glen?"

The man replaced his cap.

"I told him he didn't want to be eating all the time," the woman continued. "Weight said he couldn't help himself but he was going to do something about it. Thirty years he's been coming through, I never seen him looking this bad. Look at him. He's just a bunch of skin and bones."

The professional guy glanced hungrily at the woman in the exercise shorts, who was also mostly skin and bones, but such very nice skin, young skin, tanned from being outdoors, or maybe from being under a tanning light. Who could tell?

The girl put whatever was in her hand in the bag and moved toward other cases. Her running shoe touched the bag of tomatoes that Weight still held. She looked at Weight for a few seconds as if she were contemplating what effect acknowledging his existence, or lack of existence, might have on the plans she had made for that morning. Then she said, "Do these tomatoes belong to anyone?"

"They belong to his estate," the man in the hat said. "If he left a will. If he didn't, it belongs to the Commonwealth of Pennsylvania."

"They belong to me," the professional guy said, squatting again to pry the bag out of Weight's hand. "He picked them out and put them in and was about to make change when he . . . went down."

The man in the hat said, "We should leave everything where it is. The police might want to know what killed him."

"What killed him is drinking and eating so much rotten junk," the woman said, scowling. She filled up another bag.

The man in the hat sadly shook his head as he dialed his cell phone. To see these people robbing the dead filled him with regret. He called the *Philadelphia Press*, where there was a fellow named Ladderback who did the obituaries. He got Ladderback's "I cannot answer your call because I'm on another call" voice-mail message. He said, "This is Owen Glendower. Perhaps you've heard of me. I'm reporting that Sid Wisnitz has just died not fifty paces from where he grew up. He's sold fruits and vegetables in the city all his life. He's not famous and some people wouldn't consider him any more than an ordinary guy, but, seeing as how you give the ordinary people a write-up when they die, you might want to give him a write-up, because he provided a service, and he died unnatural. Do right by his family, Mr. Ladderback, and write the truth about him." Then he broke the connection, shook his head one final time to the harpies picking over Weight's things, and sadly walked off.

The older woman handed a pale white onion to the girl. "You'll want one of these," she said. "It's a Vidalia. You roast it with a chicken and it tastes very sweet."

The girl threw back her head to show off the tight, lithe muscles of her neck and shoulders. "I don't eat meat."

The widow picked out some peaches. "He had better peaches last week."

The professional guy opened the bag he'd just taken from Weight's hand. He exchanged some tomatoes that had been crushed in the fall for those in the cardboard boxes in the truck. He thought he saw something at the bottom of one of those boxes that didn't look like a vegetable, but he decided he'd rather look at the girl. "I've thought of being a vegetarian," he said, "but seven days a week of beans and Brussels sprouts? When you work the kind of hours I put in, I just go back to the apartment, put on some music, and grab at whatever is around."

The girl pulled off another bag and gave him a sexy look that said, *I'll bet you do.* She followed it with, "We all have our obsessions."

Their eyes met, and the professional guy decided that he was obsessed with getting this woman into his apartment. He noticed her T-shirt and said, "You know, I've always thought about buying art."

"Then I will sell you some," she said, dropping a business card into his bag, "soon."

Before he could wonder where the hell she'd kept that card before she dropped it in his bag, she was off, tossing her hair in a spring strut, across Tenth to Smartt Street. Why, they were practically neighbors!

She turned around to give him one last smile. He felt the temperature of the air around him rise.

Then he saw the widow looking at him, waiting for him to offer to carry the five bags of vegetables piled beside her. He let her wait.

She hoisted them up and said she was going home to call the cops.

He watched her go. He looked at the stuff in the back of Weight's truck and didn't want any of it. He tossed the bag of tomatoes back in the truck. What he wanted was the $20.

He squatted down, put his bag on the curb, and, suppressing a shudder, locked his hands around Weight's cooling arm and pulled it away so that the hand holding the $20 emerged from the pants pocket, followed by all kinds of stuff that shot out: money, of course, a really disgusting red-stained handkerchief, crumpled coupons that had been torn from newspapers, scraps of paper with things written on them in a tiny,

cramped handwriting, and a vial of pills that went rolling down the gutter into the sewer.

He tried to gather up what he could and stuff it back in the pocket. He
had some loose change in his hands and figured that, if the cops didn't
come, he'd use it to call them on a pay phone.

Then he grabbed the $20 in Weight's bony fist and slowly began to
pull it out.

It must have taken him a minute, no, several minutes to get it out.

His knees were killing him so it took even longer for him to pull himself up. He was almost standing when he heard the whoop of the siren,
and the clunk of a door opening, footsteps moving on the sidewalk.

A female police officer told him to step away from the body.

He had never in his life been in trouble with the police—the Parking
Authority, sure, but never the Philly cops. He'd heard things about them,
so he decided to tell the truth. "This is my twenty dollars and . . . I was
using the rest to get change for a pay phone so I could call you to come
out here."

The officer gave him a look that he swore was the same look he got
from Weight Wisnitz when he dropped the plum. "Anybody ever tell
you that 911 is always a free call?"

He was suddenly speechless.

"You also got a right to remain silent," the policewoman snapped.
"Somebody already tell you that?"

# 2 a question for mr. action

The *Philadelphia Press* newsroom carpet had been cleaned the previous day and just about everyone was too busy complaining about the lingering odors to notice that what had been industrial gray was now blue.

When Neville Shepherd "Shep" Ladderback saw the carpet, he stared at it for a while before taking off his trenchcoat and hanging it on the hook next to the watercooler. He noticed that Andrea Cosicki, the young woman who wrote the Mr. Action column, was at the desk adjacent to his, and that a pile of unopened complaint letters from readers had been shoved to a corner (spilling over onto his desk), exposing a small area of the green laminated top.

Andy was sprawled before her desk in her swivel chair, wearing a dressy midnight blue pinstriped suit, peering at an article from the newspaper's database on her word processor screen.

Ladderback sat down at his desk and saw that Andy was reading a profile of chef entrepreneur Matt Plank that the *Philadelphia Press* had done a month ago. It had been written by Jay Maculay, the *Press*'s irritable, vitamin-gobbling restaurant critic.

The article included a photo of a bald, gaunt, pencil-moustachioed man in a white chef's tunic, looking away from the camera at the construction debris near what was to become his next restaurant. The caption identified this as Matt Plank, the "morosely monosyllabic" twenty-eight-year-old chef entrepreneur whose "quirky, perversely inspired" Philadelphia restaurants had gained lip-smacking attention in national food magazines and restaurant guides. In the profile, he had said his latest restaurant was to be a "meditation on the point at which the two most passionate cuisines, the Transylvanian and the Carribean, transcend life and death."

Andy pushed herself back from her desk and said, "I'm going there for lunch. Loup Garou. Can you believe it?"

Ladderback hadn't heard her. He was listening to his voice mail. He found a message from a person who said he was calling for Danny Bleutner, saying how happy Mr. Bleutner was with the obituary Ladderback had written about Weight Wisnitz.

Ladderback reacted to sudden surprises by closing his eyes and trying to fight back the waves of anxiety. Getting a call from Danny Bleutner, even through an intermediary, could be read in many ways. Ladderback listened to the voice-mail message several times.

Then he signed on to his word processor and saw an e-memo from Howard Lange, the newspaper's editor:

**Shep: Reader left a phone # and wants a retraction about Wisnitz obit. You're slipping. Call him. Send retract to me. ASAP. Lange**

He closed his eyes again. More anxiety. Ladderback reopened his Wisnitz file again and re-read his obituary. It had been a joy to do. As soon as he heard the message on his machine, Ladderback had begun making calls, starting with the police, who knew Wisnitz because Wisnitz gave them free vegetables—whether the police wanted them or not. One of them knew a few of Wisnitz's customers. Ladderback got a few on the phone. He called the owners of companies at the Food Distribution Center from whom Wisnitz bought his merchandise, and learned that some of what Wisnitz sold was so badly damaged that he got it free.

"There's a good living in it," a loading dock operator told him, "but it's not for everybody."

The information Ladderback acquired began to form a portrait, with cracks and gaps and unformed areas: Sidney Caesar Wisnitz was born in Camden, N.J. but settled in South Philadelphia, right on Smartt Street, when Polish-born Tadieuz Wisnitz (deceased; Katrina, mother, also deceased) moved to Philadelphia after Tadieuz got a job in the U.S. Navy yard's motor pool. Some said they named their boy for Sid Caesar, the comedian. Raised in South Philadelphia (almost across the street from where the mobster Chickie Marandola lived for a while), Sid dropped out of high school and began to work odd jobs, and may have even worked briefly with his father at the motor pool (the source was confused: it was either a boy or a girl but somebody named Wisnitz worked with the father because, for a while, there were two time cards in the same slot), and he eventually began selling fruits and vegetables from a car—before, some said, he had his driver's license. Sid volunteered for the armed services but was deferred, possibly because of his eyesight. Another source mentioned that he may have had a sister, who might have moved away or something.

So Ladderback checked the census report. At around the time Wisnitz got his driver's license, the census listed only him and his parents at the Smartt Street address.

Sid also could have had some trouble with the law but nobody was around who would remember right now and, even if Chickie Marandola lived on your street, you could still see the inside of a precinct at one time or other.

Then the assistant funeral director at the Mount of Olives left a voice-mail message for Ladderback: an anonymous donor was paying to have Wisnitz's funeral there, just so anyone who was ever touched by Wisnitz's generosity could pay their respects. That there were anonymous donors confirmed a truth that Ladderback had always believed: every soul in the city was important, every absence was felt.

Ladderback asked the assistant director if anyone had a picture of Wisnitz he could run.

"None we've come across, but he's on The Wall at Orley's, with the rest of us. Only time Orley ever lent a picture was for the Marandola funeral. Only time Orley was ever known to give anything away. He's not the generous type."

"So I've heard," Ladderback said.

"You been to Orley's?"

"A lady used to take me there," Ladderback said.

"Then you know you got the entire history of the world on that Wall."

"If not South Philadelphia," Ladderback added.

"There's a difference?"

Ladderback had written the five paragraphs of the Wisnitz obituary rapidly and effortlessly. It sailed past the copy desk and landed, intact, on the small page at the center of the newspaper that he filled every day, except those when advertising was heavy or events covered elsewhere in the newspaper took up so much room that space for his obituaries was reduced or even eliminated.

He turned to Andy. "Would you like an assignment?"

Andy said, "Not now."

Ladderback tried a subtle approach. "Did you notice the carpet? The person I'd like you to profile is an authority on the color blue. This blue is very similar to the color alexandrine, the official color of Rodrigo Borgia, who became Pope Alexander VI. While he was a cardinal in Rome, he sired Cesare and Lucrezia Borgia. You've heard of Lucrezia Borgia?"

Andy could have told him that, yes, she'd heard of Lucrezia Borgia in *Contrast and Contradiction in Feminist Historiography*, a seminar she'd audited as an undergraduate journalism major at the University of Pennsylvania. During the seminar, she'd listened to an extremely tedious lecture that Lucrezia Borgia's reputation as a poisoner and incestuous lover of her father was based on the mysogynist, anti-papal ravings of a Florentine religious crank named Samonella or Sitronella or someone like that, as well as a pamphlet published by Lucrezia's husband, whose

20

actions while married to Lucrezia indicated the possibility of spousal abuse. Her professor had said that reputations can be ruined, or redeemed, on a single fragment of information. It all boiled down to what people were willing to believe.

Andy could have said all of that (and more: she had disagreed with her professor, insisting that what matters most is not what people were willing to believe, but how hard someone else had to work before people abandoned what they believed, and accepted the truth) but she could tell from the way that Ladderback's eyes had settled on her, that he was going to give her an assignment and, as his official assistant, she did not want an assignment from him, not on this day.

Ladderback took his glasses off and cleaned them on his shirt, a pale oxford that was so old that it had faded to a hue that was between colors: not what it should be, but not quite what it shouldn't.

"You might find this assignment rather interesting," he said to her.

"Not today," Andy said. "Nothing's going to beat Loup Garou."

"Loup Garou," Ladderback repeated pensively. "I believe that is the French derivative of a folk term for werewolf, though it is sometimes confused with vampire." He slid his swivel chair toward a wall of green file cabinets, opened one of the file drawers and began to search. "I may have more information on it."

"It's the name of a restaurant," Andy said. "You need a reservation months in advance, if you can get it. You must have heard of it."

He stopped searching. "I have," he said flatly.

"Aren't you impressed?"

"No." He went to his file cabinet.

Andy checked the time and thought she would go to the "Ladies" for a final check just to make sure she looked as absolutely perfect as she could possibly be, because her mother, a sales executive with a New York art gallery, was taking her out to lunch and her mother had a thing about how looking good wasn't good enough: you had to be "absolutely perfect when appearing in public to distinguish yourself from those who can't or never will be."

Going to the "Ladies" required her to skirt the cluster of desks shoved together to form the *Philadelphia Press*'s newsfeatures department. As she was going by Trina Kassein, the newspaper's waif-like book editor, Trina slowly looked up at her, as if to say Andy had no right to be over six feet tall.

The area around Kassein's desk smelled like a tropical swamp on a muggy day. The book editor had recently written a lifestyle feature on aromatherapy. Entitled "Making Scents," the article not only reviewed a handful of recent volumes on the "healing art," but included testimonials from a host of people, most of them living in California, who had experienced miraculous cures from inhaling "positive charged, antioxidant" odors. Even before the article appeared, Kassein received cases of free samples, all of which she insisted were unsolicited. She argued that even though tobacco smoking had been banned in the newsroom (a small room with a window near the emergency stairwell had been declared Fumatoria for those who just had to have a puff), the staff would benefit from an occasional aerosol shpritz of "Big Sur Mist" or "Rain Forest Morning."

The odors made Andy's eyes water and reduced Jay Maculay, the restaurant critic who sat next to Kassein, to periodic sneezing fits.

Kassein took her hands off her keyboard, shook her long, gray fall of hippie hair and, without Andy having even spoken, said that getting into Loup Garou wasn't such a big deal.

"The trend for TransCarib fusion cuisine came out of a really limp novel about a Polish werewolf living in Martinique," Trina said. "I panned it *years* ago. I mean, the book was stale, derivative as all get-out, Anne Rice on downers, and it was ancient history until they made that movie. Now it's, like, 'pass the blood sausage, mon ami.'"

This was Trina's way of telling Andy that she not only was aware that Andy was going to what was currently the city's most difficult restaurant to get into, and, too, that she wasn't impressed and Andy shouldn't be, either, but wouldn't Andy like to know how Trina found out where Andy's lunch appointment was?

Andy wanted to say that she did not care how Trina found out, but she had learned all the way back when she started writing for the University of Pennsylvania's student newspaper that journalists are the nosiest, most devious bunch of gossips on the planet, and that it didn't matter that only a few minutes had gone by since Andy told Ladderback she was going to Loup Garou: if Kassein heard it, the entire newsroom was now aware of it and each and every person on the way to the "Ladies" was going to have to weigh in with opinions that, given Andy's lowly status as a consumer reporter and assistant to the obituary writer, Andy would have to endure.

Before Andy could move, Kassein pulled a book out of an overnight mail envelope and flashed it at Andy. The book was entitled *The Angry Eater* and the cover showed a scowling, thick-set woman with brightly dyed purple hair sitting at a table with a knife held as if she was going to stab someone.

Kassein said, "They should send her there. Michelle Fragg. She hates Plank. They went to the Culinary Academy together and she went to New York and now she's notorious and Plank is merely famous. The word is," she smirked, turning away, "they were lovers!"

Janine "Bar Bet" Schroeder motioned Andy to her painfully neat little perch, the only desk among the newsfeatures cluster that did not adjoin any other writer's. During her last round of contract negotiations, Schroeder, the *Press*'s sports trivia columnist, had demanded a view "over the water," hoping that she could work at her Penn's Landing apartment and telecommute. She was told she had to show up, or else, but, as a consolation prize, she was offered a desk by herself, in front of a window that looked out onto Market Street and a distant patch of the Delaware River.

"You are going to have a blast," Schroeder squeaked, wagging a bony finger with a huge wedding ring—her fourth. "I've been there three times, and let me tell you, the Goulash Saint Barts is positively the most visually disgusting thing I have ever seen. It's made with these teeny tiny baby squid and, you have to believe me when I tell you, I sat there with a bunch of Sports Channel meatbrains—we were going over my syndication deal—and I made sure to eat it with my mouth open, you know? Those guys, if they had barf bags they would've gone to them, I mean, face *down*. They rolled over on everything I asked for. Gave me a TV/radio/website deal you would not believe."

Andy nodded and then felt the hairs on her neck rise up—a signal that someone was staring at her and that that person was not in a good mood. She turned and saw Jay Maculay glaring at her.

"You'd better not write a word about that place," Maculay said. "You so much as mention anything about food and don't clear it with me, I'm going to grieve it to the union, you hear?"

Andy's late father, a political fixer who was still known around City Hall as "Benny Lunch," used to deal with unions all the time in brokering deals for his clients. "You always got to be reasonable with people, especially the sick fucks," he would say on the rare moments when he would discuss what he did to bring home enormous fees, many of them paid for in bundles of cash. "With the sick fucks, you have to show them that you can be just as sick as they are, but you'd rather not, because, unlike them, you can be cool."

How was Andy going to be reasonable with Maculay?

She had her own ways of dealing with assholes, such as the Cosicki Intimidation-Beam, a withering stare she'd learned from her mother.

But today was her birthday and she just didn't want to bother. So she just walked past him, which seemed to irritate Maculay even more. He huffed and opened his own copy of *The Angry Eater*.

Just before she reached the "Ladies", Howard Lange, the *Press*'s short, ferret-eyed editor, motioned her over, into his narrow glass box of an office, drew the curtains and told her to sit on the couch.

The last time she'd sat on that couch he tried to paw her. "I'd rather sit in a chair," she said.

Lange made a gun with his fingers and pointed it at her. "Go ahead," he said. "Make my day."

Ladderback didn't have to look up the number. He remembered it, dialed it, and a dry, raspy male voice came to him over the phone, "You've reached Owen Glendower."

Ladderback identified himself and said, "I've heard good things about your work, Mr. Glendower."

Glendower hesitated. "You've seen it?"

Ladderback hadn't, but he knew, from speaking with funeral directors, that Glendower's talents were legendary, that he could do anything to the dead but wake them.

"You're supposed to be the best there is," Ladderback said, "and I've never heard anyone dispute that."

"That is very gratifying to hear, Mr. Ladderback. You're also the best, at least when it comes to writing about the likes of us. But the best can be compelled to do things against their judgement. And the best can make mistakes."

Ladderback kept his voice even. "To what mistakes are you referring?"

"Weight didn't die of what you said he did. In my profession, how a man dies can be significant."

Mine, too, Ladderback thought. In so many years of writing obituaries, Ladderback had received very few complaints. When readers did complain, it wasn't so much to tell him what they thought he did wrong as much as they wanted to tell him about their relationship to the decedent. They wanted someone to listen to them. By listening to them Ladderback gained insights into the reader's character that he would not normally acquire if he was like the other staffers, who hid behind patronizing explanations, or blew off the readers with polite noise.

"When I told you Weight died," Glendower began, "I had asked you to do right by his family and print the truth."

"The obituary mentions that his parents are deceased," Ladderback said.

"There's family and there's family nobody talks about," Glendower said. "You made him out to be a nice, law-abiding individual who served his community. Weight wasn't nice. He wasn't one to consider the law. He was a drunk as long as I knew him, and it was a miracle he didn't hit anything in that truck. He'd give free to the cops, so they'd look the other way."

Ladderback waited for Glendower to elaborate. When he heard only the whispy background sounds of the telephone line, Ladderback said, "I was told that he did a great deal of good."

"That depends on what you call good. Either way, it wasn't a plum that killed him."

Ladderback picked up the coroner's report. "The medical examiner's office said temporary asphyxiation leading to heart failure."

"Well, they *would* say that."

No, they wouldn't, Ladderback said to himself. Ladderback's parents were medical examiners. He heard his father's cool, authoritative voice coming through his, as he read from the report. "The plum dislodged from the victim's mouth, moved backward, covering his esophagus. The victim breathed in because inhalation is instinctive when the windpipe is obstructed. The second reaction is the choke reflex itself, an attempt to open the windpipe and expel the matter blocking it. Either could have put fatal stress on the heart."

He found himself looking at the time that Wisnitz's body was "logged in." He glanced back at his notes: Glendower had called to tell him that Wisnitz had died at 10:47 A.M. It had taken the ambulance *three hours* to drive the body from 10th and Smartt Street in Brideshead to the medical examiner's office in West Philadelphia.

"He had the plum in his teeth and it stayed in his teeth," Glendower said, "because that way he could hold the plum in his mouth, hold the bag of tomatoes in one hand and make change with the other. Weight loved plums. He always had one in his mouth, and he was always talking with his mouth full and making change. As long as I've known him, I'd tell him he shouldn't eat his merchandise in front of the customers, that it wasn't dignified and proper. But he couldn't help himself. If he got stuck with something that nobody would even steal, he'd eat it himself. He'd cut off the bad part with a knife he had under the dashboard of his truck, and he'd eat it. He'd even eat raw potatoes. I'd tell him, you can't do this in front of people, that people get strange ideas about a fellow when they see him eat a raw potato."

"The accounts I have of him say he was thin," Ladderback said.

"He was never a fat man. But the last few weeks, he was getting too thin. And he wasn't eating as much as he used to. And he wasn't drinking, much, either. It was something else that was . . . eating him up from the inside. His knees were sticking out like baseballs. There wasn't more to him than skin and bones. And, I tell you, Mr. Ladderback, when he fell over, there was blood coming out of his mouth. A man who chokes on a plum isn't going to bleed from his mouth."

Ladderback checked his notes, "Mr. Wisnitz was sixty-two years of age. It is not unusual for someone of his age to suffer impact hemorrhages. A sudden fall can bring on internal bleeding."

"When I saw him die, it was like the very soul ran out of him. He just fell to pieces, like what was holding him together didn't have the strength no more. It wasn't right, the way he died. I've seen enough unnatural cases, Mr. Ladderback. This happened in broad daylight, and there was nothing natural about it."

The urgency in Glendower's voice compelled Ladderback to write down *unnatural?* in the Wisnitz file.

"I must ask one thing," Ladderback said. "Why did you call the editor with your concerns? I would have taken your call."

"When a member of the family has an objection about my work, they don't go to me. They go to the funeral director."

Ladderback understood: given what Glendower did, most family members couldn't bring themselves to speak to him.

Ladderback changed the subject: "There's an anonymous donor funding the Wisnitz funeral. Will you be consulting on the restoration?"

"You know it is forbidden for me to speak about my work, out of consideration for the family."

"I couldn't find any living relatives."

Glendower bristled. "How hard did you look, then? There's family, and there's family in the larger sense. A fellow like Weight had people up and down the city knowing his business, and him knowing theirs. I expect, toward the funeral, some of them will probably make their presence known."

Those could be neighbors, business associates, sinners, saints—lawyers, even. "I received a call from Danny Bleutner's office," Ladderback said.

"That's a one," said Glendower. "A lot of people knew Weight. He performed many services. He connected people with people that may not have had a connection any way else. He was, like you said, part of our lives."

"About the anonymous donor," Ladderback began.

"Mr. Ladderback, it is forbidden for a person in my profession to say anything about that."

Ladderback knew that those who keep secrets also yearn to reveal them. You just had to give them the chance. He asked, "Is it possible that Danny Bleutner might be contributing?"

"You can believe Danny Bleutner never had an anonymous day in his life. You know the way he is."

Ladderback had never met Bleutner and didn't know the way he was. But now he wanted to know more and would have asked his assistant to do some kind of profile on Bleutner.

But Andy had other things to do.

"You still there, Mr. Ladderback?"

"I am, Mr. Glendower."

"You might think I shouldn't have made a fuss. I'm sure nobody else brought this to your attention. But I had to. You wouldn't think, considering my profession, that I would find it so upsetting, but this was the first time a person died in my presence. It was too awful, the sight of it."

"You cared about him," Ladderback said.

"It was a disgrace, with him in the gutter, and the rest of them, picking over his things. To steal from the dead is a disgrace."

"The police only mentioned one person at the scene. He was taken in for questioning, but they decided not to charge him."

"That was the young fellow, the professional type, who had to ask Weight about the tomatoes. New fellow, and not considerate at all. He saw it happen, and there was this young girl and the Widow Schiavone, picking at his things."

"Weeping Wilhelmina?" Ladderback checked his notes. "She made the 911 call."

"I suppose it should have been me to call them," Glendower said. "I wanted you to know first because, from reading your work, I feel we're in the same profession, in a sense. We take a person who has passed on, and, out of consideration for the living, we conceal and reveal. Someone has to care, Mr. Ladderback. What's happened to Weight should not happen again."

Ladderback hesitated. *What* shouldn't happen again?

In the next second, Glendower said good-bye to him and hung up.

Howard Lange sat close enough to Andy on the couch for his knee to rub against hers, and asked her, "What's on Mr. Action's plate for today?"

Andy would have pulled her knee away, wondering if she should stomp on the idiotic leather tassel on his loafers, but decided she didn't want to risk scratching her shoes. "Four complaints," she said, "one question."

He winked. "Any of them fabricated?"

"None," Andy said crisply.

"No complaints outside our circulation area?"

"They're all inside."

"Let's hear 'em. Who do you lead with?"

"A reader complains, she got a video home-security system and somebody robbed her house anyway. Can she get her money back?"

"You're not supposed to waste your time on nut cases," Lange said.

"This is not a waste of time. I actually solved her problem."

Lange pointed his finger at her. "Never do that again. You're not supposed to solve problems. You're supposed to give general consumer information, in the guise of solving a problem, without solving the problem, because if you get involved in solving the problem, and the problem screws up, we can get dragged into something."

"What's wrong with getting dragged into something if it's going to help?"

"Because then we become the story," he said. "We are the media. We report the story. We are not the story."

"But the story is supposed to be helping people."

"The story is whatever we want it to be," Lange said. "The day we become the story, is the day we lose our objectivity." He looked at the ceiling. "Next?"

Andy looked again at his shoe. It would be so easy to grind her heel into it. . . .

"I'm waiting . . ."

"A reader wants a dishwasher delivered, but the bankrupt appliance company keeps pushing back the delivery date. Mr. Action called the company. A spokesman says the company will deliver the dishwasher our reader paid for, but not immediately. If the reader wants, Mr. Action says, he'll call the credit card company and dispute the charge. Mr. Action tells the reader that if he doesn't get the dishwasher by the new date, cancel the charge."

"I'd lead with that," Lange said.

"This is the fourth item about that appliance company in two weeks."

"Oh, yes," Lange said, pretending that he had read the previous Mr. Action columns. "Maybe you should lead with a general, what-to-do-when-a-retailer-goes-broke guide."

"I did, the day after Dependable Appliance filed for bankruptcy protection and locked its doors."

Lange nodded, as if he remembered that. "Next?"

"A college student wants to know how to sign up for a drug testing program and how much money he'll get to be a guinea pig"

Lange held up a finger. "Didn't a college kid get killed in one of those testing programs a few years ago? I remember this huge wrongful death lawsuit."

"The suit was never filed. She was a part-time student at Philadelphia City College. The girl's mother accepted an undisclosed cash settlement from the Stoner Clinic and records were sealed. I was part of a team that covered it for the Penn student newspaper."

"So Mr. Action is telling our potential guinea pig to tell his folks that, if he dies, they should sue?"

Andy really, really wanted to stomp him this time. "No. Mr. Action gave a few addresses and phone numbers of three city drug testing programs, with web addresses. How much a student is paid depends on the specific test and what it requires. He should make sure he finds out about possible side effects and be aware that he is risking his life. He should also understand what he is agreeing to, when he signs the release forms."

Lange reached down to the floor of his office, pulled up a scrap of paper, ripped off a strip, put it in his mouth and started to chew. "Next?"

"A reader wants to break a contract with a weight-loss company. She agreed to pay so much money in installments for six months for bulk orders of the company's food products and nutritional supplements, and she says the products give her a rash. Mr. Action contacted the company. The company spokesperson says its products are safe, but it will cancel the contract if the reader sees a doctor and the doctor describes the problem in writing and the letter is sent, certified, to the company's headquarters in Des Moines."

"Lead with that," Lange said. "That's a perfect Mr. Action story. Reader asks a question, you make a few phone calls, and we print that the reader has to do something that's tedious or time consuming, or that the reader will never do anyway. I like the diet angle. Our latest demographics survey says that three quarters of our readers would like to lose at least ten pounds. The same survey found that eighteen percent of our readers are collecting unemployment or welfare benefits. You might ask how is it that people with no money get fat? All this time on their hands, so they eat!"

"That's wrong," Andy said. "Mr. Action already answered a reader question about obesity. Obesity is a symptom of several diseases and it cuts across every demographic, with the majority of occurrences in the middle and upper middle class. Very few obese people are poor because the poor simply can't afford it. The media tends to focus on, and typically ridicule, the shut-ins who are unemployed because they are mentally disabled and they tend to obesity because they get no exercise. For them, overeating may be a symptom of a mental problem, because neurotransmitters have an effect on appetite. The problem with remedies that work on neurotransmitters, is that neurotransmitters also effect mood, sexual arousal, blood pressure—"

Lange made a face. "My heart bleeds for them," Lange said, "as long as they buy the paper." He folded his arms. "This place you're going to. There's something I want you to check out. The word is that Plank has financed that place with drug money. You know what'll happen if you nail that?"

Andy did. Or, at least, she had a pretty good idea from sitting close enough to Jay Maculay to hear Maculay's end of phone conversations, even when she didn't want to hear them.

According to Maculay, Lange was annoyed that, after running Maculay's shamelessly complimentary "curtain raiser" about Loup Garou, not a single advertisement for the restaurant sprouted on the *Press*'s pages. True, the *Press*'s mostly working class, sports-crazed, inner city readers weren't necessarily the kind who would line up on the sidewalks for the $35 rum-pickled sow's ear appetizer. But Lange had seen Loup Garou ads (a fake Rousseau of a wolf about to pounce on a plate holding a malignantly blooming tropical orchid, with the restaurant's name, telephone number, web address, and the word FOOD written in drippy, blood red script) spread like bright weeds in the pages of New York newspapers and food magazines, as well as in *Liberty Bell*, the city's slick lifestyle monthly.

Lange had held off at assigning Maculay to do a "scorch and destroy" review of the restaurant because the *Press*'s annual Philly Pheed fund-raiser was coming up, and the *Press*'s promotions department wanted to include munchies from at least one of Plank's five restaurants among the fifty or so pizzerias, Chinese take-outs, Indian buffets, diners, sports bars and mom-and-pop neighborhood ravioli joints dishing out food at the Convention Center. Including menu items from the Provençal "Trellis," the "health fusion" Pulse, the "spaghetti western" Buffalo Rome, or even Loup Garou, among the mountains of meatballs, sliced pork sandwiches, cheesesteaks and other populist fare, would be a coup that, the promotions department hoped, might pry advertisements out of Plank.

Because Plank hadn't committed to the Pheed, Lange had asked Maculay to get some dirt about Plank, with the hope that the threat of bad publicity might motivate Plank to change his ways. The problem was, Plank's organization had precious little dirt in it. The restaurants were union staffed. Leftovers were donated to food banks. Plank went out of his way to employ the handicapped, and he was chummy with the right people in City Hall.

But Maculay swore that there was "drug money" behind Plank's operation—at least, that's what Andy heard Maculay say on the phone.

What further galled Lange was that, after attending Loup Garou's press opening, he could not get a short-notice reservation. He'd heard that the editor of the *Standard*, the *Press*'s broadsheet rival, *could*. What better way for Lange to impress his friends, cronies or ambitious female reporters from boondocks weeklies that Andy had seen begging him for a job ("It really has been my dream, Mr. Lange, to find a commanding, inspiring mentor and do *anything* for that person, and there is no doubt in my mind, that you are that person. . . .") than to just pick up the phone and get a table at a restaurant in less than an hour, when bottom-dwelling slime had to wait three months for a reservation? The mayor could do this. The heads of about two dozen businesses and law firms in the city could do this. Why not the editor of the *Press*, the paper that, according to its latest advertising campaign, was always "good in the 'hood"?

Because, Andy said to herself, the editor of the *Press* was not, and never has been, "reasonable" with people, least of all Andy, who got her job at the *Press*, not because she was qualified (though she was), but because her father, shortly before he died, got the city Parking Authority to forget about several hundred dollars in fines from Lange's mountain of unpaid parking tickets.

Lange dropped his hand to the floor of his office, found another piece of paper, tore a strip off, wadded it into a ball, and stuck it in his mouth. As he chewed the paper, he said, in an expansive way, as if he was getting a sudden revelation, "I have a question for Mr. Action: What is Matt Plank hiding?"

Andy said, "I'm just going there for lunch."

"When you're there, find Plank, go right up to him, and ask him that. Then, I want you to talk to everyone you can. I want to know who is in there, who they're with. Everything. When you come back, we'll go over what you have and talk about it." He pulled the piece of paper out of his mouth and tossed it toward a wastebasket spattered with globs of paper that had missed. "There's got to be a reason that Plank's holding out on us."

Andy shrugged. "Maybe he doesn't care."

"He has to care. He can't afford not to," Lange said. She stood and was about to leave when he added, "On your way out, ask Shep how he's coming along on that correction. Tell him if I don't get it in the next hour, I'm retiring him and giving the Obit Desk to you."

She stopped, "I don't want the job." This was true. If there's one job on a newspaper that no one wants, it's the obit desk.

She had to be careful, though. Lange, like most newspaper people, had an inverse prejudice about ambition, lust and greed, and who deserves what. This meant that if you wanted something from Lange— a raise, a reassignment, or just to be left alone—you had to pretend not to want it, so he would apply the journalists' standard, contrarian world-view to management decisions and thus insure that those who most sin-cerely want something must not get it, and those who don't want something, whatever it is, deserve it, and should get it.

Andy honestly and sincerely did NOT want Ladderback's job, and she had never mastered the ploy of pretending she wanted something in order not to get it. With a few exceptions, she believed that the gene-tically derived people skills that her parents exhibited had skipped her. Andy couldn't chat idly with strangers, the way her father had done, nor could she charm rich people into paying too much for art, as her mother so effortlessly continued to do. Instead, Andy grew up always feeling that she was too smart, too tall, too much aware that being too much of anything was not what people loved. Add to this, a nose that was too wide and a face that was too flat and a body that moved with the grace of a mud-spattered front-end loader ripping up blacktop on a highway con-struction project, and Andy was stuck with too much of what her father used to call "atty-tood," a crackling vehemence that radiated out from her like the acidic aroma of a pot of onion and cabbage stew that needed long, slow simmering before it turned sweet, if ever.

Except when she was alone with a basketball shooting lay-ups and nobody was watching: *then* she could fly above the ground, spin grace-fully in space, twist, turn and let the sly arc of the ball show her exactly how life should be lived.

Until she came down to earth, and asked herself why it was that, no matter what you do or where you go in this big, broad world, you're never far from an asshole.

Like the one who was in front of her, who had asked her how old she was.

"Twenty-three." She didn't tell him that today was her birthday. She hadn't told ANYONE that today was her birthday.

Lange studied her as if she were a horse being readied for auction. "The union says I can pay you the lowest and they'll let me screw you on the benefits package but, chances are, you won't need any of the benefits and you'll quit before you file any serious claims. Ladderback, on the other hand, is the oldest staffer in the newsroom. At his age, it's costing us four times what it costs us for you. With our other costs going through the roof, and what we have to pay prima donnas like Bar Bet, I have been ordered by the publisher to do everything in my power to get rid of the senior staff. This is not news. Any excuse I get, he's out."

This was coming from a man who was less than twenty years away from qualifying for the same treatment. As dour and quiet as he tended to be, Ladderback was no fool. The knowledge of the city that he had accumulated from doing his obituaries was more extensive than that of anyone else Andy had met at the *Press*, or in any other newspaper.

"Shep knows so much," Andy said. "He's got his huge file cabinet with clips from all his obits and all this other stuff he's read. Just about every time I need more information, I ask him and he gets it faster than I could get it from the Internet."

"Soon as I get him out of here, I get to dump that file cabinet and put up a row of vending machines where I can charge half the going rate and get back a quarter over costs."

Andy thought of Ladderback's files—which took up an entire wall from his desk to the watercooler and photocopy machine. She couldn't imagine vending machines there. And she couldn't imagine Ladderback had screwed up an obit so badly that the paper would print a correction.

"What's this correction about?"

"A reader left a message on my voice mail. He says Shep got the cause of death wrong on this obit he did of some guy that sold fruit from a truck."

"You believe this reader instead of Shep?"

"What I believe is, if he's starting to screw up, if he's incompetent, then I have a legitimate reason to move him out that the union won't fight. I've asked for all his sources on that obit, and a copy of the death certificate, and I haven't heard a thing from him all morning. Why do you think Shep's playing hard to get?"

"Maybe he doesn't care," Andy said.

Lange curled his lip and reached for another scrap of paper.


"I'm supposed to ask you about a correction," Andy said as she hoisted up her shoulderbag.

Ladderback looked at her for a few seconds. "About that assignment—"

Andy said, "Don't even try. I may not come back today. The column's filed, and I've done back-up for tomorrow."

"Perhaps after you celebrate your birthday . . ." Ladderback said.

Andy stepped back. "How did you know?"

"I looked at your non-confidential employee information file," Ladderback said.

"But how did you know to look in the file?"

"Your desk," he said. "You made a space on it, in that corner. Yesterday, before you left, you cleared away much of the unopened mail in a way that suggested you were making room for an object that you want to have prominently displayed. Perhaps an arrangement of flowers."

He left unsaid the fact that the flowers hadn't arrived.

Andy grabbed her shoulderbag. "I can buy my own."

# 3 compliments of the house

Just past the rough-cut, stone mausoleum entrance, a stunningly beautiful woman, tall enough, with dark skin and oriental eyes, dressed in a
richly patterned, crimson and chocolate–colored winding sheet, asked
Andy to repeat herself.

Andy was eyeing the huge stone pillars nervously. They reminded
her of the fake columns that Victor Mature had pulled down in *Samson
and Delilah*. "Charlotte Cosicki," she mumbled.

"I must ask you to repeat a third time," the woman said. "I am hearing impaired, but I can read your lips."

Andy said, "Oh. I'm sorry, um, Cosicki. That's spelled . . ."

"I understand you," the woman said, as Andy asked herself why a person who was hard of hearing was working as a restaurant receptionist.

Then she remembered, from reading Maculay's interview, that
Matt Plank employed as many impaired, handicapped, challenged—
whatever—kind of people, and that Plank stated he wanted to one day
open an entire restaurant staffed by those suffering from AIDS, "when
we find ourselves in a world in which people could get past their
prejudices."

She told Andy that the Cosicki party had not arrived.

"I can wait," Andy said. "Can I sit down at least?"

"At the bar," the receptionist said.

Andy hated sitting at bars because she was tall and men in bars tended to stare at her or try to pick her up, as if getting the attention of someone taller than they were was some kind of challenge. So she asked if she could wait at a table in the dining area.

The woman shook her head. "There are no tables open, I am so sorry. You can leave me your cell phone number. Or I have a pager for you. You can take the pager with you. The wait can be long, so some go shopping." She smiled. "If you must have something, there is also a pizza place across the street."

Was she being serious? Andy began "I don't want . . ."

The receptionist was looking past her. Andy turned around and saw, through the red-tinted glass doors, that a limousine opened up on the street and a group of people were getting out. The receptionist seemed amused. "She looks so sweet."

Andy saw a short, plump, pugnacious young woman in a distressed dark purple leather jacket, accompanied by a dreamy, handsome guy in a snuggly tailored sport coat, sand-colored knit shirt opened at the neck and dark, crisply groomed hair. "Who's the woman?" Andy asked.

"Media," the receptionist beamed.

"I'm media," Andy said.

"This is New YORK media," the receptionist said.

"But that guy," Andy said. "I know that guy. He's my boyfriend!"

The receptionist put on a wide smile, stepped past Andy and went out to the limousine.

Andy wanted to say that the guy who was fussing over the helmet-haired woman was NOT New York media, that he was Philadelphia media, specifically an underpaid *Liberty Bell Magazine* senior editor named Drew Shaw, who had been sleeping with her enough—well, not exactly enough, but sufficiently to satisfy most definitions of boyfriend, lover, paramour, major guy, main man. He had been decent enough to accompany Andy to her father's funeral and had been very loving with her, demanding, at times, that she move in with him, until she asked him if she could live with him while she looked for an apartment in the city. As soon as she indicated that she really would move in with him—for just a few weeks—he said they shouldn't be too quick, they should take time, they should get into their work, perfect their respective careers, learn how to function separately in a uniquely competitive environment, which she was very happy to do as long as they had a few of those Saturday and Sunday mornings when they didn't get out of bed until after lunch.

And then, no surprise, she found an apartment in West Philadelphia, and she had to spend a few Saturdays waking up early to go out and buy the stuff she suddenly had to have that she couldn't bring from home, and he would wake up early, too, telling her that he had to make an early yoga class, or that he had a breakfast interview, and she would wonder, how it was that a relationship could start so fast and be so good, and get better and better, until it became . . . different.

She had been thinking of that on this very morning. She'd knocked off the Mr. Action column in record time, hoping that he would call her, ask her out to lunch on her birthday to one of those cozy neighborhood bars that they loved, and then maybe take the afternoon off and go back to her apartment, or his apartment, or just walk around the city, marveling at all the small, wonderful things that you never notice until you have somebody near you who is more wonderful than anyone you can think of.

Andy had hoped, when she got to work, that she could blow her mother off, tell her that, no, Loup Garou wouldn't do, that she had a previous engagement. When the phone didn't ring, when that engagement did not engage, *when the flowers did not arrive,* she became curious, she had to find out about this restaurant that her mother was so nuts about, so she pulled up Maculay's interview with Plank and managed to not to think about Drew Shaw that much, until now.

Right now. And there he was, being so charming, so cool and quick, with this . . . this NEW YORK MEDIA BITCH!

Andy hoisted up her shoulder bag and headed toward the bar.

*   *   *

Ladderback opened the D. Bleutner folder. Danny Bleutner's law firm was among the most politically connected in the city.

Why would Bleutner care about Wisnitz's obituary? Ladderback again fought back his anxiety. He resisted an impulse to call Bleutner's firm and ask Danny Bleutner point-blank but he knew that if he called and asked to speak to Daniel Bleutner, Bleutner would probably answer, because Daniel Bleutner liked to answer every call personally and the one thing you didn't want, if you wanted anything from Danny Bleutner, was to have him answer your call.

In every print interview in Ladderback's Bleutner file, the lawyer described as "Refer Madness" or "Mr. Network" or "the Shmooze Meister" was asked why it was that he took every call possible, and Bleutner's answer was that he insisted on being "open, available and accessible to anybody and everybody. You want to get to me, you pick up the phone, if I'm in—you'll get me."

While this kind-of sounded great in print—and one of Bleutner's many skills was sounding great in print—what happened when Bleutner picked up the phone was that he said, "You got Dan Bleutner," and you had about two seconds to say something—anything—before he told you he had another call coming in, or he was in a conference, or he some-body waiting, and then he referred you to one of eight different secre-taries. These secretaries would screen the call, record what you wanted, get your name, address, telephone number and e-mail address, and tell you that Mr. Bleutner's time was prioritized and that it might take a while before action was taken or your call was returned, but Mr. Bleutner would be made aware of your concern.

A few days later, you might get a letter thanking you for your interest, even if you weren't interested, or an e-mail message explaining that Mr. Bleutner had been made aware of your concern. Then you would start getting more letters, telephone calls from telephone solicitors, junk e-mail and other communications because Bleutner's firm had "referred," or otherwise sold your name, address, telephone number and e-mail address to any of 600 different marketing concerns pertaining to whatever it was you said you were calling about.

Bleutner wasn't called "refer madness" for nothing. He defended this practice in his interviews by saying, "Ninety-nine percent of the people who call me, want something from somebody else, and most of them get it, though who's to say if what they get is what they had in mind?"

Bleutner also maintained what he called a response team. These were young, very eager kids fresh out of college. They spent the day reading newspapers, watching television, listening to radio stations and zooming around the Internet, looking for published items on subjects that had been flagged as "of interest" to Mr. Bleutner or his clients. These items would be summarized in reports sent to team leaders, who would either direct the team to commit to one of several kinds of responses, ranging from a complimentary letter or telephone call, such as the one Ladderback had received after Weight Wisnitz's obituary.

Ladderback read the article in his hand carefully. "In his spectacular office in One Franklin Tower, Danny Bleutner answers every call, from the slack-jawed delivery person asking directions to his office, to the tight-lipped editors of *Esquire* and *Vanity Fair* checking up on the star-crossed gossip about the latest mob movie being filmed in South Philly. . . ."

Bleutner explained himself as "The kid standing on the corner who knows where everybody lives, what their business is, and what's going to make them happy. When it comes along, I bring them together and it's a rush like you wouldn't believe."

Ladderback wrote down the word "rush." It was 1970s hippie lingo for a sudden pleasureable sensation, usually due to an accumulation of some intoxicating substance.

Then he re-read the quote, trying to imagine Bleutner saying it. Even if a quote is accurate, it's only a transcript. You can't hear the tone of voice, the accent, the rising or falling inflections that Ladderback had learned to listen for when he interviewed people on the telephone. You can't see the facial expressions, you can't notice the sheen of perspiration, the fidgeting gestures. You can't verify if the subject is looking right at you as he speaks, or is looking away, as if he is trying to hide something.

It seemed to Ladderback that, in the last quote, Bleutner wasn't talking about a sudden, pleasurable feeling, as much as he was indicating a need to be needed, to be of value to people. This, like the rest of the quotes, sounded good enough.

"To me," Bleutner said, "life isn't about money, it isn't about politics, it isn't about keeping score, getting ahead, or not falling behind. It's about a making a choice—are we floating a boat?"

When asked if some of the boat-floating choices he'd made might have decreased the happiness of others, Bleutner said, "They should be patient. Their turn is coming. There's only so much a poor kid out of Brideshead can do."

Who now lives in a cliffside palace in Gladwynne with a multi-million dollar art collection, is the star rainmaker of a 127-lawyer firm in an office tower whose blue glass and cobalt-hued stone was known, from City Hall to Orchestra Hall, as Danny's Inferno.

Ladderback stood and opened the "M" drawer of his file cabinet. He removed a rather thick folder called MONEY, and looked past articles on the history of money; the making of money—coins (Philadelphia had a Federal Mint located a stone's throw from Independence Hall); Atlantic City casino gambling; all the way to a four-part *Philadelphia Press* investigative series called "Where the Money Goes" that Howard Lange wrote when he was still reporting.

The series was about local political campaign financing and who the big donors were. In the middle of the article devoted to law firms was a quote from Danny Bleutner.

"My firm gives as much as we can, to everybody we can, because we want the best candidate to win," Bleutner had said. "With what I do, it's more important if they can get to me when they need me, and I can get to them. We also give because, for one reason or another, others can't."

Why, in an article as controversial and important as this, hadn't Lange asked Bleutner exactly what he meant when he said he threw money at politicians "because, for one reason or another, others can't."

It was as if Lange had found a needle in a haystack and then tossed it back because it didn't look like the rest of the hay he had been pitching.

With that quote, Lange had ignored a perfect opportunity to force Bleutner to reveal, or lie about, a crucial kind of access Bleutner, and other large city law firms, traditionally provided. These firms passed on money to politicians and kept communications open between these politicians and people and businesses whose relationship to those politicians, if made public, would violate laws concerning conflict of interest.

These people might be nice, well-meaning, criminal types who didn't want attention paid to how badly they wanted to support a politician who seemed to be on their side. The businesses might be legitimate, respectable, law-abiding and utterly aboveboard, but they needed access, and good will, from politicians who could delay approvals, pass laws or fail to pass laws, that could make the difference between sky-high profits and bankruptcy.

By getting Bleutner to admit that he provided that kind of service, Lange wouldn't change the way the city and its politicians do business. But he might have made more people aware that, when people like Danny Bleutner talk about what makes them happy, they're not talking about happiness.

Then he almost hit himself in the head for not checking the competition. He used his word processor to access the *Philadelphia Standard*'s database. The *Standard* was a big broadsheet that slanted its obituaries toward the rich, the famous, and the comfortably suburban. An itinerant city produce seller would never appear in those pages unless—

He did a search for Wisnitz and, yes, the *Standard* ran the obituary—the day after Ladderback's had appeared—without a by-line but *with* a substantial quote from Danny Bleutner.

That quote read: "I lived on the same block as Sid. My father drove a forklift at the Food Distribution Center and he'd bring home boxes, and Sid would try to sell some of it to the neighborhood. He got himself a truck and I rode along with him. I even did his route when he couldn't make it. He taught me everything you need to know about connecting with people. He kept me out of trouble."

Though Ladderback was aware that Bleutner had been born in South Philadelphia, he didn't call Bleutner for a quote when he had written the obituary because Ladderback tended to limit his background quotes to the immediate family, unless there was some special circumstance: the decedent may have distinguished himself in his neighborhood or line of work, or may have made a memorable contribution to another organization. When that happened, you got somebody with the company or the organization on the phone, or a spokesperson, and they usually said something short and nice.

Did Bleutner have one of his response team members call up the *Standard*, provide them with a statement and get them to play a request just so Bleutner could let it be known that Wisnitz, of all people, played a small but important role in his life?

Ladderback wanted to know exactly what kind of trouble Weight Wisnitz saved Danny Bleutner from.


Entering the bar at Loup Garou, Andy felt that she was coming upon this old, old place: a lavishly colorful, plant-infested, ruined Aztec pyramid. Clustered around the bar itself were tables made of awkwardly shaped, rough-hewn stone blocks and chairs made of packing crates with cushions fashioned from flour sacks.

The bar wasn't crowded as much as it was cluttered with mostly middle-aged men and women with chopped hair who slouched, slumped or sprawled with their bodies twisted to show off their baggy, shapeless, colorless silk suits. Others stood beside the waist-high stone banister at the far end and pretended not to be staring down at the privileged mob that had gained tables in the dining area below.

Closer to the bar, youthful assistants orbited about the power slouchers, wearing clinging, I'm-sleeping-with-the-CEO outfits as they muttered into cell phones, poked at palm-sized computers, or scribbled purposefully on leather-sheathed notepads with expensive pens.

Andy, in a dark gray linen suit and bone-colored knitted blouse, felt criminally under dressed. She wanted to hide. She scanned the bar for another fashion violator whose shadow she could fill, settled on a short, scruffy, scowling, stubble-cheeked guy verging on the plump who radiated such antagonism and contempt that the faux-driftwood barstools on either side of him were empty and the bartenders in purple silk tunics (one of whom was in a wheelchair), pointedly avoided him.

Andy went right for him, telling herself that, if this guy focused his festering discontent on her, she would focus her discontent on him.

But he was too discontented to notice her. His eyes scanned the restaurant as he perched on the barstool in a black jacket of some strange industrial fabric, open to a soft, electric blue knit shirt, irritably munching nuts from a terra-cotta bowl.

Andy took the empy barstool at his right, or left, actually, because he was sitting facing the bustling dining area, which was down a short flight of rough-hewn stone steps below.

She inhaled without looking at him. No, he didn't stink. The nuts he was eating from that bowl smelled rather good. What he needed was someone to clean him up a little, make him shave his face because the stubble made him appear unruly. Take those pounds off and he might look like . . . somebody familiar, but she couldn't quite figure out who.

Andy looked past him, down the bar, and saw that the bartenders had placed groupings of small, hammered metal plates holding odd, weirdly shaped hors d'oeuvres beside tulip-shaped brandy snifters and the fake-frosted, so-tacky-they're-cool pastel-hued parasol drinks. Nothing on those plates was appealing to her, but she found herself growing hungry from the aroma of the nuts that the guy was eating.

She gave him another once-over. He was definitely familiar. He reminded her of some of the guys she ran into while she was at Penn, guys who were very, very smart and knew that their parents and even some of their professors were absolutely certain that they were going to grow up and become kings, but that, for all their smartness, these guys not only had no idea how they would become kings and, therefore, were in therapy, popping pills for depression, anxiety or some poignantly tragic ailment that they couldn't wait to talk about. Others, when they weren't recovering from binges or grumbling about the grades they got from a professor who wanted more from them than demonstrations of talent, could be interesting, fun and even attractive, because they had ways of seeing and doing things that were refreshingly different from the guys who depended on their looks, or their money, to get them where they wanted to go.

Andy looked about the bar for another bowl of cashews and didn't find any.

"Where'd you get those?" Andy asked him.

"You want to know the country?" he snapped.

Andy looked down on him, way down, and found herself noticing how his eyes started out blue but faded to gray. "Just tell me how you got them," she said.

Andy expected him to be obnoxious and she sensed that he was about to insult her or say something that he thought would shock her, but that he held himself back. He was calm, almost respectful, when he told her, "You have to ask for them."

Andy waited for him to pull the bowl away, or indicate that he had some territorial command of the bowl and she should get her own. She noticed his fingers were short, delicate, clean, and marked with tiny scars.

"Now you want to try one, don't you?" he said.

Andy knew how to pass tests. Getting straight A's at Penn teaches you only one thing: figure out what the professor wants, look beyond that and see what the professor *really* wants, then study the professor to see if he can handle getting that, and, if he can, give it to him in such a way that it seems like you're not quite aware of what you're doing.

Knocks 'em dead every time.

Passing tests for a grade was one thing. Andy hated guys who tried to test her. She was about to tell this guy where to shove his nuts when the aroma again caught her nose. She touched one: it was warm, slightly soft and dusty with salt. She put it her mouth and for a moment she stopped seeing, thinking, and hearing as the salty richness of the cashew exploded between her teeth. She chewed and taste an odd, smokey assortment of spices that made her want to put another in her mouth as rapidly as possible.

She saw him waiting for her to tell him how great they tasted. She let him wait.

Finally he said, slightly peeved, "Aren't you going to tell me they're the best airline cashews you've ever had?"

Andy waved one of the bartenders over and asked for a bowl—of cashews. The bartender, another pixie, asked her if she wanted the cashews raw, scented, spiced, sweetened, roasted, or "fire thrown."

The guy shifted on his stool. Andy could tell he was about to show her that he was a regular, and that he could explain what fire-thrown meant, but she cut him off. "Just like these," she said.

"Those are fire-thrown," the bartender in the wheelchair said. "They'll take about five minutes. They're tossed through a sandalwood fire, rolled in milled sea salt and dusted with a little Tobago curry powder. Can I get you a drink while you're waiting?"

The guy smirked. "Don't you hate that when they hit you for a drink?"

"I don't mind being asked, when it's just asking," Andy said.

The guy was again about to explain something when Andy told the bartender that she wanted pepper vodka.

The bartender said, "Which one?"

Andy tried hard not to show she was impressed. When she went to a low-end bar and asked for Ukranian pepper vodka, the bartender said that they had vodka and pepper and they could put pepper in the vodka. Some of the middle-level restaurants had pepper vodka that wasn't distilled, flavored and bottled in the Ukraine. She had been to only three restaurants in the city that had the genuine item, and they had had only one brand.

"How many do you have?" Andy asked.

"Six," the bartender said, reciting the brands, explaining that three were made with conventional black pepper, one with red pepper, one with white pepper and the last was a Siberian made with scotch bonnet pepper that was very, very hot.

Once again, the guy was waiting for her to pass a test.

To hell with his test, Andy said to herself. It was her birthday, right? "I'll take the hot one, cold." Andy sat back, expecting to watch the bartender go up on a ladder or reach down into a cellar. But the bartender just turned around, rolled the wheelchair back, pulled away a section of the stone wall to open a freezer compartment, reached for a somewhat dingy bottle with a plain, orange label printed in Cyrillic script, poured an ounce in a chilled, tulip-shaped shot glass, and put it gently beside Andy's elbow.

Andy picked up the glass, aware that the guy was watching her. She wanted to tell him to stop watching her, and she was about to, and decided she would let it wait until after she tasted the vodka. She touched the glass and felt the frozen tingle of the glass. She brought the rim to her lips. She took a sip.

It was ohh-so-cold and burning, burning all the way down.

"It's what hell tastes like," the guy said.

Andy put down the glass, licked her lips, fixed the guy with a Cosicki Intimidation Beam so extreme that he almost dropped his bowl of nuts.

Then she tossed down the rest of the shot.

The guy shifted on his barstool, looked back at the dining room and began to gobble nuts again.

Andy turned and saw the bartender. "How about another?"

"You liked it?" the guy asked incredulously.

"I *loved* it," she said. She downed half of the next shot and, before she could put the glass down, the icy fire drove a spike into her brain. "It's my birthday," she said, as if that would explain everything.

She waited. Was this guy going to turn into a true asshole and ask her what her astrological sign was?

Instead the guy handed his bowl of nuts to her. "If it's your birthday, you should ask for something special. Whatever it is that will make you happy."

"You know what I'd really like?" Andy said, no longer caring if she sounded silly. "A cheesesteak. You think I could get a cheesesteak in a place like this?"

"What *kind?*" he said, turning to face her in a way that made her think of Cyrano de Bergerac responding to a comment about his nose.

The guy's nose wasn't bad. It was small and almost cute. It would look less like a baby's nose if the guy lost a little weight. Why was he being hostile? She said she wanted a cheesesteak and he got huffy . . . no, not hostile, but he was like a fighter who finally saw an opening and was about to pounce.

But not on her. He had asked what kind of cheesesteak and she was going to tell him. She tried to think of cheesesteaks and ended up thinking of the Zen proverb: don't think of a monkey. She thought of a cheesesteak eating a monkey—no, a monkey eating a cheesesteak and . . .

Was she drunk, or what?

But she could function while drunk. If some big stupid thing happened here that was news, she could jump into reporter mode, get the facts, get the quotes, get them into a story, and send it to the paper. She could do that.

And she could force herself to think of a cheesesteak: thinly sliced sirloin, fried in olive oil, covered with a few slices of provolone cheese, and dumped into a sliced Italian submarine roll. Among the acceptable permutations were the addition of diced, fried, or raw onions, a substitution of Cheese Whiz sauce for melted provolone. A pizza steak, a marginal permutation, included a shot of pizza sauce.

True cheesesteak emporia also had condiments: you could load the thing up with hot or sweet peppers and other additives, but Andy liked hers with that meaty, cheesy, greasy, throat clogging, gut-slathering, *de profundis* that is the essence of cheesesteak ingestation.

"Onions," Andy said. "I want a cheesesteak with provalone and fried onions."

"That's it?" the guy asked.

Andy said. "That's what I'd like."

"You'd like it, yes, consider the possibilities."

She was about to tell him what he could do with the possibilities, but he went off.

"Start with the meat," he began. "Thinly sliced prime sirloin, but, instead of frying it, let's toss it over a flame of hardwood coals. For extravagance, let's add a little sliced pork loin, with the pork following the sirloin into the grill, because the pork cooks faster and you want the flavors to exist, side by side, which means that the textures have to be identical. Let's consider the onions: should they be sweet, sour, red, white, slightly pickled, roasted, deep fried, sauteed? What about the kind of oil they should be sauteed in? Or would you want to go for the gusto and have them sauteed in butter? And the cheese—must we settle for industrial provalone? The temptation to be extravagant with cheese is worth giving into, though melting characteristics must be taken into account. Some cheeses will overwhelm the meat. The lesser provalones have a soapy, salty texture so why not try a slightly acidic white Norwegian cheddar, grated and dehydrated in a freezer so that when it hits meat it will proclaim itself handsomely and not run too much and get sloppy. With the bread, we must first select for dryness: the dough must absorb the juices, but not collapse. Finally, there is the matter of crusts. Crucial for presentation, the crust also adds a bitter, brittle texture. Should the crust be soft, dense and rubbery, like the common Italian sandwich loaf, or light and crusty like the French baguette? Or should we defy tradition, just a little bit, and use a tangy, but risky sourdough?

"Let's step back and ask the important question: what would make you happy? What would please you in such a way that the quotidian experience of consuming food would become a singular event that you never forget, for as many years as you have left?"

Because Andy was a little bit more than slightly drunk, she was aware that her mouth was hanging open. The grumpy toad on the barstool had transformed himself into a princely wizard. Listening to him was like hearing one of her professors back at Penn open up a new world to her, just with words. This scruffy lump used "quotidian" in a sentence. Not everyone can do that. Andy had put that word in one of her Mr. Action columns regarding a reader who complained about a neighbor who sang a loud, croaking version of Queen's "We Are the Champions" every afternoon before going to work as a telephone solicitor, ("You can get

50

used to quotidian annoyances," Mr. Action had replied) and Bardo Nackels, the *Press*'s slovenly, blustering night city editor who was always working days, knocked the word out, replacing it with "stupid," and then yelled at her across the newsroom, asking her where she got off thinking that the *Press*'s readers gave enough of a shit about her column to want to open a dictionary.

And he had used it in a question about what would make her happy.

That question stopped her. This was her birthday. She should be happy even if nothing and nobody was making her happy. This lump sitting beside her was the first person all day to care enough about her to even mention the possibility that life could be a little more (or a lot less) than putting up with all the shit she'd had to put up with.

What would make her happy, she decided, was an unspeakable, crazed, highly erotic act involving another consenting adult, perhaps Drew Shaw who (in the fantasy that was bubbling into her brain) had bought her flowers, groveled pitifully about his thoughtlessness, offered to make it up to her any way he possibly could, and then taken her back to his apartment where there just happened to be a bottle of champagne and a box of chocolates and he had actually changed the sheets in his bed and . . . it had NOTHING to do with a cheesesteak.

But she couldn't say that. She couldn't even hint about it. Not here and with anyone who was as yucky as this lump next to her.

He was looking at her, awaiting a response.

"Well," Andy said. "I guess . . . I guess you know something about food."

His face grew dark. "I don't know shit," he grumbled, and turned away from her.


Ladderback took his usual path to Jimmy D's: down to the sub-basement of the Press Building, out into the lower concourse of the Gallery Mall, past a bookstore where he saw the book that Kassein and Maculay had been waving around.

Copies of *The Angry Eater* were piled up in a pyramid, like cans at the end of an aisle in a grocery store. In front of the pyramid was a sign that announced that the author would be in the store, signing copies at 4 P.M. Another sign advised passersby to listen to the author being interviewed today at 3 P.M. on *The Scrivener's Tale,* a book chat program on the local national public radio affiliate.

Ladderback approached the pyramid cautiously, not at all sure why he was doing so other than to see what it was that had the *Press*'s book editor and food writer sniping at each other all morning. They had been arguing about who should interview the writer, who had either been born in Philadelphia, or had spent enough time in the city to realize that if she wanted fame and fortune she would have to decamp for New York. The book critic argued that the book was getting "major push-comes-to-shove type publicity and she was local, once," the food writer insisted that Michelle Fragg is "an obnoxious media punk who knows nothing about food or power. What she needs is a good spanking and I'm the one to do it."

Both had been disappointed to learn that the highly desirable luncheon interview slot on Fragg's author tour had been taken, and not even by the *Standard*'s armada of book and food writers, but by *Liberty Bell,* the city magazine that the *Standard* and the *Press* pretended did not exist, though the newspapers' staffers couldn't wait to see if they were mentioned in the magazine's gossip column.

Ladderback examined the book. On its cover was a color photograph of a stout, broad-shouldered, fiery-eyed woman glaring out from under a compacted, compressed swoop of dyed hair. She wore a beat-up leather jacket and sat, sneering like Brando on a motorcycle, at a perfectly set restaurant table, a knife in one hand, an expensive fountain pen in the other.

It was ridiculously contrived, almost a joke. But it was enough to make Ladderback open the book and read the jacket copy. Michelle Fragg, the book proclaimed, was an award-winning food writer for *En Tour Magazine*, and a regular guest on some television show where, as The Angry Eater, she "implodes the overblown reputations of celebrity chefs, pompous diet gurus, hypocritical winemakers, and other devious denizens on the high-priced food chain."

Ladderback closed the book. He was not interested in the imploding of reputations, overblown or otherwise. But he could not take his eyes off the author's photo. He looked closer at her face and saw, around and under the eyes and on the skin above the jawbone, that ruddy layers of makeup could not cover the physical signs of alcoholism, signs that he had learned to detect from his parents, who would take him into the city's morgue, point to a corpse, and encourage him, in the same playful way a father would play ball with his son, "Guess what killed him?" If Ladderback guessed correctly, his reward was a glimpse of the corpse's liver, hideously discolored with cirrhosis.

That this woman was a drunk did not surprise him. When Ladderback was hired at the *Press*, he found a newsroom of hard drinking, chain smoking men, all of whom wore badly tailored suits and seemed eager for a quick, stylish, flashy death. For a while, you were considered trustworthy, at least within the newsroom, if you didn't hide your afflictions. Real men had real vices: booze, smoke, and what the former English professor on the copy desk insisted was insulin that he injected every night into his arm a half hour past the copy deadline. Vices were supposed to steady the nerves, help you keep perspective, and bring you blessed relief from having seen too much or learned too much about why the city was going to hell.

Ladderback's difficulty was that, try as he might to swill martinis like the sassy Algonquin round table swells he had read about, he could only do so for a few drinks until he saw in the faces of his coworkers the rotting livers, straining hearts, and cancerous lungs that quickly killed them, or forced them to retire. The hard chargers were replaced by a new generation of recklessly ambitious women, and a few young men with masters degrees in journalism and awards won while slaving away at suburban weeklies and small-town dailies. They came with vices that were not vices, but components of a "higher consciousness" that would help them in their crusade to bring down the hypocritical, unnatural older generation that was impeding their efforts to change the world. After the world resisted such change, or failed to alter its course to their satisfaction, they dropped out to live on farms, write screenplays, or teach their failed wisdom to another generation for whom honesty was the struggle against vices that were so inhumanly powerful that they could only be resisted with furiously disciplined regimens of therapy, self-help books, religion, exercise, gurus that make housecalls, or new pills from any of the half-dozen pharmaceutical companies that had sprouted just outside the city in the industrial parks and suburban mill towns.

As much as one generation indulged, celebrated, or fought its vices, the physical effects of these vices never changed: the scarring skin, explosive changes of temper, the jittery movements, the dulling of abilities. What was it about journalism that compelled its practitioners to hasten the destruction of bodies and minds that had been so beautifully, brazenly young?

Ladderback replaced the book in the stack. He found himself thinking of his assistant, Andrea, who insisted that the world ignore her femininity and call her Andy. Her vice seemed to be her anger. She became easily, rapidly infuriated, at the pettiness of the newsroom staff; the tediousness of the readers' complaints that crossed her desk; the incompetence, selfishness and venality of the businesses, institutions, municipal agencies and other organizations that did not care if their actions, or lack of actions, cheated, insulted or endangered ordinary people.

When Andy became angry, she wanted to do something: she wanted to blame a bureaucrat, extract a confession from the contractor who did shoddy work, fight back as if she had suffered personally. Her efforts only increased the number of complaints that piled up on her desk, cluttered her e-mail queue, and clogged her voice mail with stories of injustices great and small.

Ladderback admired Andy's energy, though he could never bring himself to tell her that. He had once known another woman, one who was even angrier than Andy, who believed that every fight was worth winning. He'd fallen in love with her and . . . the relationship ended, as all relationships will, with one, or both parties wondering how it was possible that they could have ever fallen in love with someone who was so . . . wrong.

As he opened the door of the basement entrance of Jimmy D's, he reminded himself that relationships have a way of happening, regardless of how much better off the participants might have been had they never met. He reassured himself that, with so few years left in his life, he was fortunate that there were still people he could talk to, who would talk to him. Having them in his life, he decided, could be enough.

Andy wished her mother would hurry up. This guy was getting to her.

Andy gulped the rest of the vodka, and he smiled, and Andy was astonished—no, not astonished, but relieved or pleased or whatever it was you felt when you see that someone who talks like a jerk, acts like a jerk, and has his hair cut like a jerk, might not really be a jerk, or, at least, doesn't have to be a jerk and finally exhibits non-jerk behavior, even if it was only a smile.

Then she saw that he wasn't smiling at her, but at some group of people who were being led to a table in the dining area below.

Andy turned her attention to the restaurant itself. The overall impression was not an Aztec temple, no, it was more like an ancient European-style mausoleum that an earthquake has ripped open to the tropical sun. The servers wore uniforms that suggested old, mildewed 19th-century European military dress; the table cleaners were in tattered—no, faux-tattered—dining room service attire, as if they were survivors from a wrecked cruise ship. They carried dishes that arrived flaming, steaming, sizzling, or, more disturbingly, wiggling on the plates.

The sight made Andy look away, and it was at that instant she saw, coming out from under the stone archway, Andy's six-foot-one-inch-tall mother, with someone else! What was Charlotte "Cosi" Cosicki doing in the same room with a look-at-me-guys-and-cry blonde in a clinging, black, knock-'em-dead cocktail dress that showed off her gymnasium-toned shoulders and thighs?

"Oh, would you look at them," the guy beside her snickered. "They're trolling."

Andy didn't tell him that reading her mind was a jerk-like thing to do, that what he should have done was to let her feel horrified, and then indicate in some excessively pleasant way that muscles, hair, a cocktail dress and boobs out to *there* in no way compensated for Andy's wit, intellectual capacity, and subtle charm.

Andy did not say that, but she did notice that, as her mother and the girl approached the bar, every set of eyes EXCEPT those of the guy at the bar, turned to the girl.

"AnDREYah," her mother said gayly, leaning forward to air-kiss her ear. She pulled back, gave Andy a single glance that told Andy that not knowing how to dress could be fixed with professional help. Then she said, "We've been in such a rush. No one truly understands speed outside New York."

"McDonald's," the guy said.

Andy's mother turned her imperious *Park Avenue* skin-stretcher enhanced face down on the guy. Andy expected him to wilt, cringe or melt, as most men did when her mother wanted to be intimidating, but he only smiled again. "McDonald's understands speed. Speed has a taste, and a texture. Speed thrills but it never satisfies. What satisfies is timing. To get the right thing, at exactly the right moment—that's what you live for."

Charlotte blinked as if a fleck of dust was in her eye. She apparently decided the guy was so worthy of being ignored that it would best if he merely didn't exist. She put one finger affectionately on the girl's beautifully toned shoulder. "Andrea, meet Karyn—that's spelled with 'y'— Asgard, the gallery's newest sales associate. Karyn adores art and exercise. In addition to being with us, she's also a personal trainer. We only have her part time with us, but what a part!"

"You look terrific!" Karyn said to Andy.

Andy signaled for another pepper vodka.

"And this," Charlotte said to Karyn, "is my very special, one and only daughter, Andrea! And we are here to celebrate that, aren't we, Andrea?"

Karyn seemed only a tiny bit annoyed that the guy at the bar had not taken his eyes off Andy. Karyn flashed a perfectly symmetrical grin. "After hearing about you for so long, it's so wonderful to meet you in person!"

Andy put her hand on the third (or fourth?) shot of pepper vodka and tried not to wobble as she followed Karyn and her mother to the stairs. She stopped when she saw that she held, in her other hand, the guy's bowl of nuts. She turned to give it back but he was no longer looking at her and she didn't want to do anything to attract his attention, so she carefully moved down the stairs into the dining area.

She moved aside to let a waiter pass with something giving off fumes of dark smoke, and she saw Drew Shaw at a table with the helmet-haired woman. The woman had three empty drink glasses in front of her, and Shaw had his tape recorder out, his note pad, and the expensive fountain pen.

Something made him look up. Their eyes locked, and he looked at her in such a way that said, "Later."

Andy hoped there would not be a later. The slippery, silly mood that the pepper vodka had given her had suddenly turned anxious and awkward.

Her mother paused before a thatch-covered table set for three. Andy took the chair closest to the wall. Karyn sat closest to the aisle, crossing her legs as she opened her purse, took out a mint case and popped a tablet into her mouth. She flashed a hollow-cheeked grin at Andy and whispered, "Appetite suppressor!"

A waitress came their way. Andy found herself looking at the coral name pin on the waitress's uniform. Her name was Den. She had a bowl of warm, richly scented roasted cashews in her right hand. She put it in front of Andy.

Karyn eyed the bowl suspiciously. "You're not going to *eat* that, are you?"

Andy closed her eyes and wished that it would all go away.


"Used to be," Whitey Goohan said from the corner of his mouth, "we only had Italians working the kitchen of Jimmy D's, and they had to know somebody to get in. Now we got Koreans, Viet Namese, Mexicans."

Ladderback took a sip of the snapper soup. "The food tastes the same."

"So where are the people?" Goohan said. "Don't tell me I'm keeping 'em away."

Ladderback turned around and saw that the noisy, bustling, wood-paneled dining room had a few empty tables. He didn't see Danny Bleutner.

Goohan cleared his throat. "Used to be, lunchtime, the waiters had to fight their way past all the table-hoppers. Fellows like Chaz Shnayerson and Danny Bleutner, they'd never sit down in an hour, always moving around, acting like they was so surprised to see this one or that one breaking bread under the same roof, when the truth was they'd tipped me extra to tell them who was coming by. Now I'm seeing fewer of the old guys and none of the youngsters, and the fool I got running the dining room says he hasn't been asked in a week who's coming by."

Until a stroke had paralyzed his left side, Whitey Goohan had been the restaurant's lunchtime maitre'd, charged with the delicate task of seating the city's power brokers, deal makers, political, legal and business elite in such a way that deals were made, fights ended and rancorous disputes were settled, as they say, out of court.

After a few weeks away in therapy, Goohan had forced himself to return to the restaurant. But with a cane, and his left arm in a sling and his left leg in a brace, he could not work the dining room as he once did. So he stuck himself on a stool at the bar beside a telephone and advised a series of younger understudies that he kept firing and rehiring, as to where to put the favored, the out-of-favor, the mighty, and the fallen.

"They're gone to that Loopy Guru joint down the street," Goohan said. "As long as I've been living, I've heard it said you couldn't go wrong in Philadelphia with steak and seafood, and that louse comes in with his fancy fritters and what all, and they drop us like a burning stone."

"I see only three empty tables," Ladderback said. "Every seat at the bar is full."

Goohan dismissed that with his good hand. "So where's the line we used to have at the door? Around this time, they'd be backed out onto the street. And you see those tables? You know who used to be at those tables? Regulars that I'd see so often they'd get on my nerves like family."

Then, magically, the old, pre-stroke Whitey returned: Goohan pulled himself together, sat as straight as his curved spine permitted, and asked Ladderback with the careful sincerity of someone who was genuinely pleased to see him, if Ladderback was having a good day.

Ladderback had to think about it. "A reader complained."

"And who would have the discourtesy to do that?" Goohan asked. "If I was still working for Chickie Marandola, I would have paid a courtesy call on such a character. Would have had to call an ambulance on him, when I got done with him."

Ladderback took another sip of his soup and said, "Whitey, when you had your stroke, how did you get to the hospital?"

Goohan almost smiled. "Now that's a question. It happened right here, in this place, less than five blocks from three hospitals. I had my head waiter call me a taxi. No way I wanted to get into an ambulance."

"It would have been too slow?" Ladderback asked.

"When I was with Chickie, he had relations with some ambulance companies. You see, in some parts of the city, if there's an emergency medical call, the fire department handles it. In other parts, you call 911, the dispatcher is supposed to refer it to the ambulance company that's closest to the caller. Now I don't have to tell you that the definition of what's near and far in this city had a lot to do with how much the dispatcher got under the table. Chickie got a slice from the operation because whenever you're paying somebody under the table to perform a service, you have to be sure that you're getting what you pay for, and when that was called into question, Chickie would ask me to make sure the dispatchers understood what was expected of them. Of course, it cut both ways: sometimes the ambulance company was slow to give Chickie his slice, and I would have to visit the garages and inform the companies how easily accidents could happen to their employees or their equipment."

"You didn't want to be at the mercy of someone who might remember you?"

"Let's say I didn't want to end up cut up like Chickie," Goohan said. "He brought it on himself, you know. Every man he killed, he'd take out that knife and . . . it's not worth going into. Chickie Marandola was a monster. He was street hungry. He couldn't control his appetite. A man in his position has to be feared, and Chickie liked scaring the people, but he went too far. He was downright hated. Everybody wanted him out of the way. There was others, asked me to take him out, because I was close to the man."

"But you didn't," Ladderback said.

"A man who kills another man never rests well," Goohan said. "On the other hand, a woman that kills a man, she sleeps soundly. I think, if I'd been a woman, I could've chopped him up just fine."

"Let's give thanks for small favors," Ladderback said.

"Besides, working for Chickie had its fringe benefits," Goohan said. "Chickie would send me down to Puerto Rico, to watch over our import/export operations. I would start in Puerto Rico and work my way around the islands. There were times when I never wanted to come back."

"I understand that," Ladderback said.

"You'll excuse me for saying so, but you don't seem cut out to be the traveling kind, Mr. Ladderback."


When Den told Andy that all the food prepared in the restaurant was free-range, organic, pesticide and herbicide free, including rare imported herbs and vegetables from the Caribbean and Eastern Europe, Andy asked if she could order out for pizza.

"Page three on the menu," Den said. "The conch and sheep's milk cheese pizza is really wild."

"You have a salad?" Karyn asked, her long, silver-tipped nails on the server's arm. "I can't eat much. I have to look good in leather."

"Push it while you've got it, Karyn," Charlotte said. "It doesn't get any better when you stop celebrating birthdays."

She turned to her daughter. "Order something. Anything. An important client got me this reservation and when you see him you're going to tell him how thrilled you are to be here."

Andy was thrilled to eat the cashews. In fact, she couldn't stop eating them. They were superbly addicting, a salty, oily, nutty combination that, once introduced to the mouth, required continual feeding until . . .

What Andy really wanted was a big, cheesy, greasy cheesesteak, but she couldn't bring herself to say so. "Could I look at the menu a little longer?" Andy asked.

Den disappeared and Andy wished she could make herself small enough so that *she* could just disappear. Charlotte liked flashy places where you went to be seen. Andy had been to enough of those with her mother to understand their appeal, but, somehow, what she wanted now was the opposite: a place where you could fade in, or out, and wallow in simple food that was probably a little too rich, salty or fatty to be good for you, but that tasted great going down.

Andy could tell from the jut of her mother's jaw, and the way her mother's eyes constantly scanned the crowd, that Charlotte was in her element. Since Andy's father had died in June, mother and daughter hadn't been seeing much of each other. Andy found an apartment in West Philadelphia, and Charlotte began spending nights in a Manhattan apartment hotel.

As if to bring her daughter up to date, Charlotte said, "You should be aware, Andrea, that I think I've found a buyer for the house. He's one of the gallery's clients, the same one who got us this reservation. The realtor gave him the key and a temporary access code. I'm staying at the house tonight—there's a Wish List affair at the Museum tomorrow night, then I'm back to New York so, be a good girl, and get rid of the rest of your things as soon as you can. You'll do that, won't you, Andrea?"

Andy hadn't wanted to go back to the house, but . . . "Okay."

"If you run into the buyer while you're there, please be nice. His company is about to go public and I'm sure he has every intention of going to settlement but one never knows until the check clears. I know you've been emotional about the sale but—"

"I'm not emotional," Andy lied.

"Good girl!" Charlotte said. She turned to Karyn. "I believe it's time for a run to the powder room."

Karyn stood, grabbed her purse, touched her hair, and thrust out her chest. Just before she took a step, Charlotte said, "For God's sake girl, relax a little. Just go off, slowly, look confused. The first person you're going to ask directions from is Alex Elgin, in the leather jacket."

"*Dr.* Elgin," Andy said.

Charlotte was impressed. "You've met him!"

"I interviewed him, when I was at Penn," Andy said. "He collects Boyagians. You helped set it up."

Charlotte eyed her daughter warily. "If you ran into him again, would he have pleasant memories of your interview?"

"I don't know. I remember he asked me about my Doc Martens."

Charlotte brightened. "I bought you that pair."

"And the skirt I wore. You bought me that, too, and, he kept asking about how long it takes me to lace them up, and how tight I like them. I had the feeling he was a pervert."

Charlotte closed her eyes.

"What's wrong with that?" Karyn asked.

Charlotte opened her eyes. "I believe Karyn was going to point out that some men express their respect for a woman by making innocent comments about their wardrobe."

"It was out-of-line," Andy said. "I was supposed to be getting information and he was supposed to be giving it to me. Nothing more. And I don't think what he was asking was innocent."

"You didn't react negatively?" Charlotte asked.

"I didn't react at all," Andy said. "I tried to ignore it and I finished up with the questions, and that was it." Andy turned to Karyn. "I mean, how would you react if you were in a business setting and some guy old enough to be your father asked you if you get off on what you're wearing?"

"I'm sure he was merely gallant," Charlotte said, "Alex is absolutely *massive* in pharmaceuticals and . . . you *will* be very kind to him if you see him, won't you, Andrea?"

Charlotte turned her attention back to the dining room. "The one standing, in the blue jacket, is Danny Bleutner. Very influential. Collects blue, anything blue. Don't ask me why. Make sure both men notice you, mention the gallery and, get them to introduce you to whoever they're with."

Karyn, like a good soldier, gazed soberly at the field of battle, and marched off.

Charlotte watched her go. "You could be doing that," Charlotte said to Andy. "You could turn just as many heads as Art World Barbie over there. Say good-bye to that dreary newspaper and we'll go to New York. We'll go shopping. We'll see people. You'll have so much fun."

"Mom," Andy began, "I like what I'm doing."

"I suppose one *can* learn to like trivial things," Charlotte said.

"Mom, please. There's this really old guy who writes the obituaries in the desk next to mine. He told me that if you really want to find out how the city fits together, you don't look at the celebrities and the scandals and the stories that win all the awards. You go talk to the ordinary people, or the people you're supposed to think are ordinary. And you find out, pretty quick, that they're not ordinary at all, that they're quite extraordinary in ways you never realized."

Andy waited for her mother to say something. She saw that her mother's eyes were on the dining room. "Extraordinary," her mother finally said. "I adore extraordinary people. You meet a lot of them in the art world. My favorites are those whose checks clear."

Then she pushed her chair back and said, "You'll excuse me. I, too, must ask the gentleman where the powder room is." She waved to a man who was table hopping. He waved back and Charlotte glanced back at Andy. Andy could almost hear her mother thinking: *should he meet my daughter or not?* Charlotte turned her face back toward the table hopper.

Not.

Her mother left and Andy had one of those gaps in which nothing happens until everything happens and what made everything happen was hearing the voice she'd wanted to hear all day.

"Hey, Andy."

"Drew."

Andy failed to force herself not to look at him, and he probably saw how much she wanted him to sit down and put his arms around her, so he remained standing and started talking. "Look, over there, that's Slip Disc Chasen, the creep that's always filing slip-and-fall lawsuits against restaurants. They call that kid with him Slip Knot. You know they're checking this place out, trying to find a way to sue. And did you see that scorching babe your mother brought in?"

Andy wanted to throw a nut at him. "No, Drew. Who would that be?"

Shaw glanced over his shoulder. "Look, I know this is your birthday, but we heard that Michelle Fragg was coming through on her book tour and we had to do something with it. She used to be the magazine's food critic, and now she's the Angry Eater. She's *famous*, Andy. We just HAD to get her to lunch, and at the last minute, Fragg started having cold feet, like she wasn't sure about it. She said she was on a diet. I didn't believe that for an instant, because the truth is that, even though they have hated each other for years, Fragg and Plank were actually once . . ."

"Lovers," Andy said. "So you just picked up a phone and got a reservation."

"I called in a favor. See that guy in the blue jacket? I did this round-up of rich collectors. Bleutner has his own table here. Supposedly, he put the financing together so this place could open."

Andy remembered that Lange had ordered her to talk to people, to ask questions like what is Matt Plank hiding.

She asked, "Drug money?"

"Money from drugs, but not drug money. One of the partners has a drug factory, makes generic rip-offs out on the Main Line. Danny can explain it to you. He knows everybody."

"My father knew everybody," Andy said.

"Yeah, but not everybody wanted to know him. With Danny, it's mutual. He's says there's a writing job opening up at *Esquire* and he can get me in for an interview. Remember that article I did on the murder of Chickie Marandola and the Philly Mob? You know, the one crime nobody wants to solve? Danny said that could be a book."

Andy had to admit: Drew could make a career for himself chronicling the exploits of the South Philadelphia Italian mob. It had begun before she met him, when Drew had first started with *Liberty Bell* and had blundered into—he would say staked out and entered—Orley's Emperor of the Steak when mob boss Chickie Marandola was there. Drew had had the guts to ask Marandola for an interview, and that interview ended up being Marandola's last. A few days later pieces of Marandola began to turn up all over the city, and, when Drew's interview ran in the magazine a few weeks later, Drew became a local celebrity, featured on TV talk shows as some kind of expert on organized crime.

When Andy met Drew, she was more impressed with his looks, his flair, the fact that he seemed to know his way around the city, and that he had a wide-eyed sense of wonder about so many things. He dressed well, he chased the stories that he thought deserved the effort, he drove a sports car and—what Andy found most endearing about him—he cared for her, took her seriously, listened to her and genuinely wanted her in his life.

For a while. And then . . .

Andy wasn't sure exactly why, but she felt like she was about to cry.

Drew said, "C'mon Andy, I'll introduce you to Danny. I'm sure he knows your mother. Danny buys art all the time—as long as it's blue. I mean, you should see his house. He actually has a Blue Period Picasso."

She said nothing.

"Okay, I forgot your birthday. I forgot because things aren't good at the magazine. The publisher is looking for a new editor. I'm up for the job. But, the way it works is, I'm either going to get it, or, if I don't, whoever the new editor is, is going to fire my ass real quick unless I can come up with a book deal or some kind of major project that will turn me into something more than a guy who was passed over for the top slot. If I don't find that, I'm over, history, you know? What we had was great, for a while, but now, I have to make these decisions and . . ."

"Drew," Andy said, "go away."

"I'll let you know if I get the job," he said. Then he went away.

Andy touched the napkin to her eyes and saw a server heading toward her table. "Mr. Plank said you might care for this," Den said.

It was a steaming, greasy, Philadelphia cheesesteak! Well, not exactly a Philadelphia cheesesteak. The bread's crust has a crackling crisp texture while the interior was as soft as sponge cake. The onions were minced white, the sirloin had been delicately sliced into thin ribbons, and the cheese was definitely not domestic provolone.

Andy picked up a fork, put the fork down, grabbed the roll, stuffed it in her mouth, and bit into the best cheesesteak she ever tasted.

She looked up and saw the guy who had been sitting at the bar, now standing near the entrance to the kitchen.

That was NOT the bald, hollow-cheeked, pencil-moustachioed genius chef whose picture had run in the *Press*. He waved at her, as to say, in a gesture, *is it okay?*

Andy gave him an OK sign. Then she stood. She knew it was crazy. She knew that there would be people staring at her as she walked across the dining room floor, but she didn't care because she was a little drunk and it was her birthday and he had been the only person who was nice to her all day, and so WHAT if he had been a little bit creepy and his restaurant was an intimidating theme park—everything she'd tasted had been great and he was right about timing and she didn't care how creepy he had been, she just had to thank him.

Then she heard a crash of furniture, plates and cutlery hitting the floor. Andy saw Michelle Fragg, whose chair had fallen behind her, crouching, clinging to the edge of a table, its contents spilled around her. She brought one hand up to cover her mouth, tried to stand up but made a terrible gurgling sound, and then fell back on the floor.

Just before the room erupted in confusion, a lone voice, later identified as belonging to Slip Disc Chasen, called out, "Is there a lawyer in the house?"

# 4 overdrive

We have in us a switch, a gear shift, an inside gadget that kicks us into overdrive. You can have a pile of explanations about why and how this thing works. You can identify the numerous chemicals, substances, devices that yank your eyes wide open, straighten your spine, and shove you into the air like a ball that makes that special crack when it hits the bat that announces to everybody in the stadium that this is going to be a home run.

And so it was with Andy Cosicki. Without quite knowing exactly what had happened, she was moving, her shoulder bag with her notebook computer banging against her side, a standard spiral-bound reporter's notebook in one hand, a pen in the other.

And because Andy's entire being had shifted into its highest neurophysiological-spiritual-psychobiological level, she was no longer glum, sad, sighing, put down, put-upon or more than slightly drunk. Suddenly it was perfectly cool to be a little taller than those around her—she could see so *far*—and she chewed up the fifteen yards or so between her table and Michelle Fragg's in a few effortless steps.

The room had become noisy again, but it was a noise with an edge of panic. People who had been table hopping were sitting down. People who had been sitting down were getting up, trying to stretch their necks so they could see a waiter at Michelle Fragg's table jumping up and down, wringing his hands.

He said, "Get up! Please get up! You're not going to do this to *me!*"

Andy found the rounded bulk of Michelle Fragg sprawled on her side on the rippling, swirling, sand-colored carpet like a beached mammal, her purple leather jacket streaked with a brownish, reddish spray of liquid that had apparently burst out of her mouth and her nostrils. Her eyeglasses had fallen off and she stank of stomach bile. Near one open hand her purse had come open, scattering several small items: a nail clipper, a key chain made out of rusted barbed wire, an ancient microcassette recorder, a breath spray, a wad of Wet Naps, a container of yellow pills without the prescription label. Her brown, bloodshot eyes were open, unmoving, unblinking.

A single question popped into Andy's mind: is this woman alive? When it's your job to get answers to the most obvious questions, you get them. So Andy didn't feel any revulsion as she reached for Fragg's hand, which was also covered with the crimson goo. She caught a hideously foul stench. She put a finger on the Fragg's clammy wrist. The skin felt thin and slimey.

Andy knew how to find a pulse and she felt none. She took her hand away and saw a dark stain appearing on the inner thighs and lower seat of Fragg's baggy, gray, herringbone-patterned chef's pants.

A deep, confident voice behind her said, "Now what seems to be the trouble here?"

Andy glanced back and saw the ruddy, puffy, troll-like face of Dr. Alex Elgin. "You'll excuse me, young lady, but I happen to be a doctor."

"I happen to be with the *Philadelphia Press*," Andy said. "You saw this happen?"

"I wasn't looking in this direction, but . . ." he crouched beside her, his black wool pants puckering instead of wrinkling. He sniffed and said, "My God. How *did* she get this?"

"How did she get what?" Andy asked.

He bent his body in such a way that, if Andy hadn't been in high gear, she wouldn't have seen his left hand sweep up the vial of pills. The vial went into his jacket pocket. He came out with a cell phone, glanced at Andy, and said, "You'll excuse me, but this must be confidential."

"You're not doing CPR," Andy said. "Why aren't you trying to save her?"

"Oh, *please*," Elgin said with annoyance. He touched a single number, and put the phone to his lips. "I'm at Loup Garou and this time, it's front and center. Get Huff and a crew down here *now*." He put his hand over the phone and looked at Andy, "I'm sorry, but I can't have you listen to my conversations."

"Tell me what you think did this," Andy said.

"It's obvious. . . ." He caught himself, changed his tone. Others began to gather around them. "Who did you say you were?"

"Andy Cosicki. I interviewed you when you were at the Stoner Clinic. Now, tell me, this person is dead, right?"

"You're Charlotte's girl! You were wearing those long, nasty boots," he said, brushing his hand against her knee.

Andy moved her knee away. "Dr. Elgin, tell me what's going on. Why aren't you helping this woman? You said something's obvious. What's obvious?"

"Because this is a massive metabolic collapse involving ruptured blood vessels and she's completely, thoroughly and *obviously* dead."

Andy began to write down what he had said.

"You're not going to quote me on that, are you?"

"Any idea about the cause?"

He put his cell phone away, stood and folded his arms. "I think what you're asking is, if I have an opinion, and my opinion, at this point, is that this poor person exhibits symptoms of several serious illnesses."

"Could it be what she ate?"

"Young lady, I will not be entrapped into issuing a statement that could result in any kind of legal action against any institution in which I am involved." He looked past her and called, "Danny, get *over* here!"

Andy wrote that down and said, "Thanks. I'll get back to you."

Elgin became flustered. "Young lady, you do not have permission—"

Andy moved away and saw that Drew Shaw was still seated at the table, tapping furiously on a notebook computer, talking to himself as he wrote, ". . . she spat up blood, and then she keeled over."

She turned to the waiter. "What was she eating?"

"The Passion Pot," the waiter said, and tried to launch into a memorized spiel: "It's a very stimulating broth-based oyster stew: you take your basic Hungarian ox tail with Caribbean hot and sweet spices, some of which are reputed to heighten certain *sensual* sensations, with these special oysters—don't ask me for the name because my brain is not functioning properly—sautéed in butter until lightly browned, and then tossed in a kind of seaweed, oh God, what is the seaweed? Mr. Plank uses six different kinds of seaweed and, normally, I could remember them, but right now, I want her to get up. I want this to be over. I want her to get up. *PLEASE*, make her get up!"

"I'm with the *Philadelphia Press*," Andy said as she wrote. "I need to get your name."

"You're media!?" the waiter exclaimed. "Mr. Plank says we can't talk to media."

Drew Shaw tapped some keys on his laptop and said, "I'll take another Manhattan, now, Jonn."

Andy saw the waiter wearing a coral name tag that said, JONN. She wrote it down as the waiter fled. In his place came a perspiring, round-faced man in a muddy brown summer sweater, who shoved his enormous paunch in her direction. "I'm Fred Chasen. I saw the whole thing."

Andy asked him what he saw.

"First, I gotta tell you, I go to restaurants all the time, and a restaurant is a dangerous place. You just don't hear about how dangerous it is because, when you see anything about a restaurant in the media, it's about the food, right? But . . ." he pulled out a business card.

Andy asked him what he saw.

He handed her the card. "Before I get into that, I want you to know I'm Fred Chasen, director of Citizens Honorably Advocating Safe Eating Environments, an advocacy group with a web page and, right there's the web address, and if you go there you'll find out how I won in that $1.2 million judgement against Roland's Deli for having the mustard spilled over the floor leading to the rest rooms, right where anybody could have fallen and hurt themselves, just like I did."

Andy asked him one final time what he saw.

"I'm coming to that. I just want to tell you that, whatever you heard about it, I had three back surgeries for a slipped disc and I have another scheduled and, whatever they say about me casing restaurants trying to find things I could sue them about, it didn't have a word of truth in it. But, from what I see," he drew close, "this situation was a set-up from the word go. The food in restaurants isn't safe and that woman was going to expose it all and that's the reason she's on the carpet and you're standing here talking to me. You can quote me on that and, let me give you my cell phone number, because I'm about to have a press conference and I want you to be there . . ."

Andy was in such a high level of activity that she didn't even get mad at this asshole. She just left him standing because Plank had slipped past the ring of bystanders and was now crouching beside Michelle, gripping her hand.

"Oh my God, Michelle," Plank said, his face flushed. "Oh, Michelle, what's wrong with you?"

"I've called for an emergency medical team," Elgin said calmly. "We'll find out soon enough."

"I want to find out now!" Plank screamed.

"Stop whining!" Elgin said. "I've done all anyone can!" He stepped away and stood beside a woman that Andy might have identified as Karyn Asgard if Andy hadn't gone down on her knees next to Plank, who saw the pad in her hand and said, "You're not—"

"I know something about first aid," Andy said. She grabbed a napkin, wiped the woman's face, peered into her mouth and listened for breathing. "Put your ear right there," Andy said to Plank. "She's not breathing.

Do you have any bottled oxygen? Do you have any CPR equipment here?"

"I have a sign up in the kitchen that shows how to do a Hemlock manuever," Plank said. "I can make her breathe." He straddled Michelle, put both hands on her chest.

"That's not going to work," Andy said.

Plank pushed and a brown gout of liquid flew out of Michelle's mouth. Plank jumped back in fright, then he came around and cradled Michelle's head in his arms. "C'mon, Michelle. Wake up."

Andy took up her pad and pen. "Is there anything in the ingredients of the Passion Pot that could have caused this?"

He looked up, as if he had heard her for the first time. "Caused this? You think I wanted this to happen? This is my worst nightmare!"

"When was your last food poisoning incident?"

"You really think I do this to people! Where's Danny? I'm not saying another word to you without Danny okaying it."

She saw him grab a bread crust that had fallen on the carpet and stuff it in his mouth.

Then a pair of navy blue trousers appeared between her and Plank. Andy looked up, saw the trousers going into an electric blue blazer and then, riding over a pale blue suit and striped tie, an unremarkable, rounded, jowly face still dark and leathery from a summer in the sun, tiny spectacles riding on a bulbous W. C. Fields nose, crowned by close-cropped, gray whorls of kinky hair.

"Sheesh!" he said, putting his hands on his head. "This is a tragedy, major league tragedy and . . . and . . ." He took his hands away from his head as he searched for a word, "regrettable. That's it. This is regrettable in the extreme. Extremely regrettable. This is a tragedy."

He saw the pad in Andy's hand. "I'm Danny Bleutner and you'll excuse me if I didn't catch who you were with."

"She's media and we have to get rid of her!" Plank snarled. "I treated her decent and she's going to stab me in the back."

Andy stood and indentified herself.

"The *Press*," Bleutner said, his hands moving faster than his mouth.

"Don't be unhappy if I haven't seen your by-line. Cosicki. Cosicki. There was a guy, a Cosicki, died a coupla months go. He used to expedite around City Hall, and with the unions. What did we call him? Benny Lunch."

"He was her father," said Drew Shaw at the table.

Bleutner pointed at her. "*You're* the one Benny got into *Press*! What I heard, after he got you into there, it was like, wow."

For a second, Andy's energy level slipped. She became guarded. "What do you mean, wow?"

"Wow as in, you know, wow! Your boss, Lange, he has this way about who he likes to take on, and he didn't like having to make a place for you. A coupla days later, he was on the phone to me about that Philly Pheed business, and he was telling me how happy he actually was that you turned out to be actually decent."

Andy was shocked. "He never said that to me."

"So . . ." again, his mind searched for the words, "so . . . Lange's got you doing food writing now?"

"It's her birthday, Danny," Drew Shaw said. "She's not here on assignment."

Andy would have thrown something at Drew, but she went back into overdrive. "I'm covering this, now," she said.

"You have every right to," Bleutner said. He pointed to Plank. "You. Give her everything she needs. Unlimited access. Don't hold nothing back. She wants a meal, you make it."

Before Plank could say he already did, Bleutner motioned Andy over like a cop directing traffic, "See that guy who looks like a doctor? That's Alex Elgin. He doesn't do much doctoring, and he can be a little full of himself, but he can fill you in about medicine. He told me there's an ambulance on the way, and the guy you're going to talk to on the ambulance is the driver. He's also head of the response team, name of Larry Dettweiler, and you'll know him because he's got a lung condition so he's always using an inhaler, so they call him Huff. Tell him I said it's okay for him to answer anything you want."

Andy said she'd already talked to Elgin. She opened her pad and was about to read back some of Elgin's remarks. "He said the victim—"

Drew said, "He did not!"

Bleutner made a referee's penalty sign. "That's a word that I don't think was used."

Andy glared at Drew. She checked her notes. "You're right. What he said was—"

Bleutner said. "What we have is a dead person and if she's a victim of something or other . . ." he took into account the empty cocktail glasses on the table, "we will make that loud and clear when we know for sure, but until we know for sure, she's just a dead person, okay?"

It wasn't okay. Andy didn't like to be told how she should do her job, but Bleutner had taken charge, and Andy wouldn't have said anything further if Drew Shaw hadn't cut in with, "How about 'former lover?'"

Plank groaned.

"Drew, Drew, Drew, Drew," Bleutner said, stepping over Michelle Fragg's body to come to the table. "I know where you're going with that, and it's not going to make people happy, if you know what I mean."

"I want the same access you're giving her," Drew said indicating Andy with a Loup Garou handcarved ivory swizzle stick modeled on the wooden stakes that are nailed through the hearts of Hollywood vampires, "and I want that book deal you said you would get me, with a serialization in *Vanity Fair.*"

"Drew," Bleutner wagged his hands, "Is this you or is this you? You did that article about me in *Liberty Bell.* It was pretty good. I got you in here today. Your subject drops dead, but, hey, it's tough all over."

Drew sipped his Manhattan. "I'm the senior editor of a major metropolitan lifestyle magazine, and the most famous restauranteur in the city cooked off the menu for a no-byline consumer reporter for a tabloid newspaper," Shaw said, smacking his cocktail glass down.

Plank looked at Andy. "Did I do something wrong?"

Andy glared at Drew. "Drew Shaw is not happy."

"Such a tragedy," Bleutner said. "You'll excuse me if I mention, in passing, that, any second now, we're going to get a ton of media, and cops, and who knows what else, and they're going to take one look at this dead woman here, and they're not going to want lunch, okay?"

"What I want is different," Drew said, his eyes on Andy. "I want to write a fascinating, penetrating, gossipy, true-crime expose about our restauranteur getting his just deserts!"

"You need a title?" Andy snapped. "How about 'Chafing Dish'?"

Shaw gulped his Manhattan. "We have the most famous restauranteur in the city with a dead woman with a national reputation in his place, a dead woman who used to be his lover, a dead woman who hates his guts and the feeling is mutual."

"She doesn't hate my guts," Plank said.

"She hates you, and she hates the city, and she hates the entire state."

"She give any reasons?" Plank asked.

"Too many. She hates the state because she got busted for drunk driving and they wouldn't take it off her record."

"You can't expunge DUIs in Pennyslvania," Bleutner said. "And it's a Commonwealth, by the way, not a state."

"She hates every place in the city but one," Drew read on. "Orley's Emperor of the Steak."

"That's where we met!" Plank said. "In South Philly. We were both working there. I worked the grill and she prepped and made the soup."

"And she really hated your stew," Drew said, "that was the last thing out of her mouth, before the blood." He closed his laptop, folded his hands, and said to Plank, "It won't be me, but *somebody's* going to say you killed her."

Plank nearly jumped on him, but Bleutner put himself between Plank and the table. A commotion near the front of the restaurant made Bleutner turn and say, "There they are!" The ambulance crew, led by a red-uniformed skeleton with an Elvis pompadour, had arrived with a group of police and two TV news reporters.

Andy saw Bleutner point to Plank and say, "You are currently unavailable." He waved his hands like a magician. "Disappear!"

Plank looked helplessly at Andy, and then he slipped away.

Bleutner motioned Andy toward Drew. "Before I set into motion my famous spin, would a statement from a Philadelphia lawyer acting on behalf of Mr. Plank and his restaurant be of interest to our remaining former lovers?"

Andy blushed. Drew muttered, "That didn't come from me," as he flipped his laptop open.

"What's happened is truly regrettable," Bleutner began, "but regrettable things happen. . . ."

# 5 conflict of interest

In the end, Howard Lange employed the "reverse Solomonic" in determining who would get the lead byline position on the story about the untimely death of Michelle Fragg.

Both Jay Maculay and Trina Kassein had demanded their bylines be in the lead position. Maculay had contributed three paragraphs about Fragg's life in Philadelphia. From a press bio supplied by her book publisher, he had written that she had been born in Reading, and came to Philadelphia to study at the Culinary Academy. She worked in a succession of restaurants and then joined Matt Plank to open his first restaurant, Trellis. She then became a food critic for *The Rag*, a weekly freebie paper. She went from there to *Liberty Bell Magazine* and then, New York City and fame.

Ladderback noted that no one had bothered to see if Fragg had family anywhere. Who was going to claim the body? Who would see to her estate? Who would grieve for her?

Kassein added three paragraphs about Fragg's New York "reinvention" as TV's Angry Eater, when, as a fill-in co-host on a Manhattan local access cable TV talk show, she spit out a forkfull of sea cucumber souffle during a celebrity chef cooking demonstration, called it "crap-o-rama," and then won the chef's libel lawsuit when she forced the judge and jury to taste the concoction, thus launching her on a career as the righteously enraged champion of New York's silently suffering $150 fixed-price dinner set.

And it was Kassein who, when she wasn't spraying her desk with the nutmeg-scented "Barbados Breeze," argued the most. She wanted her byline to lead because, unless it could be established that one among an article's authors did the most work, it was the *Press*'s style to list multiple bylines alphabetically, and she did NOT want Maculay's name to come before hers.

As Maculay and Kassein struggled to prove whose contribution was the greatest, no one considered that if *Press* style was followed to the letter, Andrea Cosicki's name would lead.

It was Andy who had written the story and sent it on her notebook computer. She had included comments from diners, a wonderful "we can't say if it's murder or not" quote from Police Homicide Lieutenant Everson, and a "this is my absolute worst nightmare" statement from Matt Plank.

At his word processor, Ladderback could call up both the original version of the story that Andy had sent in, and subsequent versions that were being edited at the copy desk. She had done a terrific job, and, in his opinion, deserved to have her byline in the lead position.

But she wouldn't get it.

Ladderback's one drink at Jimmy D's had led to another, and another, making it difficult to do anything more than revise an obituary that, because of the space in the newspaper that would be taken up by the breaking news of Michelle Fragg's death, might not even see print.

So he busied himself. He cut out and filed articles from the newspapers and magazines he read every day. He checked sources and databanks on the Internet.

He also watched the way the newsroom reacted to Andy's story. He saw Howard Lange strut imperiously from his office and take a seat on the copy desk, the geographic and spiritual center of the newsroom—

everything written had to pass through the copy desk editors. Though Lange had a computer terminal in his office where he could monitor the flow of copy in private and edit whatever he wished, he worked at the copy desk when he wanted to assert himself in the newsroom.

Ladderback's terminal wasn't intended to provide access to the intimacies of the editorial process, but one of the newspaper's computer techs, in appreciation of an obituary Ladderback had written, had tweaked it so he could summon the version lists and read instant memos between Lange, in his smartly tailored suit and silk tie, and Bardo Nackels, the unshaven, pot-bellied troll who, as the night city editor who never seemed to leave the newsroom, had to approve any copy before it could be laid out and printed.

Ladderback called up the story's "O" version, the original that contained the spelling mistakes, transposed words, and other errors that Andy had made while typing the story on her notebook computer.

The "O" version also contained notes that Andy wrote for editors. A note was appended to a paragraph containing a quote from a Dr. Alex Elgin, a "pharmaceutical industry executive" who had happened to be in the restaurant and examined the victim before the ambulance arrived. "I can assure you," he had said, "that this poor person exhibits symptoms of several serious illnesses."

Elgin. Ladderback did a search of the *Press*'s database. How many Alex Elgin could there be? He pulled up a few articles that mentioned him—ending with his resignation from the Stoner Clinic, denying that it had anything to do with the death of Carol Dettweiler.

Ladderback closed his eyes. The anxiety would subside, he told himself. It always did.

Andy's note, added at the bottom of the paragrah, read [**Can't confirm, but Elgin might have been the reason my mother got a reservation at Loup Garou. Conflict?**]

Andy was asking if it was a conflict of interest to mention a source in a news article with whom you have, or a close relative might have, a financial relationship. If there was a conflict, it was trivial, but in a subsequent version of the article, Lange cut the paragraph.

Ladderback did an Internet search on Elgin and found out he was a managing partner at Alixxir, a generic drug manufacturer that was in the tiny Main Line borough of St. Anne's. He glanced at the biographical details about him, saw that he was the "third generation Elgin" in the pharmaceutical industry; born in Somervale, New Jersey, raised in Puerto Rico; Yale undergrad; MD from George Washington University Medical School in Washington; recipient of numerous research grants; former director of clinical trials at the Stoner Clinic; collects art.

If Elgin collected art, he might know Andy's mother. Not quite a conflict, but . . .

Ladderback went back to Andy's article. The next paragraph to go was a diner quote from Daniel Bleutner. Andy had asked Bleutner if he would return to a restaurant where someone had died. Bleutner's response, "Regrettable things like this happen. Matt Plank has made a lot of people happy in this city, and I have great confidence in Matt Plank and everything he does, and I think it will soon be established that he is blameless in this regard."

For the second time that day, Ladderback pulled his Bleutner file, glanced at a *Liberty Bell Magazine* article about Bleutner's art collection, and saw that among the clients Bleutner's firm represented were Plank's Constant, Inc., and Philadelphia Press Inc.

Andy hadn't indicated Bleutner's financial relationship to Plank and the newspaper—it was possible that she didn't know, Bleutner didn't tell her, or she simply forgot to include it. The newspaper's conflict-of-interest guidelines might permit the quote to stay, and, in a few versions, Lange kept it, awkwardly characterizing Bleutner as a "power lawyer with his finger on the pulse of the city's business climate" until Bardo Nackels pounced: [**Howie, I know you're a huge fan of the Weather Channel, but since when does a climate have a pulse?**]

Lange fired back a note telling Nackels where he could shove his pulse. He tried to rework the line without mentioning Bleutner's relationship with the *Press* until Nackels wrote: [**Plugging the Blue Boy is not going to get Plank to commit to the Philly Pheed.**]

[**FUCK OFF.**] Lange wrote to Nackels. [**I have my sources.**]

[Give the Blue Boy up.] Nackels fired back.

Lange asked, [What do you have against him?]

[The last time I spoke to him, he told me he wanted to make me happy. Is that enough?]

Ladderback saw Lange spit a blob of paper out of his mouth. Lange's finger went down on a key that cut the paragraph.

Ladderback then went back to the Alixxir web page and saw that Bleutner was listed as "of counsel." Ladderback was going to explore the web site but found himself distracted by the byline fight between Maculay and Kassein.

Knowing that the attention of the entire newsroom was focused on him, Lange ripped up a new piece of paper, put in his mouth and began chomping on it as if it were chewing gum. Then he positioned himself beside the writers, who could not leave each other with the last word.

Lange put his hands on his hips, so his burnt puce paisley silk tie flopped forward. This was his about-to-assert-authority-in-public position, a relaxed but intrusive stance intended to contrast with the feverish feud going on in front of him. He stood, waiting for a pause in which both writers would have to take a breath.

Maculay ran out of gas first, clutching himself somewhere below his heart. Kassein attacked with an acrid, turpentine-scented cloud called "Swaying Pines." Just as she put the spray can down, Lange called her over to his terminal and said, "How come there's nothing in the story about Fragg being a drunk?"

"Because . . ." Kassein began.

"There have been rumors," Maculay jumped in, "but we—I mean, I—couldn't substantiate them."

Lange knitted his fingers and grinned. "I happen to know that when she got her TV show in New York she tried to expunge two DUI convictions that she got down here. One of the sponsors backing her show was a winery, and they wanted to be sure there wouldn't be anything anybody could get on her to make them look bad. So she finds out what all DUI arrests find out: you can't get a DUI expunged in Pennsylvania."

Maculay was stunned, as Lange had wanted him to be. The best way

81

for an editor to assert authority over a reporter was to come up with specialized knowledge that the reporter should know, or should have considered, when writing the story. While it was possible for a reporter to call in a favor and get someone in front of a computer at the Pennsylvania Department of Transportation to do a license check and find out about DUI convictions, the fact that Fragg tried to get these convictions wiped off her record showed an even deeper level of insider lore.

Precisely the kind of lore Danny Bleutner, or one of his associates, would supply, Ladderback decided, in the form of a simple phone call that Lange could have easily taken in his office before emerging to edit the story.

"Two DUIs don't indicate a drinking problem," Kassein said. She was married to a psychologist who specialized in substance abuse cases.

Maculay, who was known to drink a bit too much before his digestive difficulties made eating restaurant food a spectator sport, waved a finger and said, "It's not pertinent."

"It damned well is," Lange said. "If she got the reputation for being a drunk, and it turns out she died because she had a reaction to the food brought on by liver damage, you'd better believe it's pertinent," Lange said.

Did Bleutner, or one of his minions, also give Lange medical information? Either way, Lange was correct: rumors about a person in the news, especially when these rumors cannot be confirmed, become newsworthy when they suggest a cause of death if none is immediately obvious.

"I'm putting it in," Lange went on. "I also cut out a lot of this crap about how famous she was in New York. This is not New York, and we do not parrot the junk we get from PR agencies."

As if Lange didn't parrot information from *his* sources? Newspaper lifestyle writers relied heavily on promotional materials about their subjects. Though they were supposed to question the fluffy press releases and carefully worded background material that public relations agencies vomited forth, they depended on them, to some extent, at least when time was short.

"I also thought we were a little wordy about Trellis," Lange said to Maculay. "I've been to Trellis and it's no big deal. What is a big deal is how much and how long she was fucking Plank. I didn't see that."

Lange had found additional flaws in each writer's work. He then delivered his notorious "reverse Solomonic."

"What's happening here," Lange went on, "is that you're both too close to this thing. You're into it too deep, and when you're in too deep, we can get ourselves a conflict of interest, and we're not going there."

Maculay was about to say something: perhaps that, in terms of perceived conflicts of interest, Lange might also be just as deep because he was trying to get Plank's company to donate food to the newspaper's Philly Pheed. But Maculay shut himself down. He had worked long enough under Lange to know what was coming. It was Kassein who, either because she was hoping to prolong the decision, or she was using her dormant, but still powerful journalistic rat-smelling talent, demanded that Lange tell her what the rest of the newsroom was eager to hear.

"Who told you about the DUIs?" Kassein said, with enough disgust to imply that, by tossing in what was an obvious smear on Fragg's character, Lange just might doing someone a favor.

Then Lange made a stupid mistake: he folded his arms, narrowed his eyes, stopped chewing on paper to indicate HIS disgust at the fact that Kassein would dare to indicate HER disgust that he was doing somebody a favor.

Which meant, he *was* doing somebody a favor.

Lange snapped, "A little bird told me, got that?" He looked around, and his eyes locked on Ladderback, who quietly turned back to his terminal.

Ladderback heard Lange say, "I've put enough work into this Fragg thing so I could put my name on it. But I'm not going to put my name on it. We're team players here. Whatever's in the paper when it goes out, we all take the credit, and the blame."

Lange had just uttered a big, fat lie, the kind typically employed by politicians who smother dissent by evoking the myths of equality and group loyalty. The *Press* had no team players: the only thing a reporter hated more than not getting a byline, was another reporter sharing credit for a story. That way, if the story won an award, the award would have to be shared and, with the exception of the Pulitzer, most major award-giving organizations liked to hand out prizes to single writers.

"I'm not putting anybody's name on this," Lange announced, delivering the reverse Solomonic. "It's going to be a *Philadelphia Press* Special Report, and that's the end of it."

Of course, it wasn't the end of anything, but it was a signal for everyone to go back to their desks and the assignments they were supposed to be completing, and, to their credit, Kassein and Maculay complied.

Because he had an old, TV-tube-type computer screen, Ladderback could see Lange's reflection as the editor approached.

"You got that retraction for me, yet, Shep?"

"The reader withdrew his objection," Ladderback said, without looking at Lange.

"I want a memo to that effect." When Ladderback didn't respond, he added, "I also want you to use whatever connections you have with the medical examiners to get a cause-of-death into the Fragg piece before the deadline."

He waited. Ladderback waited.

"Do it now, Shep."

Ladderback picked up his phone. He dialed and spoke so softly Lange couldn't hear. He waited for Lange to leave, but Lange remained by his side. Ladderback took some notes, thanked his source, hung up and turned to Lange. "Officers on the scene identified blood and stomach contents in her mouth. Cause of death is still to be determined. The coroner won't have a report until Fragg's body, which is still in transit, is autopsied at the medical examiner's office."

"In transit?"

"A private ambulance company is delivering the body."

"Not a Fire Department ambulance?"

"It's at the discretion of the dispatcher," Ladderback said. He did not mention that the same ambulance company carrying Fragg's corpse had also attended to Weight Wisnitz.

84

Ladderback let a few seconds pass. Then he said, "About that bird."

Lange blinked. "What bird?"

"The one that told you about Fragg's DUI convictions. Was it a blue bird?"

Lange blinked again. Then he got it. "Yeah. Bluebird of happiness." He pulled the paper out of his mouth and went back to his office.

Ladderback waited until he heard Lange's office door slam shut. Then he pulled a file out of his cabinet and dialed Andy's cell phone.

She sounded tired, preoccupied, distracted, annoyed: "Yeah? What is it?"

"Would you like an assignment?"

He counted the seconds that she took to recognize his voice and decide if she was going to scream at him.

"What I just did wasn't good enough?"

Ladderback pulled up the edited version of the story on his computer screen. "I have it in front of me. It's very good. The assignment I have for you regards a day-in-the-life of an emergency services technician with a company named Speed Care Emergency Transport."

"They're the ones that carried Fragg out of here," Andy said. "They came and went."

"Did you notice how long ago they left?"

"Not really. An hour, maybe."

"Could you be precise?"

"At *least* an hour, okay?" Andy snapped.

Ladderback knew it took far less than an hour to get to the medical examiner's office from the Chestnut Street location of Loup Garou. "I take it from your tone of voice," Ladderback said, "that you'd rather not do this assignment. I have another."

"I don't want it."

"Daniel Bleutner."

"Not right now. He's going to have a gathering—that's what he called it, a gathering—at his office tomorrow, and he wanted me to come because there's someone who thinks he's going to write a book and Bleutner wants me there."

"Did he say why?"

"So I can really, really annoy the guy who thinks he is doing the book."

"I can offer you another assignment if you need a reason not to go."

"I have plenty of reasons not to go. The only one that makes me want to is that Plank will be there. He is this super-arrogant type, but he's also got this nice side. I told him I wanted a cheesesteak and he made one for me, and it was a *great* cheesesteak, the only decent thing that had happened to me all day!"

"The day isn't over," Ladderback said. "Better things may happen."

"It feels like it's over," Andy said.

Ladderback could hear, from the weakness in her voice, that after the frenzied gathering of information, the rush to write it, and the final triumphant e-mailing of the story, she was making a slow, awkward return to earth.

"If you need any background about Bleutner," Ladderback said, "I have in my files a *Liberty Bell* profile done of him. It says he is a lawyer who says his job is 'making my clients happy.' "

"Drew Shaw did that profile," Andy snarled. "I wouldn't believe any of it if I were you."

Ladderback paused. "Perhaps I should ask you to do a different assignment."

"Perhaps I should take the rest of the day off!" Andy said and broke the connection. She wanted to throw the cell phone into one of the restaurant's waterfalls.

But it stayed in her hand. She told herself she was a little older now, that she'd no longer kick in walls and punch out guys who would annoy her. It was no longer cool to express anger so visibly. There were better ways to pretend she was an adult.

Like go home and do lay-ups with a basketball.

Then she remembered her mother was selling her home. Andy had an apartment in West Philadelphia, and she could use some basketball courts in a nearby park but . . .

She wanted to cry. She was still at the table where she had written her story. This was the table where she had expected to have a nice birthday lunch with her mother, but there's nothing like a sudden death to make your mother and Art World Barbie take the quick route out.

Andy took a final glance around the restaurant, at the empty tables with their half-eaten meals left on them. All the patrons had left. A few members of the staff remained, waiting to be interviewed by the homicide detectives. The crime lab technicians were still hovering about Michelle Fragg's overturned chair. She watched them scrape things off the carpet and put the scrapings in the bags. She didn't want to think what those scrapings were. She was cranky and tired from the frantic rush of interviews, the hurried writing she did on a notepad she kept in her shoulderbag, and the final e-mail.

It was over and she had no appetite, so why was she hungry? She folded up her notebook, put her cell phone in her shoulder bag, hoisted it on her shoulder, and went up the stairs and out of the place into a day that, like most Philadelphia days in the summer and too many in the autumn, was aging gracelessly: the afternoon heat, dust and vehicle exhaust gave the air a bitter, empty taste, like tea made from leaves from which all the flavor had been leached out.

Lieutenant Everson's big, unmarked Ford Crown Victoria was parked on the sidewalk, one of several police vehicles cluttering up the sidewalk. If not for the vehicles, a handful of uniformed cops keeping the gawkers at bay, and the police I.D. badge hanging on a chain across his sport coat, Everson could have been just another urban wage slave pumping up his productivity outside the office.

His mahogany-colored hair was still thick and straight, but the skin around his eyes and mouth were beginning to wrinkle at the edges, and the wrinkles weren't the kind that showed character or strength, but wariness and restraint.

She'd met him previously when she was on the scene at the hit-and-run death of a former Philadelphia city councilman. He had known her father and told her that he owed her father many things. Andy had found him to be genuinely courteous to her, as well as others at the crime scene. He didn't crack wise, he didn't lose his temper, he didn't look at his watch and rush things along and, for Andy, he didn't radiate that prickly hostility that cops had for the media.

She saw him yawn, and that made her yawn, close her eyes, and wish that she could fall asleep on the top of his car.

He said to her, "You don't look so happy."

She said, "I'm not."

He took off his sunglasses and rubbed his eyes. "I keep wishing people would lay off killing each other so I can catch up. Tough for you on your birthday." He gave her a look like he just wished she'd ask him how he found out it was her birthday.

"I'm not going to ask how you found out," Andy said.

"I hear things. People come to me and they say, hey, funny way for the reporter from the *Press* to have a birthday, don't you think? And I run a license check, and, there it is: your birthday and everything else you did that maybe you shouldn't have done while operating a vehicle." He shut down the laptop and got out of the car.

She was coming down from the beat-the-deadline pressure and caught the whiff of pizza-scented grease blowing out of the pizzeria across Chestnut Street, and she found herself getting hungry.

"So," he said, "how does it feel to be working for the enemy?"

"What do you mean?" Andy said. "The last thing I wrote up that you were involved in, I got the facts straight."

"You did your job," Everson said. "You can work for assholes and do your job exactly right, but it doesn't change the fact that you're working for assholes."

"You're in a mood," Andy said.

"I got a right to be. The one I did, this morning: A 14-year-old creep doing a drive-by in a stolen Dodge that's older than he is, misses the scumbag he's trying to hit, and instead kills some four-year-old kid playing on the sidewalk. We got the creep because he was too busy shooting and he didn't see the garbage truck in front of him and he drives right into it, which just about flattens the front end of the old Dodge he's driving, pushes it flat like he hit a wall, and we have to get the Jaws of Life to pull him out. Now, you tell me how much I wanted to let that creep sit in that car and maybe die, but, what happens, I get a call from somebody—I'm not saying who—who asks me if I'm happy. You know what it means when somebody in this town asks you if you're happy? I'm looking at this dead child and he's asking me if I'm happy.

"Then he tells me it would be good if, when I write up my report, I write it up that it doesn't appear as if the trash truck was at fault. And you know what? The truck could have been at fault because it was way out on the other side of the street with its blinkers off and I just know some lawyer's going to get ahold of this and it's going to come down to me to decide: Do I tell the truth and the city pays for this creep killer's medical bills and maybe a fat settlement on top of that? Or do I lie a little bit and hope it doesn't go to court so it won't be my word against a bunch of witnesses the lawyer is going to dig up who will make me look like I'm trying to get the city off the hook?"

"You tell the truth," Andy said.

"The truth is this kid did nothing to deserve getting killed, and the creep that did it should've died when he hit that truck, but he didn't, and all this happened on a beautiful morning. Did you notice? Sun way up high in the air, a little breeze blowing. The four-year-old kid was shot with his mother right next to him. She was holding his baby sister and the both of them, as well as the other kids on the block, are going to need psychological counseling and medications that she is probably not going to get because there is a war going on between the bureaucracies that are supposed to be providing this kind of help. Cases are backed up and the media isn't going to follow-up on this case. You report it and it's over for you, but it's never over for these people, in these neighborhoods. It just gets worse. How do you think the kids on this street are going to grow up, watching one their own get half his head blown off? So I was calling in a few favors, to get some way to deal with this mess, and then I get called out here and it looks so much like food poisoning you want it to be food poisoning because it would be so nice if it was. A famous woman that nobody likes, who makes all this money going around the country trashing restaurants and, finally, she gets it from her old flame. It would be so right if Plank put something in the soup that killed her, wouldn't it?"

Andy shook her head. "He couldn't be that stupid."

"Anybody that kills anybody else is stupid. That's a given. Would he be so stupid to blow his entire business just to take out a critic? Sure. When people kill each other, they don't think." He glanced across the street. "We are officially trying to locate him, but so far all we've been able to do is get to Danny Bleutner and Bleutner has referred us to someone who basically told us that we are not going to get a word out of Plank, on the record or off, which is okay because he probably didn't do it."

Andy said, "What do you mean, probably?" She began to type on the notebook but Everson said, "Put that away. Only reason I'm talking to you is that I knew your father, your father did me some favors, so what I'm saying to you is my way of paying him back. Okay?"

It wasn't okay, but Andy wanted to hear him out. She put her notebook away and Everson swallowed some coffee, and said, "You didn't get this from me, okay?"

Not okay, either, but she had learned when people want to take you into their confidence, you let them.

"What I'm giving you here, is for your father. He said if I ever wanted to do back for him, what I should do is, if I ever had anything that a person who worked for a newspaper would really, really want to have, I should give it to you. So I'm giving it to you. But you can't say this came from me, because if you do, I will do more than deny it."

"What do you mean, 'more than deny it'?"

"You don't want to find that out. Now listen to me. Something like what this woman died of, has been going around. I've seen about eight cases in the last two months of people dropping dead with blood in their mouth, but who are these people? Local. Decent people, some of them. Some of them, not so decent. The kind nobody hears or cares about. Nobody anybody heard of."

"You mean some kind of disease?"

"I don't know, but I don't think so. It's too weird for that. You see, with a disease, there's a carrier or a source of contamination and it usually spreads out from one area, and there are more people involved, some who almost get it, but live . . . that kind of thing. With this, it's too strange. The people that get it, they're normal and then they drop dead with the blood on their mouth, or, in one case, coming out the other end. Either way, it's strange."

"So what do you want me to do with this?"

He shrugged. "I don't know. If it was me, I'd get the hell out of here before whatever this thing is comes around and gets me. But before I do any of that, I'd first check to see if my job was secure."

"It isn't," Andy said. "I don't get a day when I don't want to quit."

"Same here." He got into the car, started it up. "Maybe you should interview the owner of that pizza place. Ask him what it's like to serve slices across the street from this theme park where you can't get in without knowing somebody, and you don't get out without dropping a couple hundred bucks."

"I don't think so," Andy said.

"Try it," Everson said. "What you're looking for, is right there."

Andy waited for Everson to drive off. A cab was coming and she looked the driver right in the eye and the cab almost hit her. The cab was going slow enough to stop, but it didn't stop because people in a car who see you think that if you've seen them you should know that they're not going to stop.

Why isn't it the other way around?

She contemplated this for a minute and then she smelled pizza grease. This is an odor that would not be seductive if she hadn't just faced a life-threatening situation and hadn't she read, in one of those stupid men's magazines that Drew Shaw kept around his apartment, that the first thing people who have been in a life-threatening situation want to do is eat, and that the second thing is to make love, and the third is sleep.

So she went in. The walls were of cheap wood paneling, adorned with faded, grimy pictures of Rome, the Vatican, Venice, the Bay of Naples and the Isle of Capri.

There was also the scent of frying onions and thinly sliced sirloin, because it doesn't matter if there is no definitive link between the cheesesteak and pizza (an Italian roll sandwich called an oven grinder that is baked briefly in a pizza oven has been cited as a missing link, but culinary anthropologists have yet to file the paperwork), in Philadelphia, you can get a cheesesteak in any place that serves pizza, though you can't get a pizza in every place that serves cheesesteaks.

Andy guessed that whatever they made here could not beat the cheesesteak she had tasted at Loup Garou, so she told the kid in the turban (yes, they had a kid who did not resemble the stereotypical pizza maker making the pies, filling the drinks, packing the sandwiches, and looking as bored as anyone who might just have been Italian, in appearance, if not in fact) that she would go for a hoagie, a Philadelphia variation of the sub sandwich that, like the cheesesteak, employs sliced onions in a long, doughy Italian roll as an accompaniment to the sliced Italian deli meats, sliced tomatoes, chopped lettuce, shots of oil and vinegar, salt and pepper.

Because these onions are raw, the consumption of a hoagie places social obligations upon those with whom you choose to eat. You expect that anyone you speak with while eating, and in the hours after the fact, will have to accept you completely, that they will love you—body, soul, onion breath—or leave the room.

To this classic hoagie Andy requested both hot and sweet peppers. She figured she could use a sugar rush, so she had a large cola. No industrial fake sugar on this birthday.

The hoagie was served wrapped in paper in a red plastic mesh basket. Her Coke was in a big waxed cup with too much ice in it. She looked to the back of the place, which had a row of skinny, mismatched chrome and formica tables and chairs. Because it was past the lunch hour but not near dinner time, the chairs were empty. At the very back was a staircase with a sign over it that said ADDITIONAL DINING.

She went up the staircase and said to herself that she knew he would be there even if Everson hadn't hinted. And why did he hint anyway? So what if she had spent most of her time, not with the shocked diners, not with Danny Bleutner, not with the Everson and his crew, but with the guy who was hunched over the table next to the window, with grease-stained paper plates piled up beside him, and empty soda cups, a ruddy square of Sicilian pie on a plate in front of him, and, within grabbing distance, a can of Planter's roasted cashews.

"When things go wrong," Matt Plank told her, "I eat."

# 6 from hunger

It was only the early afternoon, but the newsroom had developed that flat, sour coffee smell, when Ladderback made the call to the medical examiner's office to get a cause-of-death for Michelle Fragg.

He talked to one of the ME's oldest employees, a woman who had known his parents, who told him as soon as they had "opened the decedent" the evidence was "obvious and plentiful." Fragg hadn't been murdered. She hadn't died of food poisoning, either, but rather, heart failure due to temporary asphyxiation. Though she was only twenty-nine years old, and had lost some weight in the last few weeks, Fragg's arteries were "paved with plaque" and she had numerous bleeding ulcers that had been aggravated by the high-fiber breakfast cereal she had eaten four hours earlier, and then washed down with an almost stupefying quantity of gin and quinine. She got to the restaurant, had another gin and quinine, which irritated the ulcers. They began to bleed profusely. The stomach filled with blood, triggering a need to regurgitate. The blood and stomach contents came up, Fragg choked on it, the stress brought on a heart failure and she died.

Ladderback could imagine the portrait of Fragg that the *Press* and others in the media would put together: a moody, alcoholic personality that alternatively abused herself with booze and rich, disasterously unhealthy food that she ate as part of her job, food that she tried to compensate for with high-fiber, weight-loss diets.

Ladderback passed the report on to the copy desk, where bits were inserted into the "Special Report" about Fragg's death for the late city edition. Then he went back to his desk and worried about how the evidence supporting the medical examiner's conclusions had been so obvious and plentiful.

That meant it was no-brainer, another easy analysis for the presiding pathologist who either wasn't interested in, or had good reasons not to probe. The cause of death made sense in the same way that Weight Wisnitz's cause-of-death made sense.

So far, the only thing the deaths had in common, were some—though not all—symptoms, and the ease with which everyone who processed the bodies handled the cases.

Both bodies were transported by an emergency medical service and ambulance company called Speed Care, which took a little too long to bring the body to the medical examiner's office.

Ladderback forced himself to stand, and go to his file cabinet, and open the file cabinet drawer marked "D". He pulled out the Dettweiler file, returned to his desk, and sat for a while with his hands on the file of what Whitey Goohan had called his road not taken.

Ladderback met Gina Dettweiler when he had been Andy's age, give or take a year; when he could walk down a street without shutting his eyes and panicking. In addition to doing obituaries, he also took general assignments. He'd get a tip about something that was horrible, shocking, scandalous, stupid, or flat-out amazing, get clearance from an editor, go out, come back filled to the bursting with the experience, bang out the lead, throw in the quotes and description, and he'd be done. The story would move to the copy desk, where the copy editors would hack off big pieces of it so it would fit whatever space on the page hadn't been taken up by an advertisement. Maybe they'd call him over to the desk and ask for clarification or qualification. They'd want to double-check the spelling of a name, mull over the meaning of a sentence, grumble over the placement of a comma.

And then he'd be done. He could walk the fifteen blocks back to his tiny studio apartment feeling like a hero, with nothing more to look forward to than a cheap meal, a few hours watching television or reading a book, maybe a movie in one of the crumbling cinema palaces on Chestnut Street, and then the sleep that would turn the day's experience into dreams wilder than any movie, until his alarm clock rang and he woke up to start the process over again.

When he was Andy's age, every story he did as a general assignment reporter was different. He had no idea in the mornings what parts of the city the newspaper might send him. Would he get wet from the backspray as firefighters aimed great beams of water at a burning building? Would he fill up on ridiculously sweet pastries while interviewing a South Philadelphia baker while that baker denied that he knew the mobster who had been gunned down outside his shop?

While working on assignments, he would hear from one of his sources that if he really wanted a story, he should check out this one, look up that one, "Just come on down here and stand on the corner, and you'll see stuff you'll never believe."

Looking back on it, the one thing about his days as a general assignment reporter that he envied was how easy it was not to care about some of the stories he did. He would tell himself that he was just doing a job that was temporary, that was going to take him somewhere, perhaps to some slick magazine writing position where he and his fellow journalists would burn up long lunch hours being clever and witty at Algonquin round-tables. When there were facts that didn't quite fit, situations too easy to believe, sources who were hiding facts or lying to him when they had no reason to, he would just shrug these things off: he had a daily 5 P.M. deadline to beat, he would tell himself. There's only so much you can do before the clock says you can do no more.

A funeral director told him about Gina Dettweiler. Gina ran a gas station where she worked on the funeral director's hearse. She was also a legend among import car owners, especially the German imports. But if

Ladderback really wanted a story, he should do one about what Gina did as a "sport or hobby, or whatever you want to call it. It's downright crazy, that a gal that cute could crash cars so well," the director said. "She once drove one of my old hearses in a derby. Crashed it up good, but she won, too."

Ladderback got the story approved, called up the gas station, asked if she was, in fact, the woman who crashed cars and, yes, she was, and did he have a problem with that?

Ladderback identified himself, told her he wanted to do a profile about her, made the appointment, and took a cab to her gas station, and, almost before he could get his pad out, saw this short, absolutely gorgeous woman getting into a Day-Glo pink flameproof jumpsuit. She told him to wait for her in the wrecker. He got into the big tow truck, and then she was beside him, backing the truck up so she could hook it to her car, a huge Chrysler Le Baron with FEMME FATALE spray painted on the side in pink. Because it was rigged for a derby (with the lights removed, gas tank moved to behind the front seat, all glass, lights, and upholstery removed except for the front seat), Gina had to tow it to the derby, but before she did, she looked at him and said, "You should eat."

She drove down to South Philly and grabbed an early dinner at Orley's Emperor of the Steak, where Ladderback thought he'd show off by ordering the cheesesteak with Brussels sprouts. Gina topped that with her steak with raw onions and garlic and hot peppers—her "Dragon Breath Special."

Ladderback endured the breath, and more. They drove for an hour across South Jersey. On the way, he interviewed her. She told him about how her father-in-law, Larry Dettweiler Sr., the original owner of the gas station, had driven in derbies and had taken her to a few until he was killed in a robbery.

"You don't need to be mad at the world to win a derby," Gina told him, "but it helps."

Gina's list of grievances was short, and bitter: she had loved her father-in-law and had been devastated by his loss. Then, shortly after her daughter was born, her husband left her without leaving a forwarding address. Add to that the problems of being an independent service station owner: extended warranties were locking in new car owners to dealer service departments, gas-and-go convenience stores underpriced her at the pump, and national auto repair franchises could offer oil changes at below cost. Add to that the increasing complexity of the cars, especially foreign makes.

"Every year, they come out with some new design that forces me to buy a new gadget just so I can get to the engine. And parts keep going up through the roof."

So she would keep on the lookout for old clunkers that she could get from a junkyard for one-hundred dollars or less. She'd modify them for demo derby competition in a few days, spray paint the sides with Femme Fatale, and "work out every bit of anger and frustration in about in ten minutes." The worst injury she'd ever suffered from crashing cars was a strained thumb "from holding onto the steering wheel too tight. Somebody hits your front wheels, the impact is going to snap the steering wheel around. You have to hold it, or it'll pull your thumb out of joint."

They went to a dirt track at what had been an old airport, where temporary bleachers had been set up and lighting came from an old floodlight truck. Gina was in her element, cheered by a thousand tailgate-picnicking bikers, motorheads and car freaks, as well as an entire cub scout troop, as she slammed her car, mostly in reverse, into an assortment of vehicles that, after a few minutes, were spouting flames and steam from seized engines and from ruptured radiators.

On the way back, she sang songs by a rock 'n' roll band called Little Feat—not FEET but FEAT—Gina was quite specific about that. One was about a Dixie chicken, another was about skinning something back, another mentioned a "horizontal mambo," and sailing shoes. What were sailing shoes, Ladderback had wanted to know. Do you wear them on boats?

After putting the Femme Fatale behind her garage ("I always put my car in the back. Don't want people thinking you're a junkyard," she'd tell him), they went to a bar at 43rd and Biltmore "within stumbling distance" of the West Philadelphia apartment she shared with her mother-in-law, Sonja, and daughter, Carol.

At the bar, Ladderback drank martinis (the drink of choice of the Algonquin round table, he told her) while Gina knocked back Latrobe Bombshells, glasses of Rolling Rock beer (made in Latrobe, Pennsylvania) supplemented by shots of "bottom shelf, cheapest-you-got" bourbon.

After a while, she started singing again, and Ladderback couldn't help but find her goose-honk of a voice even more adorable. He wrote the article the next day and called her again, when it appeared, asking her if it made her mad—it did, and did he want to go to another derby next week? Ladderback, a privileged, sheltered kid from Chestnut Hill, couldn't help but say yes, especially when, on the night of the second derby, after an hour or two in the bar, he went back to her rowhouse, and helped her carry the five-foot-tall winner's trophy up the steps. He came in, watched her kiss her sleeping daughter, Carol, said hello to her mother-in-law, Sonja, who was watching television, then helped Gina carry the trophy up to her bedroom and despite everything Ladderback read about alcohol making it difficult to make love, had absolutely no difficulty doing it.

The relationship lasted about three months, ending when Ladderback did something he thought would please her, but actually had the opposite result. As strong and fiesty as she was, Gina was angry and hurt by her husband's absence, but she seemed incapable of doing anything to find him.

Ladderback had used the resources of the newspaper, and his own persistence and effort, to track down the supposedly missing Larry Dettweiler, who, Ladderback discovered, was not missing at all. Larry was living in South Philadelphia near Orley's Emperor of the Steak, driving ambulances for a company that Gina's garage serviced. Though they never spoke, never even wrote letters to each other, and Larry did not provide her with a cent of child support, she had known exactly where he was, at all times, and so thoroughly resented that Ladderback had found this out, she refused to see him again.

First moral of the story: it is possible to fall in love with someone who is wrong for you in so many ways, and yet to love that person, in ways you never thought possible.

Second moral: the truth doesn't always set you free.

He called Gina only twice after that: when Gina's mother-in-law died, and when her daughter died.

Now, with the file open in his hands, Ladderback looked past the clipping of the profile he had done on Gina, and the articles he saved about her daughter. He went to his notes, a suggestion she'd made for another story, if he ever wanted to do one, but a story that he couldn't let anyone know had come from her. She had made the suggestion to him when she had had a few too many Latrobe Bombshells, and she was angry at Larry. Some of the ambulance drivers at the company where Larry worked were taking illicit drugs in their vehicles, or transporting them, or both, she told him. When she did basic maintenance on those ambulances, she would find marijuana, narcotics, and other illicit substances tucked in and around the driver's seat.

There could be other reasons that an ambulance took so long to deliver a corpse, he acknowledged, but Ladderback couldn't think of any that were good.

Of course, an ambulance going slow, when it should have been going fast, wasn't the best reason to look up an old lover. Would she want to talk to him, after so many years?

He dialed the number of Gina Dettweiler's garage.

As soon as she saw Plank, Andy wanted to leave. She had been through enough that day. She wanted to eat in peace.

And yet there was something about his discomfort that drew her to him. Maybe it was the way the flab on his face smoothed out the masculine edges and turned him into a baby. It would be rude to just up and leave, and though Andy could be rude when she wanted, she couldn't bring herself to be rude now.

She sat down opposite him. She felt his eyes on her. Once again, he was evaluating her, waiting for her to pass a test.

This time, she wasn't going to put up with it. She gave him a blast of the Intimidation Beam. "Stop staring at me."

He almost jumped out of his chair. "Okay. Sorry. Let's try it this way.

YOU SHOULD EAT." He folded his arms and made a serious show of looking out the window.

Andy saw his eyes roll back toward her. He was being silly and she didn't laugh but she picked up the hoagie anyway, bit down, and felt the onions, peppers, lettuce, sliced tomatoes and Italian deli meats combine into a rude, greasy, salty, spicy explosion.

He raised an eyebrow. "Well?"

"It's okay," she said.

"Okay? Food isn't just okay." He speared a fried onion ring with a fork. "Food is all about pleasing people. All that other stuff doesn't count. Food is pleasure. Lack of food is pain. Good food is happiness. Great food is bliss so intense that you wish you could keep eating forever. Bad food is . . . a degradation, an insult, a crime. Supreme food is better than religion."

He told her he ate to feel good, a habit he developed as a child when living with his single mother, a hypochondriac who would send him out at all hours of the day or night to buy food to satisfy her weird cravings.

Andy listened absently. Some among those she had interviewed in Loup Garou had told her that Plank had achieved what others will spend a lifetime working for, and that success had happened to Plank so rapidly that he had no respect for his accomplishments. She also learned that Plank not only hated Fragg but had said many times that the restaurant industry would be better off if she died an early death.

She could imagine him saying that, but she could not see him doing it. She reminded herself that she should be wary of him, but she also wanted to know more about him, especially what it might be like to have your dreams come true.

Andy had dreams and most of them hadn't come true. She had originally wanted to work at the *Standard*, the city's solemn, provincial broadsheet newspaper that was always winning awards—sometimes even a Pulitzer—for huge, multi-part investigative stories. Her father got her a job at the *Press*, and she discovered that what appeared in the newspaper had less to do with the passionate, beat-the-clock quest to gather information that readers needed to know, and far more to do with the biases, prejudices, ignorance and fears of a newsroom staff that had stopped dreaming long ago.

Then her father died and she had prayed for the ability to solve his murder. When Ladderback helped her do that, she did not know how to feel.

Had Fragg's death been yet another answered prayer? Was Plank experiencing that sour state of elation that people get into when they find out that dreams that come true don't necessarily make things any easier?

She asked him that, point blank.

"You call this easy?" He gobbled another onion ring. "I went to the Culinary Academy because there was never any question in my mind that I would work in food. And I've hit the jackpot, okay? I've done four restaurants in seven years. I got all these people on the phone, wanting to give me money for my next restaurant. I have chefs in every part of the world, begging to work for me, and, get this: I can't go into my kitchens because they think I'm the boss, and the kind of people I hire, they go nuts when they see the boss. They need their space. They need to be creative. They need to make their art."

He stuffed some fried potatoes in his mouth. "So I can't cook anymore. I have to come up with concepts, and ways of doing things. No matter what I do, it always screws up. You may not see it. You may not taste it, but, I know it's screwing up even if it hasn't screwed up yet."

"And you let it get to you?" Andy said.

"EVERYTHING gets to me." He chomped down on a fried, stuffed mushroom. "If I would have had a choice, I would have not wanted Michelle in my restaurant, and I would have prevented it, if I had been given a warning. But I wasn't. I was blindsided, and it was a publicity stunt, and I hate publicity stunts, but I have partners who think that a publicity stunt is a good idea now and then. I have business partners who make me hire designers who tell me stupid fountains and fake rocks in my dining room will make everything so campy and ironic. And I have partners who want to me to take out advertisements in magazines so we can get coverage in those magazines, and you do these things to please your partners, or, at least, not to get them so pissed off that they become a problem."

"You told me that her dying was your worst nightmare," Andy said.

"My worst nightmare is losing control of my operation. A restaurant requires consistency and consistency requires control, and I like to control every aspect of my restaurants, and it's bad enough I can't control what a reviewer writes because, even those that give me what they think is a good review, are still mostly ignorant liars with faulty memories who invent things about me that are insulting and wrong. I've wanted to ban them all but, again, I have partners who think that publicity is important and reviews are to be permitted and, because of that, I'm in a situation that is thoroughly beyond my control, that has to do with me, personally, and not the food."

"*Was* it food poisoning?"

For a moment, he became almost furious. "My customers have had heart attacks, food allergies, a sprained ankle from slipping in the bathroom, whatever. There are at least a dozen lawsuits pending against my restaurants and they all want to settle out of court and sometimes we settle, even if we know we're not at fault, because it's just too tedious or expensive to fight it. But we *never* settle suits alleging food poisoning. I insist on that. We fight those suits until we win, and we always win. My food is not poison."

Andy paused. She had heard that, or a statement similar to that, before, but she couldn't remember where. She had a feeling of déjà vu, that she had had this conversation, or something like it, some time ago.

"But, people can get poisoned," Andy said, "even if it isn't your fault."

His face darkened "It's my fault if I haven't controlled fully what happens in my kitchens. One of the only good things about being successful in this business is that your suppliers stop sending you crap. I have 8,329 suppliers. Some of them ship me a single item, like that vodka you drank. I will fire a supplier if there is even a suspicion that an item is not of the quality specified, or if has not been handled properly."

While he had been lecturing her, Andy studied her hoagie, wondering

104

how many suppliers might have skimped or mishandled the ingredients. She decided it tasted too good to worry about.

"I want to ask you something," Andy said. "There was a picture of you in the *Press*, in an article about you that ran a few months ago. I looked at that before I came here and—"

"I hated every minute of that interview," Plank said.

"I'm talking about the picture. How come it's not you?"

"It was me, 45 pounds lighter. When I'm developing a restaurant concept, it completely consumes me. I'll take off and spend weeks traveling, tasting food, talking to people who grow it and make it. I let the concept change me. I'll get different clothes. I'll see a chair or a side bar that I have to buy and get rid of half the furniture in my apartment to make room for it. Then I go for days without sleep. I forget to eat. I become obsessed with the vision. I have a vision of what every restaurant should be, must be. It's always centered on the food, on the ability of food to please. Loup Garou was going take that as far as it would go. It started at the suggestion of one of my backers, Alex Elgin."

"I interviewed him."

"His father used to work for this huge drug company with labs and factories in the Caribbean, and he told me about how the islanders have all these strange religious traditions, because, you know, in some of the voodoo rituals they have in the islands, they use food as a kind of spiritual medicine, as a means to transform and transport the soul, which is identical, philosophically, to ritual slaughtering and food preparation for cultic feasts associated with medieval Romanian tribal warlords, which, for convenience sake, we call Transylvanian, I came up with this vision, but Elgin couldn't leave it alone. To me, the saddest day was when we opened, when what I imagined, was so different, so utterly alien. So I started to eat."

He stopped talking and Andy felt, not the heat of his gaze, but the need behind it. The need wasn't sexual, he wasn't a male on the prowl. He was more like a child, a brilliant, self-centered, self-absorbed child, who had fallen down in the playground and wanted to be told he would be okay.

And yet, of all the people she had encountered on this special day, Plank had been the only one to show her any kindness, and she could not help liking him for that, and hoping secretly that his kindness was in some way inspired by her, and not the working out of some inner need.

She decided to test him by repaying that kindness, just a little bit. "That cheesesteak you made was the best," she told him.

He seemed to grow larger. "You deserved it," he said, staring at her again.

"Stop staring at me."

"And you deserve better." He grinned impishly. "Leave this stuff. Come with me."

"I haven't finished," she said.

"You don't need to," he said. "Trust me."

You should never trust anyone who tells you to, but Plank had done *such* a good job of pleasing her that, before she knew it, she was following him downstairs, through the back entrance of the pizzeria, into an alley that let out a block away. Andy almost ran to keep up with Plank as he dashed across Chestnut Street, then, four blocks south, into maze of alley-like streets between Spruce and Pine, to the door of a tiny row-house. Plank tapped a keypad, nudged the door open into a balcony enclosed by a steel railing. The balcony ringed a basement kitchen of white and gray surfaces and gleaming, malignantly coiled appliances, that would have reminded Andy of a starship engine room if not for the glorious aroma of nutmeg and vanilla, and the curving crescent of butcher block in the center, and an array of knives.

Plank led her to the right, to an open cage of an elevator, trimmed in horizontal steel bars that reminded Andy of the over-designed, backyard play sets that sprouted on the lawns near her Main Line home. The elevator itself was so small she had to squeeze up against him. But she felt no jolt this time, no sexual heat as he closed the cage and the elevator slowly descended. The man beside her was more like a child who wanted to show her his favorite toys.

He was out before the elevator stopped moving, pausing over the knife collection to select a stubby paring blade. He beckoned her to keep up with him as he went past the table, the burners, and what seemed to be a vast walk-in refrigerator with a spiral staircase at one side and a locked metal grate on the other. He tapped another keypad and the gate clicked open, revealing banks of shelves with boxes, crates, containers of all sizes. Plank reached into one shelf, grabbed a cellophane-wrapped package, tossed it at Andy and said, "Catch."

Andy caught it two handed, as if it were a basketball.

"Open it. Those are not quite cookies. They're closer to an Italian pizzelle, not as sweet, but not as salty as to be a cracker. They're actually Dutch, made with rice flour, what the British would call a biscuit, but they come from Indonesia, from a bakery that dates back to the colonial period that has been making these things for three hundred years. Taste one. Just a nibble, you don't want to fill up. They're just a counterpoint, a contrast, a way clearing the palate. It may make you thirsty. Don't worry about that."

Andy looked at the package. The *Press*'s conflict-of-interest guidelines specified that journalists could not accept gifts from sources, but the music writer got free CDs and show tickets, the film reviewer went on all-expenses-paid junkets to see new movies, the political columnist got free meals and transportation when following politicians on the campaign trail. At the same time, Howard Lange kept yelling at staffers who ran up big expense accounts, so he said that though the staff could not accept a gift, it could make use of "unsolicited materials" that were either valueless (press box seating at sports events, for example) or whose value could not be reliably determined.

Andy wasn't going to ask Plank how much one of these damned crackers cost. He had been a source on the article she just did, but, as far as she was concerned, she was never going to write about him or his restaurants again.

She opened the package, pulled out a biscuit, took a small bite. It was crispy, crusty and slightly coarse and, yes, just dry enough to make her want to drink.

Plank fetched more containers from the shelves, giving some to her to hold, piling the rest in a stack that he carried out of the storeroom and dumped onto the butcher block table.

Then he went to a cabinet beside a large, stainless steel sink and said, "Coffee, tea or water?"

Andy hated coffee, but adored tea. She had a collection that she supplemented by monthly visits to a specialty tea shop in Queen Village. She said, "Keemun."

"Black and bitter, an excellent choice," he said, opening a cabinet with at least thirty different tea canisters. He sprinkled two unglazed mugs with dark leaves, filled them with boiling water from the tap, and then carried them to a corner just beyond the spiral staircase piled high with cushions and pillows of various sizes.

He put the tea mugs on a small wooden stool. He pointed at a large, worn but inviting cushion. "Sit."

Andy didn't move. She watched him go back to the table, pull out a battered wooden serving tray from a drawer, open the packages on the table, and slice chunks of something dark.

*Chocolate.*

The aroma hit Andy's nose and she almost melted.

"Please," he said, gesturing toward the cushions, "sit."

She collapsed on a cushion and saw a huge, flat video screen on the wall, framed by dark speakers. Near it was a shelf of cookbooks and—Dr. Seuss!?

"I can put some music on, but I'd rather not."

"That's okay," Andy said, her eyes on the chocolate.

"To me, the sounds of the kitchen when nobody's in it, are the most soothing. When I was in my first restaurant, I would stay so late that it was the easiest thing to find a place on the floor, lay out a pile of tablecloths, and fall asleep to the sound of the refrigerator compressors. I've heard some industrial ambient bands that make similar sounds, but that's kind of like reconstituting orange juice. Why add water to concentrate when you can get the real thing?"

Andy didn't want to tell him that she was tone-deaf. In the same way dyslexics had trouble reading because the letters never quite made sense

108

on the page, she couldn't hear music because the mix of sounds and rhythms never fit together. That made things awkward when she was with people who wanted to go to a concert, or to a club where they wanted her to dance to something they were hearing that she wasn't. It was almost silly when she was in a movie and she heard this loud noise during chase scenes, or when the actors were pretending to have sex: what did so many incoherent sounds have to do with anything? She kept quiet about it because it seemed to bother others when she mentioned it. They became curious. They wanted to test her by humming a few bars of a tune and then watching the way she reacted, as if it was just a matter of finding the right music and she would become normal, or cured. This became annoying because, as far as she could tell, she wasn't sick, she wasn't suffering, and what gave these people the right to think that she even wanted them to make a difference in her life?

She liked to think that, in the same way blind people are more sensitive to what they hear, this condition, that she heard was called amusa, had made her more sensitive to the nuances in human speech. She also thought she detected in his voice a faint suggestion of stress. She could imagine him, then, somewhat younger and thinner, falling asleep on the floor of his restaurant kitchen, not because he had worked so hard that he didn't want to go home and then have to come back to the kitchen in a few hours, but that his nights then were like hers were now. Ever since she had stopped sleeping with Drew Shaw, she did not want to go back to her apartment because it reminded her of how lonely she was.

Plank gestured toward a collection of teddy bears near the shelf. "You can have any bear but the crimson one that's missing the eye. That's mine."

"Does he have a name?" Andy asked.

"A. Bear, short for Aloysius." He put the tray down beside her and sat on the opposite side. Upon the tray were several clusters of sliced, crumbled pieces of chocolate.

He pointed to the mounds. "This is Dutch. This is Swiss. Two French: one with high butterfat, one with low. This is American, for comparison. This is Austrian, to compare with the Bavarian, here. Here is a

Peruvian—very, very strange—and, this, my current favorite, is Hawaiian. There's just one guy that makes it in the entire world. Grows his own beans and I don't know how he gets that smokey flavor and that incredible finish, but . . ."

He took a pinch, popped it in his mouth, and licked his fingers. "You're allowed to lick your fingers—right, A. Bear?"

Did the bear wink, just then? Andy saw Plank reach for the biscuits she had in her lap. She put the package beside the tray.

She knew if she asked him why he was doing this, she would wreck the mood. She asked him anyway.

"Because you like what I do," Plank said.

She was wary again. "I'm not the only one."

"You are now. A. Bear is on a diet. But A. Bear has something to tell you." He grabbed the one-eyed bear by the neck and moved it up to her face. He said, "YOU SHOULD EAT!"

Andy looked at the bear and she had to smile. She moved her hand over the tray like one of those vending machines where you push buttons to position an articulated, metal claw, and then, right when you're not sure if you have the claw in the right place, it descends and pounces on—the Hawaiian.

She put it in her mouth and it was like watching fireworks on a hot summer night, when her eyes would find the faint sparkling trail of the rocket as it went up, and up, and up, until the trail almost disappeared. And then the came the first sweet explosion, followed by a second that was bitter and complex, and a third that was a fusion of the two that sent spiraling flares whizzing off in all directions.

And then, just when she thought it was over, came a huge, dark, sweet smokey BANG!

She opened her eyes and he said, "Happy birthday."

"Biltmore Gas and Service," Gina said. "This better be worth it."

"Gina, it's Shep," Ladderback said.

"You still afraid of the dark?"

"Open spaces," Ladderback corrected her.

"That's whacked, you know that? I mean, if that happened to me, I would've had to change my line of work."

"Gina . . ."

"You didn't fight for me."

Ladderback said, "I am asking you for some information."

"Why don't you tell me the real reason you called?"

He hesitated.

"You were always one for hesitating, always afraid to make the first move. You could've nailed Elgin, Shep. You could've prevented him from killing others."

He couldn't say what he felt. "Gina, there's no evidence that he killed anyone."

"I told you—he had a guy working for him who could mess around with a body to make one thing look like another. And you wouldn't believe me."

"I didn't say that."

"Well, whatever it was you said, you said it."

Ladderback paused. "Do you still do the maintenance on the Speed Care ambulances?"

"After Carol died, they took their business somewhere else. Elgin had some connection to them. He wanted to hurt me. He likes hurting people. It's his *thing*."

"You told me you found illicit drugs in their ambulances."

"I was finding all kinds of shit, who was to say it was illegal? Pills, mostly. Pills in bags, jars, tin containers they put mints in. The drivers would buy direct from some of the pharmaceutical warehouses, or they'd load up from the labs. One driver told me he had this anti-hostility drug that was never released because it had too many side effects, one of them was that it would knock out your short term memory. If they roughed somebody up, they'd give him a shot and he wouldn't remember how it happened."

Ladderback smiled. He used to love it when she told him things like that.

"Did they sell these drugs?"

"Not to me. You in the market?"

"Speed Care was used to transport a decedent from the Brideshead section of South Philadelphia, to the medical examiner's office. The ambulance took nearly three hours to go a distance that would have taken 25 minutes."

"So they went to Orley's and got lunch."

"The same ambulance company took far too long to transport another decedent, a restaurant critic who died today in Center City. You knew at least one of their drivers. You may have known their habits. Is there any way to determine why the ambulances took so long to go across town?"

"What do you think? They got a dead body in the back. What's the hurry? It's not going to get any deader. I work on cars, Shep. I've always worked on cars. I don't look what's in them. All I care about is that the cars leave the shop."

"You said you saw photos in Elgin's car."

"He was screwing my daughter. When it's my daughter, I have a right to be curious. I had to go into the trunk to check the pressure on the spare and it was all there, like he wanted me to find it: the whips and the leather stuff, right next to that doctor bag with the knives and the needles. I told you all this and you could've done something and you did nothing."

He heard her voice begin to break. "I got cars ahead of me."

He remembered that she would say that when she was impatient, as if the cars were children that did not know how to wait.

She said, "Let's do a countdown, like they do at the derbies. Ready? Five, four, three, two—"

He heard the angry clatter of a pressure wrench turning the nuts on an automobile wheel rim.

And again, she slammed down the phone.

Andy made the fourth pass at the Hawaiian chocolate, having gone "around the world" of chocolates on the plate at least twice. Plank had refilled her tea mug, sat down and leaned back into the cushions and closed his eyes.

And then, what had been an afternoon of almost unbearable sensual delight, changed into something else.

Andy couldn't figure out how it happened. Plank hadn't tried to touch her. He hadn't made any comments about her appearance. He hadn't tried to be affectionate. Most of the conversation had been anecdotes from their childhoods, mostly from his childhood. He told her about his first great failures at home candy making—he'd watched candy commercials on TV, so why couldn't he just melt chocolate and peanut butter and mix it up and pour it together and have it look like something other than a pile of dog poop?

He was funny. He knew how to tell a story. And Andy was content to listen to this fat, furry, playfully childish guy who could have been a brother she never had.

But then, he suddenly grew up. Again, Andy felt as if she was being given a test to pass. Plank's need to please her with food had been sated and now she sensed he was expecting her to please him by doing something more than listening to him.

Andy said, "I'd better go now."

She might have stayed a little longer if he'd protested, if he asked her to stay, or if he went back into his pantry and came up with something else to share with her. He was intensely, easily likeable, and he seemed to care for her. There were more than a few times when, if he had been sitting a little closer to her and she just happened to put her arms around him, she would have hugged him, and shared with him the comfort, reassurance and tingling excitement that a first embrace can give.

But she couldn't escape the feeling that, in a quiet, infuriatingly passive-aggressive way, he expected—no, he demanded, that she touch him, or give him some physical sign that she approved of him.

Andy simply didn't want to do what was expected of her, especially when things had been so nice just as they were.

So she told him that she had loved sharing such wonderful flavors with him. It had made the day special.

He folded his hands and stayed on his cushions with his eyes closed. "Matt, look at me."

He shook his head.

"Matt, you took this awful day and turned it into one of the best I've ever had. You did what you said would. You made me happy, and, believe me, that's not easy."

He opened his eyes, and she saw the pout of a spoiled child. "I didn't make you happy enough."

"You did," she said. "More than enough."

He frowned and looked away. Andy asked herself why so many guys had to be so stupid, all in the same way. Why did they think that by being nice to her she would be so thoroughly enthralled that she would rip her clothes off and screw them blind?

"You don't want to stay with me," he pouted.

She didn't want to tell him to act his age. "What I want to do," she said, "is go home, and remember how nice this all was, and, maybe, look forward to it happening again."

"It can't happen again!" he almost shouted. "A meal is a unique experience. It can't be duplicated."

Andy sighed. "Pretend you're actually as smart as people say you are."

"I don't have to pretend."

"Do it anyway. This is the last time I'm saying this. What you did for me was very, very nice."

His frown turned into a sneer, and Howard Lange's smarmy voice suddenly boomed in the back of her brain: WHAT IS MATT PLANK HIDING?

So she asked him.

"What are you hiding?"

Plank said, "Huh?"

"A few hours ago, you asked me what I really wanted, and you gave it to me. I'm asking you the same thing. Right now."

"Why? I had a great mood going here. Why are you spoiling it?"

"You spoiled it first."

"Did not!

"Did too!"

114

Suddenly, just like that, he was absolutely adorable, and Andy almost put her arms around him and hugged him. But she held herself back. "Listen. I am *not* in charge of making you happy, okay? Whatever it is you think you want from me, you're not going to get it."

He grinned. "Not ever?"

"Not now."

He got up, refilled the tea, sat down slightly farther away from her. He thought for a while. "What I'm hiding," he began, "is a desire to take this day back again and start over and never have Michelle walk into my restaurant. No . . . let's go back a little farther. I would never have wanted to have met Michelle at all. We met before we went to Culinary. Both of us were working at Orley's Emperor of the Steak down in Brideshead. Orley Roberts was the most incredible ball buster I have ever encountered in a kitchen: the truest thing to a genius I've ever encountered. I would've stayed with Orley, but Michelle and I became a team, and Michelle wanted to go to Culinary, and she talked me into going with her. You been to Orley's?"

Andy had heard about it, but had never gone.

"It's everything people say it is. One entire wall is pictures of everybody that you'd ever want to know, and a lot more you probably wouldn't, in South Philly, taken by Orley himself, which is amazing, all by itself, because Orley is so drunk sometimes, you can't believe he can move. But then, he'll pick up a camera, and the shot is as steady as a bell, or he'll pick up a knife and cut meat—he'll actually slice the sirloin by hand—and he'll cut as straight a line as you'll ever see."

Andy said, "I learned how to cut an onion but . . . that's all."

"You spend a year working for Orley, it's like three years at Culinary. Orley is the only person in the entire city who would put Brussels sprouts on a cheesesteak. That man is *not* in it for the money. Except for what he spends on film for that camera, every cent he makes goes into getting better ingredients, improving the kitchen. He lives in a room the size of a closet on top of the restaurant, goes to the free clinic up the block when he gets sick. I'd ask him how come he wouldn't go to a doctor—he'd had enough doctors eating his food, they'd do him a favor—but he'd go to the free clinic because he never had any money, and he was too proud to ask for anything that he didn't feel he was entitled to."

"Tell me about Michelle."

"I was in love with her. I mean, I thought I was in love with her. She could cook and, when one genius tells another that he's full of shit . . . she told me I was full of shit, because I had this fantasy and she thought it was stupid. I wanted to get one of those trucks, with a fryer and a hot plate, and make crepes. I had a great name for it. I called it Le Truck. My idea was to develop Le Truck into a mobile franchise. You got a guy driving and a guy cooking. You call the driver. He picks up on the cell phone. He takes the order, processes the credit card, gets the directions, and, while he drives, the cook makes whatever it is and it's done by the time the truck pulls up to the address."

"Michelle didn't like that?"

"She was always getting car sick, or truck sick, but that's beside the point. I admit, it was naive, idealistic, a little bit dumb, but . . . I always thought, if you've been given some kind of special ability, some talent that most people don't have, you owe it to whatever gave you that gift, to make things better, not for those who can pay $150 for a fixed-price dinner and send the dessert back to the kitchen three times because they don't like whipped cream rosette, but for people who really need what you have to offer. There are people all over the city who are poor, or sick, or too old to cook, or too crazy, like my mother was, to get a decent meal, so, the idea was to make it a kind of meals-on-wheels, but, with meals-on-wheels, you have to take what they give you. What I wanted to do was meals-on-wheels, but the best ingredients, cooked precisely to order."

"Michelle didn't like that idea?"

"She wanted us to open the very best restaurant, make a lot of money and eat, drink and screw our way around the world. I wouldn't have minded doing that, too. But, to me, the challenge isn't in doing the complicated sauces and the special preparations and the super wine cellar— that's just a matter of getting money from an investor, renting a good location, following instructions and never, ever deviating from them. To me, the hardest thing has always been doing the simplest things, perfectly. Like sushi, before the Japanese turned it into fast food for the American market. You know, it used to take ten years of apprenticeship in Japan before you could call yourself a sushi chef, and you spent the first three years just making the rice. In France making crepes is like making rice in Japan: the recipe is a snap, but perfection is almost impossible. I say almost, because you really can achieve it, sometimes, when the pan is heated just so, and you get the texture, elasticity, color, the crispness of the edges and that buttery scent of toasting flour all coming out precisely as it should. And then, for that instant, you understand why you were born, why you studied this art, why you put up with the thousands of mistakes, failures, almost-but-not-quite-good-enoughs so you could achieve this single, flawless, undeniably magnificent crepe. And then you know what happens?"

Andy shook her head.

"You add the filling, fold it, dust it with sugar or sauce, and it's gone and you know that this moment will never come again, but getting back to that moment may be best thing you'll ever do with your life."

Andy could think of several things.

"And Michelle thought *that*," Plank said, "was full of shit."

"So you broke up with her?" Andy asked.

"Nahh. We opened Trellis, and Trellis was a hit, even if we didn't have a day when we didn't have a fight over every damned thing. Michelle started drinking from the wine cellar and . . ."

"You never did anything with your meal truck idea."

"I had a hit restaurant, but, even without Michelle draining the cellar, the expenses were so high that I was going broke. I couldn't raise prices any higher in a place with a chalkboard menu. It came down to cutting back on the quality, which I absolutely could not see myself doing, or try to realize some economies by opening a second restaurant. Some of my customers offered to invest. I found this space in West Philadelphia that was in a basement, with all this plumbing coming out of the walls. It reminded me of that enormous fake human heart at the Franklin Institute, the one where you walk through it and you pretend to be a blood cell going through these womb-like valves, and into veins and arteries and lungs, and I thought it would be just perfect for hospital food, that horrible no-fat, no-salt, no-fun junk you get after you've had an operation, but better, much, much, much better, with a little salt, and a little fat, and spices that will make it so we could charge double for the some of the same—well, not quite the same, but close enough—menu items we had at Trellis. That became Pulse. You've been there?"

Andy hadn't.

"I'll get you in. No. Better yet. We'll go to Buffalo Rome. That's in Manayunk. I created this tasting menu, tiny portions, big variety. You'll love it."

Andy shook her head.

"You don't have to be hungry, we'll just be tasting."

She said, "I want to go home now."

He shook his head. "I don't want you to go yet."

That was the wrong thing to tell her. Andy set off for the elevator and punched the button. The doors didn't open.

She heard him scramble to his feet. "There's a keypad for security reasons. Only I can open it, and so you might as well—"

Andy didn't look around for a stairway. She put her hands on the steel lattice surrounding the elevator shaft, put one foot on a cross beam and climbed up.

"You're not supposed to do that!" he shrieked.

She reached the landing.

"STOP!" he shouted at her.

"No!" she swung her leg over the railing.

She looked down from the balcony and felt Plank's mock-dramatic, but very real need, reaching out to her, imploring her to stay, to be the person he wanted her to be, to make *him* happy, and never mind that he could be a jerk when he didn't get his way.

About as much of a jerk as she was, when she didn't get her way.

"Please," he said.

"Later," she said. She opened the door and went out.

# 7 stay out of the kitchen

Ladderback did an Internet metasearch for newspaper and magazine articles about Alex Elgin. He saw the articles line up. There were too many to read in an hour, or even a day. He re-sorted them by the date they appeared, and he saw an obituary from the *Philadelphia Standard* tucked in among them.

The obituary was about Elgin's father. He was also named Alexander, but had a different middle name. Ladderback skimmed it, learning that Elgin's father was a founding partner of Matson Palmer Pharmaceuticals, and that he headed its Puerto Rico–based Caribbean manufacturing division for many years until he died in a boating accident.

Ladderback pulled from his cabinet a thick folder that contained clippings about Puerto Rico. Finally, he opened the Dettweiler file.

He re-read the small item he had clipped from the *Philadelphia Standard*'s financial page about Dr. Alex Elgin of Stoner Clinic, who announced his resignation to found a generic drug company to be located on the "pharm belt" of the Main Line. Dr. Elgin denied that his resignation was due "in any way" to the death of Carol Dettweiler and the settlement the Stoner Clinic awarded the girl's mother.

The file also contained Ladderback's first draft of an obituary he wrote when Gina's mother died.

Ladderback learned of the death of Mrs. Sonja Dettweiler through reports the paper received from the police and the medical examiner's office. He checked to make sure it was the same Sonja Dettweiler. It was.

Ladderback hadn't seen or spoken with Gina in nearly a decade. He called and Gina told him that she was cremating her mother. There would be no funeral, no ceremony of any kind. Gina did not want an obituary written. Ladderback then asked about Carol. Carol had turned into a scrappy, rebellious teenager "just after her old mom" who was forever running away—to the Jersey shore, usually, but sometimes to New York and Baltimore—and returning days, weeks, months later, like a stray cat.

"She hasn't asked me to bail her out of a single thing," Gina said proudly, though Ladderback could hear the worry in her voice. He suggested that Carol might hear about an obituary about her grandmother.

"She just might," Gina agreed.

Ladderback did not deny, to himself, that this was an excuse for him to find out if a woman he had loved, had remained the woman he had loved. When Ladderback asked her if she was living with anyone, she said, "I've had my opportunities."

She didn't ask him if he had had similar opportunities. She didn't ask to see him. The agoraphobia that had been latent when they had been lovers had become chronic. He had already moved to the Locust Street apartment so that he could go to and from the newspaper through the pedestrian tunnels and subway concourses below Market and Broad streets.

He told her that if he was going to get the obituary done in time, he would have to start it right now, on the phone. Gina told him, under no circumstances, was he to mention her husband's name.

Ladderback wrote three short, carefully constructed paragraphs about Mrs. Sonja Dettweiler, a native of Puerto Rico, who settled in Philadelphia and worked as a seamstress for the Tuxedo Park formal wear factory in North Philadelphia. She had been widowed twice. The first husband, a foreman at the factory, died of lung cancer; the second, Lawrence R. Dettweiler Sr., died from a knife wound when his University service station was robbed. After her second husband's death, Mrs. Dettweiler quit her job at the Tuxedo Park factory to help her daughter-in-law, Gina, raise her granddaughter, Carol.

The obituary didn't run. Space was tight for several days and then part of the head of Chickie Marandola turned up on a patch of turf beside a Schuylkill Expressway access ramp. Other pieces of the mob boss were discovered, in various stages of decay, scattered throughout the city, so the *Press* put a photo of Marandola on the cover with the headline: THE SLICE MAN GOETH: *REST IN PIECES, CHICKIE.*

In that issue, you almost couldn't turn a page of the *Philadelphia Press* without seeing something about the Philly mob. Mob hits always boosted circulation. The *Press* ran mug shots of past and present criminals; angry letters from the city's Italian-Americans protesting the media glorification of mobsters; an organizational flowchart showing who was currently on top; profiles of angry prosecutors and FBI men; a mob-speak glossary explaining such vital South Philly idioms as "You talkina me?" and "You gudda problem widdat?"; an Italian mob fashion spread; and a pull-out map of South Philadelphia and surrounding regions showing where other infamous characters had been shot, knifed, blown-up, poisoned, or merely found, in oil drums, in the trunks of old cars, in trash dumpsters, or floating face down in the Delaware.

On the day of the funeral, Ladderback had come to work and stood in front of the Philadelphia street map hanging at the back of the newsroom until he had memorized the route to the crematorium, a plain brick annex at the Pennsylvania College of Mortuary Science. He went down to the ground floor of the Press Building, had the doorman call a cab and, with his eyes closed, felt every twist and turn until the car stopped in what he was almost sure was the entrance to the oldest, continuously operating mortuary school in the country (Boston's was actually older, but there had been a few years during the Revolution when it had been shut down). Ladderback could not remember how he got from the cab to the building's lobby, but he did, and found the crematorium at the end of a spotless, marble-sheathed corridor.

He opened the door. The hinges didn't squeak. His eyes fell on the condolence book. Should he sign it? He opened the book and saw no signatures. He closed the book. In the rounded, warmly wood-paneled room, folding chairs had been arranged in a crescent around the coffin. Seated in one of those chairs was Gina, in a dark brown, ankle-length dress. At her right was Carol, fully grown, in black denims and a leather jacket, with her hair cut ragged and moussed up, the upper right portion of her face, including her eye, covered by white gauze.

And on Gina's left was a long-limbed man in ill-fitting dark pants and a black denim jacket. He wore thick glasses and his arm was on the back of Gina's chair, and Ladderback saw that his fingers were stained with what looked like the juice of a plum.

He didn't look at all like the photo of Lawrence R. Dettweiler, Jr. on the copy of the emergency services vehicle driver's license that Ladderback had been given from a contact in the police department. Ladderback reminded himself that identification photos could be misleading, people can change their hairstyles. Larry Dettweiler, Jr. didn't wear glasses. In his picture he had a ridiculous Elvis pompadour. The man sitting next to Gina had close-cropped, prematurely gray hair, and the vacant, pained, distracted expression of a drunk with a bad hangover.

Ladderback told himself that, even if he hadn't been Gina's former lover, he had just as much a right to be there as anyone else who may have known Gina's mother-in-law, Sonja Dettweiler. She had asked him what he did for a living when he helped Gina carry one of her ridiculously large demolition derby trophies up the stairs of the rowhouse, to Gina's bedroom, where he spent many nights. Ladderback had told Mrs. Dettweiler that he worked for a newspaper and that he was writing an article about one of the most amazing people he'd ever met. Mrs. Dettweiler had even smiled at him once or twice on the mornings when he came down those stairs, his face still flush from having made love. He remembered Mrs. Dettweiler at the kitchen table giving Carol her breakfast, saying to Carol, "That man is Mommy's friend."

But Ladderback hesitated when he saw Gina tightening her left hand into a fist, the ring on her finger glowing brightly against her skin.

A wedding band? Gina never wore jewelry on her hands because her hands got so greasy from working on cars. She certainly hadn't been wearing a wedding band when he had been her lover, and had almost been, but couldn't quite bring himself to be, her Number One Fan.

If he had seen in her face the hint of acceptance, he might have stayed. But the look he got from Gina was the same look he got from her that had ended their relationship.

Ladderback should not have been shocked to see a man sitting beside Gina that was not her husband. Ladderback should never have felt the emotional devastation when Gina told him, with a look, to *go away*. Why did he think she would want him with her to watch the coffin slide on the conveyor belt into the furnace? Why did he assume she would listen to him explain to her that a mob hit can prevent obituaries from running. . . ?

Ladderback made an embarrassed gesture with his hand, as if he had entered the room by mistake.

As Gina turned her head back toward the coffin, Ladderback slipped out and moved quickly away, going up a flight of stairs to wander through the school's halls, peering purposelessly into the classrooms with their charts and tables, examining the photographs hanging on the walls of years and years of graduating classes, and the single photographs of the recipients of honorary scholarships from companies that made products or sold services for the "dismal trade."

The recipients of those scholarships did not smile. They were serious, solemn, darkly dressed.

He eventually found a row of pay phones and called himself a cab.

Ladderback didn't hear a word from Gina until Carol's death, a few months later. Gina had another story for him, a story that he couldn't say came from her. Her daughter had been murdered because Carol had tried to blackmail Alex Elgin, and Elgin killed her instead, and altered the body so that it looked like Carol had died of food poisoning.

Some lawyer she never heard of named Bleutner was offering her some "TIGFY money," she said, not to sue.

"What's TIGFY?" Ladderback had asked.

"It stands for 'take-it-and-go-fuck-yourself,' " Gina said. "Nothing's going to bring my baby back. Elgin fucking killed her, is what he did. We have to fight for her, Shep. We have to nail that bastard."

Gina said she had found compromising pictures of Elgin and Carol while working on Elgin's Porsche. She had opened the trunk and had also found a black doctor's bag filled with medicines, and a set of costumes, with a smelly mask of leather and goat horns painted red.

There was also a loaded .38 semiautomatic handgun.

Ladderback didn't tell Gina that compromising pictures did not necessarily indicate a motive for murder. He did not tell her that he had done a search of Carol's name and had discovered that she had been questioned by police regarding what was apparently a blackmailing scam involving a mobster linked to Chickie Marandola and an unnamed casino gambler in Atlantic City.

He also didn't tell her that newspaper newsrooms were divided into tedious little fiefdoms, and that it would require an extraordinary effort for an obituary writer to get approval to do an investigative story.

He ended his conversation with her without making promises. Then he went across the newsroom to Howard Lange, who was slumped at his desk, lost in thought, chewing on a piece of paper as he listened to Ladderback.

Finally, Lange said, "Didn't we run something on this?"

"Last week, a news item about the girl's death."

"She had some reaction to a drug."

"The director of the testing program disputed that. He said she might have had food poisoning at the restaurant where she was employed. Or it could have something to do with trace chemicals in the water supply. The girl's mother is being offered a settlement in exchange for not filing a wrongful death suit."

"She filed that suit?"

"Not yet."

"So you think it would be possible to prove that the head of a drug testing program at a prestigious nonprofit research clinic is covering up what happened to one of his human guinea pigs, a school kid—"

"She was a part-time City College student. She was supporting herself as a waitress."

"Crapped out in the real world, decides to go back and get a degree."

Actually, Gina had told him, Carol Dettweiler had been quite successful. She was going back to school because Gina insisted that she stop attaching herself to older wealthy men who were into sado-masochistic sex, that she straighten herself out and do something decent with her life.

"You know what it's like," Lange said, "when you go to a party and there are people that don't know you and they ask you what your job is, and you tell them you're in the media and what happens? Everybody and their uncle hops out of the woodwork at you with a story. You gotta check this out. You gotta blow the whistle on this person or that organization. Like, you have nothing better to do."

Ladderback waited as Lange chewed on the paper. "She local, this mother?"

"She owns a gas station near the Penn campus," Ladderback answered.

"What's the coroner say?"

"Cause of death was anaphylactic shock. Anaphylactic shock is usually a response to a toxic substance, but it can have many other causes. The coroner found no large quantities of toxins in her body."

Lange nodded, trying to show that he knew what anaphylactic shock was, even if he didn't.

"What restaurant was she working at?"

"Pulse."

He brightened. "I ate there. It's kind of creepy, all those round walls and red-and-blue tubes that look like blood vessels. The food is great, though. They have these mashed sweet potatoes and you'd swear they're made with butter but it's actually some kind of sauce. . . ."

He eyed Ladderback. "I have to tell you the truth," he began, then he stopped. "What was that?"

"Nothing," Ladderback said.

Lange sat up again. "You were going to say something. I could tell."

Ladderback decided to tell him. "What does a politician mean when he prefaces his statement with 'to tell you the truth'?"

Lange glared at him. "If we start poking around with this, the very act of poking could trigger a lawsuit, and any lawsuit the paper gets sends its liability insurance premiums through the roof; and we would have to prove negligence, which is very, very difficult in cases where each side can hire expert witnesses who can say any damned thing if you pay them enough."

"We should be able to risk that," Ladderback said. "Our readers take risks. They trust us to do the same."

Lange shook his head. "The only risk worth taking is the one that is most likely to pay off. If there were something really sleazy about this, like, if they were having sex and she died because of that, I'd risk it because anything with sex in it gets attention and it would be worth it to be the first to break it. Readers think anybody who fucks around deserves what they get."

Ladderback wanted to correct his usage: "anybody" took the singular. Lange should have said, "Anybody who fucks around deserves what he gets."

Instead, Ladderback said, "This story is about getting what is deserved. It makes all the difference if a person dies by accident, negligence, or intent."

"With this, we'd need a story that's so trashy that by the time we've played it out, neither of them would be able to show their faces in this town again."

"When we resort to sensation, we lead our readers astray," Ladderback said. "We can't let lurid elements detract from what's most important: exactly how the girl died."

"You know this woman, right? It's personal, between you."

"It may have been."

"Do we have a conflict of interest here?"

"You can assign this to another reporter."

"But you want it, don't you? You're hungry. You want to rip this doctor's liver out. How about a reason why I should let you?"

"My parents were medical examiners."

"So you know the tricks of the trade?"

"I know that in any investigative situation, it is possible to leave traces and alter evidence so that the investigator—even a very competent one—is led astray."

"So what would stop you from being led astray, eh, Shep?"

"Persistence," Ladderback said.

Lange took the paper out of his mouth with his fingers, regarded it, and dropped it in a wastebasket. "If the mother sues, it's news, and we'll cover it."

Ladderback called Gina and told her to file her suit.

"That's the one thing I can't do," she said.

"It's the one thing you must do. I'm sure a lawyer will take the case just for the publicity."

"I don't want publicity. I don't want people saying my daughter took after her goddamn father!"

"Gina, you told me that she was blackmailing him."

Her voice began to break up. "I told you Elgin killed her. That should be enough for you to go after him."

"It would be for me, but not for this newspaper."

"You want me to go to the *Standard?* I don't know anybody at the *Standard*. I know you and, all my life, I've learned nobody's going to do anything for you unless they know you, or you're a winner. Shep, I've had a lot of bad things happen to me, and I will not call myself a loser. If it gets out that Carol was anything but legit, I go down."

"Then you should take the money, Gina," Ladderback said. "If you sue, Carol's affairs in Atlantic City will come out."

"You found that out, too, didn't you?"

"It was a news report in the *Atlantic City Star* and, yes, I found it out because things that appear in newspapers are a matter of public record."

"Elgin met her up in that restaurant she worked in. He sold her on it. Carol told me he said he'd get her all kinds of drugs, stuff they make but can't sell that does all kinds of things."

"And what did Carol offer him?" Ladderback said.

"She offered to put on some stupid mask, tie him up with these hand-spun ropes, and hit him with a whip made out of pigskin. Shep, this is my daughter. You saw me kiss her goodnight. You know I loved her. I tried with Carol. I tried as hard as I could, but she was street hungry, just like her father."

Ladderback had heard similar emotions from parents who suffered the death of a child: that you could have done more; that you could have done better; that, somehow, you could have kept your children alive, and, failing to do so, you will strike out at what took your child from you.

"I know you loved her, Gina," Ladderback said. He heard her sob and he wanted to crawl through the phone line and be with her, as he had been with her on those nights when she was angry or hurt, or in any of the ways it was possible to feel less than peaceful, and he just stayed with her, touching her in the dark, holding her, waiting until she noticed that there were ways to feel good without winning, without fighting back, without doing anything more than being with another person who loves you so much that he couldn't be anywhere else.

It is so mysterious, this attraction that brings us to another person, Ladderback thought. Mysterious, risky, fraught with danger, regret, and so rarely right.

But when it's right, it's all you need. "Gina . . ."

She said, "What if tell him I kept one of the pictures of her doing it to him?"

"Then my editor would want to see the picture," Ladderback said.

"Then you'd do the story."

"Someone else would do the story, and it would not be the story you want to see," Ladderback said.

"You wouldn't do the story because you know me. It would be, what do you call it, conflict of interest?"

"I wouldn't do it because anything purporting to be journalism, with that picture reproduced in part or in full, would impede the truth. You might gain the satisfaction of embarrassing this man, at the expense of Carol's memory. But we might never know how Carol died."

"You won't fight for me!" she sobbed. "You're a wimp, like Larry, only you don't use that goddamn inhaler to take your fear away, you hide behind that newspaper."

He listened to her cry. Then he said, "Do you really want to know how Carol died?"

She slammed down the phone. Ladderback held the phone against his ear until he heard the dial tone. Then he put the phone down, put on his coat, left the newsroom, and called in sick for two days.

He did not know how long the Dettweiler file lay open before him. Eventually he looked around the newsroom. He saw reporters on the phone. He saw others writing furiously to make the 5 P.M. copy deadline. He found himself in one of those strange moments you get into when you've let your memories take you so far back that you can't figure out how you got there in the first place, or why.

His hands were on a clipping, the last clipping in the Dettweiler file:

### CLINIC PAYS BIG FOR STUDENT DEATH.

The Stoner Clinic paid a undisclosed sum today to the West Philadelphia mother of a Philadelphia City College student who died last month while taking experimental drugs as part of a testing program.

In making the settlement, the Clinic was not admitting wrongdoing, according to Daniel Bleutner, a lawyer acting on the Clinic's behalf.

"This is an unfortunate situation that no amount of money can change," Bleutner said. Because details of the settlement had been sealed, Bleutner could not reveal the sum, though he added that, "low six figures wouldn't be unrealistic."

Andy slowed down when she smelled the coffee brewing in the Court of Kings Coffee Bar.

She went up the chocolate-brown, thickly painted, wooden steps leading to a wraparound porch on what had once been a Second Empire mansion on South 43rd Street. It had been carved up into apartments, one of which was hers.

She found herself again on the steps that she would climb to the big, ugly, frosted-glass door. She could see herself following a well-trod path: open the door, put the mailbox key in the mailbox, dump the junk mail in the basket, put the front door key through the inner door, go up the creaking steps to the second floor, down the hall that always smelled of curry, to the second stairway at the back, then to the door in the center of the hall. That door opened into a small kitchen and eating area, then, up an open staircase to a glass-enclosed balcony that was just large enough to hold a night table, a low bookcase, and a queen-sized futon mattress, in what had been the mansion's cupola.

She had found the place by accident. She had been looking for a place to stay in the city after her father had died, and she had been on the street checking out another apartment when she saw the woman she would soon know as Mrs. Vardigadavan sitting on a faded wicker chair chained to the wraparound porch, scowling at her. Andy always scowled back at people who scowled at her. She found out later that Mrs. Vardigadavan thought she was someone else who had made an appointment to see the "top room." Andy never asked if that person showed up. Andy signed the lease the moment she climbed into the cupola and looked out onto the squirrels racing across the gray slate–tiled roof, and just beyond it, a tangle of green trees.

Later, she discovered that it took far too long for the hot water to come up, the refrigerator in the kitchen was too small, and that the slightest breeze rattled the cupola's windows. She took down the bent tangle of blinds and hung over the windows billowing layers of white muslin that could be tied back to let in summer breezes, or, when drawn together, give her a feeling of being in a four-poster bed.

She could see the cupola and the curtains from where she stood, outside the mansion, the coffee fumes dancing around her. Drew Shaw drank brutally strong cups of espresso, and she had thought that they would first go to the Court of Kings Coffee Bar, where they had a reasonable but not remarkable collection of bagged teas. They would get a bag of fresh-roasted beans to take out, and then go to her apartment, where he would spend the night, and she would make espresso for him the following morning with a machine she bought in anticipation of his stay.

But all their nights together had been at his apartment in Old City and, now, standing on the steps, the bittersweet tang of chocolate still in her mouth, she wanted to go up those stairs, open the top window of the cupola, and toss that espresso machine down, past the fire escape, into the alley in the back. She wanted to get rid of it to make room for . . . whatever was worth making room for. Maybe something back at her old house?

She didn't want to go there. Her mother had done things to it after her father had died. Her mother had changed all the locks and put in an elaborate, very expensive pinhole camera video surveillance system. She told Andy that she did it because she had the gallery's art on the walls and now that there was no man around people might want to break in.

Andy mentioned this to Ladderback one morning when she opened a letter addressed to her at the newspaper. It was from her mother's gallery, and she found a list of new keypad codes that would open the doors and deactivate the alarm system.

Ladderback had told her that survivors—that's what he called friends and relatives of anyone he was writing about—often made changes to their physical surroundings. "It is a way to cope with loss," he told her.

Andy didn't see the changes as a way to cope. Her father had never locked his car, never locked the front door of the house when he was home, and hated the first, non-video, alarm system her mother had put in, because "It's like putting up a billboard that says, 'You want something worth stealing, we got it, right here!' "

No, Charlotte had changed the locks and put in the video cameras because her husband would never have permitted it when he was alive.

Sure enough, two days after the surveillance system was installed, Charlotte informed Andy that the house was going to be sold. Andy drove up, cried a few times, filled up the car, which wasn't that difficult to do, sank one last ball in the basketball hoop over the garage, and left, resolving never to go back, unless she had a reason.

So how was it she had to get *almost* seduced before she had a reason? Back at her house in Merion were a few boxes of college notes and articles she had written for the student newspaper. Ladderback had an enormous filing cabinet containing everything he wrote, and piles of things he clipped from other papers and magazines. Andy didn't want anything like that cluttering her life, but there *was* room in her apartment, and whoever was buying the house would probably throw the boxes away when he moved in.

She didn't feel any of the alcohol she had consumed a few hours before. It had been purged by the article she wrote, the tea, the long walk back. She looked up the street at her dented Ford Focus. It was still where she had left it, parked in front of the Court of Kings, its fire-engine red paint dulled by grime, a few of the first withered leaves of autumn scattered across its hood.

She went up the stairs, through the door, not even bothering to open her mailbox, changed her clothes into a pair of shorts and a faded BUY ART T-shirt that her mother had given her way back when the gallery had printed them up. The shirt was oversized, supposedly designed by some artist with the gallery. What Andy liked about it was how soft the cotton became after a few washings. The inner seams were cut close enough so that they didn't rub on her skin when the shirt absorbed perspiration. She could put it on and feel almost as if it wasn't there.

Andy told herself that she was going to give herself a birthday present: she was going back to her house and do some basketball layups, the way she used to when she was tense, upset, annoyed, cranky. Andy never played basketball in high school or college—she hated getting into any of those idiotic competitive trade-offs with girls, or guys, who had something they wanted to prove. She did lay-ups by herself because, after a few minutes, she would get into this groove. Stay in that groove and her entire life became a process by which a basketball went into, or failed to go into, a hoop.

She'd do those layups and forget about Drew Shaw forgetting about her, that dead restaurant critic, a lame seduction, and a tip about some disease that was killing people.

She sat down on the edge of her bed and put a sock on one foot. She saw the late afternoon light playing through the trees and found herself sinking deliciously into the bed. She put on the other sock and then, impulsively, let herself melt into the mattress. She heard a mild gust of wind blow through the trees outside the cupola. She closed her eyes to listen to it, wondering what it might be like to be a bird and lose herself in that rush of sound.

She closed her eyes, to hear it better. She'd only rest for a minute, and was asleep before she knew it.

# a black swan

If Ladderback had been a religious man, he would have trusted that all he had to do was walk in righteousness and that his prayers would be answered, and every problem solved.

But Ladderback was not feeling religious as he took the elevator down from the newsroom into the basement of the Press Building, going past the security guard, through the glass doors into the underground pedestrian shopping mall, with its bright neon food courts and cheery franchise shops. He saw that the pile of *Angry Eater* books had been removed. His eyes lingered on a record store. Should he go in and find out if they had any new Mozart recordings? He could do with another version of Mozart's 29th Symphony, the one Mozart wrote when he was eighteen to break free of the frilly Italian-style compositions he'd been performing to impress bored royals and aristocrats. Listening to the first movement was like being young again. You could almost get inside Mozart's skull, and feel that it was only a matter of time before you had the world at your feet.

He decided to make do with the version he already owned. He kept walking and the mall ended at the grimy, dreary, balefully lit tunnels that wrapped themselves around the Market Street subway, branching off into concourses beneath City Hall and Broad Street. After going about a quarter mile heading south below Broad, he would turn west and take a smaller tunnel that followed the Locust Street Hi-Speed Line, where he would open a locked door with a key and enter the sub-basement of his apartment building.

Ladderback walked slowly, the weight of his creaking, sagging, graceless lump of a body shifting from one dusty black leather brogan to another, so that he seemed to be swaying from side to side instead of going forward.

As he moved, the pop tunes that echoed in the underground mall gave way to the brutal rumbling of the subway trains. He pulled his hat down lower on his head. That hat was an old taupe fedora that would have been so swell in another era, as would the baggy raincoat.

The hat and coat made him uncomfortably hot in summer. The coat never kept in enough warmth in winter, but that could have been due to his circulation, which was never good and certainly wasn't getting any better. Now that it was September he felt almost comfortable. Though it wasn't cold at night in the concourse, there was no warmth.

Still, he wore his hat and coat every time he walked the underground pedestrian concourses because the ceilings occasionally leaked and, as much as he loathed the open air, he dreaded even more the possibility of being pelted by drops of filthy, oily water sluicing off the city's grimy streets.

The liquids that leaked into the tunnels below Market and Broad Streets did not always come from the heavens. Pipes burst in all seasons. Sometimes there could be run-off from firemen's hoses. Once, a film crew brought tank trucks filled with water (the city refused to let the crew use the fire hydrants) to the corner of Broad and Sansom, where the drably grand Union League mansion was recast as a mad millionaire's haunted house. The water was pumped through sprinklers to fake the visual equivalent of a dark and stormy night, and the water followed so many paths of least resistance that, though the film was released to mostly bad reviews two years ago, lawsuits were still pending from businesses and property owners—some of them situated several blocks away from the site—claiming irreparable damage from errant flooding.

The city was like that, Ladderback admitted. Philadelphia specialized in characters who made entire careers out of taking unfair advantage of others, picking fights with those who couldn't fight back, blocking new developments that might benefit everyone just because they didn't get a kickback, or what they imagined to be the proper respect.

And then, just as he was about to condemn the city as a Gomorrah of petulant, scheming ne'er-do-wells, he would discover among the ranks of the newly dead, a person of such compassion, simple dignity, and moral rectitude, that Ladderback could believe his purpose in trudging through the city's grim tunnels, sitting in his worn and squeaking swivel chair (that he refused to relinquish for the newer, black-composite-polymer and blue anti-static fabric seats the newspaper introduced when it installed its computerized word processing system), was to bring this person's uncelebrated life to print so that the readers, dispirited by so much media fizz about the wealthy, the famous, the powerful and sensationally vile, would see that the city was blessed with an abundance of quiet heroes who left their world a better place.

Instead of feeling enervated from writing about one of those heroes, Ladderback was tired and grumpy. He had spent his last hour in the newsroom on the Internet, pulling up digitized Philadelphia police reports and death certificates with the hope of finding one case that might act as a "black swan."

The English economist John Stuart Mill had come up with what he called the "black swan problem" as a way of extending the skeptical arguments of Scottish sourpuss philosopher David Hume. As Mill stated it, you couldn't prove that all swans are white, because, to do so, would require the observation and listing of every swan currently alive on the planet, a task that, back in the 18th century, was as impossible for Mill, as it was now for Ladderback, despite having the Internet and other fancy 21st century technologies.

Surveying an infinite number of white swans confirmed nothing about their color. But only one black swan was required to prove that not all swans were white.

As it turned out, finding an actual black swan wasn't that difficult. Upon discovering the continent that became known as Australia, explorers noted the existence of a dark-hued bird that they called *cygnus atratus*, a black swan.

Ladderback had been searching for a record of at least one more death that might have shown some of the symptoms of Fragg's and Wisnitz's, or one death in which the ambulance company took an inordinately long time to transfer the body from the place of death to the medical examiner's office, or the funeral home.

You would think that, in a city of such size and complexity as Philadelphia, there would be a central database recording the time, place and cause of every death occurring within the city limits, possibly including the ring of Pennsylvania and New Jersey counties surrounding the city. This database would also include names and affiliations of those who handled the decedent: examining physicians, coroners, pathologists, transport staff, burial service, and final resting place. This database would be easily accessible on the Internet, so that anyone now, or in the future, would be able to determine the manner and procedure by which fate, and human beings, attended to the fifty to hundred people who died each day within the *Philadelphia Press*'s circulation area.

You would think that for someone such as himself, there would be such a database, and that this database would be updated regularly and reliably, and that the merely curious would not require a passel of passcodes, access keys, and other cumbersome tools to access it, and that the result would be an Australia for the dead: an unimaginably dense trove of information from which Ladderback could easily bag a black swan whenever he needed one.

You would think that, and you would be wrong.

The task of even beginning to extract that information was so tedious that it turned Ladderback into a sputtering grump. There were too many databases, and they were inaccessible, incomplete, or inexplicably unavailable.

Worse yet, Ladderback didn't know what he was looking for. This, in itself, wasn't an obstacle: part of the fun of being a reporter, even if your beat was confined to the newly dead, was the joy in stumbling upon a stray fact or observation that converted a jumble of incongruous quotes and meaningless biographical detail into a convincing human portrait.

But Ladderback's hunt for a black swan had not been fun. There had been no telling details, no vital clues, that would reveal to him that what he now suspected was correct. In the hundred or so cases he had explored, he found a few vague similarities, but he had to dismiss those. Any random search will reveal patterns and congruencies that almost make sense.

But almost wasn't good enough.

In the best of all possible worlds, in the rigorously fundamentalist faith of his Mennonite grandparents, any and every search for truth was actually a prayer for divine revelation. Because God was the essence of truth, God was constantly revealing Himself in ways big, small, mysterious, and obvious, so the search was a mere preliminary step, an uncomfortable preparation for the epiphany that would answer all questions and set everything right.

Of course, you never know how long you must suffer before your God decides to show you what you're looking for. Even then, what you're shown might replace old questions with new ones.

Ladderback's parents had abandoned their religion when they left their Lancaster County homesteads to pursue medical degrees in Philadelphia. Matters of faith were ridiculed in the small, meticulously appointed Chestnut Hill home of the Doctors Ladderback. On weekday evenings, before they moved to a retirement home in Arizona, his father liked to swish around brandy in a snifter and say, "Let's see God unboil an egg."

Ladderback maintained the family skepticism when he became a newsman, but he never imposed it on others. Faith was the first, and last, resort of the aggrieved. And though the newspaper rippled with accounts of cruelties propagated in God's name: homicidal fanatics, larcenous clergy, parents who let their children die instead of getting them adequate medical care; for every horrible deed, Ladderback knew there were even more acts of religiously inspired generosity and sacrifice, most of them unreported (unless they were done by the famous or the fortunate) because such crucial human achievements were not considered "news." People were presumed to be good, lawful, and respectful, with the media filling the sky with ghastly black swans to prove the presumption untenable.

So why couldn't he find a black swan when he needed one?

As he walked he tried to ignore the foul odors of the Broad Street concourse. He asked himself if he would have spent so much time on his swan search if this had been his birthday, or would he just take the afternoon off, as Andy had, and cut and run.

Then he noticed an emaciated man in filthy, foul smelling clothing sprawled against a pillar. One of the man's eyes had swollen shut. His lips were cracked and peeling. Most of his teeth were gone. The skin on his face had erupted in crimson sores, and small bloodstains extended down his soiled, gray pants leg to a rotting, torn sneaker stuffed with newspaper.

Ladderback passed this way twice a day and recognized most of the panhandlers and homeless people. He hadn't seen this one before.

The man's single, functioning eye hadn't been aimed at Ladderback, but he sensed Ladderback approach. "Got something for me?" the man wheezed.

Ladderback had a dollar in his hand but hesitated to offer it. A dollar wouldn't do this man any good. He needed to be hospitalized.

"I'll take it," the man said, extending his fingers toward Ladderback's dollar in a fashion that reminded Ladderback of Michelangelo's painting in the Sistine chapel of a muscular Adam blithely extending his fingers toward a bearded God.

Ladderback let him take the bill. Then he said, "You need a doctor. You should be in a hospital."

"Already been," the man said, examining the dollar bill as if he wasn't quite sure what to do with it. "Was all set to see the doc at the clinic, then they carry in this body bag, and he says ' 'Scuse me but I got a emergency.' And you know what? He hain't had no emergency. What was in the bag, was not moving. See? I'm moving. I got some time yet." He rolled his open, yellow eye toward Ladderback. "I figure, I die, and they'll see me faster."

"Do you want some food?" Ladderback said. "If you wait here, I can get some."

"You got pills, man? They gave me pills at the clinic. Don't need no food, as long as I got my pills."

Ladderback didn't carry a cell phone. He hated the obnoxious sounds they made when someone called. He was only thirty yards from a bank of partially vandalized pay phones. He set off for the phones and then, after about ten yards, he stopped and turned around.

The man was gone.

At night, in his studio apartment with the windows shrouded and a light on at all times, Ladderback wore a smoking jacket. He didn't smoke, but he came upon the smoking jacket in a Salvation Army used clothing store a long time ago: a maroon, quilted, decadent, belted robe with ridiculous black velvet lapels and huge pockets that could carry all the remote controls that came with all the electronic media equipment he couldn't stop himself from purchasing. He'd come in the door, slide carefully out of his shoes, stick his stocking feet into a scuffed pair of leather slippers, hang up his coat, wrap the smoking jacket around himself, reach into his pocket and pull out a remote control, any remote control, smack his thumb on the button marked POWER and watch that high-definition video screen blink to life. Or maybe the remote control would wake the CD player, with Brahms's fabulous First Symphony thudding like a stumbling, bearded, beer-swilling giant: boom, boom, boom, boom!

Then he'd put the mail on the narrow shelf in the galley, open the refrigerator, take note of what was about to spoil, and then mix together another preposterous, over-spiced, thoroughly ludicrous food pastiche that looked foul and tasted worse. He would dump whatever he'd made on a plate, carry it into the studio's single room, put it on the side table that also held a telephone, a memo pad and pen, a computer keyboard and mouse, and a photograph of a sunset over his grandparent's Lancaster County farm.

Then he'd fetch himself some kind of liquid, with alcohol in it, or without, and drop into the recliner, rock it back until his feet were in the air, and then he would begin to consume: food and drink in his mouth, food and drink odors in his nose, music (or words, spoken or sung) filling his ears, and visuals from the screen flying before his eyes, rushing from the cable channels, the Internet, or a movie disc.

He surfed the channels on cable and paused at a rerun of the Carol Burnett television variety show. He chuckled for a few minutes and then he shut off the set.

He could remember telephone numbers but dates were difficult. Dates and street numbers . . . that, and he would need to see a picture of Weight Wisnitz. Family resemblances could be misleading, but, if he did have others in his family, they would have had to have left the Wisnitz residence on Smartt Street before the census was taken.

He could get that photo of Wisnitz in one of two ways: he could ask his contacts in the police department for a driver's license photo, or he could go to Orley's Emperor of the Steak and look at The Wall.

No, there was another way. Perhaps Wisnitz was among the hundreds of South Philadelphia locals who had been recruited for what was one of the worst, but, in it's own way, most revealing Philadelphia movies ever made.

Called "The Bassos," it was an unreleased, two hour pilot for a TV show that was supposed to be based on the lives of a South Philadelphia crime family. While dramatic treatments of mobsters were not hard to find, this one was unique in that it was written and filmed on location in South Philadelphia, and financed by California off-shoots of the Marandola family.

Ladderback had found the tape in the discount bin of the record store he passed in the underground concourse on his way to and from the Press Building. It was a tangle of improbable sub-plots pertaining to the unsolved murder of Tony Basso, a stand-in for Chickie Marandola, at whose funeral the pilot begins.

Though "The Bassos" was never broadcast, it provided a priceless point of view into the epic fantasies its creators believed, about themselves, their neighborhood and numerous city denizens who begged them for help, basked in their glow, envied their so-called freedom, took money from them, exploited them, and ultimately betrayed them.

Ladderback took the unmarked tape from a shelf and put it into his video recorder. He fast-forwarded past the opening credits to the slow, jerky aerial pan over the flat roofs of South Philadelphia rowhouses and factory sheds. Where had they filmed this view? From one of the Franklin Towers, looking south, most likely. He paused the tape in places. He peered carefully at the vehicles on streets. His agoraphobia didn't trouble him. A recorded image of the outdoors didn't bring it on.

He fast forwarded again to the funeral scene, where a short, formidable woman in a dark veil and black clothes rips off her veil (showing how real tears have left dark streaks of liquified eye-makeup on her wrinkled cheeks), leaps up from a folding chair, and pounces on a casket, an open casket that is supposed to contain the carefully restored remains of Anthony Basso. She bangs her fists on the casket, shouting, "Ant'ny, Ant'ny, you shouldn't've had to die!"

Ladderback stopped the tape. He remembered a telephone number, picked up the phone at his side, and dialed. When the woman answered the phone, Ladderback asked if it was too late to speak with "the famous Weeping Wilhelmina."

"Never too late for you, Shep," she said. "You going to write me up again?"

"I didn't write you up the first time."

"That's right. You gave it to your assistant."

"He wasn't my assistant. He was the editor of the newspaper, Howard Lange. He writes a column occasionally. When I asked him if it would be a conflict of interest if I wrote you up, he took it for a column item."

"I guess I have to get myself dead before you'll write me up."

"As I told you, Willie, I was concerned about the appearance of a conflict of interest. It was important to make it seem that the *Press* wasn't doing any special favors for the Mount of Olives, whose funeral personnel I speak with from time to time when doing obituaries, and who also happen to employ you."

"I was not, and never have been, employed," she said. "I perform a service. The honorariums I get mean nothing to me. And, let me tell you, it hasn't been exactly a picnic since that article appeared. You know, everybody that wants to make a movie wants to come to South Philadelphia. They want mafia this, they want mafia that, and, naturally, they have a mafia funeral, they want to do at the Mount of Olives, and they want people who can, you know, do what I do, and there really aren't that many who can do a quality job, day in, day out, with consistency and proper elocution. Half of these new kids, they don't know languages, they don't know the dialect. They don't know nothing. Used to be, there wasn't a funeral director in all of South Philadelphia didn't say, you want the job done right, you get the Widow Schiavone."

"I never thought you had any competition, Willie."

"Well, for what I get for a funeral, it's not an arm and leg, but you get people, seeing what I do, they think it's easy. They go out, they buy a black dress, they think all they have to do is sit where the family can see them and think sad thoughts. Some of them try to force it—they come in with a tiny onion hidden in their purse and, when nobody's looking, they come out with that onion in their hand and they make like they're covering their eyes. That works—for five minutes! Six minutes go by, seven, eight, and somebody smells the onion and, by then, these amateurs are out of gas, and that can be very embarrassing for the families, especially when Father Aveni is doing the eulogy and he's going on, and on, and on. The amateurs don't know how to pace themselves. They lack depth. They have no sense of loss. But they're getting work and I'm not, and what I am hearing, is that I am too famous. They are telling me that since I was on the TV and in the movies, they think I've raised my price. What price? I get no hourly rate. And then, what I hear is, some of the families say they can recognize my face and they know that I am an actress, and not just a person who knows how to sit and blend in with the crowd and cry so its believeable—so the people that need to cry, but can't bring themselves to do it, can feel comfortable. I tell you, this

144

being a celebrity—you can have it. Sometimes I wish I could turn it all back to the way it was before I got famous."

"But you're still getting work, right, Willie?" Ladderback said. "Are you doing the Wisnitz funeral?"

"Personally or professionally?"

"Either."

"Well, I been living by Smartt Street all these years, I remember the donor, you know? The one who's paying without saying who she is. She had a hard life. Had to start it all over again, you know? I should be there for her."

She said *she*. "I thought the donor was Danny Bleutner."

"Danny won't show himself. He don't come back to the neighborhood, now he's got his own building and all. He'll send flowers, sure. But not Danny. No. The donor is somebody that truly loved Weight."

"A lover?"

"More like a sister. You should've talked to me before writing him up, Shep. I would've told you plenty. I know you talked to Glen. He probably told you a bunch of stuff. I wouldn't believe none of it."

"He told me you were there when Weight died."

"If I was on the street, and he was coming by, I might take a peek at his truck. So I was taking a peek and he just, you know, keeled over."

"The police report said you made the 911 call."

"Last one I'm going to make, too. The ambulance they sent in to take him away, made so much noise, it wasn't decent. I was just performing a service."

"Didn't you buy from him?"

"Never! I don't buy discards. I don't buy seconds. But I'd go because . . . it was so sad, him dying like that, in the gutter."

"You sound like you saw it happen, Willie."

"Did I ever? As it happens, I was there, when he was hawking about the tomatoes. And would you believe it, he falls into the gutter, and one piece a shit, one of those professional types, reaches into his pocket and steals his money. Right out of his pocket! And next to him, this creature— I wouldn't even call her a woman, she was dressed like such a tramp in that underwear they wear when they're exercising—starts stealing Vidalia onions, right out of the back of his truck, in broad daylight. Like vultures, they were, both of them."

Ladderback dipped the pan a third time. "Did you happen to see anything in the back of his truck that wasn't what he normally sold?"

"The grapefruits were hard as baseballs."

Ladderback didn't ask how a person who claimed to never have purchased anything from Weight Wisnitz would know how hard the grapefruits were.

"He was carrying nothing out of the ordinary?"

"Nothing in the truck. He had some pills, in his pocket."

Ladderback wrote *pills* on a pad. He drew a circle around it. "What kind of pills?"

"When that professional piece a shit went through his pockets, a jar of pills rolled into the sewer."

"Did the jar have a pharmacist's label?"

"I didn't see one."

*No label on pills—no prescription. Illicitly obtained?* "What happened to the pills?"

"The tramp got them."

"The woman in the exercise clothing?"

"She took it up like she knew what it was."

"You don't happen to know who she is?"

"You think I'm nosy? You think I ask people about their business?"

"Perhaps you may have seen her at some funerals?"

"Never. None of mine. I mean, none of the ones where my presence was requested. I seen her around, though: Dresses always in black, when she isn't looking like a tramp. Except for the T-shirts. She wears these T-shirts with stuff on them."

Ladderback wrote *stuff?* on his pad. "What kind of . . . ?"

"You think I'd notice? She had one with words on it. 'Buy art.'"

"By whom?"

"Art," she said. "You know, the stuff they put on walls?"

Ladderback paused. "I was told Weight performed other services."

146

"You want the honest truth?"

"Is there any other?"

"There's the truth you tell the people you know, and there's the truth you tell the people you don't know; there's the truth you hear about, and the truth you read about in the newspaper."

"How about the truth that makes sense," Ladderback said.

"What makes sense ain't always the truth."

"I'll take what I can get," Ladderback said.

"Funny you say that, because, with Weight, it was all about taking what you could get. He wanted you to do that, he really did. There was a time, a few weeks ago, he was feeling sick on account of those pills he was taking"

"The ones you saw in his pocket?" Ladderback asked.

"I don't know. It was some kind of pill that was stopping him from drinking, if you could believe that. What it did, was, it gave him a permanent sore throat, sometimes going all the way down to his stomach, and it would get worse if he drank anything. Made him grouchy, excitable. So he gives me a call and tells me he has the truck loaded up, and he just called me up and said he couldn't make his run and I should give him a twenty and take what I want. I says to him, he should be so lucky I can come down and save him from the indignity of a truck with rotten stuff that he can't sell, and he said it was okay.

"See, he wasn't a total piece a shit. He could be generous. The beautiful thing about Weight was, if you had something you wanted to get rid of, and it wasn't going to cost Weight anything, he'd know how to get rid of it. If he knew you needed things, and he could get them, he get them to you, and he'd charge you, but it would never be an arm and a leg."

"What kind of things did he get rid of?" Ladderback asked.

"Wouldn't you like to know."

Ladderback waited. "Yes, as a matter of fact, I would."

"Well, you know those pieces of Chickie that turned up over the city? You look at where he used to drive that truck of his, you might've found a way they could've got where they did. He lived on the same street as Chickie, for a while."

"I believe Marandola was no longer living on Smartt Street when he died."

"But he was always around. Marandola couldn't leave nobody alone."

"You're saying that Weight Wisnitz killed him?"

"I'm not saying that. I'm saying that, if anybody knew how to get rid of Chickie, Weight could."

"Aside from body parts, what else did . . . Weight distribute?"

"Well, his father—Taddy Wiz, they called him—Taddy Wiz had a job in the motor pool at the Navy Yard. Some of those spare parts would have a way of coming home with him, and Weight, if he had some of those spare parts, he'd stop by some gas stations and body shops that might take them off his hands. And Chickie, he lived across the street from Taddy Wiz, that was how Chickie got started, you know? Chickie saw himself an opportunity. He moved in on the family and he got Weight to start running car parts to gas stations all over. And then it was the pills and the drugs and the other stuff. It was never a lot that he carried, but it was enough, you know?"

"Was he ever robbed?"

"He had that knife of his. He used it to cut the bad stuff off whatever he was eating, but he could handle a knife."

"From what I learned about him," Ladderback said, "I can't imagine him paying any attention to anyone like Marandola."

"That's because you don't know Chickie. Chickie was good for nothing, but he was a charmer. The fathers on Smartt Street would lock their daughters into their rooms when Chickie walked by, but it didn't stop Chickie. Chickie was a total piece a shit. He was the kind that liked to pal around with the father, and be the best friend of the brother, while he was giving it to the sister when nobody was looking. For a while, Chickie and Weight were like brothers. It was because of Weight that Chickie started up with a blade. They was friends, for a bit, because Weight liked having Chickie ride with him."

Ladderback remembered a scene in the Basso TV pilot of a young

Tony Basso worming his way into a trusting Polish family and getting the sister pregnant.

"When did Marandola break it off with Weight?"

"When it got so Weight was going to kill him. You see, with a guy that's a piece a shit, you can only tell yourself that he's not a piece a shit for so long, and then, one day, you get what they call incontrovertible evidence that a piece a shit is a piece a shit and, then, you want to kill him. That's when Chickie disappeared, but he'd come back, now and then, when Weight wasn't around. Weight stopped with the drugs because he hated Chickie so much. But he'd provide other things."

She was holding something back and Ladderback had a difficult choice: try to get her to tell him why precisely Weight Wisnitz came to hate Chickie Marandola, or let the conversation flow in its own direction.

He decided to go with the flow. "What other things would Weight provide?"

"Sometimes, it was just news about somebody. My husband, when he was alive, told me Weight was just like the peddlers they'd have up in the hill country in Italy. Before they had telephones, people who didn't normally keep in touch would hear about things in the other villages, from the peddlers. It was the same with Weight. He'd run into all kinds of people—some of them who couldn't stand each other, wouldn't step into the same room with each other—and he'd hear things from them, and when he saw you, he'd fill you in. Of course, he'd expect you to tell him something in return, or buy something from him, but, the way he saw it, he was providing a service."

Ladderback groped for a pad and pen he kept on the table. "Could you give me an example?"

"Well, there was a ambulance driver moved into where Chickie used to live on Smartt Street. He was supposed to have a wife and kid up in West Philly somewhere that he wasn't on speaking terms with. They say Weight would see him on a Tuesday and see her on a Wednesday and that's how they'd keep in touch."

"This driver wouldn't be Larry Dettweiler, would it?"

"Could a been. He had that kind of name. His wife's supposed to be real good with the foreign cars."

"Weight was a go-between."

"You know Weight did time?"

"It was mentioned that he may have got himself into some kind of trouble," Ladderback said, "but no one could confirm it."

"That's because it was wiped off his record. What do they call it? Ex-sponged."

Ladderback wrote down *expunged*. He did not correct her pronunciation.

"What did he do?"

"Nothing actually. It was Danny B that got him into it, when Danny B was trying to be a piece a shit. He tried real hard but he couldn't quite pull it off. I mean, to be a piece a shit, you need a certain talent and Danny, he was a charmer, but he didn't have the devil in him, like Chickie did. Danny got Weight back into running pills and pot and all kinds of things out of the truck. Weight used to hide the pills in the Brussels sprouts because nobody used to like Brussels sprouts and, wouldn't you know, Weight comes up on a cop that likes Brussels sprouts and the cop wants to pick his own and Weight tries to say no, but the cop starts picking anyway, and Weight did two-to-seven for possession. But, because Danny B isn't a total piece a shit, the first thing Danny B did when he got out of law school was ex-sponge him."

"Would that be Danny Bleutner?" Ladderback said.

"Could a been. He had that kind of name."

# the view from the seventy-third floor

When Andy came into the newsroom the next morning—early, as usual—she found so many flowers on her desk she couldn't see her mail.

There were actually two displays. One was a hugely intricate explosion of color, suspended from dozens of wires and levers, that folded, opened and swiveled back and forth. The card, addressed to "Ms. Action," described this as "another unique creation from McCorey's Flowers for All Occasions, Eustace McCorey, Master Horticultural Engineer."

Who did it come from? She could think of at least a dozen—no, two dozen, maybe three—who knew that she was Mr. Action.

The second arrangement was smaller, but exquisite: a row of small, peculiar, but breathtaxingly intense orchids in brown, red and yellow hues, affixed to a simple, sawed-off slab of lumber.

Not a slab: a plank.

The card said, "For the morning after."

She smiled and lost herself in the chore of making a place for the arrangements. What a difference flowers can make! A typical morning becomes . . . not so typical.

Then she signed on to her word processor and began checking e-mails. Then she had a hunch and did a search through the *Press*'s data-bank for obituaries containing the words "McCorey" and "florist." She found one done two years ago, about Loraine McCorey, a florist, who, before she died of diabetes, became somewhat famous in horticultural circles for the elaborate mechanical devices built into her arrangements by her husband, Eustace, a former pipe fitter at the Philadelphia Navy Yard. Eustace was quoted as vowing to continue the business as best he was able.

N.S. Ladderback had written the obituary.

At nine o'clock, she made a call to a law office, confirming that the lawyer was going to represent the reader who had complained about her surveillance system. Yes, it was going to happen!

Andy wrote it up, checking to make sure the story flowed. While she was writing, Ladderback came in and stared quietly at the flower displays.

"Thanks," Andy said.

Ladderback said nothing. Then he said, "You were speaking to me?"

"For the flowers."

He frowned and she could imagine him thinking whether he should maintain the secret. He took off his glasses and wiped them on his shirt. Then he said, "Have you seen today's paper? You did excellent work."

Andy hadn't seen the paper. "I'm on a roll with this Mr. Action about this video system. It's a great story. The company is a South Philly business, a pair of twin brothers who used to work for the phone company. They're very concerned about their reputation. A year ago they hired a salesman who turned out to be the worst mistake possible. He was a commission-junkie who has since been fired. The salesman may have made promises the company couldn't back up."

Ladderback listened quietly. Reporters frequently become enraptured with their work. The smallest incidents, the tiniest of facts, had a way of becoming overwhelmingly exciting. He envied her enthusiasm.

"It gets better," Andy said, "Or worse, actually. The salesman may have been involved in a burglary ring. Or more than one ring. He would sell the systems, collect the commissions, then sell the layout to a team of burglars. If he sold you a system that wired the front door, he'd take money up front, or a cut from the loot, in exchange for telling the burglars to go in through the back."

"Did the police find him?"

"They think so. But the salesman, through his lawyer, is currently trying to sell himself as an informant. He wants a deal for turning in everybody he knows."

"Will the woman get her money back?"

"If she can get a lawyer who will work for cheap. You see, her house is insured, and the insurance company was supposed to lower the premium if she had a security system installed. She got the system put in, but they never lowered the premium because they don't like her system. But her policy doesn't have language specifying the system. Hers is video surveillance on the front door and an intercom wired up to a slow-speed tape recorder. She taped the claims adjuster telling her to go fuck herself."

"Verbal abuse generally isn't sufficient grounds for a lawsuit."

"The claims adjustor is the one who burgled her home."

Ladderback said, "Amazing."

Andy said, "She called him to come and inspect the system. He did an exterior inspection and didn't see an alarm box. They had an argument out in front of her house. She insisted he come in so she could explain the kind of system she had. He followed her in, and before she could tell him about the system, he saw this samurai sword her late husband brought back from World War Two. He told her he could get a good price for it and offered to take it on consignment. She said the sword was staying there and he told her that she was a crazy old bitch and she could go fuck herself and he took it out of her house."

"Did she call the police?"

"They told her to get a lawyer. They said they don't get involved in he-said, she-saids. So she wrote to me. The twins that have the home security company that installed her system told me they have a sister who is a lawyer. I called and told her about this, and she's taking the case, for free."

"You've accomplished something," Ladderback said.

"It feels good," she said. "It feels so good. It makes up for all the times I want to quit."

Ladderback nodded quietly. "I can offer a Mr. Action that might bring you a similar feeling. It concerns the reliability of drugs prescribed by the free health clinics."

"Later," she said.

She attacked the pile of mail, sifting through complaints, enjoying—loving—what she was doing, imagining herself righting wrongs, sticking up for the little guy (or gal), backing those venal, craven, victimizing jerks into corners, when she felt a hand clamp down on her shoulder.

Howard Lange said, "So what *was* Matt Plank hiding?"

Andy took her hands off her keyboard. She spun her chair around, forcing him to take his hand off her shoulder.

"That he's a pathetic, neurotic, self-absorbed jerk," Andy said, "who would probably be happier making crepes out of a truck for shut-ins."

"I didn't see that in your article," Lange said, chewing on a blob of paper. He glanced at the orchids. "He's the kind of jerk sends you that? Or did you tell him, if you like what I write, say it with flowers?"

Andy stood up. She wanted to step on Lange. She was curious if she'd hear that squishy, crunchy sound that cockroaches made when she squished them.

"You're being disgraceful, Howard," Ladderback said. "Ms. Cosicki did not solicit those flowers. You should treat her with more respect."

"You're right, Shep," Lange said. "Here I was, all set to be disrespectful to our star staffer, but because you just told me to respect her, I've got to change my ways. I have an assignment for her, as a matter of fact."

Andy clearly didn't want to be taken away from her work.

"I have given her an assignment," Ladderback said.

Lange rocked back on his heels. "Oh. Excuse me! Who authorized this assignment?"

Ladderback looked him right in the eye. "I authorized it. In addition to her duties as Mr. Action, when time permits, she can do background research for the obituary desk."

"Well, Shep, Father Time ain't as permitting as he used to be." He stared up at Andy. "I want you to profile somebody you ran into yesterday: Slip Disc Chasen, that delightful, admirable, thoroughly respectable individual on the restaurant scene."

Andy made a face.

"They're having a press conference for him in Danny Bleutner's office. You know where One Franklin Tower is?"

Andy said, "Can I ask why you want to give it to me?"

"No," Lange said. "You can't."

Ladderback said, "If it's a restaurant, it's Maculay's beat."

Lange pointed to Maculay's empty desk. "But Mac doesn't get in until a half hour before lunchtime and this deal starts at 11 A.M. That, and a little bird told me that Matt Plank appreciated our coverage of the Fragg death. Plank is catering this press conference and, of all our many, dedicated, highly talented staffers, he would most like to see Ms. Cosicki chow down on his spread, which is fine with me, because if we keep Plank appreciative, we get him in the Philly Pheed and maybe got a few full-color, full-page ads."

"I'd rather not see Plank again," Andy said. "Just the other day you were going to use me to threaten him."

"I still might," Lange said. "You keep your eyes and ears open, especially about that drug money."

"Is this about Chasen or Plank?" Ladderback asked. "Ms. Cosicki should be informed of precisely what she is expected to cover."

"It's about you going back to your little obits," Lange told Ladderback, "and letting Ms. Cosicki do what I tell her to do."

He turned to Andy. "Just wind yourself up, and go. Don't ask stupid questions. Don't piss anybody off. When you get back, we'll sit down together and go over what you've got."

"We're not supposed to get personally involved with the people we write about," Andy said. "It goes against ethics."

"I'm not asking you to get involved," Lange said. "It's more like, don't bite the hand that feeds you, okay?"

They watched him go back to his office.

"Chasen is a total waste of time," Andy said. "And there's something screwy about the timing. Yesterday, Bleutner told me that he was having a little get-together at his office, and he wanted me there."

"And so you're going," Ladderback said.

"Shep, why do I get the feeling that somebody's pulling my chain?"

"Because that's exactly what is occurring," Ladderback said. "You are being manipulated. As members of the media, we are subject to constant manipulation. We're no different, in that regard, from politicians, or anyone else whose opinion or deeds can have wide significance. This shouldn't surprise you."

"It doesn't surprise me. It just, like, I have better things to do, you know?"

"You will have the opportunity."

She picked up her shoulder bag and saw that Ladderback hadn't moved. "You want to ask me if I want an assignment, when I'm done with this one," she said.

"There are many that I could give you, but, at the moment, I'm concerned about what is expected of you," he said.

"You don't have to worry about me," she replied, hoisting up her shoulder bag. "I've handled worse."

"I have a great deal of confidence in you," Ladderback said. "I'm just hoping that no one will ask you if you're happy."

There were two Franklin Towers in Philadelphia, and both were blue and topped with neon zigzags that glowed at night to suggest the Promethean lightning bolt that zapped Benjamin Franklin's kite so long ago and, thus, established Philadelphia as a sacred place where heaven and earth came together.

Franklin Towers were part of a late-twentieth-century building boom set off when a group of developers stopped spending enormous sums on legal fees designed to thwart each other's progress, and discovered that a series of bizarre zoning complexities, tax deferments, and nearly incomprehensible accounting procedures, made it easy to turn a quick profit by building the first of what were intended to be a pair of slightly dissimilar towers in the space that would have been occupied by one.

Though they weren't the tallest structures in the city, the Franklin Towers loomed like two huge, spoiled siblings who refused to behave, and thus, drew all attention to themselves. On a clear day, you can stand just about anywhere in the city and see the towers and know that you weren't in the center of things. Where an earlier generation of Philadelphia factories created hats, clothing, cans, candy, patent medicines, containers, baked goods, arcane electronic devices built on government contracts that made sure missiles did what they were told and the bombs they delivered exploded at exactly the right time—things that the rest of the region, if not the country and the world, was willing to pay for—these buildings manufactured envy. It took months—sometimes years—of working in the city to resist the urge to wish, on days rainy or bright, that you were inside one of those buildings, preferably in the first-born One Franklin Tower, where you might stand and gaze past the slightly stunted Two Franklin Tower, at the the the rest of the shorter, plainer, timid buildings surrounding, and know in your heart that, though the rest of the city's complicated architectural heritage was interesting and perhaps even distinguished in its groveling, modest way, being anywhere else was simply not as much fun.

The building known as One Franklin Tower was the first to break the traditional, forty-story, "no higher than the brim of William Penn's hat" limit that had been imposed on the city's skyscrapers for the first part of the 20th century. In shooting up so arrogantly, it transformed what had been the city's unifying center, the oversized, broad-hatted statue of William Penn atop City Hall, to a quaint lump, one more ornamental chunk of the city's past suitable for tourist photography. The presence of Two Franklin Tower, and subsequent post-modern knock-offs of far more interesting landmarks in other cities, emphasized that what was intended as a "green country town," a utopia of plain, unpretentious, egalitarian sixteenth-century Quaker ideals, was now a city whose business was, in the words of an American President (Hoover? Harding? Coolidge?—one of those high-collar guys), *business.* The guy who worked behind the scenes to make Franklin Towers happen was Danny Bleutner, who had modestly agreed to locate his law firm on Floors 68 through 73, in exchange for sheathing the buildings in blue glass, blue marble and blue steel "because it's my favorite color and I always play favorites."

The cab left Andy off at the hotel entrance, which, in keeping with the Towers' 1980's postmodern need-for-greed pomp, was a gaudy gold, glass, dark-wood and chandelier-encrusted portal (with blue, aqua and teal accents) that was supposed to evoke the louche license and aristocratic privilege of a Regency-period London gambling club.

She took a gray and blue marble-slathered corridor to the lobby of One Franklin Tower, which, differing from the hotel, had all the warmth of a squash court. Cavernous and over-lit, it had no chairs, no kiosks selling coffee and muffins, no sundry shop with magazines and overpriced snacks—just a broad bank of rigidly geometric, marble-and-steel-sheathed high-speed elevator islands, and a single black desk where a group of security guards dressed like lawyers politely but firmly demanded to know whom she was seeing and "have a look at what you're carrying, if you don't mind."

Andy took off her shoulder bag and said she was seeing Danny Bleutner. The guard asked for her name, checked a list, and handed back the shoulder bag without searching it. He said, "This is your first time visiting Mr. Bleutner."

"So?"

"Take Elevator Four. You won't find any buttons in the elevator. It goes directly to the seventy-third floor."

The elevator doors opened as she approached. Only a slight pressure in her ankles told her that the polished obsidian cube was moving. It didn't creak and groan like the elevators in the *Press* building. The lights didn't buzz or flicker. Her ears popped and the elevator doors opened.

Andy stepped into a view so sweeping that she felt as if she were a seagull catching a thermal that had sent her soaring over the city.

Straight ahead, radiating like beams of orderly, imperial power at the gardens of Louis XIV's palace at Versailles, was the furious, tightly packed geometry of the streets laid out by William Penn. The streets extended southward toward the factory sheds, sports stadiums, oil refineries, and the gentle curves of bridges and superhighways, culminating in the boldly skewed pattern of runways at the city's international airport.

Andy looked down on the roofs of buildings. The easiest to see were the parking garages, followed by the painted targets that drew helicopters and, over there, a glass enclosed swimming pool. She only recognized one feature: an proud ornamental cupola atop an art nouveau residential tower that had seemed like an eagle's aerie from the street. From the seventy-third floor of One Franklin Tower, it was a tiny thimble studded with cell phone antennae.

"It's like a game board," Drew Shaw said behind her. "Everything looks like it fits perfectly together."

She told herself that it was the view that made her not want to look at him. But she kept her eyes on the view because she didn't want him to see in her any signs that she hadn't figured out a way not to care. Not yet.

"Some things you should know about Chasen," he began, as if all he wanted to do was help.

"Drew, after the way you treated me yesterday, and the things you said to me yesterday, I can't believe you have the guts to talk to me."

"That was our thing. We both have guts."

"You can take yours somewhere else."

"I will, mostly. But, it's possible that you'll see things and find out things that I'm going to want to know. About Chasen, for example."

"I spoke to him yesterday," Andy said. She had also done a web search while in the taxi. "He's a former butcher. He cut the tendons in his right hand so he can't handle a knife and now he's into food safety."

"You find out the settlement he got when he sued the company that made the knife? The suit didn't come to court, but he supposedly got some heavy TIGFY money. You probably don't know what that is."

"Take-It-and-Go-Fuck-Yourself money," Andy said.

Drew did not reveal if he was impressed. "Chasen's made a career of it ever since. He goes to some low-rent restaurant, tells the owner there's some kind of safety problem, and wouldn't he like to make a donation? If the owner doesn't donate, Chasen or one of his proteges slips and falls and sues. How he got into Loup Garou I don't know, but he didn't get to Plank. Instead, Danny got to him. The press conference is about Chasen getting this grant to launch an alcohol-in-restaurants abuse awareness program. Chasen is going to say this was all inspired by Michelle Fragg's oh-so-tragic death."

Andy couldn't help herself: she had to ask him how he found this out.

"I asked him. Chasen. He's here stuffing his face with the rest of the city's eating press. If you're eating press, you always show up early to a Danny Bleutner press conference because he puts out the food early and the food is always very, very good—I once did an article about the sizes of the cocktail shrimp at various press conferences and the ones they give out for the Orchestra and the Ballet—so tiny you wouldn't believe it—but Danny, he always puts out these humongous prawns. And blue crab claws, of course."

He moved up until she could see him on her left, at the very edge of her peripheral vision. "The other reason you come early is The Show: Danny in action. He hasn't left this place since yesterday. He's got his own apartment right off his office, with a bed, full bath, whirlpool tub, sauna, and a dozen changes of clothes. I'll show it to you. You shouldn't miss it."

If there was something she wasn't supposed to miss, Andy figured that she should see it. But she didn't want to see it on Drew Shaw's arm.

He came closer. "Andy, it's coming together for me. The book deal—everything's coming out the way it should. This kind of thing happens only once and, I assure you, when I get to where I'm going, if there's a place for you, I'll . . ."

She hit him with a near-lethal blast of Cosicki Intimidation Waves.

And then, like a wish come true, she heard Plank say, "Yo, Andy!"

She turned to her right and saw he was in a baggy gunmetal suit, black silk T-shirt, with his face shaven and his hair trimmed short and neat in such a way that it almost made him look interesting.

He grinned. "You hungry?"

Andy glanced at Drew, who appeared as if he had just swallowed something that wasn't going down.

She turned back to Plank and said, "Sure. Lead the way."

Ladderback spent the morning among his files.

He reread the profile he did of Gina Dettweiler. He saw an article in the Penn student newspaper that he had clipped about Carol Dettweiler's death and noticed that it had been written by Andrea Cosicki.

He poured over his notes. He remembered how investigations always yield more information than is needed. They also reveal incongruities, contradictions, complexities that, when writing the profile about her, he chose not to mention. Gina said she had been born and raised in West Philadelphia, that her maiden name was Coca.

Then, and now, Ladderback couldn't find any evidence of a Coca family living in the numerous neighborhoods that constituted West Philadelphia during the years when Gina said she lived there. He could not find Philadelphia County birth certificates for a Regina or Gina Coca during the year Gina would have been born. Checking the years before her stated birthdate, just in case Gina had wanted to be younger than she was, also came up empty.

Gina told him she hadn't gotten married with any ceremony, and that she was visibly pregnant with Carol at the time. Perhaps Larry had hesitated until she insisted.

On the rare moments when Gina compared Ladderback to Larry, she told him he hesitated too much.

And yet, some of the character flaws that a person condemns in another might be the same flaws that person sees most prominently in himself.

Or herself.

The first place Plank took Andy was a long, book-lined conference room whose lustrous mahogany table was arrayed with mountains of finger food, a few too many of which were conspicuously blue. At its end, three chefs stood before a carving station, an omelet and crepe station, and a raw bar.

Matt put his finger to his lips and strode to the crepe station, where he bowed to the chef, who stepped aside. Plank took up a cloth, wiped his hands, put down the cloth, folding it into a perfect rectangle, then lit a portable gas burner, stirred the crepe batter, placed the crepe pan on the burner, tossed in a blob of butter, angled the pan so the butter melted over the cooking surface, stirred the crepe batter again, looked at Andy, stirred the crepe batter a third time—

He said, "A drum roll!"

The chefs huddled together and said, "Barumba rumba rumba rumba . . ."

Plank's face relaxed. His eyes seemed to lose their focus. He ladled the batter into the pan, moved the pan in a circular motion over the flame as the liquid batter turned into a paper-thin crust.

He held up a finger and the vocalized drum rolls ceased. In near silence, he flipped the pan over and the crepe fluttered down onto a plate.

And he groaned.

Andy eyed the crepe. "Something wrong?"

"Three bubbles, two brown-spots!" Plank fumed. "It's that damned domestic butter. The moisture content is entirely inconsistent."

"It looks okay to me," Andy said.

"It might look okay to *you* but it is not okay to *me*! It's a disgrace!" He tossed the pan down and stomped off.

"Matt, I'll eat it!" Andy called after him.

"You will not!" he sputtered. "You said you did this interview and now you can't eat. A perfect crepe, you would eat. You would have to! You wouldn't be able to do anything BUT eat it."

He went out of the room. Andy caught up with him and told him to stop acting like a jerk.

"I'm not acting," Plank said. "I'm the head of a multi-million-dollar restaurant company, and I can't make a decent crepe. Michelle could have made a better crepe than that! And Michelle would have eaten it, even if it would've killed her. Michelle could eat anything, anytime, anywhere, no matter what she did before. I mean, she once even made sausage at Orley's. Have you ever seen sausage made?"

For a moment, Andy tried to remember who it was who said that people shouldn't see laws, or sausage, being made. Was it Alexander Pope, or Ben Jonson, or Samuel Johnson?

"Can you relax, please?" Andy asked him.

"If I were Michelle, I would go off and cut meat. You know she used to do that when she was mad and she couldn't get a drink? She'd open Orley's walk-in refrigerator and whatever he had—it didn't matter what he was going to use it for, she'd chop it up into little itsy-bitsy pieces."

Andy saw Chasen, in a snugly fitting pinstripe suit, and headed for him.

Plank caught up to her and said, "Wait. Let me take it back and try again."

"Matthew, it's not important."

"But you're important," he said.

She stopped. His eyes were saying, *I like you!*

Andy said, "Thank you for saying that, and thank you for the orchids you sent me. They were great. Now, if you don't mind, I have to inter- view him."

"I do mind and you don't have to. Everything he's going to say has been written down in advance. You'll get a copy."

"I still have to talk to him. I can't just take what's written on a hand- out as the truth."

"Most of the other media people do." He raised an eyebrow. "C'mon, we should eat."

"After I interview Chasen."

"You haven't seen the dessert tray. I used that Hawaiian chocolate that you had in a rum tart that is absolutely cosmic. You have to try it."

"Matthew . . ."

"Stay here. Don't move." He dashed down the hall and came back with a crescent-shaped pastry shell holding a dark swirl of chocolate.

"Hey, hey, hey, it's a buffet! You can eat a meal completely out of order. You can even have dessert first!"

She turned on him, hoping to fix him with a blast of Intimidation Waves but he suddenly seemed so adorable that, before she could stop herself, her arm was around him and his was around her and she leaned against a wall that wasn't made of blue glass, in a corner of a corridor where nobody seemed to be looking, and suddenly the touch of another human being felt so *right*.

Andy didn't know how long it was before she let go. She looked down at him and he looked back at her and she realized he *liked* her.

She took a bite of the chocolate tart and she *liked* that, too. She really, really liked it.

She hugged him again and, this time she let him almost kiss her. She glanced down the corridor, saw a door that also wasn't made of blue glass, led him to the door, opened it, stepped into a room filled with the dry, inky aroma of reams of paper and legal stationery and boxes of blue pens that probably wrote in blue ink.

"You said it's all written down," she said, "what Chasen is going to say?"

His eyes were shining. "Somebody in Danny's office wrote his speech. If he deviates by one word, he doesn't get any money."

"You can get me his phone number, for original quotes?"

"Easy," he said.

She looked at him again and saw that he really, *really* liked her.

She liked being liked. She kicked the door closed and said, "Let's finish dessert."


Whitey Goohan told him that the oysters were in. "It's still September," Goohan said. "Any month that ends in an 'r' is good for oysters."

Ladderback had a Rich Boy Special, oysters dipped in a corn batter and deep fried, served on a bun with sauted onions, mushrooms and a sour cream sauce, with a side dish of buttery succotash. "It's our version of the New Orleans Poor Boy," Whitey said proudly.

After saying that the sandwich was superb (and it was), Ladderback asked Whitey Goohan to tell him more about what he did in Puerto Rico.

"Ahh, that was long ago. I saw the sights. I tasted the rum. I lived fast."

"You said Marandola sent you there. What kind of business did Marandola have in Puerto Rico?"

"Pharmaceuticals. Many of the drug companies have factories in the islands. Pilferage occurs. I was to sent down to make sure some of what was walking out of the factories came into Chickie's hands."

From his pocket, Ladderback pulled out a clipping that had been in his Puerto Rico file. "There was a shake up some time ago regarding a version of the birth control pill. It seems that some pills were tested illegally through the Puerto Rican clinics that treated charity cases. The drug companies paid cash to workers at the clinics to give the pills to poor women without telling the women what the pills were supposed to do. The clinics were supposed to keep track of the women and report back to the companies. Did you hear anything about that?"

"Ahh, it's terrible, the disregard some of those drug company executives have. They're so careless, and, you know, carelessness leads to accidents."

"Just after the scandal broke about the testing of the birth control pills," Ladderback said, "a Dr. Alexander P. Elgin died in a boating accident."

"Now I wouldn't tell you anything because I can't remember a thing about my previous life. But, being an orphan as I am, I might let my emotions get the better of me, had I heard of such a thing. I might have used my persuasive abilities to identify the person in charge, and, because islands are surrounded by water, and it's just a few dollars to rent a nice big boat, with a full bar and all the amenities, and have a party where the responsible and the irresponsible might get to know each other, and, with all that liquor going around, a man can fall over the side, or just disappear, get himself tangled up on the propellers, and pieces of him might turn up later, so they can serve as a lesson to the greater community, if you understand."

Ladderback said. "Were you on that boat?"

"I might have been. And, if I was, this would have been the kind of incident that inspired me to question my previous employment. I began to ask myself if I was doing any good. Soon as you try to knock some sense into some stupid s-o-b, there's another to take his place. At least, with the food business, you're as good as your last meal, as long as nobody looks too closely at what goes on in the kitchen."

Whitey snapped his fingers and two Jimmy Deets appeared.

"This isn't going to help," Ladderback said.

"This time you're buying," Goohan said.

"Whitey, did you ever hear about a pill that would make it more difficult to eat or drink?"

"If I had I would forget about it the moment I saw it," Goohan said. He lifted his glass and said, "Banish misfortune," and downed it in a single gulp.

# 10 sentimental resonance

Andy pushed Matthew Plank away and turned on the light.

"So I'm oral, so what?" he said, blinking.

She straightened her clothes. "Not so fast, okay?"

"But, in this day and age of fast food—"

"Didn't you tell me yesterday that 'speed thrills but it never satisfies. What satisfies is timing'?"

"Yeah. Sure. That was when I was in a mood and you were in a mood and the one thing that would have gotten us out of our mood was the one thing we couldn't do, so . . . I got philosophical."

"Later," Andy said. She picked up her shoulder bag, opened the door and slammed it behind her.

She went down the corridor to a gallery area where Drew Shaw and other reporters were seated, taking notes. Behind a single blue-tinted glass panel, in the center of a broadly open work area with tables, chairs and an entire wall of oversized video screens, was Danny Bleutner, his hands flapping, chopping, fluttering, his jacket off, blue patterned suspenders crawling up his shirt, glasses sliding down his nose, a wireless headset clipped to his ear.

"So," Bleutner said, his voice amplified so that those in the spectators' gallery could hear, "are we in agreement?"

Behind him, on one of several oversized video monitors hanging from the wall, was a digitized photo of an executive, male, mid-forties, who, according to what was printed on yet another monitor, was a mid-level functionary in a media company.

"In principle, yes," the executive's voice came back. "You're saying that, in exchange for quitting any prior or future claims against your client, we get all rights to publish a collaborative cookbook between your client and ours."

"A collaborative *memorial* cookbook that my client will assemble from notes left when your client and my client were a team," Bleutner said, "to be called . . ." He waved his right hand in a circular motion at a row of four assistants seated at keyboards. On another screen, a row of titles appeared. "MORE THAN THIS . . . it's a . . ." he watched as the assistant who suggested the title typed in some background data, ". . . reference to a Roxy Music song that is still played on classic rock stations, so it's sure to get major boomer-type recognition. Baby boomers were the major audience segment of your client's television show, and they make up the widest demographic of my client's restaurant business."

Andy could hear, from the speaker in the gallery, faint keyboard taps in the background—could this executive have a similar bank of assistants, recording his statements and augmenting his thoughts?

The executive's voice asked, "And will your client be willing to promote the book in all media, including but not limited to, a tour, in which your client will personally prepare recipes?"

Bleutner said, "He's a natural."

"We've heard he can be moody. We want him up for this."

"You want up, you'll get up." He looked at Dr. Elgin. "We can do up."

"The cover will have them together," the exec continued. "When we put him on TV, we'll want to emphasize that they were lovers and that these recipes were what they ate before they went their separate ways."

"We'll come up with a preliminary graphics package," Bleutner said, as one of his staffers filled a screen with an assortment of photos of

Plank: bearded, clean-shaven, fat, thin, brooding and sublime. Andy recognized one of the photos: it had been used to illustrate one of the articles about Plank that had appeared in the Penn student newspaper when she had been a student reporter.

"Wait here," Plank said suddenly to Andy. She hadn't seen him approach. He went past her, through a tinted glass door isolating the gallery from the row of assistants. He approached one of the assistants, whispered something.

On another screen appeared: PIC OF PLANK + FRAGG TOGETHER & IN LOVE ON WALL AT ORLEY'S.

"Get this," Bleutner said, touching the earpiece of his headset. "There's actually a picture of them when they first met, when they were an item, working in this fabulous, fabulous local's joint and . . ."

*Fragg, pre-purple hair, thinner, ok looking.*

". . . You're going to love it," Bleutner said. "It's from Michelle's pre-purple-hair period, when she was a knock-out. You could put her on the cover of *Cosmopolitan*."

The exec snorted. "Are we talking about the same person? I can't imagine our Angry Eater as a babe."

"You won't have to use your imagination when you see this."

Plank came back into the gallery and motioned Andy to a corner of the gallery so they could talk and not be overheard. "That blue screen you see over there, the last one in the row of monitors? It logs the number of phone calls, staff contributions and service time, by the minute. You could buy an entire cab company for what it costs to keep Danny's meter running."

"You're paying for this?" Andy asked him.

"I really don't know. Danny likes to run with things. What started him off on this was that ass—I mean, your former boyfriend."

"You can call him an asshole," Andy said.

"Danny had been talking about me going national, but, with Shaw wanting to write a book about me and Michelle, Danny figured we might as well go for it now, turn what happened to her into a tragedy about thwarted love."

"C'mon," Andy said. "You, *thwarted*?"

"No, Michelle. The concept is, she visited my place, now that she and I had achieved our youthful dreams of success, because she couldn't forget the good times and she was just about to tell me that when, alas, she died."

Andy said, "No way."

"Actually, it has a very high credibility factor among a specific demographic group, mostly aging baby boomers who have achieved a level of success and want to believe that the stupid, cruel and selfish things they did to each other when they were in love, still have a kind of—I think Danny's cultural anthropologist called it 'sentimental resonance.' "

"Matt, that is complete, utter and total bullshit," Andy said. "You told me you hated her because she drank up your profits, and that she trashed what you really wanted to do. From what Drew read back of his conversation with her, she came into your place to put your place down so she could put herself up."

"Yes, all that might be true."

"All that IS true," Andy said.

"But she had to go, and, sadly, expire. She could not make her feelings known to anyone other than that asshole. Umm, you really don't mind if I call him an asshole? The way you were getting on each other's nerves yesterday, I figured you'd slept together, at least."

Andy said, "I actually like hearing you call him an asshole, at least."

"The pleasure is mine," Plank replied. "Danny has just about fixed it so that your asshole—I mean, not your asshole specifically, but this guy you slept with who happens to be an asshole—"

"Maybe you should just use his first name."

"Okay. Drooooooooop is going to publish something about this, either in *Liberty Bell* or, if Danny can set it up, *Esquire* or *Vanity Fair* as a prelude to a book deal."

"That's what he wants," Andy said.

"It's also what Danny, and all the other people who own my business, want," Plank said. "The strategy is, Drooop—can I call him that? Droopy-poopy-scoopy? I'm sorry, am I being too cute?"

"Close," Andy said.

"We're going to let Pooper Scooper write whatever he feels like, negative or positive. Danny says that, instead of paying people to say what you want, it's much easier and cheaper to get somebody else to fight for you in the media once someone has taken a highly publicized position, because, as soon as media people see someone has taken a position, they have to trash it. Danny said it has to do with most media people being a bunch of lazy, jealous, spiteful, abusive, vindictive, egotistical pricks—present company excluded. You agree?"

Andy thought about it. "Let's say, I don't disagree. Not completely."

"So, just as the media storm peaks, a cookbook will come out with recipes from the time Michelle and I were supposedly in love, and that will be timed to coincide with my next restaurant, which will open in either Las Vegas or Manhattan, depending on what kind of deals we can get on a high-visibility location. The menu will be based around traditional, classical and contemporary aphrodisiacs, some of which, we'll hint might work. That's the kind of theme that can go national, international, even."

He noticed Andy had curled her lip. "You don't . . . you don't approve?"

"You told me that one of things you couldn't stand about Michelle was that she said the things you believed in weren't worth it. You told me you wanted to have a fleet of trucks doing gourmet meals-on-wheels so that people like your mother could eat a decent meal."

"That was a very complicated, non-profit concept possibly requiring government involvement, which means paperwork and politics, which almost guarantees failure."

"What's wrong with that?" Andy said.

Plank furrowed his brow. "Huh?"

"What's wrong with failing?" Andy went on. "You would have the satisfaction of doing something that's really important to you, of seeing where it takes you. Maybe the only thing you'll get out of it is the knowledge that it wasn't meant to be, but I think you'll probably get a lot more. One thing is certain: you'll never know what you'll get until you do it."

"I'll tell you exactly what I'll get from it," Plank said. "I'll get trashed. Failure is unforgivable in my business. Did you know that seven out of every ten new restaurants fail in their first year? I have four restaurants and none of them have failed. And I'm about to become more famous than I ever believed because Danny and his team are going to turn my worst nightmare into a completely bogus concept that people will believe because it's exactly what they want to believe."

She watched Bleutner flapping his hands as he spoke on the headset to another caller—this one, according to the identifying data on one of the monitors, was a lawyer for the holder of Michelle Fragg's life insurance policy.

The lawyer's voice, amplified so that the reporters could hear, was like a dentist's pick probing for a rotten tooth. "We're still not convinced about the negligence question," the lawyer said.

"Joe, Joe, Joe, what are you smoking?" Bleutner replied. "You trying to tell me that my client killed her, right?"

"We haven't reached a definitive position on that question, yet," Joe said. "But we're going to launch our own investigation and if we identify negligence or some other matter that would suggest the possibility of wrongful death litigation, we will inform her parents. Ms. Fragg did not have a will, but her parents could be beneficiaries of the policy and, thus, if a negligence issue were to be identified, would be willing to seek further redress."

"Redress? What is this with the redress? They don't like the clothes they're wearing? Seriously, Joe, I'm not aware of how much you know about this family, but I believe if you check into their backgrounds . . ."

On cue, one of the monitors came to life with a list of Carlson Fracchiano's convictions for child abuse, Sheila Fracchiano's arrest for possession with intent to distribute crack cocaine, references to evaluations from social workers that resulted in the placement of two younger Fracchiano daughters in foster homes.

". . . you will gain an understanding why Michelle ran away from her home several times, finally coming to Philadelphia—"

He turned to the monitor that had a list of data for a Michelle

Fracchiano "where she was arrested for an assortment of misdemeanor offenses that, depending on our ability to open juvenile records, may include larceny, substance abuse and prostitution. None of this information, I might add, has been included in media reports about her death, though I have a feeling, they are about to come out in the next few days—with the exception of two DUI convictions that occurred after Ms. Fracchiano had her name legally changed to Fragg, but, I'm sure you're aware, that, some things have a way of coming to light."

"I'm sure you're aware, Mr. Bleutner—"

"It's Danny, Joe." He made an "S" motion with his finger. One of his assistants picked up a phone.

"—that my company," Joe continued, "has participated in several successful civil litigations regarding wrongful death."

"Actually, Joe, I'm not aware of your company's litigations because . . ." Bleutner pointed at one of his assistants, who made a thumbs down gesture . . . "none of them have been successful in the Pennsylvania Commonwealth courts, which, I am sure you do not need to be reminded, have their own peculiar bias against out-of-state insurance companies."

"That may very well be," Joe said.

The assistant who had dialed held up his thumb. One of the monitors showed the photograph of a handsome man whose face was either Native American or Asiatic. The text identified him as Juan "Johnny" Sungaigutung, M.D., Director Brideshead Free Clinic.

"Permit me to cut to the chase, if I may," Bleutner said. "I have Johnny Sungaigutung on the other line. He's an M.D., runs one of the free clinics in town. He's been a resident of the city for quite a while, comes to us from Puerto Rico, interned at the Stoner Clinic, am I right, Johnny?"

A sharp, lightly accented voice said, "Yes, Danny, my father was from Thailand, but my mother was an American citizen, and I am an American citizen and proud to be one."

"And we're proud to have you, Johnny, who, I want to add, we would naturally have weigh in on any matter regarding the health, or lack of it, of Ms. Fragg. Johnny, you've seen the autopsy report on Ms. Fragg, have you?"

"I've done a lot more than that, actually, Danny. I took an interest in this case because it is of a local nature. Before she went to New York, Ms. Fragg worked at a restaurant close to the clinic. This was before my time here, but the clinic still has her records from then, as well as a recent visit, in July of this year, actually, when she came in complaining of pains in her stomach. At the time, I noted evidence of long-term inflammations and other symptoms due to self-inflicted substance abuse of a possible suicidal nature that, in my mind, may render the payment of benefits null and void."

Joe was startled. "You're saying that two months ago this woman was trying to poison herself?"

"It is a position I would investigate further," Dr. Sungaigutung said. "When we consider the arteriosclerosis and the visible symptoms of alcoholism, we have a very, very sick patient."

"That's just too tragic, Johnny, given Ms. Fragg's positive feelings for my client," Bleutner said. He scanned the gallery. Plank waved. Bleutner waved back. "Now, Joe, let me anticipate your next response by assuring you that we'll send to your office by overnight mail a copy of Dr. Johnny's records regarding Ms. Fragg. I think this will establish that any discussion of my client being negligent, in food preparation or service, will not, as we used to say where I grew up, grow hair on an egg. Do we have an understanding about that, Joe?"

The pause was long enough for Andy to see Bleutner grin with triumph.

"I wouldn't describe it as an understanding," Joe said. "We don't fund suicides."

"And we're all happy you don't," Bleutner said. "Now, if you'll excuse me, I have another call. . . ."

Andy left the gallery. Plank followed her. They were in the same corridor that led to the stationery closet, or one just like that corridor, when she turned to Plank and said, "I want the truth: was Michelle suicidal?"

"She was pretty messed up, physically, psychologically," Plank said. "She was also brilliant. She knew how to cook. She had everything she needed to be a magnificent chef, an important chef, possibly more important than me. She also knew how to cut meat, which is a completely different skill. But she had no confidence, no faith in herself."

"Did you ever see her do anything to harm herself?"

Plank looked away. "Not really."

Andy shook her head. "And you're proud of this? You think it's cool, that Bleutner can just keep feeding people what they want to hear, so you can get famous and he and his clients can make more money off you?"

"Andy, you don't get it," Plank said, taking her hands in his. "What I liked about you the second I saw you, was that you just don't get it. We spent a lot of money on that bar so that a certain kind of person would walk in and say, 'Wow! This is fun! This is silly! This is amazing! This is so pretentious that a typically pretentious asshole can be his typically pretentious self and *fit right in!*' And you didn't get it, then, and you didn't get it when I took you to my place after."

Andy took her hands away. "What I got was that you wanted to seduce me to take your mind off your problems."

"See? You still don't get it about me. I'm a compulsive pleaser. I'm just like Danny in that, I see people who aren't happy—well, not anybody, but the right kind of person, a person who is interesting, who is smart, who knows things, who doesn't look like anybody else because she looks better than everybody else . . . when I saw you, pleasing you became an obsession, a challenge. After you left, I stayed awake half the night, working, and trying this and trying that, until I got that Hawaiian chocolate tart just right, because it had to be right, for you, and it was!"

"Matt, I think I *do* get it, some of the time. What I'm getting right now, is, that you think that Bleutner and Elgin and all these people who are backing you, are there for your benefit. They're not. They're not helping you, with this thing with Michelle, they're in this for themselves."

"They are helping me to the next step," Plank said. "This is a business of steps. You can't sit still. You're either going up or down, and I will not go down. I can't."

"Not even to make your own dream come true?"

"You mean Le Truck?"

"I mean do something where you please yourself!"

Plank became confused. "Why?"

Andy wanted to smack him. "Why not!" she said, and set off in search of Slip Disc Chasen.

Ladderback had two obituaries written that still hadn't been printed, so he spent the rest of the afternoon moving between his files of old clippings and articles and any other interesting information that he'd saved over the years, and numerous web pages on the Internet. The quest was intuitive: he let his interests lead him where they might, to web pages for Alixxir, Dr. Elgin's privately owned Main Line drug company, to that of Kaplan Gallery, where Andy's mother was featured prominently as a vice president, and the daily events calendar of the Philadelphia Museum of Art.

Along the way he read about the career of the painter Anton Boyagian. He hunted down some of Boyagian's paintings, identified some of his major collectors. When doing a web search for more background about Alixxir's products, he came across an article written by yet another bloviating financial analyst, about "IPOs we'd like to see."

Of course, it was illegal for a company to even hint that it was preparing to make an initial public offering of stock, but, this analyst said, "If you put your proverbial ear to the proverbial rails, you can hear the proverbial train a 'comin' "

Proverbially so, Ladderback agreed.

Alixxir was one company among a dozen that, this analyst said, would probably issue a stock offering within the year, but, like many small, relatively new companies, it had "challenges" and "issues." For Alixxir, the challenge was to come up with a very strong new product that would make the company's stock worth a little bit more than zero. As a generic drug manufacturer, Alixxir had limped along in the greater Philadelphia "pharm belt," making cheaper knock-offs of more expensive patented

176

drugs. Elgin wasn't much of a manager, he preferred collecting art and making gassy statements about the industry instead of devoting himself to research and development.

But, there had been rumors, based on comments from Elgin that dated back before he founded Alixxir, when he was in charge of drug testing at the Stoner Clinic, that he was sponsoring research on some kind of orally ingested drug based on Caribbean plant sources that would reduce the desire for food and alcohol. Such a drug would make billions if it worked as anticipated.

But the punishing legal judgements against the manufacturers of Fen-Phen had raised the bar on diet drugs. If Alixxir was cooking up an original appetite suppressor, it would have to be in near perfect shape BEFORE it was tested, because, the analyst said, "The pharmaceutical industry has become a veritable elephant's graveyard of small drug companies whose great white hopes tested poorly and failed to win FDA approval."

Veritably so, Ladderback agreed.

Alixxir's "issues" were with its assets: the company didn't have enough. Alex Elgin was certainly wealthy, but he had almost none of his own money in his company. He—or rather, his company—had one of the best collections of "second rate Boyagians" in the country, and Elgin had been using the collection to leverage acquisitions of real estate and other, more solid, assets. But, unless the value of those Boyagians increased (and the soft art market suggested that they would not), Alixxir's IPO would be no more than "a virtual dream."

Virtually so, Ladderback agreed.

He continued to let his curiosity guide him. He searched through a directory of the city's free clinics and saw that one was located rather close to where Weight Wisnitz lived. He learned of strange plant substances used in arcane Caribbean cult rituals. He discovered an odd side-effect of a second-generation appetite suppresser that was later abandoned by the company Alex Elgin's father worked for, because ingesting this drug interfered with the metabolizing of a common sugar, creating inexplicable cravings for fruit and sweets.

He worked on, vaguely aware that other reporters were scrambling over five-alarm fires in distant neighborhoods, economic troubles causing lay-offs, speeches that the mayor had made about the city wage tax, rumblings from team owners about the future of overpaid athletes on the city's sports teams, a movie that the film critic had just seen that was by far the worst of its kind—what were they thinking, the film critic asked out loud, again and again, as he struggled for the right words to express his righteous disgust.

Ladderback paused, for a moment. He took his fingers off the key-board and remembered how Andy had glowed, early that morning, when she had told him she had gotten involved in another's problem, and had solved the problem. He glanced at the newsroom, caught the aroma of coffee and tea as some of the reporters raced to meet a deadline, while others talked on the phone, or just yawned and read their mail, or another newspaper, or just killed time until they could creep away with-out arousing suspicion or contempt.

Ladderback glanced around and felt content. Then he jumped back into the flow of information, learning about the practices by which art galleries would let their favored collectors "borrow" works for impor-tant parties, and how the collectors would hold onto those works so long that art scholars, critics, and even bankers, would think that the works belonged to the collectors.

At around four in the afternoon, Howard Lange told him to tell Andy to write the Chasen profile "short" because space in the paper was being taken by a train derailment in Delaware.

Ladderback went back to the Alixxir web page and examined some of those holdings. He saw a Main Line address he recognized. He got out his Cosicki file, containing an obituary of Andy's father, City Hall fixer Benjamin "Benny Lunch" Cosicki. Ladderback had written that obituary with Andy's help.

The time went remarkably quickly, as it tended to when Ladderback lost himself in research. He looked up and saw Andy had returned.

He told her that Lange wanted the Chasen piece short. Andy went to the city desk and asked fat, growling Bardo Nackels, the night city edi-tor who was always working days, "How short?"

"Is it bullshit?"

"Mostly," Andy said.

"How about," Nackels said, "not at all?"

"Another thing. Danny Bleutner dug up something about that critic that died yesterday. She changed her name to Fragg. Under her old name, there were a lot of arrests when she was staying here, including prostitution."

"You believe it?" Nackels said. "Don't. I don't have to tell you, just because somebody says they got it, doesn't mean shit. You ever heard of Sacco and Vanzetti? The were a pair of Italian guys got busted for killing a guy and holding up a shoe factory payroll in Massachusetts in the 1920s. The state had no case. The evidence sucked from the get-go, but the state came up with these eyewitnesses. They swore they saw the whole thing, and these eyewitnesses, none of them could agree on the color of the getaway car. Now, if you tell me you dug through the records, if you tell me you found stuff out about this woman that the others missed, we'll talk about it and I'll ask to see those records or I'll get your sources or I'll just sit on my butt and think about it before I decide to run that.

"But if some guy just tells it to you, what's the one question you're supposed to ask?"

"What's in it for him," Andy said.

"Exactly," Nackels said. "Now where's Mr. Action?"

"Coming," Andy said. She sat down at her desk and wrote furiously for the next fifty minutes, and finally sent it to Nackels. He called her over, asked some questions, fiddled with a few sentences and then sent it through.

She returned to her desk and sat down with a sigh.

"Dinner?" Ladderback asked.

Andy said, "Sure."

"Did you drive in, this morning, or take the train?"

"I drove."

"Good," Ladderback said. "We'll walk."

They went to Jimmy D's through the underground concourse. Andy didn't know if this was Ladderback's favorite restaurant. Her father had used it as a place to take his clients and she felt uncomfortable, imagining his ghost haunting the dark wood dining room.

"No one asked you if you were happy?" Ladderback said after he'd ordered the crab cakes.

Andy shook her head. She nibbled absently on her lamb chops, her brain full of jarring memories and impressions, acquired in Danny Bleutner's office, that had yet to cohere.

She found herself liking Matt Plank, just a little. She just couldn't figure out what he saw in her.

She and Ladderback said little through dinner. Perhaps he sensed that she needed time to decompress. He could be cold and focused when he gave her assignments, but he could also be very kind. Where did this kindness come from, she wondered, what did this old man see in her?

His eyes seemed to lose their focus behind his glasses. He said nothing for a while, then Andy noticed his eyes were on the table, on the marks that diners were permitted to carve in the wood with their steak knives. This one said *Gina*.

Andy had offered to pay half the bill, but Ladderback shook his head and handed his credit card to the waiter. Then he said, "I want to meet your mother tonight at the Museum."

"Why?"

"I want to see how she reacts with a specific collector," Ladderback said. "It has to do with a death that might have been similar to the one you witnessed yesterday. I am also interested in how events may be arranged to help, or hinder, the collector's business plan."

"You must mean that wishlist thing." Andy said. "It's a thing they have every three months or so where the collectors get together and listen to some guy at the museum talk about his wish list, you know, what works the museum would like to have but doesn't want to buy outright, so wouldn't it be nice if these collectors either ponied up the money, or just gave whatever they had that the museum was wishing for, as a donation."

"That's one way of describing it," Ladderback said.

"There isn't much else that happens, unless one of the old guys shows up with a new wife who is, like, still a child, or somebody drinks too much, goes for a walk to find out where Rocky did that run up the steps in the movie, and falls down the stairs. I thought they'd turn it into an Olympic event, you know? Give medals to whoever can pick himself up at the end of the fall."

"Like a demolition derby," Ladderback said.

"I guess," Andy shrugged. She didn't know what a demolition derby was. "Can I ask you something?"

"A demolition derby is a contest in which drivers manipulate vehicles that have been adapted to withstand low-speed collisions, in a confined, but open space for a limited period of time, or until only one vehicle is capable of movement."

"Something else, actually. This death you want to find out about, it's not somebody you knew, was it?"

"The person was related to someone I knew."

"But that person is dead and buried, right?"

"Cremated," Ladderback said.

"But you want to know exactly how he died."

"I know exactly how she died."

"Why is her death important to you? I mean, I know you do obituaries, and deaths are important, but what makes this one special?"

She saw him thinking again. "When we love someone, we want to give our best to that person. The one who died was the daughter of someone I cared for."

Andy smiled. "It's about unfinished business?"

"No. All transactions were concluded long ago. But, sometimes, a way to care, or to express that one cares, is to provide information."

"But you said you already know how this person died."

"To have information is not the same as having the opportunity to express it. My hope is that I can express this information, in such a way that the woman I cared for will not feel any more pain."

"You mean this mother doesn't know how her daughter died?"

"She has her beliefs, speculations that only lead to suffering."

"And you want her to know the truth."

"I want her not to suffer."

"So just tell her the truth."

He shook his head.

"You should've taken math in college," Andy said. "There was this guy, Kurt Gödel, who basically proved that you can't know everything, sort of what Heisenberg did with the Uncertainty Principle, but with logic."

"I did not go to college. I disagreed with my parents about the direction I wanted my life to take."

"My father never went and my grandfather never went. My grandfather ran a bar, but he had half the city in his pocket over the stuff he let them get away with upstairs at his place. And my father had the other half in his pocket, greasing the wheels around City Hall. It was my mother that went to college, but, if I can say anything decent about my parents, it's that, early on, they figured out early on what bullshit smelled like, which half the people you meet in college are still not sure about, you know?"

"You studied journalism," Ladderback said.

"I took a lot of courses, but the one that made the most sense when it comes to people was that math course. Another thing that Kurt Gödel proved was that all systems are incomplete, including the system that defines completion. Therefore, you can never be one hundred percent certain. It's like, you can go someplace but you'll never know if you're there. Or you can be someplace but not know where you're going. But you can't know both."

"Gödel was describing logical notation," Ladderback said. "Heisenberg was defining the ability to determine the speed or location of electrons. Human beings are not electrons and are therefore exempt from such simplifications."

"What's that supposed to mean?"

"That it is possible to be correct."

"Possible, sure, but what do you get for it? You want to be correct all the time, you end up being alone."

"Yes," Ladderback agreed, as if that was the most important and most elusive thing in his world.

He insisted on going back through the kitchen, and out into the tunnel, which was lonelier and more depressing than it had been an hour earlier. When they rose to the street level, he closed his eyes and asked her to lead him by the arm to her car.

"I have difficulty in open spaces," he said, as if that would explain everything.

Andy had driven the car to work because she had planned to drive back to her parents' house in the leafy, luxe Main Line suburb of Merion, and bring back some of her old things.

She liked the fact that Ladderback had his eyes closed as she walked him to the lot where she'd parked her dented, faded red Ford Focus. When her father had bought it from one of his clients, he had told her, "This is one of the most recalled cars in the history of the automobile. Nobody's going to want to steal it."

The Focus's narrow backseat was littered with old newspapers, idiotic circulars that unseen denizens stuck under the car's windshield wipers that she'd pull off but never throw away, old styrofoam cups that had held tea.

Andy opened the door for Ladderback. She wondered if her mother felt this way, when she played chauffeur to Mrs. Brickle. Mrs. Brickle was the majority stockholder in the city's oldest bank, and one of the art gallery's best customers. She was also legally blind. When Andy asked her mother why people who are legally blind collect art, Charlotte told her, "because they like it."

Andy got into the Ford, gunned its engine, watched the engine heat gauge fluctuate wildly for no reason she could guess.

She glanced at Ladderback. He sat beside her gripping the door handle, his eyes locked shut. This was definitely not the kind of person who knew a decent mechanic.

"You mind explaining to me how it is you are all eyes in your office, and now you have the terminal squints?"

He clutched the door handle. "I prefer walls around me, a ceiling overhead, shuttered windows, locked doors. I feel better when I am enclosed."

Andy shook her head. "My mother's a little on the extreme side.

She'll rip you apart if she doesn't like you, or if she thinks you're wasting her time. You're not going to waste her time, are you?"

"I don't waste time," Ladderback said.

The engine heat needle went way up as Andy steered for the magnificent Greek Revival structure rising from the rock scarp at the end of the Parkway, then swerved onto the ramp leading up. "I'll need you to help me to the entrance," Ladderback said.

She guided the car past idling limousines and taxicabs that actually looked clean, away into a space, shifted the gears into park. "It isn't far," she said.

"I am agoraphobic," Ladderback announced.

"The opposite of claustrophobic?"

"It's not the opposite. Claustrophobia is a range of responses brought on by the illusion of physical entrapment. Agoraphobia is an aversion to situations in which limits are not readily verifiable."

"You get that from somebody sneezing on you?"

"No." He put his hand on the door latch, felt the door open beside him, felt Andy's arm wrap around his. She moved him slowly, warning him about the flight of steps next to a thing with skinny people and a woman holding her hands in the air.

Ladderback said, "It's not a thing. It's a Jacob Epstein bronze called Social Consciousness."

"What do you call that wall of metal boxes across from it?"

"Beautiful. It's a Louise Nevelson. Did you take any art history courses?"

"My mother always said that if you want to learn about art, look at what people spend their money on."

Ladderback made a disapproving grunt. He asked her if there were any people standing around the entrance. He said he could smell cigarette smoke.

"Some old guys with dumb hair," Andy said. "One has a transplant, I think. You can always tell a transplant because the hair looks like it showed up for the wrong party but decided to stay because the drinks were free."

Ladderback made another disapproving grunt.

"And there's a group of women closer to the door. They're the dropouts. They're either bought out or they can't take the competition, but they can't quite leave yet."

"I hope we don't need an invitation," Ladderback asked.

"My mother could get us in if I ask for her. But let's see if we can crash it," Andy said. "Let's walk in as if we belong here but are arriving late because we had more important things to do."

She held his arm, and as they neared the entrance, Andy sensed a strange energy in the man at her side. He stood straighter, moved his shoulders back and his paunch forward. Instead of taking small, halting steps, his legs swept ahead of him, and his shoes claimed ground that was rightfully his. He was still letting her lead, but it appeared now as if he was escorting her, a woman with an older man, a woman who was *not* his mistress.

She looked ahead. The whole point in sneaking into clubs when you're underage is not to fool the bouncers into thinking you're someone you're not, but to act so completely cool that you just *belong*. Could she make it into the museum's semi-annual donor-buying binge with this lumpy old guy?

She took a quick glance at the thick, swarthy security guard in a blue sport jacket stationed in front of the art museum's revolving door. Like the bouncers at nightclubs, the guard would observe how the people standing outside reacted to Andy and Ladderback. If the tall girl and the lumpy old guy with his eyes squeezed shut seemed just a little too strange to these smokers, the guard would block them.

If the outsiders ignored them, or made polite hellos, Andy and Ladderback would slide right by.

When her footsteps were close enough to echo against the museum's façade, she heard the women standing outside stop talking. She felt them fix deliberately on her. Then the men made small movements—a shift of a foot, a hand raised to scratch behind a neck, folded arms going down into pants pockets—that positioned them so they could check her out without appearing to want to.

She sensed hostility from the women. They were her mother's age, or older, and they wore the flashy, high-contrast evening wear that looks great hanging on tall women with narrow shoulders and beanpole legs, and silly on just about everybody else.

Andy was tall with narrow shoulders and beanpole legs and these women hated her.

She and Ladderback swept through the revolving doors, past the guard and the membership desk to a corridor that ended at the rental gallery. To the left of the gallery was an opened door to an auditorium. Near that was a service bar, with a guy in a white dinner jacket and black bow tie standing behind it.

Andy broke away from Ladderback and found herself in front of the bartender, who was young, with closely trimmed dark hair, a muscled face with thin skin as pink as the inside of a steak cooked medium rare. The way he diverted his gaze reminded her of the servants in Mrs. Brickle's house. They were not allowed to look directly at the people they served. Mrs. Brickle's son had said that the custom descends from European court manner.

The bartender did not look at her when he bowed his head ever so slightly and asked, "Something from the bar?"

Andy asked for pepper vodka.

"On ice?"

"Only if it isn't really cold."

"Ice it is."

The vodka was nowhere as good as what she had had at Loup Garou. She had the glass in her hand (and it was a glass, nothing plastic for this crowd) when she saw Ladderback looking at her expectantly. She tilted her head back, poured the firewater down her throat, felt it burn all the way down.

She saw Ladderback ask directions from a guard and then go into the auditorium.

The heat from the alcohol radiated through her stomach, up and down her spine, and out to the tips of her fingers. She was exhausted, emotionally drained, and suddenly sleepy. She had a second, then tossed the glass to the bartender, who caught it with one hand and gave her a wink.

Her head seemed to leave her neck. It floated up as the rest of her stepped down into the darkened auditorium. She was at the top of a descending rows of chairs. At the bottom stood Lionel Tropea, the museum's curator of contemporary art, in his French-cut café-au-lait suit, with his face glowing from the lectern's reading lamp. He held a cordless microphone like a TV game show host as he discussed the splash of red and black colors projected on a screen behind him.

The screen was large enough to be in a movie theater and the colors momentarily disoriented her. She put a hand out to steady herself, heard Ladderback go, "*Oof.*"

"*Oof* yourself," she whispered. She saw people in the auditorium sitting in groups, muttering among themselves, some with a forced loudness, as if directed at a listener with a hearing aid, as Lionel pretended to ignore it, prattling about paintings as if he were describing something wonderful he'd found at a yard sale and just couldn't wait to tell us how much he didn't have to spend.

"This Boyagian," Lionel piped, "was clearly executed as the artist was approaching his prime. It's a portrait of a Sect Rouge mambo—a priestess—of a Caribbean tribal sacrificial cult. She's wearing a horned headdress that is soaked in plant substances that are supposed to work their way into the wearer's skin to create feelings of power, anger, control. In this series, Boyagian dramatizes the dark, dominant power of the feminine over the masculine. The work is vital for understanding the synthesis between pain and creativity in Boyagian's mature work. Some of us, when viewing this work, might feel that it is possible to have too many Boyagians, but we don't think so, do we, Dr. Elgin?"

Andy saw Elgin stand up in the front row, wave, and sit down again. Karyn was at his side in one of the gallery's BUY ART T-shirts.

Andy whispered to Ladderback, "He talks good, but he is very creepy."

"He also needs to show assets for an upcoming public stock offering for his company," Ladderback said. "The assets were to be a new drug. But the drug hasn't tested well so he needs something else."

"But what's that have to do with . . ."

"Watch," Ladderback said.

Lionel said, "If we meet the collector's price on this and the late de Kooning, we have something that we can put together right now against the Pollock show that the Modern is planning for next fall."

Andy saw Danny Bleutner stand up. "I'd take the whole lot, but it won't go with my sofa."

That got some laughter. Ladderback told Andy, "Bleutner is on the board of Elgin's drug company. It's in his interest for the value of Elgin's assets to increase."

Then Andy heard the high, cutting voice of Belisaria Brickle: "Why can't we get him to donate it, then kill him and grab his swag for nothing?"

Even more laughter fluttered through the auditorium. Lionel broke up as if he had never heard anything so hilarious.

Andy searched the room, saw, about three-quarters of the way back, Mrs. Brickle's small, silvery swirl of hair beside Charlotte Cosicki's larger, blond swirl.

"As usual," Lionel said after the laughter had crested, "we can depend on Mrs. Brickle to offer the most expedient suggestion."

"Oh, please, Lionel, I'm just being *cheap*," she replied, getting a bigger laugh.

"A virtue if there ever was one," Lionel agreed.

"Let him take his late bloomers to auction," Mrs. Brickle continued. "Let's see how many are bought in and then we'll wait for him to come to us."

"A painting that is 'bought in' at an auction," Andy explained to Ladderback, "is a painting that doesn't get the minimum of what the seller wants."

Ladderback didn't react, but somehow he gave Andy the impression that he knew more about art and auctions than she did.

At the mention of an auction, Lionel seemed to shrink. "We all know that this belongs to an important collector. The Rouge Sect series represents Boyagian's realization of the relationship between pain and creativity. It's the transition from the Pain God paintings to his masterpiece, his icon of consuming passion," he switched to a slide of a painting of a dark, blurry, malignant beast, "the Loup Garou."

"We shouldn't waste our energy on what we don't want in the hope that we'll be first in line for what we do," Mrs. Brickle insisted. "If you want to bed a prince, you don't sleep with the soldiers."

That brought an even bigger laugh. Andy listened as others in the auditorium expressed opinions about the paintings, though none as loud as Mrs. Brickle. Andy looked at Mrs. Brickle, and saw Mrs. Brickle whispering quietly with Charlotte.

Then Mrs. Brickle announced, "Let's conclude this. Alex, tell your butler, if you have one."

"I'm between houses, actually," Elgin called back to her. "But I've made an offer." He gazed at Charlotte. "I've been told the neighborhood's good."

"Then crate them up and send them to the museum," Mrs. Brickle said. "I'll give fifteen million to take care of his separation anxiety."

The room was silent for a second. Then Danny Bleutner stood and started to applaud. Elgin and Karyn Asgard followed, with the rest of the room rising until, last of all, Charlotte Cosicki rose, her arms in the air like Rocky dancing on the Art Museum steps; as Mrs. Brickle remained seated, glorying in it.

Ladderback stood and rapidly moved back toward the exit. Andy followed him. "Didn't you want to meet my mother?"

"Perhaps another time," Ladderback said. "In a less social situation. I wanted to determine if there was a relationship to Dr. Elgin."

"You could have asked me. Elgin got her my birthday reservation at Loup Garou."

"I believe you should refrain from writing about Dr. Elgin in the future," Ladderback said as he left the auditorium. "A financial relationship now exists between you and Dr. Elgin—or, rather, Alixxir, his company. He's buying your house."

He saw that she was confused. "I will explain if you are willing to drive me to my apartment building."

"I've, uh, had something to drink."

"I can trust you to handle yourself competently."

She led him outside and back to the car. She was heading back toward Center City when he said, "The manipulation you have just seen has tripled the value of Dr. Elgin's art collection, even though Dr. Elgin doesn't own it. The collection is owned by Alixxir, his company, even though half the paintings in it have been lent by your mother's gallery. Alixxir is using the entire collection, as well as the highly inflated value of your house, as corporate assets so that Dr. Elgin can realize a windfall profit when he takes his company public, even if the diet drug he's hoping to sell remains dangerously defective."

"How do you know *he's* buying my house?"

"His company has listed it among its assets as already bought."

"But my mother said they haven't gone to settlement."

"A gallery such as your mother's will lend art to important collectors for indefinite periods with the hope that collectors will eventually purchase them. Or the gallery will sell the art to the collector but not request payment for months or years, while the collector behaves as if he owns the work. Some collectors use this art that they are pretending to own to leverage acquistion of more art, as collateral for loans, or as corporate assets. Your mother's gallery website lists those paintings that Mrs. Brickle just purchased for the museum, as being 'placed' in the Alixxir collection. Placement means that Alixxir has taken possession and agreed to purchase. This confers value, even if no money has changed hands. I'm sure if you ask your mother, she will tell you that she has found a buyer, or that she's placed the house, but that the check, as they say, is not in the mail."

Andy parked illegally on Locust Street. "Would you like me to . . ."

"Please," he said, "though I would hope you might return to your car safely."

"I can handle myself." She walked him up through the door of his apartment building. "Something about Elgin has always bothered me," she said. Andy told him that she had interviewed Elgin when she was a Penn student.

"I read the student publications from time to time, and I put your article in my files," Ladderback said in the small lobby with his back to the front door. "I recall your tone was quite respectful, but, I could sense your feeling that Elgin wasn't being as open with you as you would have liked."

"I had the feeling he was thinking of me as a piece of meat."

"We must be careful when we make statements about how people think," Ladderback said. "Though, from what I've learned of the man, I suspect that Dr. Elgin's thoughts were much worse than that."

The elevator arrived. He stepped in and bid her goodnight.

# lle truck

At a little after 9 A.M., Andy came into the newsroom to find Ladderback going through digitized city records on his computer terminal.

She removed a few flowers that had withered from the arrangement and signed on to her word processor and went to the list she kept of Mr. Action's Questions of the Day. All of the questions were supposed to come from readers, but she was permitted to invent a few, as long as the answers she found were accurate.

She looked at the orchids on the wooden plank. How do you care for orchids? She had heard that they weren't like normal plants, so . . . did you water them? If so, how often?

She went on the Internet, did a search for "orchid care," and was overwhelmed at the result.

Later, she decided. She went back to her list and couldn't help thinking of Plank. He had been very good at solving the mysteries of the fasteners, buttons, and zippers that fashion designers employed so that a woman getting into clothing had be a contortionist to get herself dressed. And he had been definitely *oral*. No question about that.

She didn't imagine anything serious developing between them, but she enjoyed the food he made for her and the attention he gave her, when he wasn't talking about himself. Had he been right about her not getting things? As a journalist, she was supposed to figure out what was true and go with it.

She heard Ladderback's fingers clattering on the keyboard at the desk beside her, and her thoughts returned to last night's trip to the Art Museum. She remembered her car's overheat gauge, and said out loud to herself, "How far can a car go when its engine heat gauge is in the red?"

Ladderback said, "I can give you a source you can call who can answer that."

"That's okay," Andy said. "I can probably find it on the Internet."

His eyes seemed to light up behind his glasses. "What you would find on the Internet would most likely be too much data, or information that was much too general. This source is local. She is a mechanic and female mechanics are still rather rare. There is also a feminist angle: she grew up at a time when cars were perceived primarily as symbols of male power and so became interested in them as a way of challenging this power. You could ask her, for example, how far one could travel on one of the major roads if there were stop-and-go traffic on the Schuylkill Expressway, or along the city streets with many stop signs, such as Tenth Street in South Philadelphia."

"How does somebody with agoraphobia know about feminist car mechanics?"

His eyes dimmed. "I was not agoraphobic when I was younger."

She studied Ladderback, asked herself, what was she not getting? *What was Shep Ladderback hiding?*

"This source you want me to call," Andy said, "is a woman you used to know?"

He looked away and Andy saw the blush crawl up his face. "My relationship to the source is not . . . would not . . . create a conflict of interest if you were to make the call."

Andy put a notepad on his desk. "You write it down, right there. I'll be happy to give her a plug."

He took a long breath. Then he wrote the number down and handed the pad back to her. Andy put the pad in her shoulder bag. She could tell he wanted her to make the call immediately, and she didn't quite want to. Not yet. She went to her stack of mail.

The fifth letter had odd stamps on it. It was from Germany, from a visitor who had come to Philadelphia to research an ancestor, one of the Hessian mercenaries who fought for the British during the Revolutionary War, deserted, married, and never returned. While in town, he stayed at an "economy" hotel that he had booked on the Internet, and was dismayed to find that the room was filthy and the bathroom plumbing inoperable. He found subsequent rooms in the hotel to be less than satisfying and, when he tried to check out, he was told that he would only get a partial refund, because city taxes were levied on visitors upon check-in, regardless of how long the room was occupied.

So he ended up spending the week in the hotel, where, in addition to spending sleepless nights because of noise, he found a copy of the *Philadelphia Press* in the lobby, and thought he would write Mr. Action as a way of warning other visitors about this situation and, perhaps, inspiring a public outcry that would end what seems to be a deliberate victimization of tourists.

The address of the hotel was within the 12th Street loop, a sixteen-block area in Center City that, at night, was used by male prostitutes. This hotel was probably one used for sex, but, even if this visitor was what he said he was (the hotel happened to be within walking distance of one of the city's genealogical archives), he did *not* receive accurate information about city room taxes.

Andy began making calls to various offices in City Hall where the person she wanted to speak to was not available, or not at his desk at the moment, or had been transferred to another department, or was not at the extension she had dialed, but if she left a brief message after the tone . . .

She left messages. Along the way, she tried to find out if there was a person who was supposed to inspect city hotel rooms to determine if they were even minimally habitable. She made more calls and left more messages.

At a little after 11 A.M. she reached that point when she could not make another call because she was absolutely certain if she made another call, any of the twenty people she had been trying to reach would call right back and she'd get that annoying beep, or the newsroom receptionist would wave at her that she had a call on another line and . . . she just wanted *somebody* to call her back.

And then, the phone rang. Andy picked it up.

"Hey, Andy!" It was Matthew Plank, sounding like he was underwater.

"Hey, Matt," she said. "You calling me on a cell phone?"

"A real cheap scuzzy model that was not cheap and scuzzy when I bought it, that I use on remote operations."

She took the bait: "What's a remote operation?"

"It can be when I'm scouting locations, visiting suppliers or, you'll excuse the cliche, making a dream come true."

She smiled. "Is this dream one of mine, or one of yours?"

"Both, I think, but I'll let you take the credit. Now, are you, at this very moment, pissed off, annoyed, feeling neglected, unappreciated, unfulfilled and possibly even *unloved*?"

"Matt, we have to talk about this."

"How are you dressed?"

"What do you mean?"

"Action gear? Formal wear? Meet-the-public suit? Business casual? Don't-fuck-with-me black pants and a ripped tank top?"

"Black pants, blue *blouse*, not ripped."

"Shoes that you can stand in comfortably?"

"Every shoe I wear I can stand in comfortably," Andy said. "I'm in an old pair of lace-up Doc Martens."

Cars honked in the background as he asked her if that particular shoe came with heels.

"I was six feet when my mother bought these for me," Andy said. "Since I graduated, I've actually grown an inch. I'm just about six-foot-one. I didn't do heels then. I don't do them now."

"Great. I'm outside your building, Market Street entrance, in a bus zone. It's going to be lunchtime soon. You should—"

He said he was in the bus zone. She imagined him parked at the curb in some bright, lethal-looking sports car. "What car should I look for?"

"Not a car," Plank said, "Le Truck!"

Ladderback watched Andy hoist up her shoulder bag and take long strides out of the newsroom. He had been waiting for an opportunity to give her an assignment but, from the way her face brightened during the last phone call, he decided it might be best to let her go.

He examined his mail. The October issue of *Liberty Bell* had arrived. The cover was a picture of a couple around Andy's age: white, Anglo-Saxon features, flawless teeth in wide smiles. They were peering up from behind the dashboard of a red sports car, wearing expensive suburban casual clothes: a suede jacket on him, a thick sweater on her.

Beside them, big yellow block type shrieked, TEN GREAT FALL GETAWAYS! And, in a smaller column, MOB TREK: THE NEXT GENERATION.

Ladderback opened the magazine, turned to the article, and saw that it had been written by Drew Shaw. It was just another round-up of familiar names and faces. The first paragraph began, "It was all over for the Brideshead boys long, long before Chickie Marandola's severed ring finger turned up stuck in the sewer grate at Smartt and Tenth. The finger had been wrapped in a napkin, like a hot dog somebody tossed half-eaten from a passing car. . . ."

The article was a lurid recap of the last few years of violence. Shaw had nothing new to say, but having nothing worth writing about never stopped an ambitious journalist, and Ladderback could tell, from the way Shaw kept talking about all the dark secrets in the dark corners of the city, that he was sending a message to his readers, as well as his editor—you ain't seen nothing yet.

Shaw was desperate. Ladderback didn't know why, but journalists go through periods of noisy desperation, and this was Shaw's.

He glanced at Andy's desk. Until last night, he had wanted to give Andy a series of assignments that would help him identify what killed Weight Wisnitz, Michelle Fragg and, possibly, others. But Dr. Elgin's

197

tangled financial relationship with Andy's mother might make things difficult for Andy. Concepts of conflict of interest and journalistic integrity are impossible to maintain when family, or loved ones, are involved.

Ladderback was certain of one thing: Andy could pursue the truth, tenaciously and competently. But, because of the petty rivalries, hierarchies and rigid classification of responsibilities among the *Press*'s reporters, if Andy stayed with this investigation, she would either have to share a byline with another staff reporter, or she would have the story lifted from her after she had done the ground work, and have her efforts blended into yet another *Press* staff report.

Ladderback looked about the newsroom. He knew many of the reporters by their first names, but he did not know if they would want a story about Elgin. He could imagine Howard Lange shooting it down, for too many reasons.

Ladderback dialed the editorial office number of *Liberty Bell Magazine* and asked to speak to Drew Shaw.


Andy went through the revolving door at the street entrance of the Press Building and saw, blocking traffic, a rusting, dented, ice cream truck whose menu of dessert treats had been painted over with gray primer paint. Plank, dressed entirely in chef whites, was at the wheel.

Andy jumped in and Plank pulled the panel truck away.

Almost immediately, the engine stalled. He started it again and went west, toward the traffic circle around City Hall. "If we can make it around the circle, we're good to go for the rest of the day."

"You're going to do it?" Andy said, hugging him. "You're going to deliver food to shut-ins?"

"As you said yesterday, not so fast," Plank said over the noise of the engine. "This is an interim step. Today's challenge is to make the perfect mobile, on-demand crepe."

The engine stalled again. He started it again and entered the circle. "What I'm looking for is a system whereby a crepe can be made while the vehicle is in motion, so that when the order is placed, the chef can make the crepe in transit and it can be delivered relatively hot and fresh."

Andy looked behind her, at the chopping block and a pair of hot plates bolted to what had been the tops of ice cream freezers. "I don't know how to make crepes."

"You'll be my assistant," Plank said. The truck stalled again. Plank pumped the gas pedal and the engine wouldn't turn over.

"I'd rather drive," Andy said.

"This isn't a suburban SUV."

"I've moved people in and out of dorm rooms," Andy said. "I learned how to drive light trucks like this." She looked at the dashboard. "You can't start in this gear."

Plank downshifted, turned the key again and the engine screamed to life. They went around City Hall and came back on Market Street, heading east this time, until Plank made a right run onto Tenth Street. He said, "The way this thing sounds, I don't think we should try to go fully mobile today."

"Where did you get this?" Andy asked.

"An absolutely fascinating used car lot next to a donut bakery in the North East. It was either this or an old fire truck."

The truck lumbered past the high-rise hospitals around Walnut Street, the stiff rows of subdivided mansions on Spruce and Pine, beyond the playground and the supermarket on South Street to Queen Village and Bellavista and, finally, Brideshead, the part of South Philadelphia that everybody thinks about when they think of South Philadelphia: a swath of old, closed-up factories and corner bars with TV sets everyplace you could look, churches anywhere you tried to go, a bread bakery pumping out an aroma that made you want to throw open every window, and an open-air market street selling vegetables, fresh fish and meat that, even before the sun started to turn the rooftar into a sticky black industrial soup, made you want to shut every window and wish you lived on the Jersey shore. Andy gazed at shops that were carved out of the front parlors of the rowhouses where the workers used to live, at delicatessens that didn't even have signs on the front windows, street corners where shifty-looking men in ill-fitting clothes stood beside piles of boxes of shoes or microwave ovens that they were selling for cash. Ask where these boxes came from and you would be assured, that, just as it is possible to buy a single lottery ticket and win a hundred million dollars, marry the person of your dreams, or go out onto the street and have the right bus pull up exactly when you need it, it is also possible to be standing on a corner with no thought in your mind and nothing to do when boxes of these very shoes and microwave ovens fall out of the back of a truck and land on the street, and what else are you going to do but pull them out of the street and make a little display so you can make an honest buck in this great city of ours?

Plank took the truck past neon-lit cheesesteak palaces, where the sidewalks were dark with splattered Cheese Whiz and fried onions and red-tablecloth Italian restaurants where everybody swore the house wine was made in somebody's basement and some old geezer or geezerette was supposed to sing operas every Saturday night. As the sun rose to its noontime height, Andy looked out from her seat by the truck's passenger window and could almost smell the long, fat, golden brown loaves of Italian bread in the storefront bakeries.

She peered down the narrow streets and couldn't help but wonder if, somewhere around here there might be someone who knows someone who knows someone in The Mob. Depending on who you talked to, Philadelphia could have so many criminal organizations that it's a wonder how you could cross a street without somebody jumping on your back—but there was only one Mob and you had to go to South Philadelphia to find it. You could take tours of the places in South Philadelphia were mobsters were shot, poisoned, drowned, incinerated, strangled, beaten to a pulp, or blown to pieces from dynamite planted under the steps leading up to their houses.

Even before it was a tourist attraction, the Mob was an industry, as Italian kids of all sizes in fabulous clothes got busted by black or Spanish cops. Then mobsters got Jewish lawyers to defend them and, depending on who you talked to, the mobsters were either locked up, like the no-good scum that they were, or they were insulted, demeaned, lied about and shamelessly framed in court by Irish prosecutors in baggy gray suits and ties you wouldn't want to get buried in.

And the one thing everybody in this industry had in common was that they were all born within a couple of square miles of each other, or, if they weren't, they could feel as if they were, because, as much as South Philadelphia was a home, it was like most working-class city neighborhoods: a launching pad, a place to grow out of and get far away from.

Because the mob kids would either get acquitted or "take time on the inside" of a jail, after which they'd get out, and, by then, the cops who busted them got jobs with the federal government or with the casinos in Atlantic City, and the prosecutors became defense lawyers and everybody would make nice and move to some leafy half-acre in the suburbs with great schools and convenient shopping right down the road, while, back in the neighborhood, the old house, the old bar, the old places where you used to hang out and make trouble, as well as those where you ran to get away from the trouble you made, were going over to the Vietnamese, Laotians, Cambodians, Thais and Koreans.

Andy was lost in it all when Plank pulled the truck up to the corner of Tenth and Smartt Street, right in front of a fire hydrant, and cut the engine. He went to the back of the truck and tossed her a white, crisply pressed apron and a long, white-paper chef's toque. "Put this on. Now stand up."

Andy did and her toque smashed against the roof of the truck.

"Figured as much," Plank said. He tossed Andy a worn, but brilliantly white cotton jef cap. "This is yours?" she asked him.

"I bought it when I opened Trellis. At Orley's, we had to wear the paper, Emperor of the Steak hats."

"You should be wearing it," Andy said.

"I got plenty of hats that fit. You put it on."

Andy did so. It fit snugly. She looked at herself in the truck's side mirrors. "I like it," she said.

"Me, too," Plank said, letting his gaze linger on her.

"I told you, I don't know how to make crepes."

"I'll make the crepes. You'll hand them to people, right? What we're going to do, is just what my mentor, Orley Roberts did: fire up the stove, make only from fresh ingredients, let the aroma advertise what you're selling, sell what you can, give away what you can't, and hope you have enough money at the end of the lunch shift to make change."

He stepped out of the truck. Andy followed him out and helped him open and secure the side panels. She saw the fire hydrant.

"Aren't you going to get a ticket if you stay here?"

"This is South Philly and I'm performing a service," Plank said. "Besides, any cops you see, they get free. Whatever they want."

"What are we giving them?"

"Whatever WE want." He went back in the truck and came out with a sign that said, "COD."

"It stands for Crepes on Demand. Anybody asks for fish, you tell them they have to have it in a crepe," Plank said. He opened the freezer compartments, took out containers of eggs, milk, sugar, butter, cream and flour.

"Everything here was flown in from France," Plank said. "The flour alone cost me more than this truck."

"So what are we selling these for?"

"Two bucks a pop, three for five dollars, because it's easy to make the change."

"How many do we have to sell to break even?"

"Being able to do this, with you," Plank said, "I've already broken even. More than even." He looked around at the ruddy brick rowhouses and cars baking in the noontime sun. "You made this happen."

Andy put her arm around him. "Now you're not getting it. You made this happen."

"But I needed you to do it."

He had a look, like he would kiss her if she let him. She let him. She let him again.

He broke away and brandished a wire whip like a fencing foil. " 'And with the refrain,' " he said, quoting from Cyrano, " 'I thrust home!' "

Andy helped him feed flour into the batter. He gave her a knife and told her how to chop the fruit, the mushrooms, the chocolate ("Two French, one Dutch and one very, very Hawaiian") more than a dozen cheeses ("This goat cheese will put you on the moon!"), the prosciutto ham, ("Because if you're Italian, and you're still living in South Philadelphia, and you see somebody cooking French on the street corner, you have expectations that must be met."), and other ingredients that he would use as fillings.

Then he fired up the hot plates.

"You want a drum roll?" Andy asked.

"Nahh. I'm not out for perfection today. Let's just see what happens." He ladled the batter onto a pan, let it darken, flipped the crepe. "Not good but not bad." He asked her if she wanted to eat now, or later.

"Both," Andy said.

Plank gazed at the array of possible fillings. "It's not here!" He dropped and pulled from a cabinet a container of brownish goo. He popped the lid, stuck in a spoon and flipped out a blob of the goo onto the crepe, folded the edges, nudged it onto a piece of thin white paper—"If this were France we'd use newspaper, but I figured you might find that a little extreme"—folded the paper into a loose cone, and handed it to her.

"You should—"

"I will," Andy said. She tasted the crispy, yielding, flour shell and then tasted the rich, smokey flavor of roasted cashews and . . . fire!

"It's those fire-tossed cashews you liked, ground while they were still hot and then allowed to soak into that pepper vodka you liked, then roasted in just a little bit of butter to combine the flavors and . . . does it work?"

It was so delicious, Andy didn't want to open her mouth. She could only nod and hope that he could see, from the expression on her face, that this was as close as she had been all day to pure pleasure, and she *was* getting it.

"Now we work!" Plank said.

Ladderback got Shaw's voice mail. He began to describe the story when Shaw picked up.

Ladderback introduced himself and began again to tell why he was calling.

"Wait a minute. I know all about this. I was there when she died. You're saying Fragg was on drugs? I didn't see her take anything."

"She could have had the drugs in her possession. They may not have been identified and collected by the police, or someone could have taken them from the scene. Her body may have been tampered with in some way after it was transported to the medical examiner's office, so that it would not indicate the presence of the drug, or that the symptoms might be mistaken. I've spent much of the morning gathering data about deaths of this sort, going back over the last three months, and—"

"Hold on. You're telling me that Michelle Fragg did not die because of clogged arteries, or alcoholism, or suicidal tendencies, that she was popping this pill? What's the name of the pill?"

"It doesn't have a name yet. It is most likely being developed by Alixxir and distributed through the free clinics to which Alixxir gives research grants."

"Wait a minute. Alixxir is Alex Elgin. I just got a call this morning about Alixxir. They own this fabulous collection of Boyagians, that just became super valuable. We're thinking of profiling them as a Hot Property." He paused. "Let me ask you something. How much is Danny Bleutner paying you to tell me this?"

"I've never met Mr. Bleutner," Ladderback said crisply.

"Okay, so it isn't Danny. But you know the way he is. He knows people who know people who know people. So who told you to call me?"

"I am calling you because I believe this information is worth journalistic investigation and exposure," Ladderback said.

"But you don't want to do it, right? Or you can't do it because the *Press* doesn't give a shit. Or maybe you don't even work for the *Press*."

"My byline has appeared daily in the *Philadelphia Press* for the last forty-two years," Ladderback said.

"We get the *Press* here. What section do you write for?"

"The obituary desk," Ladderback said.

"I don't read those. I used to know someone who works for the *Press*.

204

It's a truly terrible newspaper. A total embarrassment. I can't believe you've been with them as long as you have."

"Some days I can't believe it either, Mr. Shaw," Ladderback said. "I apologize for taking up your time."

"And tell Danny that I'm not as stupid as he thinks. I don't just swallow what I'm fed."

"We must be careful when we make statements about what people think," Ladderback said. "But, from what you have told me, and from what I've seen of your work, I believe Mr. Bleutner is aware of the extent of your ability."

Ladderback hung up and tossed the magazine in the trash. After a few seconds he pulled it out, and opened it again to Shaw's article about the mob.

What was Drew Shaw hiding? Ladderback asked himself. By the end of the article, Ladderback had a very good idea.

Plank was correct: the eggy, buttery aroma of the crepes, as well as the numerous hot and cold fillings, did draw a few passersby. For the first few minutes, Andy gave all the crepes Plank made without charge. Andy took money from people who wanted drinks (Plank had an assortment of bottled sodas, juices, iced teas and coffees), and from those who asked for specific crepes.

An old woman in a Sixers cap said, "What is this? You give me for free, but when I ask, I have to pay?"

"The choice, ma'am," Plank said testily, "is yours."

"But I'm a celebrity around here," she said. "I been in two movies and a TV show. You treat me good, I'll tell people how good it is, and you'll make more money."

Plank touched his toque in abject humility. "A celebrity? I'm sorry. I was completely mistaken." He pointed at the woman and said loudly to Andy, "Anything she wants, on the house."

He apologized again to the woman. "I should have paid closer attention but, I suppose, this happens to you now and then, when you're incognito."

"What I'm in," the woman huffed, "is none of your business." She accepted her prosciutto ham and sweet onion crepe, and ate it solemnly. "I could eat another one a these."

Plank gave Andy a second one to hand to her. "Thank you for reminding me, ma'am," Plank said. "It isn't enough to meet demand. We must anticipate it."

And older man in a black jef cap stood blinking on the curb. "Why, this is amazing."

Andy asked him what he would like.

"That you would come back, to this corner, as many times as you're able," he said. "Just saying you can make a Welsh rarebit and have it in a crepe . . .

"A miracle!" the man said as Andy gave it to him. He sat quietly, eating it cautiously, as if afraid that any bit of it would escape him. Then he saw a paunchy, professional type approaching and he moved rapidly away.

The professional type almost swaggered up to the truck. "I'll take the shitaki mushroom, scallions and green pepper."

"Would you like the mushrooms sauted in tamari or sesame oil?" Plank asked.

"Both!" the guy said.

Plank frowned. "There is such a thing as overkill, but, you will get what you pay for."

The guy seemed confused. "I'm not paying for this. This is supposed to be free."

Andy explained the rules.

"This is South Philly," the guy said. "People do business differently here. There was this fruit seller, keeled over and died right here, and, one after another, people came, took what they wanted out of his truck, and guess who the cops busted?"

"The fool who took his money," Plank said to Andy as he sauted the mushrooms. "As I heard from my produce distributor, some idiot actually searched his pockets!"

"Yeah, well," the professional guy said awkwardly, "whoever that guy was, he didn't know how business is done around here."

"You do, I'm sure," Plank said. He turned his back to the man but stood close enough to Andy so she could hear him muttering to himself.

"I happen to be a consultant," the professional guy said.

"That means he's unemployed," Plank said.

The guy handed Andy a business card. "See, I was in my office a few days ago—it's right up the block here—when I saw the fruit seller with his tomatoes. Well, he didn't just sell fruit, he had some vegetables and . . . anyway, after I got back to my office, I started thinking about the way business is done around here and I've studied it."

"His unemployment compensation has run out," Plank said, tossing in the scallions.

"I used to be in software management, and I've been on the inside of a lot of companies, seeing how they set up things."

Plank muttered, "Can't keep a job, then." He sliced the green pepper, tossed it twice, then flipped the ingredients into a crepe. He said to Andy, "He's going to try to talk to you so you'll forget to ask him for the money."

"I'll ask for it," Andy said.

"Let him talk. The initial rush has tapered off. As long as we have people in front of the truck, others will approach."

Andy handed him his crepe. "Not bad," the guy said. "But if you really wanted to clean up, you'd set yourself up by that free clinic on Washington Street, just past Orley's."

Plank turned to him. "And how would we clean up, sir? By selling crepes to people who have no money?"

The guy clearly liked being called "sir."

"Well, they do get a lot of people that have no money. I mean, most of them, or probably all the people that go in there are sick, or they don't have any benefits where they work. It's a sliding scale, they told me. You pay what you have."

"I'm sure that you did," Plank said.

"I didn't," the professional guy said. "I mean, I didn't have to pay anything because I was just, you know, asking them how they did business. They're funded, you know that? They get stuff from the city and the state, and there's also a pharmaceutical company that hires them to do tests and things."

Plank moved to the batter bowl and gave it a stir.

The guy turned to Andy. "But the clinic also gets the ambulance drivers. Speed Care has a garage over by 12th Street, and you can stand out on the street, and watch the ambulances come in around the back of the clinic, between the clinic and that trailer behind the clinic. What they do, ambulance crews are always coming out with stuff, looks like body bags, you know? And Doctor Johnny goes into the trailor, and the ambulance crew, they have nothing to do for an hour or so, so they go to Orley's, have lunch or dinner or whatever, come back and load the body bag back in and off they go."

"Would that be Dr. Johnny Sungaigutung?" Andy asked.

"That's him. Looks like he's oriental, but he speaks Spanish like you wouldn't believe. You know him?"

"Matt," Andy said. "Dr. Johnny, the one that Danny talked to the other day, his place is right up the block."

Plank stared down at the professional guy. "I suppose you'll be wanting another."

"If it's no problem," the guy said. "But this time, seeing as how you been testing your business on all these people that aren't sufficiently sophisticated, how about with . . . bok choy?"

Plank let his contempt show, for just a second. "Sir, I am not testing a business, I am fulfilling a dream. And, when it comes to food, *everyone* is sophisticated. My job is to exceed expectations."

He fetched the bok choy from one of the cabinets, put it on the chopping block, sliced it, and tossed it into the saute pan. Then he nearly threw the crepe batter into the pan.

"What's his problem?" the professional type asked Andy.

"He has a need to please people," Andy said.

"Hey," the guy said. "I'm perfect for that job. I'll tell you what you're doing wrong, what you're doing right—"

That's when Plank yelled. It wasn't a cry of pain, but it wasn't pleasureful, either. Andy turned and saw him staring at the crepe pan. He lifted the pan, flipped out the crepe, stepped back and opened his mouth but nothing came out.

Andy came up to him. "Matt, are you okay?"

His face was contorted in shock. He pointed at the crepe. It was a flawless, pristine, luminous circle, full and round and splendid like the moon rising over the horizon on a misty night. "It's . . ."

Andy was about to say "perfect" when Plank glared at the professional type and said, "Wasted!" He stomped off to the chopping block, grabbed a green pepper, brought down the knife and said, "Mmmp."

Andy saw the blood leap up from this hand. "Matt, your hand!"

He dropped the knife and grabbed his left hand. Blood gushed on his white chef's jacket. "Flesh wound," Plank said, his face growing pale. "Chef's blood is an important ingredient in every recipe."

"Let me see that," Andy said.

Plank shook his head. Andy knew enough first aid to know that Plank had cut something deep, and major. She tore off her apron, yanked his injured hand out, clamped the apron down, hard, and demanded that he tell her where the ice was. Before he could tell her, Andy had opened three of the drawers until she found it. She wrapped that in another apron and said, "Hold this over the cut as hard as you can. If you can feel where the blood is coming out, push in the opposite direction. Try not to move. Where are the keys?"

"Ignition," Plank said, a dazed expression on his face.

"Sit down and don't move."

"The hot plates . . ." he said.

"You have a kill switch anywhere?"

He nodded at a red button. Andy punched it and said, "Sit down and don't move." She went to the front of the truck, turned the key, heard the engine groan.

She called to the professional type. "Where did you say that clinic was?"

"Down the block and, when you see the Mount of Olives, you go right. You pass Orley's on your left, it's just after that. But you're not going to find any parking right around now. Cars coming to Orley's for lunch fill up the whole neighborhood. But if you go just past the clinic, there's that driveway where the ambulances go. It's kind of hard to see."

"Get in and show me," Andy said. She moved the shift, stomped on the gas pedal, turned the key again, the engine awoke and she was off.

"We are not a hospital emergency room," Dr. Sungaigutung told Andy after he came into the clinic's grim, grimy waiting room. "But I am in great admiration of Mr. Plank's cooking. The fried plantains at Loup Garou remind me of home."

He stood with his back to an ancient television set that was chained to the wall: a small, compact, meticulously groomed man with shiny black hair, gold-trimmed spectacles, a patterned silk tie knotted precisely at the center of his throat, in a dark green wool suit that fit so snugly that it had be custom-made.

Andy rose from the cracked, dull green fiberglass chair. "Is he okay?"

"Yes, yes, he is okay!" Dr. Sungaigutung said. "I stitched him personally. I am to stitching what Mr. Plank is to spices. My father was a tailor. He came from Bangkok and did all the rich doctor's suits in San Juan. From him I get my appreciation for the fine things."

He made notes on a PalmPilot. "I tell you this because if he forgets, you will remind him. He must see a specialist with the hands. He has lost blood, so he must get rest and drink fluids, fruit juices. Normally I would ask you to wait for him, but I see you want to see him now?"

"If it's okay?"

"Yes, yes. Come with me, then." He went through a door marked STAFF ONLY into a narrow concrete-block hallway that had been painted over so many times that it seemed as if the blocks were melting into beige-colored sludge.

"He has been given a tetanus shot, but if he develops a fever, or if the wound appears to be infected, he should have something." He stopped in front of an iron door, inserted a card in a slot, opened the door. Andy followed him into a room of floor-to-ceiling shelves so close together that she involuntary sucked in her stomach to try to make herself thinner.

Each shelf was crammed with plastic bottles, some transparent, others opaque, containing medicines, most of them pills.

Two of the larger bottles held yellow, football-shaped pills that Andy had seen before. One variety had a blue dot at one end, the other had a red dot. She thought hard: she had seen the red-dot pill go into the mouth of Karyn Asgard, just before she sat down at a table and ordered food at Loup Garou.

And the blue-dotted pill *might* have been among those Dr. Elgin swept away when he examined Michelle Fragg.

Dr. Sungaigutung found a plastic vial, waved his finger like a magic wand before the bottles, selected one bottle, and dropped a few pills into it.

"We are also not a pharmacy, but we get samples and other things of interest." He put a lid on the vial and gave it to Andy. "This is for pain, if he has any, and this . . ." he filled another vial, "is a very interesting antibiotic, a generic, that might be as good as the original, might not. One thing we do, we get these samples from the drug companies and we don't charge to dispense them, but . . ." he ducked behind a shelf and came out with two thick, pre-addressed, buff-colored envelopes. "We ask the patients to fill out simple easy questionnaires and send them out. See? No need to put on stamp."

Andy noticed both addresses were for Alixxir Pharmaceuticals, in St. Anne's. "How many of these should he take?"

"Recommended dosages are in with each questionnaire. If he needs them, he takes them and tells the company what happens, and the clinic is compensated, in terms of research grants and other fees. Follow me this way."

He stuck his card in a second door, opened it, went though an office so luxurious that Andy gasped. At one corner of the 19th century secretary desk was a TV monitor whose camera was trained on a huge Mercedes sedan surrounded by a gated, chain-link fence. A coffee table was piled high with *Architectural Digest*, the *Robb Report*, and other high-end lifestyle magazines and, above it, a swirling, angry, red and purple painting. "My study," Dr. Sungaigutung said. "I appreciate the finer things."

"Is that a Boyagian?" Andy asked.

"It is!" Dr. Sungaigutung said. "A gift, or a loan, from my mentor."

"Dr. Elgin?"

"You know him?"

"A little."

"All this is because of him. My father used to do his suits. Funny story—my mother had just died, and I was a sad little boy, and I told Dr. Elgin I wanted to be like Jesus and raise the dead. Dr. Elgin said I would have to be what they call in those silly voodoo cults an olo-kou-in-we, a child of Baron Cimetiere, or I could be a doctor or an undertaker. I say, why not all three? Dr. Elgin said two out of three, and he got me scholarships to all the best schools—for pathology and mortuary science. Then, when he goes to the Stoner Clinic, he makes a position for me and, when he leaves, and I come here, he makes the grants so I can have a place to do my stitching! Come, follow."

He led Andy through an exit door at the rear of his office. The exit opened into the driveway where Andy had left Le Truck.

"This is his, yes? You must move it. The ambulances come and go and they have to go through. You will move this?"

Before Andy could say she would, Dr. Sungaigutung stepped around the truck and went up a metal ramp to the entrance of a featureless, windowless office trailer. He inserted his card into the door and opened it into a spotless, gleaming, operating room where Matthew Plank lay on the table, the thumb of his left hand in a huge gauze bandage, his other hand holding a remote control to a wide screen television tuned to a soap opera.

"Not a hospital emergency room," Dr. Sungaigutung said. "Better."

But also, different. The room had the bright lights and precisely arranged rows of shiny, sharp instruments. But every television and movie portrayal of a hospital operating room Andy had seen, had also included views of machines that beeped, buzzed, chirped and charted the life signs of the patient on the operating table. This room had no such machines.

It was as if the work done in this room had nothing to do with the health of the patient.

Andy came around where Plank could see her. "How you doing?" He was still wearing his toque. She took it off and ran her hand through his hair.

"You ever watch these shows?" he said. "They're all about people who are fabulously good-looking but behave like they're total scum. And when you see these people eating, what is it? Rubber roast chicken? Yuck! I'd want something rare and juicy and salty and rich and nasty, fuck cholesterol and fuck the calories. I mean, where is your typical overpaid young to middle-aged professional with an expense account going to go if he or she wants to blow it out, break the rules, gloat, or act a little bit depraved? Imagine: a red and black color scheme, lots of flowing drapes, polished candelabras, shiny black velvet and campy Goth flourishes. We'll price it high enough to hurt, have a cold buffet and supersaturated sugar desserts, and call it, Revenge!"

"You give him anything for pain?" Andy asked Dr. Sungaigutung.

"Local anaesthesia, but side-effects and other complications are inherently unpredictable, which makes the work I do for Dr. Elgin so interesting."

Plank was annoyed that Dr. Sungaigutung was competing with him for Andy's attention.

"Can he travel?" Andy asked.

"He is okay to walk."

Suddenly the room shook with the baying whoop of an emergency siren.

"You must move the truck," Dr. Sungaigutung said. "And you must go. I need this space. Now. Go!"

Andy helped Plank to his feet. They went outside and down the ram where a large Speed Care emergency services vehicle with lights flashing had pulled up behind the truck.

A tall, skeletal man in a red Speed Care uniform and an Elvis haircut swaggered out of the cab. He put an inhaler in his mouth, gave himself a blast, and said, "Is that your piece a shit?"

"They are about to move it," Dr. Sungaigutung said.

"Is there an emergency?" Andy asked.

"No," the driver said, giving himself another blast from the inhaler. "Now, you going to move it, or I move it for you?"

Andy led Plank to the truck. Andy tried to start it but the engine just groaned.

"You can leave this here. I'm done with it," Plank said.

Andy jumped when the EMT vehicle siren went off. She heard a voice from the EMT's p.a.: "I SAID MOVE IT!"

Andy wiggled the shift, started the truck, and gently let in the clutch. It moved a few feet and stalled. She tried again and then felt a jolt as the EMT vehicle shoved the truck forward.

Andy got out to see if the truck, was damaged when the driver opened his door, jumped down, and brought up a hooked, serrated folding blade pointed at her neck.

She stopped. "Are you crazy? I want to see what you did to the truck."

"Get back in the truck," he said, "and move it the fuck out of here."

"I think I'm going to call the police instead," Andy said. She was just as tall as he was. She stared him right in the eye.

He brought up his inhaler, took a third shot. "I don't think so," he said, his eyes locked on her, his hand waving the knife, his legs taking long, confident steps closer.

He was just a little too confident, or he would have seen Andy's kick coming. She had aimed for his groin but he had an odd, wobbly swagger when he moved so she ended up putting the big, round, reinforced toe of her lace-up Doc Martens into his shin.

His yell started out as a high yelp, from surprise, and then dropped into a yowl, from the pain, as he went down, dropping the knife but holding on to the inhaler. Andy kicked the knife under the EMT vehicle and stood ready to stomp on the driver when Dr. Sungaigutung came between them, and said to her, "Please. Please. Just go."

"If there's anything wrong with the truck, he's paying for it," Andy said.

"Send me the bill," Dr. Sungaigutung said, checking the driver's leg and admonishing Andy to leave.

Andy took her time getting back into the truck. She hoped it wouldn't start, but it did, and she moved it slowly forward. She watched in the side-view mirror as Dr. Sungaigutung helped the driver stand. The driver spun around and flailed in Andy's direction, but Dr. Sungaigutung restrained him. Then both went to the back of the truck, the driver limping painfully.

The driveway curved slightly as it led into an alley behind the clinic. At the very end of the driveway was the Mercedes sedan surrounded by the chain-link fence that Andy had seen on the monitor in Dr. Sungaigutung's office.

Andy shifted the truck into neutral.

"What are you stopping for?" Plank asked. "I have to get back. I have to set down this concept while it's still in my mind."

"I want to see this," Andy said. She watched in the side mirror as the doctor and the driver went back to the EMT vehicle. The driver got into the cab, moved the vehicle a few more feet forward, as Dr. Sungaigutung pushed a folding gurney from under the trailer. He brought the gurney around to the rear of the vehicle. The driver turned off the vehicle, limped out of the cab, opened the rear doors. Andy could barely make out something dark—a body bag—sliding out onto the gurney. While the driver searched under the truck for his knife, Dr. Sungaigutung pushed the gurney around the side of the EMT vehicle, up the metal ramp, and into the trailer.

"Can we get going, please?" Plank said. "God, I hate this truck. This was so stupid."

Andy put the truck in gear, let out the clutch, and drove into the alley. "It wasn't stupid," Andy said. "You made some great things for those people."

"And I almost cut off my fucking thumb," he growled. "I hate failure. I hate every bit of it. Just drive this thing into the river. There's a place on the right on the Schuylkill, right off West River Drive, where they're pulling cars out all the time."

"Matt, did you, or did you not make the perfect crepe?"

"I should have given it to you. All of this was because of you. But it was wasted on that asshole."

She took a long breath. "Matt, you saw the look on that guy's face when he had the Welsh rarebit crepe. Do you really believe all this was wasted?"

"Will it disappoint you if I say, yes, I really do think it was all wasted? Because if it will disappoint you, I won't say it."

"You can say it," Andy said. "It's just . . ."

"What?"

"Every once in a while, it's nice to be wrong about someone."

# 12 hoops

Andy put Le Truck in a parking space near the West Philadelphia apartment building whose basement contained Plank's second restaurant, Pulse. Plank's Constant, Inc. was located in a suite of converted apartments on the second floor.

He thanked her for her "help" and asked her to excuse him, he had a concept to research and when he had a concept to research, "It just takes over. I don't sleep, I don't eat, I don't see people."

She let him go and caught a trolley on Lancaster Avenue. She rode it east where it went underground at 36th Street, crawled through the tunnel beneath the Schuylkill River. She changed to the Market Street subway at Broad Street, went east two stops, came out in the concourse beneath the Press Building, and took the elevator up to the newsroom on the 11th floor.

She sat down at her desk and checked her phone messages. Not one of the people in City Hall had returned her calls. She went to Mr. Action's list of questions and thought she might add another to the list: What do you do when something screwy is going on involving the man who is buying your house?

You get your things out of the house, close the door, make sure the security/fire prevention/surveillance system is on, and you don't look back.

She looked through the other situations Mr. Action was looking into: a lost magazine subscription; a computer printer that broke one day after the warranty expired; a telephone solicitor who keeps calling even when the reader says her phone number is on the Do Not Call list; a complaint about CDs and DVDs whose edges are so sharp they cut a reader's skin; who is responsible when your car hits a pothole and the impact blows the tire and dents the wheel rim?

She went to the Internet and got basic information about some of these, and other situations. Mr. Action supplied the information: it was up to the reader to contact the magazine subscription service's 800 number; yes, CDs have edges that can cut skin—but so can a simple piece of paper; you're out of luck if the warranty has expired, but here is a list of places in the city that will repair your printer, but the repair bill will probably end up costing you about as much as a new printer; complain about the telephone solicitor by dialing the Do Not Call list's 800 number and leaving a detailed message including your own phone number; the city, and commonwealth, and even the federal government, are all responsible for fixing potholes, depending on whether the pothole is on a city, commonwealth or interstate roadway, but you're better off paying for the repairs caused by potholes out of your own pocket. If you use your insurance to pay for the damages to your car, your premiums will go up, and Philadelphia's automobile insurance premiums are among the highest in the country. . . .

If she had been feeling better, she might have called a lawyer to find out if you could take the pothole-fixing agencies to small claims court, or hunted down some spokesperson for the Do Not Call list to find out how fast they act on complaints. She might have made more phone calls, gone the extra distance to find out why these specific problems had occurred, and maybe even solved them.

But, on some days, a job is just that: something you do for a while so you can get money and do something else. She wrote the column, filed the story, waited for Bardo Nackels to edit it, and then sat, staring at the flower arrangements.

She heard Ladderback stop using his keyboard. "No, I don't want an assignment," she said without looking at him.

"I wasn't going to give you one," Ladderback said.

"But you were going to say something," she said.

"Did you call the mechanic? Her garage is near where you live."

"I'm in the middle of a mood, if you don't mind," she said.

"You seem disappointed."

"I *am* disappointed."

"Then you should talk to this mechanic," Ladderback said. "She has also been disappointed by a man."

"I didn't say anything about a *man*," Andy said.

"I apologize." Ladderback averted his eyes. "I did not mean to pry."

"But you do. Or did. You ever ask yourself why you can't just leave it alone?"

"Yes, I have asked myself that," Ladderback said. "I believe that it is a way I show my concern."

"So what happens when people don't see it that way?"

"Then I experience disappointment," Ladderback said.

"That makes two of us," Andy said. She hoisted up her shoulder bag and left the newsroom.

She took the subway back, changed to the trolley, walked to her apartment house, went in without checking the mail, opened the door, shut it, sat down on her bed and looked at the trees.

Then she tossed off her clothes, put on a pair of cross trainers, grabbed her shoulder bag, locked her apartment and went down to the street, where her fire-engine red Ford Focus was parked in front of the coffee bar.

She promised herself that, before she did anything inside or outside her house, she was definitely going to do some layups. After a sweat-soaked hour or two, she knew she would feel calm, clear, and not so much alone.

She got in, turned right onto Biltmore, and saw that the car needed gas. She pulled into a service station on the next corner. It was one of the oldest stations in University City, trimmed in curved, glass-tile blocks and radiating art deco aluminum stripes.

But what never failed to catch her eye were the two, banged-up, windowless old cars parked on the side of the garage bays, just behind the tow truck. One car had been painted a hideous pink that had weathered into primer gray. On the other, across streaks of faded red, some graffiti artist had spray painted FEMME FAT.

Andy pulled up to the pump island, got out, opened the car's gas cap, and started filling the Focus with unleaded regular. She heard the sound of an air gun and watched a small woman in grease-stained work clothes wrestle a tire off the axle of a car suspended on the hydraulic lift.

As if she were aware someone was looking at her, the woman turned and Andy saw her bright red lips, hardened jaw, blunt nose, deeply lined face, and mop of gray hair spilling out from under a black baseball cap.

Andy couldn't remember the woman's name, but she recognized her from the picture accompanying the series of articles about the City College student who had died after enrolling in one of the Stoner Clinic's drug testing programs. This was the mother of the student who died, and she had refused to talk to anyone from any of the media.

Every time Andy had bought gas at this station, someone else had come out to take her money. Now, Andy watched the woman glance at the others working in the garage. Then she wiped her hands on a rag and came out toward the pump island.

"Evening," she said to Andy.

Andy returned the greeting, and then, emboldened, perhaps, by the slightest residue of that firey vodka, she said, "I've been driving past this place for years and . . . why do you have a car there that says Femme Fat?"

The woman narrowed her eyes. She took in Andy's long, wiry legs and the faded T-shirt, and she said, "It's not Femme Fat. Do I look like I ever been fat?"

Andy shook her head.

"Didn't think so. What's on there is Femme Fatale. You know what that is, a femme fatale?"

"A female villain."

"More than that. Much more than that. And not always a villain. But trouble. Always trouble, if you know what I mean."

Andy didn't quite know what she meant, but this short, scrawny woman was so intimidating that she couldn't bring herself to say so.

The woman said, "I used to drive that car."

The car was so battered that Andy couldn't imagine it moving. "In a race?"

"The kind of race you win if you finish last. You ever heard of a demolition derby? They used to have them all over the place, but now, they've kind of died out, because it's hard to get the right cars—you need the big boats they used to build up to the mid-70s. That one's a '72 Chrysler Le Baron, back when the Le Baron was Chrysler's biggest car. I've had to rebuild the engine a few times, replace the rear end twice, but it's as strong as an ox, even in a head-on."

The gas pump clicked. Andy pulled out the nozzle, replaced it, and took out a twenty. "Why does the car need to be strong?"

The woman took her bill and pulled a wad of singles out of her coverall pocket. "In a derby, you do everything possible to immobilize the opposing vehicles. You can hit any part of the car, as long as you don't pull any head-ons and driver-side front-end impacts. Last car moving, wins."

Andy was amazed. "And you do that?"

"Used to."

Andy heard the regret in her voice.

"What made you give it up?"

"Some said I was too old, but that was never the reason. I suppose you could say I lost my spirit." She counted the bills into Andy's palm and said, "Thanks for stopping by."

Andy said, "What do you mean, you lost your spirit?"

"I got cars ahead of me," the woman said, and walked slowly back to the garage.

Her hands turned the Focus's steering wheel gently to meet the curving of the streets, so lush and leafy in the fading light. Her foot moved lightly from the gas pedal to the brake pedal, and back, in answer to the demands of stop signs and traffic lights. These demands, Andy had learned from her course in Civic Spirituality: Myth, Ritual and Sacred Spaces in a Pluralistic Society, had little to do with traffic safety and pedestrian rights (most of the streets in her section of Merion Township had no sidewalks). The function of what her professor had called "insertions of civic iconography" was to force both resident and visiting automobile travelers to make ritual obeisances, tiny genuflections that acknowledge the higher authority of government, and thus, turn quotidian movement into a sacred journey.

Quotidian. The word reminded her of Plank, and she realized she was hungry. Maybe she should drive somewhere and eat.

She imagined, if things had been different and the relationship had gone far enough so that they might wake up together, she would ask Plank to fry an egg and listen to him tell her about which kinds of oil or butter he would use, how the eggs from this place are different from the eggs from that place, the semiotics—there's another academic word he'd probably use—of an unbroken yolk.

Andy almost stopped the car short. She'd forgotten what semiotics meant! She wasn't even a half year out of college, with a diploma that cost more than most people spend on a house, more than half the people in the world will make in an entire lifetime, and her brain was turning to Swiss cheese.

"Not Swiss!" she imagined Plank shrieking, telling her that there were over a zillion different cheeses made in Switzerland and not all of them had holes.

She came around Albemarle Way and stopped the car just in front of the driveway. Something about the house told her things had changed. The light over the door was blazing, and the landscape service had kept the rosebushes pruned and the lawn precisely trimmed.

But the side windows lacked drapes.

She looked at the front door for the video cameras her mother had installed, and she couldn't see them. There wasn't even a sign out front that said the house was protected by some alarm system company. That was supposed to be the newest thing in surveillance systems. The current generation of burglars now broke into houses whose owners put up alarm system company signs, because they'd gotten wise to the fact that most people who put up alarm company signs were either too cheap to put in a decent system, or had no system at all.

In addition to pulling off the sign by the front door, the current system also did away with the tiny white light by the front door knob. The house seemed perfectly defenseless.

Then Andy started down the driveway. The little pagoda lights on the side of the driveway winked on, one by one, just before her car passed them. The doors to the garage were closed. Her father had always kept the garage open because his automatic door opener was always screwing up.

Andy pulled the door opener out of the Focus's glove compartment. She didn't activate it, or didn't think she did, before she heard a hum of machinery as the doors—all three of them, instead of just the one that had been hers—rose slowly, like the curtain in a theater.

The bays were dark and empty. She aimed for the bay on the far left. Before her father died, he had parked his yellow Buick in the center bay. Her mother put her silver Mercedes in the right bay.

As she entered the bay, a light winked on inside. The lights had never gone on automatically before.

Then she got it: the house let you know it was secure and protected by doing things automatically that it didn't do before. It had become intelligent.

Andy got out of the car and went to the bin where she stored the basketballs and a bicycle tire pump with a cracked handle. She tried each ball until she found one that made a bell-like tone when she slapped it down on the garage's concrete floor.

She told herself to remember to put the balls and the bicycle pump in her car as she dribbled the ball out onto the blacktop.

A floodlight came on over the garage. Another winked on over the back door of the house.

In the past, she'd shot hoops at night in the dark. The lights had been there, but she'd turned them off because on nights when the moon was out, her eyes would adjust to the silvery glow.

There must be some way to turn the lights off, but she didn't want to look for it. She focused her attention on the hoop, tapped the ball down so it hit the asphalt and rose back into her hands.

The first shot would miss, but the sharp smack from the backboard told her that better things were in store. She let her feet grow light. She took a gentle leap and snatched the ball out of the air, touched it with both hands, and shot it down so that when she came down, her knees bending to absorb the impact, the ball rose up into her right hand, and she was off, dribbling the ball in a series of pirouettes. The idea was to spin around so many times that she could no longer be certain of where the backboard was, and then, to jump up and let go at just the right speed so that the ball would go up and into the hoop without her even seeing it.

She missed again. The ball went past the backboard and banged into the garage. She put herself under it and did the pirouettes again, in the opposite direction, feeling that odd warmth in her elbows and her knees as she sent the ball up again. This time the ball caught the rim and bounced off. More pirouettes, another miss, another miss, and then the ball went right in.

She wasn't sure how much time had passed before she no longer cared if the ball went into the basket. She aimed to be just in front, or just behind the ball, even if she couldn't determine how it would come off the backboard. She soon eliminated as much of her wild movements as possible until her body was almost weightless and she didn't feel the perspiration flying off her face, didn't hear the wet flap of her sweat-soaked T-shirt against her skin, didn't think about anything other than the ball dropping, flying, wobbling around the rim, falling through to begin the cycle again.

After a while, a part of her mind woke up and she became aware of what she was doing. The awareness led to a slow heaviness that made it more difficult to be in the exact spot where the ball wanted her to be. She lost it a few times, running out to chase it along the side of the garage and once into the tangle of thorny rosebushes.

Crouching to pick up the ball, she noticed that her socks were wet, so she must have been doing layups for at least an hour and a half. She stood then, with the ball in her hands, and she looked up, past the edges of her house and the tops of the trees to the twilight sky where jet planes were zooming back and forth and the stars had come out, and she believed that if she wanted to, she could reach up and pull down one of those stars, hold it in her hand and toss it right back up again.

She felt good. She felt better than good. Why was it that, of all feelings to get, this one was always the easiest, and, yet, it seemed to take forever before she could find the time? She hadn't given herself as many layup sessions since she'd moved out—a woman on the public courts around the University got hassled, no matter how good she was with the ball, especially if she did not want to share the ball, but wanted to shoot hoops because it reminded her that being able to stand, alone and at peace at the end of a long day, was really all she needed.

In the tiny galley kitchen of his studio apartment, Ladderback gazed suspiciously at the contents of his refrigerator. He saw numerous things that had dried, wilted, darkened, lightened. Some had been nearly eaten. Some lay in paper bags from take-out shops. A few had been enclosed in transparent plastic bags. He should have been able to look at the bag and tell what was inside it, but things in plastic bags, in time, have a way of turning into other things and, with some of them, Ladderback wasn't sure what they had become. Leftovers don't get better with age.

Few things do.

The refrigerator's compressor rattled to life and Ladderback stood, with the door still open, and imagined how his life might have been different if he had gone to cooking school or got a restaurant job and become a chef. He might not have been a great chef, but he would have known what to do with so many aged things.

His desire for an evening snack turned into a desire to see things on a screen, to hear sounds coming out of mesh boxes. He closed the refrigerator door and went to the other area of the studio, the one that held his recliner, his computer, his video screen and his music system.

He picked up a remote control. He turned on the video and began surfing the cable channels, and it was like looking into another refrigerator.

Maybe it was because of the location on the dial where he had begun to surf, but he got the feeling that everything he was seeing was an old movie, an old TV show—a leftover that had been wrapped in plastic somewhere and had aged: the colors were faded, the sound was fuzzy, the scenes jumped where pieces of film had been badly spliced.

Then he saw a grainy, blurry black-and-white image, what appeared to be an old TV show preserved in kinescope form. The kinescope was a movie camera aimed at a TV screen, and the effect was like looking at something through a plastic bag.

He saw a tall, manic, rubber-faced comedian waving his hands, speaking in a pompous shpritz of pseudo-German. Then he saw a woman acting in a skit with him. She was short, doe-eyed, and utterly adorable.

Across the bottom of the screen was a band that identified what he was watching as *Your Show of Shows*. This was the comedy variety show that had followed Milton Berle's *Texaco Hour* into history as the second most important show on the new medium of television. The comedian speaking German was Sid Caesar. The woman acting as his foil was Imogene Coca.

Ladderback watched the show until it ended. He didn't get all the jokes, he didn't hear all the dialogue, but, for a few minutes, he was entranced, enraptured, thoroughly taken up in the manic silliness of his parents' age.

He turned the screen off, and in the sudden silence, everything became clear.

He went back to his refrigerator with a renewed appetite. Some things *do* get better with age.


Andy put the ball into her car and went across the blacktop to the back door, where a new keypad had been installed. It responded to the same disarm code, but this time, as soon as she opened the door, the garage doors began to close.

The first thing she noticed was how stale the house smelled. The kitchen racks had been stripped of the pots and pans. The counter tops seemed too big and broad now that the black-and-chrome appliances had gone.

The butler's pantry that her mother had converted into a 1960s-themed Tiffany-swagged, lava-lamped, Haitian-cotton-draped, "rec room" office, was no more than an empty box. The shelves that had held her mother's art books and exhibition catalogs were dark, horizontal parallel lines floating in space. The wire from the cable/Internet hook-up flopped uselessly on the shag carpet, where grooves and pits showed where a couch, a table, a chair and a vintage '60's "entertainment center" had been.

She went into the dining room, and the motion detectors sensed her and turned on the picture lights. But the pictures were gone, and only a slightly darker area on the walls indicated where the china and silver cabinets stood.

She went through the double doors and into the parlor—now an enormous enclosure, without furniture, where rugs from other rooms had been rolled up and stored against the walls. On one of those walls remained the painting her father had called "the Art": an immense orange and green Boyagian that, according to her mother, was one the "large scale abstractions" executed by the Puerto Rican–born artist *before* he synthesized his horror of the Turkish massacre of his Armenian ancestors with the Caribbean voodoo cults.

Andy had grown up with "the Art" and had ignored it for most of the time she'd lived in the house. But now, in the barren room, its bright, furious slashes and splashes unnerved her.

She took the steps of the central staircase three at a time, glanced in at the bathroom where the faucet still leaked—in larger, louder drips than it had when she left. She went past the closet that had been her father's office and saw that the door had been replaced. The door was closed, something that never happened when her father was alive.

She put her hand on the door knob and gave it a twist. It was unlocked. She opened the door and instead of seeing her father's narrow desk, his chair with the back brace, his telephone and his collection of cassette tapes, she saw a column of dark steel shelves holding computer equipment and several rows of TV monitors that kept switching to different views of the house.

This was the new security system's nerve center. She saw, at the bottom of the column of monitors, what appeared to be a stack of video recorders. She watched the cameras cycle through views of outside of the house, and the first floor rooms, lingering on the staircase, the parlor rug, the Art, the second floor hallway and, incredibly, the room she was in. For a moment, she saw herself on a monitor, a flat-faced, fuzzy mop in a faded, oversized T-shirt with bony legs, knobby knees, one hand on her hip, the other over her mouth. . . .

It was too strange. If there were other arrays of cameras, she did not linger to see what they were seeing.

The door to her room was open and the window shut. She wanted to open the window because her father liked open windows. She went to the sill and looked down on the asphalt where she had been shooting hoops, at the unfinished brick barbecue and the wall of trees that marked the neighbors' land. In the decade she'd lived in this house, Andy had only seen her neighbors a handful of times. She couldn't remember their names but they did seem to have a few years when they traded up from Chryslers to a Volvo station wagon and a BMW sedan. Then, a few years later, they were driving used Honda Accords. The loudest sounds she had ever heard coming from the neighbor's house were from the heat pumps. According to Andy's mother, the neighbors were nice people. Andy once asked her if the neighbors had any children.

"You never know," Charlotte had answered.

Andy let the window stay closed.

She sat down on the naked mattress that had been her bed and saw, against a wall, a row of boxes holding the papers, books, discs and other effluvia of her college career. She pulled one of the boxes toward her. It contained notes and assignments, some handwritten, some on computer disks that probably wouldn't open anymore, from her college classes. She pulled a notebook out, and the doodles on the margins brought her back into classrooms that were either too hot or too cold, with chairs with mostly right-handed arm rests. Though she was right-handed, Andy would occasionally sit in the few chairs with left-handed arm rests, just so she could feel how it might be to be left handed, and have to use chairs designed for people who were different than she was.

In another box were issues of the student newspaper that contained work she did as an un-bylined stringer in her freshman year, a bylined reporter in her sophomore and junior years, and then, in her senior year, as an editor.

She couldn't help but cringe as she re-read her first tentative efforts. The lead paragraphs were too long. Descriptive passages didn't quite make sense. A few grammatical mistakes hadn't been edited out. She even found a quote whose source she had failed to identify adequately.

About a third of the way in, she found the series to which she had contributed about the dead City College student. The interview with Dr. Elgin, Director of the Stoner Clinic's Department of Clinical Trials, had been among the major assignments of her sophomore year.

She had first called and asked to interview Elgin. Elgin had refused. Then she went to Lancaster and 36th Street and stood outside the Stoner Clinic's octagonal, 19th century neo-classical brick-and-column rotunda, under the sign that told how the clinic was established by Brighton Stoner, whose success with the Ladies Home Tonic helped establish Philadelphia as a leader in the pharmaceutical industry.

She went in and asked at the front desk about signing up for the drug testing program. She was referred up a creaking, plushly carpeted spiral staircase to a room of battered old wooden tables and stacks of forms. She was told by a receptionist that she could either fill out here, or bring back later, or fill out electronically and return as e-mail, but she would have to sign them in the presence of Dr. Elgin, or the deputy director, Dr. Sungaigutung.

Andy asked what kind of name was Dr. Sungaigutung.

"Thai. But, he's actually from Puerto Rico."

Andy sat with the forms and looked around the room. The door was open and she saw that the walls of the corridor were lined with paintings by artists Andy thought she recognized.

She took the forms with her and then called the student newspaper's editor, and said, "I think I can get to Elgin. Give me twenty-four hours."

The editor told her to take forty-eight.

Then she called her mother and asked if the gallery was still selling Boyagians.

"One doesn't sell Boyagians, Andrea," her mother said. "One arranges the possibility by which the client may acquire the work, or rather, a work, because there are almost none on the market now. His appeal is narrow, but his collectors are fiercely loyal."

"You know who all his collectors are, right?"

Charlotte became careful. "Possibly."

"I want you to tell Alex Elgin that your daughter wants to talk to him."

"In reference to what?"

"I need help on a school project."

"About Boyagian?"

"Just set it up."

"Andrea, I can't risk the gallery's reputation—"

"I'll wear a skirt to the interview."

Andy got her interview in twenty-four hours, wrote it up in two hours, and got it into the paper.

She found her notes from the Elgin interview, and a tiny tape cassette. She rummaged through the box and found the cassette recorder, with its little earphone. She couldn't remember when she'd changed the batteries. Would it still work? She popped the cassette into the recorder, put the phone in her ear and—yes, it still worked!

She listened to Elgin's voice and it brought back even more memories. His grandfather, he explained, had made a fortune in patent medicines and, though his father didn't have to work a day in his life, he chose to become an executive with Matson Palmer, eventually relocating the family to Puerto Rico where, in the Caribbean, "part of the next generation of plant-based drugs was being discovered."

Through trial and error, Dr. Elgin had told her, the descendants of escaped slaves, European colonials, and Carib Indians had "discovered a diversity of plant-based medicines and incorporated some of them into their religious beliefs. There were psychoactive derivatives that would put the worshiper in a variety of trance states, of course, but there were also remedies that, purportedly, increased male sexual potency, limited sensitivity to pain, even suppressed appetite for ritual fasts."

After his father's untimely death, Elgin, too, found himself "of amply independent means. As your mother probably told you, I could fill my time collecting art, but there was no question that I would carry on our family's mission, which, as I see it, is to develop and refine the technologies that transform suffering into pleasure."

Andy heard herself ask about a little model of an ambulance on his desk.

"That's what we call an emergency services vehicle," he said, explaining that when he was growing up in Puerto Rico, his father would take him to the local free clinics that would sometimes conduct trials for experimental drugs, and, while his father was talking with clinic personnel, the young Alex would climb into the driver's seat of the ambulances and pretend he was driving one. "I have a small financial stake in one of our local emergency services companies. These people accomplish so much more than you'd imagine. It's really a very thrilling business."

Then Elgin got a little bit creepy. Out of the blue, he asked about how tightly she laced her Doc Martens.

Andy changed the subject. She asked him, point blank, what happened to Carol Dettweiler, and he gave her such a long, smoothly authoritative answer that she would have thought him completely reasonable if he had, just once, taken his eyes off her boots.

He enjoyed "inventive cuisine," he said. In fact, he met Carol Dettweiler while dining at Pulse. She was a waitress, and he had suggested to her that if she or any of her friends needed money, they might consider participating in one of the Clinic's trials.

"The chef at Pulse, a quite brilliant fellow, really, uses minimally processed spices and other plant substances imported from the American equatorial region, some of which have been incorporated into the folk medicines that my father originally studied. This raises the possibility, in my mind, that Carol suffered a reaction to one or more of these substances. I am aware, from our conversations, that she had not visited the islands. The likelihood that she was related to anyone of island extraction is very narrow, so it's conceivable that she did not develop tolerances to substances that, while not toxic, could be recognized as such by her immune system, bringing on a fatal case of anaphylactic shock."

It sounded so believable and Andy wanted to believe him, just so she could come back to the newspaper and tell everyone that she got to the truth.

This was the end of the interview, when you asked the important, potentially awkward questions that could bring the interview to a premature close. She asked him that most important question of all: what kind of drug had Carol been testing?

"That," he sighed, "I'm afraid, cannot be revealed. When we conduct trials, we're bound by the manufacturer to a very rigorous confidentiality."

"But she would get some kind of idea what she was taking?"

"Carol was very much aware of it, yes. She was quite enthused, as I remember. She knew of others who might benefit from it."

His eyes stayed on her boots. "If you want to do a really important story, you should examine the true costs of medical research, of which the testing we do here is only a small part. You examine the history of any successful medication or therapy, and you'll find that human beings had to suffer and die, sometimes horribly, before the illness could be understood and a therapy devised, and that, even with several therapies available, people will continue to suffer and die because no therapy is perfect, no drug works precisely the same way with every individual. We would be living in a very different world if more people would only accept that."

Then he said, "I'm having such a good time speaking with you, that, if you don't mind, I'd like to continue this over dinner. I have a few telephone calls to make and I'll get us a table at Trellis. . . ."

Andy didn't go out with him. She had things to do, and he was *too* creepy.

But she did get some names and telephone numbers from him of other personnel at the clinic if she ever needed more information about drug testing, including a Dr. "Johnny" Sungaigutung, who had examined Carol Dettweiler moments after she died.

"He's a fascinating fellow, a simply brilliant pathologist. Just don't get Johnny talking about his work, if you have a weak stomach," Elgin said. "It's not the kind of thing that makes for dinner conversation."

Elgin had a copy of an autopsy performed by Dr. Sungaigutung that, he said, confirmed everything he said. Carol had been at the Clinic undergoing an interview about the drug she had been testing when her body went into shock.

Andy turned off the tape recorder and put it back in the box. She found, in the next issue of the newspaper, an interview with Matthew Plank. The headline read: "BEAT IT," SAYS ANGRY CHEF/OWNER WHERE DEAD STUDENT WORKED. Next to the headline was a photo of a bald geek with a full beard. Andy had to study the photo before she could make out the crepe maker.

She read:

Matthew Plank, owner of the recently opened Pulse restaurant, threatened to "eject" a team of journalists who tried to question him about allegations that a Pulse waitress may have died from food poisoning.

He admitted, however, that Carol Dettweiler had been one among his "tasting club," an informal group of employees and diners on whom he would try out new recipes.

"My food is not poison and never has been poison," Plank yelled, visibly disturbing some of the patrons at his busy establishment, whose curving walls and painted plumbing is said to be inspired by the Franklin Institute's human heart exhibit.

Claiming that he had "a kitchen to run," a noticeably distressed Plank at first refused to comment in any way on the death of Dettweiler, a part-time City College student who had also been enrolled in a confidential drug testing program at the Stoner Clinic.

But then, in an apparent change of mood, the chef invited the journalists to the restaurants' curvaceous bar, where he restlessly commenced eating from a bowl of nut-like objects and spoke of Dettweiler, in what can only be interpreted as a wrenching outpouring of emotion.

Andy made a face. When she became an editor at the paper, she would never permit such lousy writing to appear in print. A bar can be rounded or shaped in a curve, but never curvaceous. Soldiers might commence firing their weapons, but nobody commences eating—you start eating or you begin to eat. And what is a "nut-like object"? Either the reporter had forgotten to ask Plank what Plank had been eating, or he wanted to suggest that Plank had peculiar eating habits. If Andy had been editing that story she would have cut the insinuations.

Plank did not deny that Dettweiler was among his more capable employees. "I make a point of giving breaks to people who need breaks. She said she had waitressed in Atlantic City. She said she liked jobs where she could talk to people."

When asked what kind of people she talked to, an exasperated Plank said, "Hungry people, okay? We never had any complaints about her, and I guess her tips were par or above par."

Then Andy turned to the color picture of Carol Burnett Dettweiler. It was a reproduction of Dettweiler's student I.D. photo. Her hair was short and spiky, with the spikes moussed back with very dated, post-punk blue highlights. Her mouth was wide and severe, a hard, nasty slash of crimson lipstick, and she had a sharp little snip of a nose that had probably been fixed but it fit in so well that you almost didn't see the small shadow of a welt on her cheek under her left eye, which seemed to be a little larger than her other eye. The welt looked like a ruddy teardrop.

Comments from teachers, other students, and those who worked with her at Pulse, described a lively "people person, with an edge," who was "trying to put her house in order."

Andy put the article down. She tried to continue reading but she began to get dizzy. She felt a sudden numbness in her arm, or was it around her throat? She tried to move. She felt herself struggling, and she heard a voice that she might have heard before, about this not going to hurt a bit, and then she was suddenly on her back, her head on the mattress, her mind sinking into that dark sleep that is so deep that you know you're sleeping, you know you're dreaming, and you want to wake up but you can't so explore the dream, and then came this squeaky, high pitched, happy voice—a voice that smelled even though voices aren't supposed to smell—of carpet cleaner—saying, "Somebody call an ambulance?"

# 13 two little words

"Don't look at me," Andy muttered.

Ladderback did not tell her that he wasn't looking at her because he was and, again, he marveled at the talent of some people to know when someone was looking or staring in their direction.

Ladderback had wanted to look at Andy's hands when she dragged herself into the newsroom that morning at 10:52. Though there were no fixed hours for the day shift staff, anyone who wasn't traveling or on deadline had to be in by 10 A.M., to go to meetings, catch phone calls, take abuse from Howard Lange, to read the paper or delete e-mail. It almost wasn't worth it to come in any later, because arriving late insured that your absence would be noticed and used against you.

In the few months since she had been hired at the *Press*, Ladderback had found Andy to be fanatically punctual. On most mornings, Andy did not merely show up for work, she blew into the newsroom with a long-legged, get-out-of-my-way stride, took her swivel chair like a fighter jet pilot, tossed off her shoes, planted her legs like outriggers under her desk and attacked her mail. Mr. Action got the second greatest amounts of e-mail and regular mail, bested only by "Bar Bet" Schroeder's sports trivia column.

On this morning, Andy's clothing was neat and unobtrusive: ash gray slacks and a baggy, oversized, cable-stitched navy sweater roomy enough to sleep in.

But she moved sluggishly. Her stride was off, her gaze was downcast, her shoulder bag weighed heavily on her right side and she appeared as if she had to tell herself to put one flat-heeled black pump in front of the other.

She had set herself gently into her swivel chair and didn't move for a few seconds. Ladderback saw that her face was puffy, with a bruise developing on the left side of her face, and on her neck, what resembled a love-bite.

Could she have, perhaps, tried to drown her disappointment last night with the wrong person?

She must have had a hell of a night.

Ladderback busied himself with the death notices. Through the corner of his eye, he saw Andy grind her palms into her eyes. He heard her say, "Guhhhh."

The *Press*'s morning edition was on her desk. The refer-line across the top could only have been written by the paper's gleeful Bardo Nackels: MORE THAN WE CAN CHEW? MAYOR CALLS FOR NEW TAX ON RESTAURANTS, JAY MACULAY REPORTS INSIDE.

Ladderback had already read the *Standard*'s version of the story: a windy, cluttered, overlong string of disjointed comments from other restauranteurs, with the newspaper's food critic contributing a gassy, thoroughly preposterous "analysis" about how the tax might discourage drinking $100 bottles of wine and eating out five to seven times a week, which was the norm for a "certain class of individual that now flocks to the city."

Andy saw the copy of the *Press* on her desk and opened it to Maculay's article.

Then Andy said, "I'm going to be sick."

Ladderback slid his swivel chair away. As Andy put her hand over her mouth, Ladderback saw that her wastebasket was under her desk, pinned against the wall by her leg. His can was filled with discarded trimmings from the newspaper and magazine articles that he clipped for his file cabinet. He bent down to reach it, his paunch compressing uncomfortably as Andy stuck her neck forward, opened her mouth, leaned forward and said, "No. No way. I will not . . ."

Nothing came out.

Jay Maculay peered at her from behind his monitor and stage whispered, "A little over the top, aren't we?"

Andy turned slowly in her swivel chair. "You want to say something to me?"

"Only that there are better ways to express an opinion."

"You call what I just did, expressing an opinion?"

Maculay folded his arms. "That's my work you almost barfed on."

"I happen not to be feeling okay," Andy said.

"Just because you don't get bylines, doesn't mean you have to denigrate the paper in front of me."

Andy went to his desk. "What I did wasn't about you," she said. "I've been sick all morning. The only reason it wasn't worse than it was, was that I'd already gave up most of it, on the way in."

"I know you're seeing Plank," Maculay said triumphantly. He stood and folded his arms. "Plank likes to cook off the menu, especially for women he wants to sleep with. Are you going to write us up a review?"

Andy wanted to smack him, backhanded, across the face. Or kick him any place that would cause pain. She knew Maculay was baiting her, that he wanted her to do something that she would regret later, that would demean her in the newsroom.

But she could barely stand up straight. (She couldn't drive her car: she left it in the garage, staggered to the Merion station, took the R5 into 30th Street Station, a SEPTA trolley to her apartment, made it up the stairs, showered and changed and took the subway surface car into work, vomiting intermittently along the way.) But some parts of her brain were working.

He probably wanted her to apologize or defer to him in some way. She was about to do that and, maybe he sensed it, because he then did something even more repulsive so that she wouldn't just be pushed over the edge—she'd leap.

He licked his lips.

A fuse blew inside Andy's brain and she had to smack him. She couldn't help it and he saw that she couldn't help it and he fluttered his tongue in delight.

She tried and it just didn't happen. Her muscles grew thick and sluggish and again, the nausea bubbled up and rocked back and—

*Something* came out.

Maculay leaped back in horror as Andy pulled herself up. She put her hand on her face. She saw what was on Maculay's desk and she immediately regretted it. She was about to apologize, and look for something to mop it up, when she heard what sounded like two hands clapping. No, not two hands. Several hands coming together in applause.

She looked around the newsroom and saw a dozen staffers, some of whose names she didn't know, standing and cheering.

"You are HORRIBLE!" Maculay said. He went red. Then he spun around and stomped out of the newsroom.

Kassein jumped up from behind her wall of books and let loose with a stingingly florid mist called "Accentuate the Positive." She put the spray can under her arm. Then she lifted the blotter on Maculay's desk and marched toward the recyclables bin at the back of the newsroom near the lavatories. Andy followed her and pulled the lid off as Kassein dropped the blotter and everything on it into the bin. By the time Kassein sprayed the bin's contents, and Andy replaced the lid, the applause died down.

"Don't you worry," Kassein said. "It's all organic."

Andy covered her mouth, aimed for the lavatory, when her phone rang.

Not her office phone, but the cell phone in her shoulder bag that was hanging from the back of her swivel chair. She'd programmed the phone with different rings so that when specific people called her, it would chime in such a way that she'd know that this was a call she didn't want to miss.

238

There were only three people who could make her phone ring that way. One was Logan Marius Brickle, a rude, supremely rich slacker whose mother owned the city's oldest bank. Andy had grown up with Logo because her father had done some rather deep and lasting favors for the Brickles and, with Logan's father also dead and his mother even more impossible than Andy's mother, Logo was the closest thing she had to a brother, even if he was definitely not the kind of brother she would choose to have. Logo was in Europe now, spending piles of his inheritance in an effort to find himself, but he did occasionally call her at odd times and this could be one of those times.

The second was Drew Shaw and that was enough for Andy to turn her back and not even think about Maculay because if Drew Shaw was calling her at just the right time to tell her that he was made editor of *Liberty Bell*, she did not want to take the call.

But habits are tough to break. Andy spun around, went back to her desk, yanked the phone out of the shoulder bag, fought back the nausea as she sank into the chair, and tried to make herself as small as possible as she put the phone to her ear and said, "You got me!"

And found herself talking to the third person that would make the phone ring that way because she had given the phone to Andy and had shown her how to program the special rings.

"This," Charlotte Cosicki said, "is your mother."

As Andy struggled with her telephone call, Ladderback tried to focus on his work. He had selected two possibilities for obituaries: a Bogota-born woman who came to America with her brother, never married, worked as a secretary at a South Jersey tool-and-die company and gained some fame as a competition Monopoly player; and a rabbi whose ability to speak was lost to throat cancer, and, until a stroke rendered him immobile, led services for the deaf in sign language at a Belton Park synagogue.

Ladderback wished he had met these people when they were alive. He would have had to ask the woman, why, of all the games in which to develop proficiency, did she choose Monopoly? Did she have a mysterious, innate talent, or did she practice, sweat and work at the game like an athlete? And what were Monopoly competitions like? Were there coaches who could help players win? Were the rules different from casual play? Did contestants fight over who would have the ladies boot, or the battleship?

The rabbi tugged at Ladderback's heart. Here was a religious man who certainly believed in a God that could do anything: how did the horrible destruction of his vocal chords strengthen his faith? And what was the silence like, at the very end, when he could not speak to anyone but his God? Did, perhaps, the angry, jealous, mysterious, thunder-and-lightning God of the Old Testament reveal to him the reason for such a final deprivation?

There was a third possibility, much more difficult to do than the others because the decedent, a four-year-old boy, was so young. The *Press* had a small item on the shooting in the police round-up section. The funeral details had not been established because the family was very poor.

"What kind of God is it that takes children so young?" Ladderback wanted to ask the rabbi. Would the rabbi refer him to God's famous question of Job, "Where were you when I made the world?"

Then he heard Andy say into her cell phone, "How did you know I was at the house?" He saw, from the corner of his eye, that she was hunched over, nervously twisting her fingers.

"Mom, I told you," Andy said, raising her voice, "I don't KNOW where Karyn is. I went to the house to take whatever was left that I wanted and I was reading some of my old papers from college, and I passed out. I don't know why. If she was in the house with anyone else, I didn't see it. I don't know if the alarm system was on. The videos were. I remember that. And carpet cleaner. I smelled carpet cleaner and I woke up really, really sick. I don't know why."

Ladderback's eyes went to the love bite on Andy's throat. He had a feeling that it wasn't a love bite, but he had to get a closer look.

He brushed the printout of death notices off the side of his desk, muttered, "pardon, please" and, bent over to pick it up, he saw that it was not a love bite at all, but the kind of bruise made when an injection is administered to the carotid artery, and the injection is either done in haste, or the subject won't stay still. The bruising is the result of the needle jammed in too forcefully.

Ladderback had seen these on the corpses of drug addicts that his parents had showed him when they took him to the city morgue.

Andy broke the conversation with her mother, folded up the phone and said, "I can't deal with this."

Ladderback asked, "What happened to you?"

Andy kept her hands over her eyes. "I don't know. I honestly don't know."

She didn't sound as if she were lying to him. Ladderback watched her yawn. She said, "What am I supposed to be doing here?" and glanced at the pile of mail. She picked up an envelope that, on any other morning, she would tear open with her fingernails like a hungry carnivore. She tried to hook her fingernail under the paper flap and missed. She tried to open the envelope again and it dropped from her hand.

Ladderback sniffed. "Vertigo, nausea, short-term memory loss."

Andy said, "You talking to me?"

"You are exhibiting the symptoms of cannabis intoxication."

Andy became testy. "I do not smoke anything and I have not smoked anything."

"What about drugs?"

She narrowed her eyes at him. "Yesterday the only thing I had for lunch was a crepe. That's it. That's all."

"There is bruising on your face?"

Andy pulled a folding mirror out of her shoulderbag and said, "Oh my God. I never saw that. I must've fallen down, or rolled over, when I passed out."

"You were alone when you passed out?"

"I don't even remember passing out." She put the mirror down and made a point of not looking at him. "You have work to do, right? I have work to do. I've thrown up everything I've eaten between here and my doorstep and I'm incapable. I'm incapable of smacking Maculay in the face, which is exactly what he wanted me to do, which would normally make me kind of sick but not so sick I couldn't smack him, but I just can't do it. I don't know why. It's like, I think of violence, I think of food, I get real sick, and then I forget what I was thinking about, and then I remember exactly whatever it was I was thinking of before I got sick, and . . ." She paused. "Yes. I was alone when I passed out. I must have been completely alone."

"What happened to your throat?"

She picked up the mirror again. "I don't know what that is. Maybe I got scratched or something."

Andy tried to think, and some of the images from the dream returned, with different images: the Elvis man with the high voice, a TV screen, a girl with bright blond hair and a red mouth on the living room carpet, the smell of carpet cleaner and this feeling of being trapped, or pinned down, or paralyzed while a maddeningly familiar voice said, "Be still."

The Elvis man: she had kicked a guy just like him yesterday. He had driven that ambulance.

Andy signed on to her word processor, went to her file of sources, found the number of Double-Czeck Home Security, Inc., and dialed. Bernice, the wife of one of the twins, answered. Andy identified herself as the person who wrote the *Press*'s Mr. Action column, mentioned that she had spoken with Tom about a woman who had had one of Double-Czech's surveillance systems installed and had a problem getting an insurance reimbursement and that Tom had referred her to his sister Julie Lynn, the lawyer, who had agreed to take the case pro bono—

Bernice said she saw it in today's paper and it was very good and they were already getting calls about it.

"I need to find out about another kind of home video surveillance system, the kind with an intercom and recorder attached to it. I need to know how you can get the recorder to playback."

Bernice didn't know, but Tom or Don probably would, but both were out and were not expected back until after lunch time. Did Andy want to leave a number?

"They have my number," Andy said, and promised to call back anyway. She hung up and turned to Ladderback. "Did you ever have a feeling about something, something really, really bad, but you weren't sure about it, and you couldn't get to the one thing you needed that would tell you if you were right?"

"Yes," Ladderback said.

She tried to slam her fist on the pile of mail but the fist wouldn't quite form. "One thing I'm sure of: there is no way I'm going to sit here and read letters and deal with all these people whining and complaining or wanting something from me until I find out if I'm right."

"You could have mentioned to the person you had called that it was an emergency."

Andy asked herself why she didn't say that. "I couldn't use the word. I am really, really bothered by emergencies and ambulances right now."

Ladderback said, "Would you like an assignment?"

Andy said, "Sure."

Ladderback gave it to her.

Ten minutes after she left, a reporter who happened to be talking to his wife on the phone, put down the phone, and said to Bardo Nackels that he was talking to his wife on the phone and she had the 24-hour newsradio on in the background and he heard what sounded like a mob hit—

Two little words and everybody went into high gear. Lange bounded out of his office, turned on a TV set over the copy desk to where a TV news reporter was standing, with a worried expression on her face, in front of a cordon of police cars on a street that appeared to be South Philadelphia.

"Yes!" Lange said, smacking his fist into his palm. "Yes! Yes! Yes!"

# 14 the art of restoration

You ask half the people in Philadelphia, and the four big counties surrounding the city, the cause of just about every civic pain and frustration, and you won't hear about the wage tax, racism, parking in Center City that doesn't cost an arm and a leg; no, they'll say one five-letter word:

SEPTA.

Short for South Eastern Pennsylvania Transit Authority, a hopelessly snarled cat's cradle of bus, trolley and train routes that employs many serious, earnest, dedicated people who will tell you that mass transit really does work, that it can be the answer to stopping congestion, pollution, and the Pennsylvania Department of Transportation wanting to build a six lane superhighway under your kitchen window.

These same earnest people will say that the only reason that SEPTA may seem NOT to work is that, in a system of such enormous, antiquated complexity, little things that go wrong have a way of becoming ENORMOUS problems. A patch of street construction on City Avenue that forces two lanes into one, a bunch of soggy autumnal leaves on the train tracks, a determined cheat who insists that his monthly transit pass is up-to-date when it isn't and thus forces the trolley to sit in place on the street like a tiny kidney stone causing unbelieveable agony—when these and other intensely little things occur, they get big so fast that the system squeals, shudders, grinds, collapses, and otherwise stops. People who were stuck in whatever in-between thoughts they get when they're in transit, wake up, look around, see things they never saw before, while they begin to rage and curse and fume and come up with hundreds of explanations as to why they've stopped (most of them made up of some combination of the words "incompent," "stupid," "idiot," "assholes") here, of all the godforsaken places.

And then, after what could be a moment, or several years, the big thing shrinks to the tiny inconvenience from which it had grown, or simply goes away, and things begin to move again.

So, when SEPTA didn't mean noise, pain, suffering, going nowhere fast, too much money for too little a ride (or, to an entire subgenre of Philadelphia lawyers, one government organization that practically rolls over and prays for mercy at the scent of a personal injury lawsuit), it can also mean, *risk*. Get on a bus, train, or whatever, and who *knows* if it will get you where you want to go. Andy had even done a Mr. Action about how SEPTA could not be held liable for delays, even if the delays were due to a bus breaking down, because, legally, riding SEPTA is like listening to the weatherman: you aren't getting a service, you're getting the possibility that the service will perform, which is why, on cloudless days, one out of every four people elbowing you away in Center City is carrying an umbrella, and damned proud of it, too.

And yet, there are times when SEPTA just appears, right there, right when you need it, and getting on that bus is the simplest and best and easiest thing to do.

Andy was going to take a cab from the Press Building to the South Philadelphia address Ladderback had given to her when she saw, right out front on Market Street, a bus pull up heading south down Tenth Street.

There was no better place to be then a big, rattling and, given that it was mid-day, rather clean SEPTA bus. It came onto Smartt Street, and then passed it before she could yank the cord, punch the rubber strip, and then get out of her seat and rush up to the driver and say "You can let me out here."

Of course, the driver—a massive, imperious black man who didn't steer as much as he caressed the wheel, teasing it this way and that—played that game the bus drivers always play: they wait until the last possible second before acknowledging that you want to get off, because the drivers only stop at officially designated stops (unless they knew you or owed you one) and, when you got into the neighborhoods, the official bus stops were always in some weird place a block or two away from where anybody wanted to get off, so the drivers would wait until the official stop was in sight before nodding, and sighing as if having another passenger depart into the world was the saddest thing that would happen to them all day.

"Looks like something," the driver told her.

Andy tried follow his gaze, but only saw cars and trucks on the narrow street ahead.

"When it's somebody famous, you can't get past it," the driver said. "It can take an hour to go two blocks. Look, they've already got the cops out, telling me where I can go, like I don't know my way around."

He popped the door release and said, as if he really meant it, "Have a good one."

Andy hoisted up her shoulder bag. She certainly wanted to have a good one, and she marveled at how a few kind words, spoken with just a little bit of sincerity, from someone you don't know and probably won't see again, can be just the thing to lift you up out of whatever mood you were in, and set you down in the place you've always wanted to be.

She said, "You, too," to the driver, and then she was out on the sidewalk with the warmth from the sun touching her face as the bus groaned and diesel fumes swirled around her, and she saw she was standing a little less than half a block away from a bone-white knock-off of the plantation gothic mansion in *Gone with the Wind*. What was the mansion called? She'd seen the movie and remembered noticing how utterly wrong Clark Gable looked with the woman who played Scarlett

O'Hara, but she couldn't remember the name of the house. Her memory was still screwing up, but she was sure that this was exactly the effect whoever had built this place had wanted: in a neighborhood where just about everything you saw in any direction was brown brick (with a few awnings and shiny aluminum trimming around the doors and windows to lend a sense of peculiarity and individuality), here was this big white whale of a thing with columns going up to the sky and windows with white curtains behind them and floodlights on, even though it was almost noon, a white sign just by the broad, ceremonial double doors, where bold, gold letters proclaimed MOUNT OF OLIVES.

Andy didn't see anything on the building that said what it was, or what was supposed to go on inside. But, like anything that you find in a neighborhood, you look hard enough, you can get the hint. The hint, in this case, came from the delivery truck that was double-parked, blocking the bus that Andy had just left. One of a pair of cops, speaking with an accent that proclaimed that he was not from Brideshead, was yelling "Move it!" to a mountain of blue-and-white flowers emerging from the back of the delivery truck like one of those ridiculous floats in the Mummers Parade.

"Inna minute!" a voice from under the mountain shouted back.

One of the cops said there was a delivery entrance around the back, and the mountain trembled and shook and a scrawny, fat-nosed, white-haired guy in a jef cap and black tuxedo stepped from behind the mountain and said to nobody, that in all his years of "makin' arrangements" for the "Mounda Oliffs" did he ever make a delivery in any way but through the front door.

The cop had motioned his buddy to come beside him when Andy stepped up and asked the guy in the tuxedo if he needed a hand.

"If I needed a hand, I woulda brought a hand," the guy said to her, then he saw she was wearing a blue sweater. He became apologetic. "You a friend a the family?"

"You want help or not?" Andy said.

The cop told the man to put the flowers back on the truck and move the truck or he was getting a citation.

"C'mon," Andy said to the cop. "If I take one of these and you take the other, we can get it in, and he'll be out of here faster than it would take him to put this back on the truck."

"I'm *sorry*, ma'am," the cop said, as if anyone could believe he was sorry, "this man is blocking traffic and . . ."

Andy hit the cop with a blast of Cosicki Intimidation Waves. She didn't even look to see if the waves made him back off. She turned and put her hands on what felt like a frame of twisted-metal coat hangers at the bottom of the flower arrangement.

"Easy with that," the guy said as he went around the other side. "Up we go."

And up it went, with Andy in the lead, toward the doors, which opened with an audible electronic whir, into a olive-wood-paneled corridor with green-and-gold spangled carpeting, crowned by a fabulously gaudy Venetian glass chandelier. Tall trellises of blue flowers had been placed against the wall.

"They're all fake," the man carrying the arrangement wheezed. "It would have to be me that gives what's real. Go through that set of doors to the left."

She did, and was surprised how effortlessly one of the great, ornately inlaid, olive-wood doors opened as they entered a dimly lit cavern of a ballroom that was almost stifling with the odor of cut flowers. The man directed Andy to carry the arrangement down the center aisle, to the lectern.

"Don't put your eyes on that one," the man carrying the arrangement said of the frail, elfin fellow in a muddy brown, plaid suit, who stood with his hands clasped below his waist staring intently at the open casket.

"Morning, Stace," the man at the casket said.

Stace and Andy set the arrangement down beside the lectern.

Andy recognized the man at the casket. Less than twenty-four hours ago, she had handed him a Welsh rarebit crepe. He did not seem to recognize her, though his eyes seemed drawn to her hands.

Stace untangled some twist-ties. Sections of the mountain opened up, down and to both sides until it revealed a seven-foot-tall flower-encrusted replica of a weighing scale, with a big "W" spelled in white orchids on the dial.

"You know they won't want it where you've put it," Glen said quietly. "They'll want it with the others."

Andy saw rows and rows of floral monuments.

"But there's no one like this one. Considering Danny Bleutner paid me for it, it's going front and center," Stace said. He removed his cap and peered into the coffin. "My word, Glen, he was as thin as a stick when he died. Now he's got pounds on him."

"A few," Glen said. "You know I was there. I saw it all. He had a plum in his mouth and they said he choked on it. But don't you believe it. His heart gave out, that's what did it to him."

Stace made a low whistle. "You've got him in a suit. I didn't know he owned one."

"It was bought new," Glen sniffed.

"You made him so young, Glen. They're going to say he went too soon."

"So he did," Glen agreed.

"So long to you, you old scoundrel," Stace said to the coffin. He adjusted his cap. "Well, I'm off."

Glen said, "Aren't you going to thank the lady, Stace?"

Stace turned around. "Ah, yes. My appreciations, ma'am." He opened his tuxedo jacket, took out a card, and presented it to Andy. "Eustace T. McCorey, ma'am. McCorey's Flowers for All Occasions."

"I got one of your arrangements," Andy said. "It was wild."

He became solemn. "I don't do wild. I am a master horticultural engineer."

"I mean . . . I really liked it," Andy said, quickly.

"I make arrangements for the most discriminating individuals," Stace said. "This one's from a person who grew up here, who made such a name for himself, he could have any florist in the world make an arrangement for him. He calls me up, and says, 'Stace, you do it right for Weight.' "

"For who?" Andy asked.

"Sidney Caesar Wisnitz," Glen said, touching the casket. "His service is here this afternoon. There was a rather fine obituary for the man in the *Press* a few days ago, though it had some mistakes in it."

"How could it?" Andy said. "I know the guy who writes obituaries, and he's good."

"As good as possible, perhaps," Glen said. Andy looked at Glen and saw the pale, fragile face of a man who spent most of his time indoors. "Mr. Ladderback took that from the coroner's report. I get a copy of the report with every subject. There isn't much room on it to describe the cause of death. It isn't meant to be an explanation as much as it is a judgement made in relative haste based on available evidence. It's never one thing that ends a life. It's always too many things."

Andy said, "Shep knows a lot about that kind of thing. His parents were medical examiners and a lot of times they'd take him to the morgue and show him things."

"Some things are not meant to be shown," Glen said.

McCorey made a face. "Got to run. Those police better not give me a ticket."

Andy watched him go.

"Is it me you had something to ask, ma'am?" Glen asked her.

Andy unfolded the paper on which Ladderback had written a name and address. "I'm Andy Cosicki and I'm with the *Philadelphia Press*. I'm looking for an Owen Glendower. He's supposed to be an expert at the art of restoration and, well, I have an assignment to write about him for an article. He's supposed to have an office on Smartt Street, but I was told he could also be found here. Is he here?"

He did not smile. "Many have the name of Owen Glendower, Ms. Cosicki. He was the last great Welsh hero, a nobleman who proclaimed himself Prince of Wales and led a rebellion against the English usurper King Henry IV in 1400. It was rumored that he knew magic and could make the weather do his will. His rebellion ended in defeat in 1409 but his body, like that of King Arthur, who was also most likely a Welshman, was never found. For a family of the Glendower line to name a son Owen, is to put the chain of destiny around his neck. It is as much a burden as a blessing."

Andy sat down in one of the empty chairs. "The man with the flowers—McCorey—called you Glen. Is that short for Glendower?"

"For Mr. Eustace McCorey, it is. His wife was in the flower business and he's tried to make a run of it after she passed away."

"Good." Andy took her notebook computer out of her shoulder bag. "I need to ask you how old you are, and if you live in Philadephia."

"I'm 56 years of age and I live on Smartt Street. I don't have an office but I have lived on Smartt Street for many years."

She typed that on the keyboard. "That's where you do . . . what is the art of restoration? You're not directly connected with this place, right? Restoration has to do with building or fixing things so I guess you fix up old caskets?"

Glendower moved away from the casket. "May I ask how it is I have become your subject?"

"It was an assignment," Andy said. "Shep—Shepherd Ladderback—said he would call to tell you I'm coming. He said I normally do the Mr. Action column, but sometimes I work with him as an assistant, and he said you'd tell me everything I needed to know."

He removed a cell phone from his breast pocket, checked his caller I.D. list, and saw that Ladderback had called. "Is that all he said, Ms. Cosicki?"

"He said that he had always wanted to have a story about you in the paper, but he couldn't do it, because, as an obituary writer, he deals with funeral directors and it might be seen as a conflict of interest if he wrote you up."

Glendower sat down near her and put his short, thick-fingered hands on his thighs. Andy noticed he wore no jewelry, that his fingernails were immaculately groomed. "It is difficult to talk about what I do, Ms. Cosicki."

"How so?"

"Forgive me for asking this, but have you eaten today, Ms. Cosicki?"

"Not a thing."

"Do you intend to?"

She shook her head. "I can take you out to lunch, if you're asking that, but it's not going to be anything expensive, and I won't be eating anything."

"I'm not asking you to take me to lunch, Ms. Cosicki. I'm trying to determine how much I can tell you without causing discomfort."

She smiled. "I woke up with some kind of twenty-four-hour bug this morning. I don't know how I got it, but there is absolutely nothing left in me that I can get sick over. I told Shep that before he gave me the assignment."

Glendower kept his eyes on his hands. "I don't work on caskets, Ms. Cosicki. The art of restoration is a term specific to the funeral business. You are not at the age, I assume, when you go to funerals."

"I went to my father's," Andy said.

"Forgive me for presuming. Was there a viewing at your father's funeral?"

Andy remembered the dark gleam of the casket's lid. "Not at all," Andy said.

"My specialty concerns open casket funerals. It has to do with preparing a subject for a viewing."

"So you do the embalmings," Andy said, her mouth going dry.

Ladderback came back from the men's room and passed the desk of the newspaper's photo editor. Howard Lange had his hand on the shoulder of the photo editor, a woman with studs of metal in her ear and azure blue-dyed hair that could have been singed into shape by a blowtorch.

She sat in front of a broad video monitor. The monitor showed the two-page spread on which the mob hit story would run. The text had not been written yet, but a headline and cutline (a smaller block of text that would appear in a column in boldface) had been inserted.

The headline read MOB MURDER AT STEAK SHOP, with the cutline DISMEMBERED FEMALE VICTIM FOUND IN TRASH: CHICKIE ALL OVER AGAIN?

In the righthand corner of the editor's screen were tiny, thumbnail-sized digital photos. The editor clicked her cursor on each photo, enlarging it. She clicked on one photo of the front of Orley's Emperor of the Steak. Judging from the cars parked in front of the dark, odd-shaped restaurant, the photo may have been taken back in the days when Ladderback went to Orley's with Gina Dettweiler.

"Too old," Lange said.

The editor clicked on another photo that included a few police cars, an ambulance and more up-to-date car models.

"Look, see, on the side? You can see the garbage dumpster," Lange said. "We'll use that."

She dragged the photo over to the mock-up of the newspaper page, and kept clicking on it until it fit the page.

"It's too cute," Lange went on. "You look at that, and you want to take your kids there. Give it a Hitchcock treatment. Think *Psycho*."

The editor brought up the tone controls. She darkened the photo, added a grainy texture to the garbage dumpster, deepened the shadows under Orley's neon sign. A bright, cheery daylight shot became menacing and grim.

"Now we get us a Chickie," Lange said.

The editor called up another file of photos. Ladderback saw that they were shots of the Philly mob boss Chickie Marandola. As she clicked the photos, Ladderback viewed a series of mug shots that could be dated by changes in Marandola's hairstyle, two shots taken from FBI surveillance agents, and another of Marandola in a suit outside Federal District Court in Philadelphia, with Marandola giving the finger to the photographer.

"I like the finger," Lange said.

"These all suck," the photo editor said.

Ladderback said, "I remember several photos of Chickie Marandola on The Wall at Orley's. It shows him in front of his car. Marandola used to drive a Porsche. It was supposed to be his way of distinguishing himself from the other mobsters, who were all driving domestic luxury and muscle cars."

Lange said. "Shep, we need anything about the mob, we know where to get it."

"The photo of Marandola was supposed to have been the only photograph Orley ever lent from his Wall," Ladderback went on. "It was used to reassemble Marandola's face for the viewing."

"Cut off that finger," Lange said to the photo editor. "We're a family newspaper."

The photo editor cropped the photo on the screen, so although Marandola's finger couldn't be seen, the arc of his arm and the expression of his face made the gesture unmistakable.

Then Lange turned to Ladderback. "Forget about any of the obits you've done seeing print tomorrow. This is a mob hit and we have to play it as large as possible. Where's the Cosicki girl?"

"On assignment."

"Pass it on, if you see her. Mr. Action is inactive for tomorrow."

"You don't require me in the newsroom for the remainder of the day?"

"Not unless you can tell me who killed Chickie Marandola."

"I believe I know someone who has that information."

Lange came up, put his arm around him. "Then, Shep, I want you to go out. I want you to find that person. I want you to get that story!"

"Are you giving me an assignment?" Ladderback asked.

Lange let go. "I'm telling you to take the afternoon off. You're getting on my nerves."

"And if I should find out who killed Mr. Marandola?"

"Sleep on it," Lange said, and went back to the photo editor's desk.


"Embalming is an aspect of what is called the art of preparation. All funeral homes provide that service. Restoration is required when the subject's condition is not immediately conducive to a viewing."

Andy's fingers paused on the keyboard.

"Perhaps the subject passed due to a lingering, disfiguring, wasting kind of illness, such as cancer or AIDS. Or, the subject had been dead for several days before discovery, and decomposition has begun. The subject might have been exposed to the elements, had contact with insects or animals, or was underwater for an extended period of time."

"By contact with animals, you mean. . . ."

"I mentioned that it is difficult to talk about this," Glendower said. "We need not get into the details."

"We can get as detailed as you want," Andy said. She transcribed the quote and she felt her stomach sink.

Glendower added, "There are also suicides and victims of extreme violence."

"Like what the mob guys do to each other?" Andy asked.

"The traditional Mafia execution entails two gunshots to the skull, behind either ear, sometimes both. The effect on the skull and soft tissues, even from very small caliber rounds, is devastating. We are also living in a period of homicidal experimentation, especially as it regards torture and disfiguring. The use of inflammables, caustic substances, and explosives can render portions of the subject nearly irrecoverable. And then there are other complications."

Andy found that as long as she focused on her job, that of asking questions and recording the answers, she would not think about the utter horror of what Glendower was describing.

"Chickie Marandola was dismembered," Andy remembered. "Some of the pieces were never found. When that happens, I guess, you would tell the families that want a viewing, that a viewing is not going to happen."

"The family is never denied, Miss Cosicki. What happens is, the funeral director meets with the family. Then the funeral director directs the family's wishes to me. The family tends not to want to see me because my presence can remind them of the manner in which the loved one died. They can meet with me, if they wish, and some do."

"To do . . . what?"

"To tell me what the subject was like. They give me a photograph of the subject before the occurrence of the illness or the incident leading to death. Sometimes an item of clothing or jewelry that was familiar to the subject can be significant. An anecdote can provide insights into the subject's personality."

"But there is no personality. I mean, they're dead, right?"

He indicated his annoyance by tightening his lips. "The art of restoration removes the sting of death. I am considered a preeminent restoration artisan. I am consulted in what you might call extreme cases. I restore the subject's facial features and hands. I also dress the subject and apply ornamental and decorative materials."

Andy swallowed. "What kind of . . . never mind." She forced herself to think of more questions. "Did Chickie Marandola's family want a viewing?"

"My profession forbids me from speaking directly about the family, but, because the funeral was held, I can tell you that a viewing for Carmen Gigliano Marandola took place, and that we provided services in that regard."

"You mean you put him back together?"

"As much as it can be discussed, yes."

"What about the parts . . . they couldn't find?"

"The essence of the art is confined to the head and hands, with the hands being the most important, because the hands are what the mourners view first. The condition of the hands determines the way the mourner will evaluate the face. The presence of rings or a favorite wristwatch can be very significant. When areas of the hands and face have suffered damage or decay, I can use specific materials to render a likeness. The detailing of the material is very important, as is the quality of the manicure, the presence of scars, or, in some rare instances, tattoos and other identifying markings. These are not what we notice when we meet people for the first time, Ms. Cosicki. But I have learned to remember these things."

Andy got a sense that Glendower was holding back, that he wanted to tell her something about the work he did on Chickie Marandola, but he wouldn't unless she asked the right question. How do you ask the right question if you don't know what you're asking for?

You don't. You don't ask any questions. You sit and you wait and you let the silence settle in and you see what fills that silence.

More silence.

Then Andy noticed he was looking at her hands. "You want to read my fortune?" she asked him.

"I was thinking that you may work with food, Ms. Cosicki, because I saw someone yesterday who resembled you. But those who work with food have dry skin, from washing all the time, and evidence of cuts and small burns. I see that your nails are cut short, without any polish or decorative enamel, and there are callouses on the pads of your fingers. You are involved in some kind of sport involving a rough object that you must hold and release. But I also see your knuckles are bruised. I see a few small lesions that are made when knuckles encounter soft tissue with a degree of force. I believe you have taken a punch at someone in the last twenty-four hours. I suppose you would tell me that I should have seen the other guy?"

Andy shook her head. "I did my layups last night, but there was no other guy."

He seemed disturbed by this. "Forgive me, but I am rarely wrong about hands, Ms. Cosicki. Can you tell me what caused those cuts on your knuckles?"

"Nothing," Andy said. "I never even noticed them."

"Perhaps a nightmare, when sleeping."

"I have never beaten up my pillow. I slept like a rock last night."

"And—you'll forgive me for asking—you were ill when you woke up? The passage of digestive materials through the lips can cause the swelling, scarring, and the slight chapping around the corners of your mouth."

She turned away from him. "I didn't punch the toilet when I threw up in it, if that's what you want to know."

He apologized. "I notice these things and I must remind myself that physical traces can be deceptive, especially where my own memory is concerned."

"You've worked on . . . ," she used his word, "*subjects* you've known?"

"You mentioned a case in which I restored the subject entirely from memory."

"Chickie Marandola?"

"He lived on Smartt Street for a time. He had the hands of a person who played with knives. Scars around the fingernails and on the pads of the fingers, an erosion on the pad of the thumb from testing the blade. Though I restored the hands completely, the family decided his hands were not to be shown because the newspapers publicized the fact that only one of the fingers from his hand was recovered."

"The one they took the print from." She typed that in. "I'm sure that cost a lot."

He frowned. "Do we have to go in this direction, Ms. Cosicki? I don't mind telling you about restoration, but I will not have you misinterpreting me. I consider myself blessed to be able to perform this service. I do a great deal of my work for the Mount of Olives, but I have no exclusive relationship here. Some of the work I do is for families that have little or no money but need my services for reasons that I don't have to describe, and I perform those services without charge. Yesterday, for example, I received a call regarding a family . . ."

He took out a handkerchief. "You'll excuse me." He held the handkerchief tightly in his fist. Andy saw his knuckles turn white, and the hand begin to tremble.

She asked, "Is there something wrong?"

"Yes, Ms. Cosicki, there is something wrong."

She waited for him to answer the question. He stayed silent, and finally put the handkerchief away.

She said, "Can you . . . elaborate?"

"I'd rather not, Ms. Cosicki, and I would prefer if you did not mention this, because, in my profession the display of any emotion beyond that of compassionate respect, can only increase a family's suffering. In most situations, I am able to keep myself . . . in line. I like to think that reason pertains to my heritage. For many centuries, the Welsh have been a conquered people. We have learned to love our neighbor. We have learned to live in peace. We have fulfilled God's will, even if we have had to do extraordinary things to maintain that love."

He went to the casket and told Andy that he didn't want her to write down what he said. He had to show her something. "The donor who is sponsoring this burial specifically asked for my services. I was told to make him appear healthy, in the full of life, and I believe I have succeeded."

The first thing Andy saw when she approached the casket was an immaculate blue business suit, the silk tie perfectly knotted, and thin, bony hands folded calmly on the suit.

"I spent a great deal of time on these hands. The joints were enlarged and the effects on the skin of incipient starvation more than readily apparent."

To Andy, the hands seemed . . . normal. "I don't see anything that looks like starvation," Andy said.

"I've had other subjects like this, those that had cancer, or were anorexic, or suffered some other element of wasting, as if their bodies stopped replenishing themselves. It's possible to make the symptoms less obvious."

Andy steeled herself and forced her eyes up from the hands, toward the skin above the shirt collar. It was lifelike. The lips were closed but not clenched, the eyes shut as if they might open if anyone made a sound.

"Regardless of what he died from, Mr. Wisnitz lived a long, full life," Glendower said. "I have no difficulty with subjects who have had their three-score-and-ten, or the equivalent, no matter what condition they are in when I receive them. In addition to the wasting illness, this subject passed blood and gastric juices through his mouth, and a rather hasty autopsy was performed on this subject and the effects of an autopsy on a subject can be more devastating than the most extreme violence."

He moved away from the casket and took out his handkerchief. "It was only yesterday I received a call from the police, about a young child who was playing on the street when he was killed by . . ."

Andy remembered what Lieutenant Everson had told her. "He was four years old. It happened on a drive-by shooting."

He turned away. "I haven't seen the subject yet. I was told of two shots in the skull, that they came in from the front, over the right eye, and that the rounds were angled downward so that they . . ." He squeezed the handkerchief tightly. "I don't even know if there will be a viewing as such, or a funeral, because the family is very poor. The family is in shock, the entire neighborhood is in shock. I was asked if I could help heal the family and I said I could not be certain. But I have seen enough people helped when they can look upon a loved one and see something other than what took that loved one away."

He began to dab his eyes with the handkerchief. "I tend to lose my emotional control when my subjects are young, Ms. Cosicki. When God takes the young, I feel the anger that led my namesake to start a futile rebellion against a worthless English king. I fight the God that takes children. I fight with everything I have even if the cause is lost from the start. I know, better than anyone, that we cannot bring them back. But we can . . . I can, make them beautiful."

He sat down, opened his handkerchief, blotted his eyes, folded and refolded his handkerchief, blotted his eyes again, and was folding the handkerchief a third time when Andy forgot that she'd ever been sick.

Andy pointed at the casket. She said, "You've seen others like him?"

"Not like him, but . . . some who have had what he had."

"What would that be?"

"You are asking only for general details?"

"Sure."

He became eager, almost childlike. "Nothing I've seen before, though I don't pretend to have seen everything. The predominant characteristic is in the blood vessels that serve the throat and upper digestive system, which makes the embalming process much more complicated. You see, because of the embalming procedure, I have to first drain the blood and replace it with—I'm sorry, am I disturbing you?"

Andy forced herself to shake her head no.

"Think of the body like a house. In the house you have the plumbing. If something corrodes the plumbing going through the walls near the front door, and the plumbing isn't repaired or replaced because the process that would do the repair work is not getting what it needs, then pipes get weaker and weaker until a sudden increase in the heart rate, a stressful situation, or perhaps even a pleasurable one, and one pipe blows, or a group of pipes blow, and, because so many of the pipes around the front door and the hallway—the mouth, the throat, the upper gastrointestinal system in general—have eroded until they're next to nothing, you get a sudden flood and the whole house comes down."

She opened her notebook. "Tell me about them. All of them."

He folded his handkerchief. "Ms. Cosicki, I'd rather not cause you any discomfort. In my entire life there has been no one I can remember that I have been able to discuss these things with, outside my profession."

Andy took a deep breath. "Until now," she said.

# 15 happy with what you have to be happy with

Ladderback put on his coat and hat and took the elevator down to the Press Building's sub-basement, to the underground food court and shopping mall beneath Market Street.

He went into a record store, and then took an escalator into the dark wood and white marble lobby of a convention hotel. He moved slowly past the bar, where a handful of men wearing golf shirts and suit jackets slouched over drinks while a woman at a piano played the Elton John song "Philadelphia Freedom."

He checked his watch. His timing had to be correct and, he admitted, she might not even be at the gas station when he arrived.

He paused in front of the bell captain's station and caught the doorman's eye. He tipped the doorman and asked him to call a cab. He followed the doorman as far as he could until the light from the front doors crossed his path. Then he closed his eyes. He heard the rush of sound from the street as the doorman went out. He heard the doorman say, "Yo! Over *here*!" He guessed, from the shrieking squeal of brakes, that a vehicle had stopped somewhere in front of him.

Ladderback opened his eyes just a crack, so he could see light through his eyelashes. He forced himself to take a step, and another, until the street sounds surrounded him and he smelled the odors of dust and engine exhaust that told him he was outside. He put one hand in front of him and blundered into the edge of the cab door window.

He heard the door shut. He sank into an unevenly padded seat. The cab had the fake fruit syrup smell of air freshener.

Ladderback gave the driver an address. The driver hit the meter and the cab lurched forward.

Something was wrong with the cab's brakes: they made a continuous screeching sound. What if the cab broke down somewhere and the driver told him he'd have to get out and walk? He forced himself to concentrate on the swaying motions, the stops and starts that indicated to him the cab's progress across the city map. He felt the cab make a series of turns onto Market Street, stop at a light, then turn left as it went around the City Hall traffic circle, bearing left to cross John F. Kennedy Boulevard and then right onto Market Street, heading toward West Philadelphia.

"You from here?" the driver asked him.

Ladderback guessed from the driver's accent that he was Asian, possibly one of the thousands of Vietnamese who were moving into what were formerly Italian, Irish and Jewish neighborhoods. "Yes," Ladderback said.

"I see you have eyes closed. Something you don't like?"

"I'm a little tired," Ladderback lied.

"Go to sleep. I wake you when we get there."

Ladderback said, "Okay." The cab stopped suddenly and Ladderback groped for the door handle.

He heard the driver bang the steering wheel. "Problem with city," the driver said. "Nobody know how to drive."

Ladderback tried not to think of what he might have to do if the cab got into an accident. His hands were beginning to cramp from gripping the arm rest when the driver said, "You wake up now."

Ladderback tilted his head forward, pulled the money out of his wallet. He shut his eyes tightly, opened the door, put a foot on what felt like

264

the street, moved his foot forward until it bumped into the curb. He stood slowly.

"Hey, you forgot to close door."

Ladderback had let go of the door and suddenly he wasn't sure where it was. He turned, heard the door shut. The driver said, "You get some sleep now."

He heard the cab squeal away. He thought he smelled gasoline but he wasn't sure. He heard traffic on the street. He felt the breeze of larger vehicles moving loudly just a few feet away. He told himself that he was safe; that he could stand on the street in the open on a nice day with the light from the sky warming his skin and that nothing awful would happen to him; that the terror he was feeling was thoroughly insubstantial, irrational; that there are *pills* he could take to reduce the anxiety, and that he could get these pills if he ever forced himself to see a therapist or a psychiatrist, which he wouldn't do because every time he thought of seeking treatment, he told himself that he didn't really have a problem, that what he had to do was just take deep breaths and think it through, even if the only thing he could think of was that his skin was growing moist and that he was probably shaking or trembling somewhere. His anxiety was so overwhelming that he wasn't sure exactly what his body was doing though he was reasonably certain that he wasn't moving. Would people stop and look at him and think he was just another ancient urban nut case who should be in a mental institution? Would he find himself knocked down on the sidewalk so that some creep with larceny in his heart could take his wallet?

No, Ladderback told himself. Gina wouldn't let that happen, *if* Gina was at her garage today, instead of dressing for the funeral. Gina would be at the garage because she wanted an excuse not to go to the funeral. What would she tell them at the Mount of Olives, if anyone asked? That she just used to buy produce from Weight Wisnitz and that she was so sorry he died?

So he hoped that she would be looking at the street in front of her garage and would happen to notice him. If she didn't, he might crawl on the ground and stand on the pressure hose that rang the bell when a car approached. He remembered that Gina liked to be everywhere at once. She'd work on cars with the mechanics she employed, but she'd also put down her grease gun to go out and pump the gas, because, she had told him, she was terrified of going out to pump the gas and seeing her ex-husband in a car. Gina had never told him what she might do if that dream came true.

Then he heard her voice. "'Scuse me, sir, but you got a problem standing out here?"

"I have a gift," Ladderback said, handing it to her.

"Oh, my God, you couldn't be . . ." He felt her take the bag from his hand. "Feat!" she exclaimed. Then she wrapped an arm around him and almost squeezed the wind out of him. "Unbe*lieva*ble!

She squinted at the CD, held it away. She took a pair of spectacles out of a small pocket on her overalls. "They have three versions of 'Skin it Back.' You know what it means, skin it back?" She eyed him. "You don't want to know."

He asked her gently if she could lead him somewhere indoors. "The truck," she said. "Wait until you see the truck."

Ladderback never saw the truck. He held his eyes shut as she took him to the side of the station where she parked her wrecker. From the sound of the door opening, Ladderback knew it was different from the truck that he used to ride in with her when they towed the Femme Fatale to a derby.

But it was appropriate to go to the truck because, in addition to having the best police radio and, in those days before cell phones, the best citizens band radio that money could buy, she also had a superb sound system. And, as it was for those of their generation, the music she played—most of it a mix of rock 'n' roll, blues and jazz called "underground" or "progressive"—would act as a soundtrack to the movie they were pretending to inhabit. The music would infuse their moments with drama, give cues on how to behave, tell them when to get angry, when to make love.

Gina slammed the door with a thunk. "What I been listening to lately is King Crimson. British prog band, though three of the four guys currently in it are American. It started out progressive and strange and now they're loud, tricky, nasty and wacky. They have this song that says you have to be happy with what you have to be happy with. Really! I've been listening to that lately."

"So you've been happy?"

"Shit no. I'm just telling you what I've been listening to." He heard her slide the disc into the CD player.

He was trying to see the lines of her face, how some had grown softer, others harder, much harder than when he'd touched them.

Then he was blown back by a blast of dissonant, grinding heavy metal power chords and a man singing about, how, if you want to be happy, you have to be happy with what you have to be happy with. The music was clearly rock 'n' roll, but, with its whip-sawing diminished chords and rhythmic slipperiness, it reminded him of the spare, disquietingly dissonant Bartók string quartets, especially the Third.

She punched the stop button when she had the cellophane off the Little Feat CD he bought her. She replaced the King Crimson with the first CD, went down the tracks to "Day or Night." The music came on and she covered her face with her hands. "There it is. Oh, God, Shep, what were we doing back then?"

Ladderback forced his eyes open and felt himself fall in love with her all over again. It was so easy that he couldn't think of anything to say.

Then those three little words came into his head. "We should eat."

Should she take a cab? Andy wanted to rush back to the newspaper when she left Glendower. Once Andy got over how ghastly all of this was, she had to admit she found it fascinating how just a few little changes could turn an object of horror and revulsion into the image of innocuous repose.

That, and what he told her about some of his other subjects, tended to confirm what Lieutenant Everson had said: that there was some kind of strange disease—Glendower called it "unnatural"—that had been claiming some people for quite a while.

267

So she was outside and taking big, long strides toward the corner of Tenth and Washington, where she might flag a cab, when she saw the block was clogged by police cars, crime lab trucks and TV vans. Uniformed police were keeping spectators back. Andy saw Lieutenant Everson. He let her through.

"About that disease you told me was going around," she said.

He shook his head at her, as if to say don't bring the subject up. Then he asked her if she was also representing the newspaper. "They've sent someone, but I'd rather talk to you."

Andy said, "Talk."

He turned his back on the cluster of technicians crowded around the garbage dumpster. "She was found by Orley Roberts, the owner of this cheesesteak place. He was taking out his garbage and he opened the dumpster and there she was. Female victim. Mid-twenties. The theory is that this is a message-killing, a kind of statement being made, even if is pretty damned sick: a copy cat of what happened to Chickie Marandola."

"What do you think?"

"I'm thinking that I want to be anywhere but here. We don't have a face and we don't have the hands, but this victim was beautiful. I'm not making any official statement about this, but, we have personnel in the department who sort of specialize in mob stuff, and they're saying that it's the same person who did Chickie."

He scowled and she said, "But you don't think so."

"The person that did Chickie knew how to cut up a body. He used a variety of knives, including a big butcher's cleaver and each cut went in just right. This girl was done with an axe, like she was a pile of wood. He left pieces of her clothes, so we'll start tracing them as soon as we get her out."

He put his hand over his mouth, as if he were trying to choke back his nausea. "And there's something else: remember I told you about this thing going around? How it involves blood coming out, either the front or the back? This one had the blood coming out the back."

"I want to see her," Andy said.

"You don't," Everson said. "It's sickening."

"After what I've been through," Andy said, "nothing can make me sick."

"You want to know what's sick? There's a crew down here from the crime lab, and there are those guys that drive the ambulances. They hang out here all the time, and there is a bunch of them inside that place and eating lunch, even while we're out here."

"Now that," Andy said as she came close enough to see the dumpster, "is sick."

"I think there are some things we're not supposed to get used to," Everson said as he brought her closer.


When Ladderback heard Gina tell the mechanics in her garage that she was "stepping out for a while," this meant that if she had thought of doing anything else during the afternoon beyond work in the garage, she hadn't told them.

Then she hopped back in the tow truck and Ladderback, his eyes shut tight, said, "I don't want to tell you where we should go, until we get there."

"So we're going to have a magical mystery tour."

It would be much more than that, Ladderback thought.

"You're just going to give me directions?"

"Turn left and go east toward the University City on-ramp for eastbound Schuylkill Expressway," Ladderback said.

"You better not get me lost."

"Have I ever?"

She laughed and started up the truck. She drove the truck powerfully through the city, the Little Feat CD roaring loudly through open windows.

With his eyes shut tight, Ladderback remembered that how difficult, but how ultimately rewarding it had been to make love to her in the front seat of an earlier version of her tow truck. He then tried to visualize, based on the jolting turns Gina took, the route they were traveling. He held two images in his mind: one was the map of Philadelphia hanging in the *Press* newsroom; the other was the incredible skyline shot from the failed Bassos TV epic—taken from what could have only been the top of One Franklin Tower—of South Philadelphia.

"Not here," she said when the restaurant came into view.

"Why not here?" Ladderback said.

"There are all these cops around."

"That might make it easier to get a table," Ladderback said.

She stopped the truck, backed it into a space.

"You'll have to help me," Ladderback said.

"You mean you're expecting me to sit here and believe that this disease you've been saying you got is real?"

"It's real to me," Ladderback said, his eyes shut tight. "It is entirely internal. I'm aware that there is nothing about the outside that I need fear. The feeling isn't quite like fear, but close enough."

"What'll happen if I don't help you?"

"I will stay here for a while."

"Then what?"

Ladderback said nothing.

"You know I've always had a problem with anybody that wimps out," she said. "Everything I've ever gotten I've had to fight for. It's been a struggle from day one. I see you sitting there, expecting me to help you, and it really, really gets to me."

"I'm sorry," Ladderback said.

"You sure this isn't something you're pulling, to get something out of me? You can do that. You've always been able to do that. You can get things out of people whether they want to give them to you or not."

He paused for a few seconds. "Most of what I obtain is given voluntarily. I can also sense when something is being withheld. Sometimes, the person who is withholding really wants to give, but is resisting for specific reasons that . . ."

"What?"

"May not be reasonable. No more reasonable, perhaps, than the irrational anxiety I feel when I am outside. What I feel does not make sense, but it is not necessarily a weakness."

"You're telling me that you're sitting here looking like you're about to burst into tears, because you're such a tough guy?"

"Not at all. What I am telling you is that, for me, it is unreasonable to see human behavior in terms of strength and weakness. To dwell on any extreme can distract us from more important matters."

"Such as," she said, "how two people who are absolutely wrong for each other could stand each other long enough to do what we did?"

"Such as what you're going to have at Orley's."

He heard her chuckle and, though his eyes were still shut, he could imagine her smiling. "I don't know. I haven't been there in years."

"How many years?"

"We're too old to keep counting, Shep."

Ladderback mentioned a year. "Did you stop going then?"

"I could've. What's so special about that year?"

"It was the last time I saw you. Your mother-in-law's funeral." He opened his eyes a crack and saw that there was no wedding band around her finger.

She was quiet for a while. "Okay, it's been a while. You got to promise me something. You will not get that steak with the Brussels sprouts!"

"It was very good, as I remember," Ladderback said.

"You got it because you were trying to embarrass me, weren't you?"

"I was curious, young and in love, so I took risks," Ladderback said. "What kind of risk would you be taking, in coming here with me?"

He could sense her apprehension. "Too many."

"I won't order the Brussels sprouts," Ladderback said.

She said, "You win." She helped him out of the truck and, surrounded by the aromas of frying potatoes, sizzling onions, and sirloin browning in olive oil, she took his arm and guided him toward the entrance.

Andy tried to run but was still too dizzy, so she managed a fast walk, heading west, past Orley's Emperor of the Steak and the free clinic, to the corner of Washington and Eleventh Street, where she turned and saw the bus that would take her back to the newspaper was two blocks away.

She got on when it came, took a transfer ticket, found a seat as far away from the other human beings as possible, and pulled out her cell phone.

She dialed her mother's number and got her voice mail. "Mom, you have to call me," Andy said. "You have to call me as soon as you hear this."

She hung up and closed her eyes, trying not see the pieces of shredded, blood-soaked BUY ART T-shirt adhering to Karyn Asgard's muscular upper arm.

She hadn't told Everson who the victim was: she had wanted to tell her mother first. Her mother had called her earlier, telling her that Karyn had gone to the house with Dr. Elgin last night, and that Karyn didn't check in this morning.

Charlotte had also wanted to know if Andy was okay, and Andy told her that she was definitely not okay.

"It'll probably wear off," Charlotte said, "whatever it is."

And how did Charlotte know Karyn had gone to the house, Andy had asked. Her mother said that Karyn had used a temporary access code. She had given one to Elgin but Elgin had said Charlotte could tell him all about codes and security *after* the house went to settlement.

So Karyn had used her access code and the security system recorded the time and date of entry. Charlotte went on the Internet, accessed a web page, entered a password and got a list of every access code—including Andy's—that had been used that night.

Charlotte knew that Elgin had been with Karyn because she also uploaded images from the surveillance cameras.

"But I was there all the time," Andy had said. "I don't remember anyone being there."

"I'm happy that you don't," Charlotte said. "If you hear from Karyn, tell her to call me."

After she had spoken with her mother, Andy had called Tom and Don at the Polidos Double-Czech Home Security company to get someone to tell her about her mother's system. Even if they hadn't installed it, they might know how she could access it. If anything had happened at the house, the video recording system would have captured it.

Now Andy wanted to push the bus faster. Memories were beginning to come back—why, she wasn't sure, but she now vividly recalled that, sometime last night, she had been hit in the face and kicked in her side. She examined the knuckles of her hand; yes, she had punched someone in the face last night!

She got off the bus on Market Street and, for a moment, she didn't know if she should go back to the newspaper, or grab the R5 train to Merion Station.

She looked up at the Press Building. She should go up there and tell someone who the murder victim was, that this wasn't a mob hit. Karyn Asgard had an apartment in South Philadelphia, but she didn't know anyone in the mob. She was a Philadephia sales associate for a New York art gallery, and the last person she had been seen with was Alex Elgin.

Andy saw his face swim into her memory and she remembered how she had hit him, right, under the jaw, and how the stubble on his skin had raked the skin on her knuckles.

She went for the train.

# the wall

Some places, you go inside and you know exactly where you are because nothing matches but everything fits.

Ladderback had heard a name for it: Contractor Gothic, in which walls, windows, moldings, lights, floor tiles, panel strips, and plumbing fixtures were bought at close-out sales, or had been scavenged from other buildings about to be torn down, or snatched off the shelves of a mom-and-pop, bought at a hardware store that was going out of business because it couldn't match the prices of the Home Depot on Delaware Avenue, or fell off a truck.

Nothing matched inside Orley's because Orley's was a monument to the people who had been brought up in families where you threw nothing away. You used what came to you, no matter how it came to you, because your grandparents lived in a country where they had nothing and their lives depended on getting as much as they could from every little thing. They say Orley learned how to cook in a prison kitchen, and that he made the food so great that the hard cases stopped filing for appeals. Which jail he went to, and for what reason he did his time, nobody knows because in Brideshead, going to jail is like going into the army in peacetime, it's one more thing to do if you're young and you don't have a relative in a union or an uncle in a business and you haven't learned that when you hear a police siren, you *disappear*.

So, way back before there was a dining room, and a big sign on the front, Orley reappeared in this building, opened up the windows, and when the traffic light turned red and anybody in a truck had to stop and wait for the damned light to turn green, they might smell heaven rolling out of a makeshift kitchen that, for reasons nobody knows, was built two feet higher than the ground level so a guy in a truck waiting for a light to change could look over and see a little cut in the curb where he could drive his truck over, right up to that open kitchen window, where Orley took his order, made him a sandwich, and handed it to him, with a coffee-to-go.

But it wasn't a drive-up window that made Orley the Emperor of the Steak. It was having no room for a decent refrigerator. He had one of those wheezing little boxes, big enough for a six-pack, where he kept the cream containers for the coffee and a tray of ice. Anything else wouldn't fit, so Orley made arrangements for small hourly deliveries with the Brideshead butchers, cheese sellers, drink distributors and bread bakers. Every sandwich Orley made was cut, sliced, chopped, ground, or baked so fresh that even if you smoked a pack of cigarettes, you could taste the difference. There were times when the deliveries screwed up, and Orley would either work with what he had (sign in the window: Special Today: CHEESE ANCHOVY NO MEAT STEAK) or, when he had too much and it was hot out and everything was going to spoil, he'd dump it all onto his grill and cook it up, shovel it onto sliced Italian rolls, open the back door (that became the front door) and yell to the world in a voice that could stop traffic, that people should eat.

And people ate.

Now any politician, priest, marketing maestro, welfare office clerk, or soup kitchen chef will tell you that giving away free food on a regular basis doesn't make you friends. People who eat the food come to think that they deserve it, and they may even resent you if you reduce the portions, use cheaper ingredients, or dish out what doesn't measure up to their standards.

But when it's random, when a person can be walking down a street or passing in a car or hopelessly lost in a part of the city where the orderly grid that William Penn laid down three centuries ago starts to break up, and you hear this foghorn voice tell you that you should eat, and what the fat man hands you is purely and totally free, with no obligation, no strings attached, no questions to answer, no card to fill out; and when you taste it, it is so fabulously wonderful—even if it is filled with vegetables, cheeses, meats and other ingredients that you normally wouldn't consume in any combination—then mere food becomes a transcendent, orgasmic, explosively delicious gustatory apotheosis of nothing-matches-everything-fits Contractor Gothic.

And that turns a free meal into a unique experience, an event that people will never forget, a moment of exquisite perfection that they will long for but never be able to repeat, no matter how they try, no matter how many times they return to that triangular intersection, no matter what they order, and how many times they order it.

From contingency, success can grow. A tiny kitchen can expand, with gas burners, a gas grill, a vast walk-in refrigerator and—most significantly for a fat man who turned to drink because his knees and his feet ached from standing up all day—a place to sit down, in front of a window that had a view of a parking area where he would take pictures of people he knew with a cheap camera. Later, the parking area was enclosed—without any attempt to secure zoning variances or appease the city's building code inspectors—becoming a dining room that included three different light fixtures hanging from a dropped ceiling, a row of pews from a church that nobody could remember, twenty-one different tables—including two from a nightclub where Mario Lanza used to sing—and a jukebox, where every third song was sung by some guy from New Jersey named Sinatra.

So nobody wondered why, when the stucco on one of the walls got blotchy and cracked, Orley glued one of his snapshots to the wall. It didn't matter that the picture was so high up nobody could see it. When the crack grew, Orley put up another picture, and another. People who were famous gave him autographed pictures. People who said they were famous also gave him autographed pictures but, then, there were people who wanted to be famous or were certain they were going to be famous soon, and they didn't have pictures, so Orley took their picture and put it on the wall, and it was no surprise that these people would come back and point to their picture and say, "See?"

Orley took pictures of others that he felt deserved their place in the plaster firmament, creating strange, mystical patterns that only he could recognize, until nothing matched and everything fit and a wall became The Wall.

Ladderback opened his eyes when the outside door closed. Usually at this time of day he would not have been able to enter Orley's so easily. On most weekdays, by around 11 A.M. a line extended out the door of the restaurant. Once inside, the line split. You went to the *right* if you were waiting for a chair at one of the twenty-one tables to open up. You went to the *left* if you wanted take-out.

But today the take-out line held only a half-dozen or so, ending at the broad open counter of Orley's kitchen, where a stooped, frail sack of bones sat at the chair Orley used to occupy, talking with an impeccably groomed journalist. The journalist was waving his hands expressively.

That sagging sack of bones was Orley Roberts? The last time Ladderback had seen Orley, the man could have dressed as the Liberty Bell for the Mummer's Parade without needing a costume. Orley had been that big. At a time when lean and mean became watchwords for jogging yuppies, Orley Roberts was hugely, grandly, defiantly fat, with a mane of midnight black, biker-hair falling halfway down to his waist.

The stooping, hollow-cheeked sack of bones in a faded Orley's Emperor of the Steak sweatshirt was infuriated at the reporter. Ladderback saw that one of Orley's hands gripped a stout black cane. The great mane of hair he used to tie behind his head in ponytail had faded to a few wisps that scudded over his mottled skull like a fog burning off a landfill.

Ladderback glanced around the dining room and saw a few open chairs.

"His business is off because of all the cop cars and TV trucks outside," Gina said.

"The mob hit," Ladderback said. She still had her arm in his, and he felt her suddenly drop his arm.

A person who looked like an elongated skeleton in an gray-streaked Elvis pompadour had been sitting with his back to the jukebox. He was wearing the red uniform of a Speed Care emergency services technician. Ladderback saw dark stains on the uniform's sleeves. The man had been sitting, alone, with his back to The Wall. Both the sandwich and the soda in front of him appeared untouched. Beside the soda was an inhaler, a folding knife and a small, open tin of mints. No, not mints, Ladderback saw: pills, tablets, capsules of various sizes and colors.

"Shep, I changed my mind," Gina said. "We're going someplace else."

"He may not recognize you," Ladderback said.

"I'm not worried about being recognized."

"Neither is he," Ladderback said. "You ended our relationship when I told you I had obtained your husband's address and a copy of his driver's license. That address is on Smartt Street, about three blocks from here, near the Speed Care garage. Assuming that he still lives near his place of employment, it's likely that he would come here for his lunch, though, I suspect he has other reasons for lingering."

"I'd rather not be in the same room with him," Gina said.

"I told you, it's unlikely that he'll recognize you," Ladderback said. "You look better than you used to."

"You think so?" The compliment disarmed her. She brushed back her hair and almost blushed. Then she searched his face. "You'd better not still have feelings about me. I never should have let things go as far as they did."

"You put up a valiant struggle," Ladderback said, "but I swept you off your feet."

She smiled and Ladderback felt ten feet tall as he led her to a table in a corner and gallantly moved a chair for her.

"I don't want to sit with my back to him," she said.

"Looks can't kill," Ladderback said.

"But if he sees me, he'll come over. He's normally a wimp. But when he's sucking on that inhaler, he turns into somebody different. The drugs take all the fear away from him."

"If he comes over, we will say hello," Ladderback said. He did not ask her why a woman who liked to crash two-ton automobiles would be afraid of a man so gaunt that a sudden breeze would knock him off his feet. She didn't marry Larry because he scared her. She may have been attracted to his fecklessness, but that would not be enough.

Then Ladderback saw some of the pictures on The Wall and he figured it out. From doing so many thousands of obituaries, Ladderback was aware that the reasons people married were not the reasons that they stayed together. Something else had to happen after the knot was tied, the honeymoon bills paid. Whatever this thing was, it had little to do with the arrival of children, but a great deal to do with learning to care for another human being in ways that were not always obvious.

Ladderback looked past Gina and saw that it was unlikely that Larry Dettweiller would come over in the next few minutes. Larry's attention was aimed at the journalist. Larry was seated too far away to hear what was being said, but he seemed fascinated with the journalist's gestures. It was the same fascination Ladderback imagined he would see on the face of an arsonist, someone who would squat in the shadows of a roaring inferno as firemen struggled to contain a building that he had set on fire.

For a moment Ladderback wondered if he could get Gina to take him outside so he could find Lieutenant Everson, or some police officer investigating the body in the garbage, and tell that officer that there was a man sitting inside who was savoring the commotion, and that this man just might have some information about how that body got into the garbage.

But Ladderback stopped himself: he had no proof, other than a lifetime as a journalist persuading people to tell him things, which gave him a sensitivity to people. It also gave him a temptation to believe an easy truth, and he had only recently been in a situation in which that temptation—regarding the anonymous donor who was paying for Weight Wisnitz's funeral—had led him astray.

Fortunately, he had found his way back.

"One of us is going to have to order," Gina said. "Orley never had table service."

Ladderback turned his attention back to her. "Permit me," he said. He stood.

"Aren't you going to ask me what I want?"

Ladderback said, "I remember what you used to eat before a derby."

"You came up with a name for it," Gina said.

"A Dragon Breath Special."

She shook her head. "Is there anything you forget?"

"My age," Ladderback said.

The girl at the counter in a gold, green and purple Orley's Emperor of the Steak T-shirt did not help Ladderback feel any younger. She was probably in her late teens and her red hair had been snarled into an unruly tangle of dreadlocks that spilled out from under the gold, green and purple Orley's Emperor of the Steak paper cap like an exotic tree fungus. Sharpened, polished pieces of metal stuck out of various places on her face.

Ladderback knew that the fashion for body piercing was into its second decade, and that, like the Elvis pompadours, it had become so much a part of the cultural gush of American life that it no longer signaled identification to any specific group, but it still annoyed him. He reminded himself that his generation did things that were disturbing and annoying to his parent's generation, but he could not figure out why body piercing had persisted. What kind of life do you live when you have an oversized, chromium-plated safety-pin partially embedded in your lip? What happens when you drink a hot liquid? Does it heat up the metal?

He watched the girl go back to the kitchen and return with a bagged take-out order. She gave it to a uniformed cop who was standing on the take-out line, took money from the cop, and made the change. Ladderback acknowledged another custom peculiar to Orley's: everybody paid. Orley's was one of the only restaurants in the city that took money from cops. The cops paid, not merely because they were supposed to, but because, when you can get just about anything you want for free, you will pay proudly for what you can't get, if it is better, or if you happen to be working a case right outside and it doesn't get any more convenient than this.

The officer was a young, dark-skinned man with a shaved head, pencil moustache, and a narrow, triangular patch of beard under his lower lip that an earlier generation would have called a duster. He leaned on the counter to indicate to the girl that he might be interested in her if she was interested in him, and he asked if she put in extra catsup packets.

She gave him a look that said she might be interested in him, but asking for catsup packets was a stupid way to start a conversation. She reached under the counter and came up with three packets, then she turned to the decrepit man at the end of the counter and asked him where he kept the catsup packets.

The journalist paused in his questions to permit Orley to say, in voice that, at one time, could have been heard over the wail of a firehouse siren, but had now been reduced to a low, grinding grumble, "In a box on the wall on back of the cooler, where they always been."

The girl was about to go when the cop said he'd come back later for more. The girl turned to Ladderback and asked him what he was having.

At that moment Ladderback saw that the reporter was one question away from death.

Or a fate that might be worse than death, because journalists who die in the line of duty achieve a level of fame within their profession, regardless of how much they may have contributed, because of their ignorance, negligence or overweening ambition, to their demise.

But journalists who are thwacked on the skull with a cane and end up blowing their deadline while waiting to have their X rays read in a hospital emergency room discover that their editors have plenty of time to postulate that the reporter may have done something stupid to antagonize the source.

Orley Roberts certainly seemed antagonized. The hand holding the cane was shaking, the knuckles white.

From doing obituaries about shopkeepers and other small business-men who dealt with the public, Ladderback had learned that anyone who dealt with the public on a daily basis, and had a cash register nearby, usually kept some kind of crude weapon—a baseball bat, a monkey wrench, or a length of pipe—under the counter, in easy reach. These weapons only rarely stopped robberies because most robberies happened so fast and, if the shopkeeper came out with a weapon instead cash, the stick-up man would shoot to kill, and flee.

The under-the-counter weapon's true function was giving the person at the cash register an object that, in the best of all possible worlds, would encourage obnoxious customers to take their business elsewhere. According to legend, Orley Roberts's weapon of choice had been an enormous meat cleaver, the same cleaver that he used to cut impossibly thin slices of meat for his steak sandwiches.

But Orley also had bad knees, so it stood to reason that he'd might use a cane. From the way Orley was gripping that cane, it might very well have been a meat cleaver, and, as Ladderback approached and heard what the journalist was saying, it was easy to imagine Orley using it.

"I said it at the beginning and I'm saying it again," the reporter announced, waving the hand that held the pen. "I'm not leaving until you tell me."

"I already told you what I told Everson," Orley said in a voice like unlubricated metal parts grinding together. "Somebody cut up like that, with no head and no hands, it could be anybody."

"Orley, we've been through this. You were there when Chickie talked to me. You heard him open up to me," he said, making stabbing motions with his pen. "I can stand here all day until you tell me you at least have an *idea* who her father was."

Orley's face grew dark. He pulled his cane back so he could whip it over the counter when Ladderback stepped in and quietly asked, "Are you Drew Shaw?"

Shaw paused, turned. "Do I know you?"

"You write for *Liberty Bell*," Ladderback said. "I've read your work."

Shaw nodded. "Well, if you'll excuse me, I'm conducting an interview here."

Ladderback turned to Orley. "I've admired your food for many years, Mr. Roberts."

"We try," Orley said.

Shaw gave Ladderback a look that said he was really annoyed that Ladderback was in the same room with him.

If you were watching him, you wouldn't be able to see quite how he did it, because, in the next few seconds, nothing about Ladderback seemed to change. But, if Andy Cosicki had been in the room, and you asked her, she would tell you that Ladderback had a way of transforming himself from a soft, flabby, harmless old guy you wouldn't pay any attention to, into a presence so quietly formidable that you could not ignore him, no matter how hard you tried.

Ladderback introduced himself. "I write obituaries for the *Philadelphia Press*."

Shaw tried to hide his annoyance. "Right. I think I know somebody who knows you."

"You did the write-up about Weight," Orley said. "How come you didn't come to me about Michelle?"

Ladderback did not explain that obituary writers are rarely asked to contribute to news items. He could tell that Orley would rather talk to him—or anyone—than suffer under Shaw's questions.

So Ladderback gave Orley an opening. "I'm sorry you were not called," Ladderback said. "What would you have told me?"

"I woulda told you a lot," Orley said. "She started here. Michelle did. And, you know, she went on, she opened those other places with that other kid, Plank, but she always came back. She always kept in touch. Even when she moved out, to New York, she'd come in and share a word. She wasn't like they say she was. Sure, she had a gripe, she was angry a lot, but Michelle had a hard life. She had a problem with drink. Like I had, but I licked it. Last time she was here, a coupla months ago, she ask me, how I did it—I told her. She'd tell me how she tried this and that but nothing was working, and then she found what she thought was working. I told her, nothing's going to work for you, when it comes to food or drink. You gotta control it all by yourself. You gotta do it for yourself. You can't rely on nobody or nothing."

Ladderback wanted to ask Orley if what Michelle Fragg thought had helped her with her drinking problem was a pill, but Drew Shaw said, "She talk about Matt Plank wanting her dead?"

"They was a pair," Orley said. "They both worked for me. On again, off again. I caught them going at each other in the cooler."

"Fighting?" Shaw asked.

"Fucking," Orley said.

"Great," Shaw said. "Now, I still have these questions . . ."

"I believe Mr. Roberts has already answered them," Ladderback said to Shaw. "Your speculations are wrong."

Shaw frowned, as if to signal to the world that he did not want interference from a mere obituary writer, but because Ladderback was interfering, and because Ladderback was a journalist, and because Shaw had told Orley that he would not leave until Orley answered his questions, Shaw said, "When I got Chickie Marandola to open up, before he was hit, it was right here, in this very place, and I saw he had a ring on his finger, it was stuck between the joints on his fingers so he couldn't pull it off, and I asked if he was into family values, and he told me that it wasn't a wedding band, that it was actually a metal gasket, a part for his Porsche, and that some girl put it on one day after he screwed her, and he never took it off because he found he could get more women to screw him with him being a mob boss with a wedding band on, than not. I said, 'So much for family values,' and he got this faraway look in his eye, and he told me that he really did have a daughter, with this girl when he was around my age, and that I shouldn't mention it in the article because, if I said that, some people might figure it out and go after her to get to him and . . ."

"I read your interview, in which you said nothing about Mr. Marandola's daughter," Ladderback said. "In your current piece you mention a 'next generation.' What you attempted to hide is that you have no idea who that next generation is."

"Chickie said he'd find me and kill me and eat a piece of me if I did," Shaw added proudly.

Ladderback looked across the dining room. "Where were you sitting when you did the interview?"

"That table next to the jukebox where that ambulance guy is," Shaw said.

Orley said, "That was Chickie's place. He'd have the jukebox going when he wanted to talk. He figured anybody wearing a wire, the music would drown out what he said."

"What did he eat?" Ladderback asked.

"It varied," Orley said. "He was a big eater. He liked double portions. He couldn't leave nothing on his plate, he'd have to finish it all. He was big on the garlic sausage, and the hot sausage, too, with this cheese from Italy he asked me to bring in just for him that really put out a stink. He liked anything that would make his breath bad. He liked to go up to people and breathe on 'em and watch 'em wilt. Except at the end, though. He would come in and meet people and he would order but he wouldn't eat."

Ladderback made sure not to look at Larry Dettweiler when he asked, "Would he meet with the ambulance driver who is sitting in there now?"

"Not him," Orley said. "That's Larry Dead Elvis. Lives on Smartt Street, in Chickie's old place. He comes in here, orders what Chickie used to, but, most of the time, he sits and plays with that folding knife. All the EMTs carry knifes like that so they can cut off people's clothes if they have to get to them. But Larry Dead, he'd play with the knife because Chickie had a knife and he liked being like Chickie. When Chickie was alive, Larry Dead would always get out of that seat when Chickie'd come in and go sit someplace else, or leave, most of the time. You see people like Larry Dead, around the mob guys, they act like the mob guys, eat what the mob guys eat, dress like 'em, if they can afford it. They want to be a mob guy because they think the mob guys got something they don't."

Shaw said, "Chickie was a man of respect."

"He was a piece a shit, is what he was," Orley said. "It's only you guys in the media that play up scum like him. We all knew he was scum. It was only a matter a time before he'd get himself dead."

Ladderback asked, "When Mr. Marandola left, would this ambulance driver return to the same table?"

"He would," Orley said. "But he'd gas himself with that inhaler thing first."

Ladderback turned to Shaw. "You believe that the woman who was killed today was Marandola's illegitimate daughter."

"You bet I do," Shaw said. "It's obvious!"

"It is not obvious," Ladderback said. "It is reckless, sensational speculation that will draw attention to you and your magazine, but this attention might also become embarrassing if the police, or any other source, proves your guess incorrect. Because you don't want to be blamed if your guess turns out wrong, you're trying to extract from Mr. Roberts the kind of answers that you can quote to make it appear that he is the source of your speculation."

Shaw pointed his pen at him. "The daughter was killed by the same people who killed the father. It makes sense. That's the way these mob guys think. Probably some Spanish mob, or the Asians. They're supposed to be coming on strong."

"We must be careful when we make statements about how people think," Ladderback said. "It is possible that the opposite might be true: that whoever was responsible for Mr. Marandola's death, would want his daughter to live, as an atonement for the sin of taking her father's life."

"You're the one who's wrong," Shaw said to Ladderback. He turned to Orley. "If you won't tell me what I want to hear, I can find somebody who will."

He put his pen in his jacket pocket and walked out.

"I should've hit him," Orley said. "Woulda messed up his face."

"It wouldn't have helped," Ladderback said.

"But it would've hurt."

"What else would you have told me about Michelle?" Ladderback asked Orley.

Orley looked him over. "That would depend on what you asked me."

"I would ask you why you cared about her."

"And I'd've told you that, of all the folks I give breaks to, Michelle was the only one that would come back and visit. Some of them, they go on, they get rich and famous, they don't want it known that they worked in a steak joint. Not Michelle. She was proud of it, every day of her life."

"I would ask you what she ate when she visited."

"I'd give her an apron and turn her loose. She knew what it was about. You have the best ingredients, you don't try to force 'em to be anything than what they are, you have respect for the people that's doing the eating, and, it don't matter much how you put it together or what you call it, it's going to taste okay. It's going to satisfy. Michelle learned that from me."

Ladderback looked Orley over. "I would also ask you if she was on medication that last time you saw her."

"She was taking those pills they tried to give me at the free clinic. The ones Dr. Johnny said was interesting."

"That would Dr. Juan Sungaigutung, the director of the Brideshead Free Clinic?"

"I go to the Clinic when I need to, and he said to me one day that they was giving the pills out for appetite reduction—you were supposed to take 'em and check back with him. He just put 'em in my hand and I've never been the kind to turn down what somebody give me, but I didn't take 'em, because, I saw Chickie take 'em, for the same reasons, and he keeled over right stone dead in front of my eyes. When Dr. Johnny put them pills in my hand, I said to myself, enough is enough. No more going overboard on the drinking and the eating."

"Some people would have a problem explaining how Mr. Marandola died. Others might not have believed he died from the pills."

"People believe what they want, no matter what you tell 'em."

"So this body had to be disposed of."

"Your food's getting cold," Orley said. "You want to find out about all that stuff, you ask the lady you came in with. She was there."

"I'm sure she was," Ladderback said. "With her daughter. She was visiting the father."

"That was her."

"But not her husband."

"I told you, Larry Dead stayed away when Chickie was around."

The food arrived. "Thank you for speaking with me, Mr. Roberts," Ladderback said.

"You should eat before it gets cold."

Ladderback turned and took a few steps. Then he paused to gaze at The Wall. It reminded him of the huge portraits, made up of thousands of Polaroid pictures, that the artist Chuck Close used to do. The Polaroids themselves contained a variety of peculiar, contradictory images, but, when arranged as part of a composition, the images became subsumed into a vivid, larger-than-life effigy.

On The Wall were snapshots of people, most of them seated, nearly all of them smiling and holding a sandwich. A few pictured were seated in wheelchairs, or had crutches leaning against a table, but all you really saw was varying degrees of happiness as a function of proximity to food. The Wall showed none of life's misfortune, no bad breaks, no missed opportunities, no delineation of the sinned and the sinned against.

He noted a few faces that he thought he recognized, such as the shot of a young but elegantly dressed Drew Shaw hunched down at the table by the jukebox, seated before a pale, starved Chickie Marandola, his black hair flecked with gray, and in the background, out of focus, was a woman with a young girl and that girl looked like she had some kind of patch on her eye.

It was one of several photographs of Marandola. One, of a much younger man, showed him holding a baby in one hand, and a sandwich in the other, and the baby looking as if it had every right to get its picture taken.

Ladderback saw a flash of the uniform Gina used to wear when she went to the demolition derbies. Was that him, that youngster gazing lustfully at her, with the glasses and the badly knotted necktie, holding a sandwich with tiny Brussels sprouts popping out of the sauted sirloin? The picture was so old, most of the colors had faded—the Brussels sprouts in the sandwich were now blue gray, instead of bright green. But Gina's uniform was still a bright, Day-Glo pink, her lips red and open, her eyes glowing with child-like delight that Orley had wanted to take her picture.

Ladderback saw that this was not the only picture of Gina on The Wall. There she was, again, beside the man she had been with at her mother's funeral, a man who was definitely not Larry Dead Elvis.

And there was the same man with an apple—no, a plum, in his mouth—holding a sandwich in one hand, a plastic bag of what might be vegetables—no, plums, in another. Ladderback could almost hear the man saying, "You've got weight!"

He let his eyes wander and saw a photo of a young Matt Plank and—yes—the Angry Eater herself, Michelle Fragg, with a face that was not yet marred by alcoholism. She held a sandwich across her chest and a huge meat cleaver in the air, aping the Statue of Liberty. Both were wearing grease-stained aprons and paper Orley's Emperor of the Steak hats.

Could that be Danny Bleutner sharing a sandwich with the man who, in another picture, had been sitting next to Gina and Carol?

And was that Dr. Alex Elgin with some bizarre sandwich on his plate, next to a Asian-looking fellow in a white lab smock?

Ladderback was aware that Larry Dead Elvis was staring at him. Ladderback kept his attention fixed upon The Wall.

If only Shaw were still here. Ladderback would show him these pictures, and others, and then ask him if, after seeing these pictures, his half-baked speculations were as obvious as he might have wanted them to be. Then he would lead Shaw back to the counter, and show Shaw that, from where Orley sat, these pictures formed a larger image of the city, a great work of art that didn't answer questions as much as it presented itself, as an answer.

What was the answer? That people were linked in ways they would never fully know or comprehend, that those who had something they liked, or that they thought might help them lose weight, stop drinking, control themselves, wanted nothing more than to share it. If the pills were from a drug factory, or deliberately sold into the underground economy, or secretly tested on the poor and uneducated who patronized the city's free clinics, those pills did not stay put. They were given to others who might need them, or benefit.

Ladderback set the tray of food and drinks down in front of Gina. "I want to meet your husband," he said.

Gina pretended she hadn't heard him. She was inhaling her Dragon Breath Special. She gave a sour eye to the sandwich that Ladderback had ordered for himself.

"What the hell is that?" she asked him.

"Scungilli sauteed in scallions, with melted Asiago cheese," Ladderback said. "Orley described it as an experiment."

"I can think of another word," Gina said. She watched Ladderback take a bite.

"It's delicious," Ladderback said, sipping a birch beer.

She bit into hers, closed her eyes. "Yes," she said. "Oh, yes."

"Is it like you remembered?"

"Close enough," Gina said.

Ladderback waited.

She took another bite, chewed and swallowed. "Why you want to meet Larry?"

"He may have information I need."

"He ain't going to give it to you."

"He might if you're with me."

"There have been no words between him and me since he walked out."

She was lying to him. He let the silence descend. Then he heard a cell phone ring with the opening bars of "Love Me Tender." Ladderback saw Larry remove the phone from a uniform pocket, put it to his ear. Within seconds, Larry had packed up his pills, his inhaler and his knife, and was heading out of the room.

Gina watched him go. She relaxed then.

"I could never figure out why you were so afraid of him," Ladderback said.

"I wasn't," Gina said. "Even when he was on something, I knew I could beat him. I always could. I just didn't want him around. He was doing drugs before I knew about him, back when he was driving the wrecker for his father. He never liked working on cars. He never liked minding the station, or doing the books, or anything else that would've made him useful. He never even liked girls, which bothered Larry, Sr. like you wouldn't believe."

"Did it bother Sonja?"

"More than it bothered Larry, Sr. She was always trying to fix him up with girls. . . ." She closed her eyes and Ladderback thought he saw her forcing back a tear.

"She fixed him up with you?"

She shook her head. "Shep, when I met you, and you did that article, I was more scared of you, because I didn't know how much you'd find out. I was more scared of you than anybody I'd ever met."

"I never imagined that you could be afraid of me," Ladderback said. "It was never really my nature to pry."

"But you did it to me anyway."

Now it was his turn to hold back, to have the secret that he so dearly wanted to tell. She had to ask the right question.

He chewed on his sandwich. Gina wasn't asking him the question. She was starting to cry.

"Gina," Ladderback began as she put a paper napkin to her face.

"Shut up," she said.

"I have to tell you . . ."

"Whatever you have to tell me, I don't have to listen."

He wanted to tell her that the only reason he pried was that he had really loved her, and that when you love someone, you feel that everything you do for another person can be the right thing, the best thing, the very thing that other person needs. He wanted to tell her that he became a journalist because he thought it would be swank and stylish, like those martini-swilling, New York wits at the Algonquin round table, and that he never, ever wanted to investigate anyone or anything, but, when he met her, and her daughter, and saw how much pain she was feeling about her marriage, he had believed what little she had told him about Larry abandoning her, and that he believed, naively, that if she couldn't find him, he might.

He wanted to tell her that, in wanting to help her, he had discovered a new world of records and record keepers, dusty City Hall storage rooms, obscure sources and endless Internet addresses.

"You married Larry because he did you a favor," Ladderback said.

"Larry?" she snapped at him. "He couldn't do a favor for a dog. He'd sit around, listening to music in the wrecker, with the police radio on, so he could hear about traffic accidents. Then he'd suck up that stuff, go out with the truck, to try to get the tow. That stuff he took, it rotted his brain."

"You knew this, but you married him."

"I took what I could get," she said. She bit into her sandwich. "Shep, you're going to drop this right now, or I swear, I'm turning around and leaving you here."

"I'll drop it," Ladderback said, "if you agree to take me somewhere else."

"I'm not some goddamn chauffeur."

"We can walk. I'll help you if you'll help me."

"I don't need your help. Where you planning on walking?"

"The Mount of Olives," Ladderback glanced at his watch. "We should arrive promptly."

"For what?"

"Your brother's funeral. You paid for it. You should see if everything was done to your liking."

# 17 street hungry

The R5 Paoli local had just left the Overbrook Station and had gone ten yards into the tunnel under City Avenue when it slowed and stopped. After a minute, Andy asked the conductor what was wrong.

"Track work," the conductor said. "Beautification project. They can't do the work during peak hours so, this being off-peak, we're down one line. There's the Amtrak to Harrisburg coming up about two minutes behind us. We have to let Amtrak pass."

Andy sat down. She tried to call her mother and got her voice mail again. The connection began to cut in and out because the train had stopped in the tunnel. "Karyn's been killed," Andy said. "I think Elgin had something to do with it. Call me as soon as you can. I'll be at the house."

She didn't hang up because the connection had cut out. She tried dialing again but the phone was down.

She was less than a mile from her house. She asked the conductor if she could get out of the train and walk.

"You ever read the *Philadelphia Press*?" the conductor asked her.

"Sure," Andy said. "Why?"

"Well, there's this thing in it called Mr. Action, where people ask questions and somebody asked Mr. Action why it was, when the train is stopped, they can't get out and just walk on the tracks, like they couldn't slip and twist their ankle or get run over by an express. Mr. Action said, 'What are you, stupid? You can't wait like a normal human being? Train tracks and people don't mix.' "

The statement was grotesque. Andy never called a reader stupid. Besides, train tracks are made of metal, people are made of flesh! Andy would never write anything so clumsy. "When did you read this?" Andy said.

"A year ago. I used to read it all the time but now they have some new guy doing it and . . ."

"And what," Andy asked.

"It isn't as good. The new guy's too serious, you know?"

Andy sat down and waited. And waited and waited.


They were back in the truck, but Gina wouldn't start it.

"I can't, Shep. I can't go into the Mount of Olives. All those people used to know me. . . ."

"We can just sit here, then," Ladderback said. "We can remember him here."

"What I remember, when I'm here, isn't Sid. It's Chickie. Chickie and Carol. We used to come here and meet him, when he wanted us to meet him. Chickie never stayed away from Carol, and Carol never stayed away from him. I couldn't stop the man from visiting her—she was his daughter. But I didn't like him coming around the station. He'd drop his car off, and I'd work on his car, but it got to the point . . . he'd have to send another of his goons around. Sometimes even Larry would come by."

"So you did see him."

"Not as rarely as I liked. I didn't want her growing up to be like either of them. I kept telling her not to make the mistake I did, not to have sex with the first guy that came along—wait until you're treated decent. But I don't know what went on when he took her away with him. He used her in his scams and I hated that. I hated all of that."

Ladderback said nothing.

"I know what you're thinking. That, if I was so much a fighter, how come I didn't fight him. Because that would be a fight I'd lose. I wimped out. He took her down to Atlantic City and got her into the blackmailing racket. She got in a lot of trouble, that girl, but, from as much trouble as he got her into, he also kept her out of worse."

"The Atlantic City gambler who dropped the charges?"

"More than that. She was doing that whip thing with some jerk, and it came back and took out a piece of her face, right under her left eye. Chickie got a plastic surgeon to fix it, but it took a long time."

"Did Marandola want her to go after Elgin?"

"That I don't know. I know that she'd get restaurant jobs in Atlantic City and use the jobs to scout out the kind of men who would want what she had to offer. But, from what I heard, she got the job by herself. She met Elgin and it was his idea to put her on the drug testing program so he could pay her for the things she did to him without it coming out of his pocket. That's when she started coming back from his office with the pills."

"The appetite suppressor?"

"He was supposed to be testing an early version of one. She got some pills because she thought Chickie would like them."

"To sell?"

"To take. Chickie had put on some pounds. He rode in that car with the seat all the way back. But the real problem was he liked to . . . anybody he killed, he'd use the knife . . ."

"He would consume a small portion of the flesh," Ladderback said. "Some serial killers have the same tendency. I came across the case of a Russian serial killer who also carried a frying pan, olive oil, and a heat source."

"Shep, please. There were other reasons I couldn't marry the man."

"So Carol thought the drug would restrict his cannibalism?"

"I guess. She gave the pills to him. What she didn't know was that Chickie was never the kind who took his medicine as directed. He ate the pills like candy—at least, I'd see him doing that when I'd take Carol to meet him at Orley's."

"Did you notice any physical change in him?"

"Plenty. He stopped eating. He stopped drinking. He'd try to force himself, but it was like he was starving to death."

Ladderback remembered The Wall's final picture of Marandola as he was being interviewed by Drew Shaw: he was pale and cadaverous. "The drug irritated the lining of the throat and upper gastrointestinal system," Ladderback said. "In every situation, the victims coughed up blood."

"Well, with Chickie, it came out the other end. It was horrible. What happened was . . ."


It was late enough so that anyone eating dinner had long gone home. When Chickie walked in, just about everyone in Orley's Emperor of the Steak got up and left. Most people who knew him didn't like hanging around in his presence. And, unless he turned on the charm, those who didn't know him could sense from his jerky movements and expensive but ill-fitting clothes, that Chickie reeked of the kind of trouble that nobody wanted.

Drew Shaw came in and didn't recognize Chickie. Few people did because the hair Chickie had kept dyed midnight black was streaked with gray. His eyes were bloodshot, his skin was the color of caulking compound and hanging off his bones like a lavatory papertowel that somebody had used but didn't pull down and throw away.

Shaw swaggered up to the counter and announced that he was doing an article for *Liberty Bell* magazine in which he went around to various places in the city and tried to find the "most unique" junk food in the city, and what did they have to offer?

Orley Roberts, who was as huge as the Liberty Bell itself, gave Drew the once over, and decided that Shaw just might be for real. He replied, "You should see what people eat."

Shaw made a crack about the guy by the jukebox talking with Carol. "What does he think he is, some kind of wiseguy?"

Chickie looked up. "And who do we have here?"

"Depends on what you're eating," Shaw said. "If it's strange, I just might write you up in *Liberty Bell*."

Chickie looked at Carol. "Wow. Such a treat. Sad thing to say, I ain't been eating much of nothing. Not as much as I should."

Still, Chickie had a sandwich in front of him that he hadn't touched. It was not as spicy as his usual, because the pills made it impossible for him to eat hot peppers. He could eat sweet things, though. In fact, he'd developed a ravenous appetite for plums.

"This here is, I guess you could call it a sweet steak. It's got the meat and, these things in it, those are plums."

Carol pretended to put her finger down her thoat. Chickie gave her a look that said, beat it. She went back to the table where Gina sat, hoping Chickie wasn't going to kill anyone tonight.

Shaw came close enough to examine the sandwich. He didn't see Chickie reach into his sport coat. "I never heard of anybody putting fruit on a cheesesteak," Shaw said. "That's almost disgusting. You're not really going to eat that."

That's when Chickie got that wild look in his eyes like when he was driving and he was about to run over a pigeon. "Nahh. You're going to eat it."

"Actually, that's not necessary. All I do is just ask you some questions—"

The knife came out, just like that, and because Chickie was Chickie, the point of the blade wasn't at Shaw's throat, or in one of Shaw's nostrils.

No, Chickie had the blade right under Shaw's eye, where—Shaw wouldn't know this but Chickie did—Carol got hit with the whip.

Orley growled from the counter, "Put it away, Chickie. This is a place a business. Act respectable. Both a you."

Shaw being Shaw, he moved back a tiny bit. Then he moved back a whole lot. He stepped back so he could see Chickie and Orley, who seemed unperturbed, like he was used to yelling at cadaverous, half-dead smartly dressed guys named—

"You're Chickie Marandola!" Shaw exclaimed.

Chickie being Chickie, he didn't much like it when just anybody used his street name. He folded the knife and said, "Mr. Carmen Gigliano Marandola to you."

"Damn!" Shaw said. He swallowed. He looked at the sandwich. Then he sat down in front of Chickie, picked it up and took a bite.

And, you should know, that though it is unlikely in Philadelphia to find anyone who would put plums on a cheesesteak, mobsters do have some influence, and, to the command "could you do something with plums," Orley's latest chef had peeled and sliced the plums and then simmered them in plum brandy, sugar, and just a dash of grated lemon peel, so that, when tasted with lightly grilled—not fried—sirloin, and the grilled red onions tossed in to create a color transition, the flavors combined into an explosively rich sensation similar to the more startling chutneys, beet relishes and Cumberland-type berry sauces, slathered over perfectly seared beef.

"This is spectacular!" Shaw said with his mouth full. "You eat this all the time?" He pulled out his pad and Chickie smirked and said, "You write down what I eat, I'll kill ya."

Shaw stopped chewing.

Chickie began to talk with his hands. "A man in my position," Chickie went on, turning on the charm that is given to the lethally insane, "has to guard his reputation. You put it out that Chickie's eating freaky, people'll think Chickie's not so much a badass motherfucker anymore, so I'll have to, you know, cut somebody open and eat a piece of their flesh or a take chunk out of one of their organs, you know, just to restore myself to respectability. But why bother when you and me can sit here and I can watch you as you eat, and I can remember what it was like when I wanted to eat every single thing on my plate, and your plate and his plate, and every fucking plate in this city."

Shaw put the sandwich down.

Chickie stuck his finger in the juices leaking from the sandwich and rubbed it against his lips. "This is as far as I get now. I take a taste. It hurts when I swallow. Burns like the hell people think I'm going to. I try to eat now, and I can feel it waiting for me. But you can take it all. You can put in ya mouth. Yeah. Right like that. Put ya teeth on it. Don't worry about the juice on your face. Let it come out. Let it get all over. That's it."

He watched Shaw eat for a while. Then he said. "So. Let's be honest. You didn't come here to bullshit around about food."

Shaw had, actually. But he couldn't say that.

"Nahh," Chickie said. "You want to know why somebody like me, who can eat in any place in town, would be here, right here, in this very spot. Am I right?"

Shaw nodded.

Chickie said, "Get out that thing you write things down on. Get it out. You ready? I am here because I am hearing from my very own daughter that I am too much street hungry. You don't say nothing about my daughter, but you can say I am a street hungry type. And get this: I am learning to control my appetite."

So began Chickie Marandola's last interview, which, this being Orley's, was of interest only to Drew Shaw. Carol had heard her father talk about himself and knew that once he got on his favorite subject, he was lost. Gina thought about the cars she had waiting for her and hoped this ordeal, like all the times she and Carol came to Orley's to meet the man who ruined Gina's life, would be over soon.

It was, soon enough. A grateful Drew Shaw got the remnants of his Sweet Steak wrapped up to take home. He went over and thanked Chickie again, but Chickie waved him off. Shaw left and Chickie closed his eyes. His hands were still and it was only until Shaw left and Chickie did not move that Carol came over and saw the blood on the sides of her father's shoes, and on his socks, and on the insides of his pants. She touched his cooling skin, and figured that he had gone to the hell that everyone had wanted him to go to, including her.

She came back and whispered in her mother's ear, "He's gone."

And that was when Carol learned that, as much as her mother had hated her father, she had not wanted him to go.

No, even for the worst, most miserable, piece-a-shit, son-of-bitch in the world, there was someone who would grieve.

For one minute. Or two.

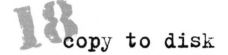

# 18 copy to disk

She called her mother on the way to the house, and this time, her mother picked up, but she was in a cab in New York and her phone started cutting in and out, though Andy heard her say that she had called Dr. Elgin and that Andy didn't have to go to the house, she should go home, instead, and sleep it off.

"Sleep WHAT off?" Andy shouted so loudly that some birds in the trees on Albemarle Way fluttered off.

"Whatever it is you got," Charlotte said, and the connection died.

To make sure it wasn't her cell phone, Andy dialed the number for Double Czech Home Security. This time Tom Polidos was in and, yes, he could tell her about some of the newer zoned video security systems with Internet access, but there were many, many kinds of systems out there and—

"Just hold on, I'm trying to remember my access code," Andy said. She was standing at the kitchen door of her house. "My memory's been screwing up all day. Some things I remember, some things I can't. Some things I don't want to remember."

"It's usually a birthday," Polidos said.

Andy punched hers in and, yes, it was.

She was in the house, smelling that chemical aroma, and up the stairs, into what had been her father's old office.

Polidos asked her to describe the equipment. She did. Polidos said he had seen one of those systems demonstrated at a security technology show in Atlantic City. "State of the art," he said, "for about five minutes."

Andy asked him how to get a video playback. Polidos asked her if there was a keyboard plugged into one of the modules and Andy said there was.

"If you have a chair handy, you'd better sit down."

Andy looked around and saw her father's old chair. She pulled it up and sat in it.

"Depending on how much the owner of the system trusts you, your access code should act as a password."

"The owner is my mother and I don't know if she trusts me. I never trusted her and I can't remember ever asking her."

"Well, you never stop learning about family. Type your code in, hit 'enter' and tell me what happens."

Andy did so. One of the screens went dark and Andy heard a hard drive hidden somewhere make gurgling sounds.

"She trusts me," Andy said, waiting. "She trusts me not. She—"

The screen flashed HI ANDREA!

"—Trusts me." Andy smiled.


"Whose idea was it to cut him up?" Ladderback asked.

"We didn't know what to do with him," Gina said. "We couldn't just carry him out. People might see something. A guy like Chickie, he would have people working for him who might get the idea that we killed him, or we set him up to be killed. It would have started another mob war and we didn't want to start anything. We wanted it all to be over.

"So Orley locked the front door, sent his cooks home. He cleared the place out of everybody but him, Carol and me. Then Orley called Owen."

"Glendower."

"He came in through the back, with a black bag, like doctors used to carry. He said we had to carry Chickie out to the Mount of Olives but there was no way any of us were going to touch Chickie. Owen said he wanted to call an ambulance but with Chickie having a piece of the ambulance company, we didn't want that, either."

"It was Carol who told Owen that he had to do something to Chickie so nobody would recognize it was him. Owen said there was no way he'd do any such thing, out of consideration for the family. That's when Carol said that she was his family. Owen thought about it for a minute. He told Orley to get him as many paper towels as he had, and to keep his oven on so he could burn the clothes and the towels when he was done."

"What happened to his shoes?"

"I never asked. I never asked about his knife, either.

"Then Owen said I should have my brother meet him at the back of Orley's in two hours."

"So your brother scattered his remains," Ladderback said.

"It wasn't Weight. We couldn't find him. Well, I found him, in my old house, drunk and passed out in the same bed he slept in as a kid. I found the keys to his truck, but it wasn't him."

"You?"

"I drove. Carol tossed out the parts."

"No one saw you?"

"Plenty of people saw us but they thought we were doing what people do all the time when they're driving around the city and eating something. When you're done with it, you wrap it in a napkin and throw it out the window. Owen had everything wrapped up real nice in those no-name paper napkins Orley had. There wasn't any blood. They didn't really look like pieces of anything that you could fit together. We threw them wherever we didn't think anybody would look. We did it all over so that, even if they figured out it was him, they wouldn't know how it happened, or where, or with who. Nobody would fight about it because nobody would be sure who did it. And nobody would want to know."

"As I recall," Ladderback said, "the first part the police identified was the ring finger of his left hand. He wore an automobile part, a valve of some kind, in place of a wedding band, and the finger was found with the ring removed, though traces of metal were found on the skin. The finger was found on Smartt Street, near the house he used to live in."

Gina said nothing.

Ladderback asked, "Was that what you were wearing when I saw you and your brother and Carol at Sonja's funeral?"

"He put that on when he first got to me," Gina said. "I said there was no way I was going to make love to no man in no car unless he had a ring on his finger. I asked Owen to give it to me. I put it on for a while. I wore it when we said good-bye to Sonja."

"That was your brother I saw you with, at Sonja's funeral."

"Larry said he had to work that shift. I invited him though. She was his mother. But he didn't show because Sonja never liked him much. She wanted him to be something other than what he was."

"What is he?"

"A loser."

He took her hand in his. "You're not wearing it now."

She let his hand stay. "I put it in a coffee can I have. Spare valves. It's a Porsche part. You don't want to just throw Porsche parts away."

With his other hand, Ladderback opened his coat and handed her a CD.

"What's this?"

"A collection of songs by Billie Holiday. She lived in Philadelphia for a while. Did you know that?"

"Shep, if you're trying to tell me something with this . . ."

"It's just something to listen to on the way."

"To where?"

He gave her an address in Brideshead, on Smartt Street. "It's the house you used to live in."

"I don't want to see it anymore." She put the CD in the player. Billie Holiday broke into "God Bless the Child."

"When you lived here, you went by the name of Imogene. Imogene C. Wisnitz. Your parents named your brother after a very popular television

306

comedian. They named his sister Imogene after Sid Caesar's foil, Imogene Coca."

"I hated that name. Didn't you hate being called Shep?"

"I learned to accept it," he said. "A name need not shape our destiny. It is, like most gifts from parents, more meaningful to the giver. I take it that you, and not Larry, named your daughter after Carol Burnett?"

"I was pregnant and feeling down and I had the TV set on and she made me laugh."

"No doubt your parents felt the same way, or your mother did, when she was pregnant with your brother."

"My mother threw me out when she found out Chickie got me pregnant. I had to go somewhere. Larry Senior's gas station was on my brother's route. My brother and I didn't look that much alike, so, when Sid brought me up, he pretended like I was just another bag of tomatoes he wanted to unload. He went up to Larry Senior with me, told Larry I knew all about cars from helping my dad, and he said the magic words, 'You got weight,' and Larry Senior let me work, let me sleep in the office when I told him I didn't have a place I wanted to come back to. Larry Senior took to me like the son he never had. It was him that wanted me to marry Larry Jr."

"But he did marry you," Ladderback said.

"All Junior cared about were uppers, because Larry liked to drive and driving on uppers can be a blast, if you like uppers. Later he got into inhalers. I never had any need for them: I liked stuff like booze, that slowed me down. But as long as Chickie kept Larry in uppers, he was fine, driving the tow truck, and then delivery trucks, finally getting his EMT license so he could drive the ambulances. Larry and I slept in the same bed, but he never touched me because, he knew Chickie'd kill him if he did. Also, guys who are on uppers, some of them, they just can't follow through. On anything. Then, when Senior got shot in the holdup, Larry walked out."

Ladderback waited as Billie Holiday sang a wounded, but bemused, "I Get a Kick Out of You."

She was quiet for a while. The song changed to "Say It Isn't So."

Ladderback said, "You asked me once how it's possible to fall in love with the wrong people, and I didn't have an answer then and I still don't."

She let go of his hand. "You were always so fucking smart. You'd get freaky sometimes when we were outside. You read books and listened to classical music and you didn't know shit about cars."

"I listen to popular music. Most of what we call classical music was very popular in its day. Billie Holiday was very popular in her day. The music you listen to was also popular. I enjoyed learning about cars from you. I could not . . . get enough of you."

Ladderback forced his eyes open and saw the tears shining on her face. He groped for her hand. "You fell in love with the right person, Gina. It's my fault that we didn't stay together. When you ended what we had, I should have fought for our relationship. I should have fought you, I should have convinced you that it would have been better for us to stay together."

"You would've lost. I didn't want you finding out about me. I didn't want you knowing how I felt about myself. But I guess, you found out about that, too. Is there anything you didn't find out about me?"

"I never found out why you fell in love with me," Ladderback said. "But I'm not one to pry."

"So how come there's no sound?" Andy said as the security system began scanning for recently recorded images.

"Funny thing about the surveillance business," Tom Polidos explained to her on the phone. "You can set up a camera and capture anything that happens on your property, because, as the owner, you have a degree of ownership over visual events on your property as long as you don't intend to publish or sell images you've obtained of another person or a copywritten object, without consent. Got that?"

"I think so." The video images began to appear in thumbnail windows on the screen.

"Don't feel bad if you don't. Now, if it's your property, and you put up a camera, you don't even have to warn people that you have a camera on site, unless people are paying you money to use the space and that part of what they're paying for is the presumption of privacy. If they haven't paid for the use of the property, if they're just passing through, then the property owner is considered an amateur photographer making home movies."

She saw some of the images contained two people, others three, one had four, but they were too small to see distinctly.

"But if you put in a microphone to record sound, or you rig the phones to transmit ambient sounds, even when they're not in use, you're eavesdropping, and that's protected by the Constitution and you need a warrant, or you'd better have one, if somebody finds out their voice has been recorded without their consent and you want that recording admitted as evidence in a criminal proceeding."

"So anybody can take anybody's picture, but nobody can listen in?"

"Not quite. But that's why you have no video and sound in home surveillance systems, not yet, at least." She heard him tapping on a keyboard. "Every surveillance system has an image recorder. This system saves to the hard drive and then dumps on an older analog videotape recorder, but it will also upload images over the Internet."

"So my mother can watch from New York."

"Which means the images are first digitized, so if there's a DVD burner . . . yes. There is. But you have to run it from your end."

"Can I see what I want to record first?"

"Easy. You have a time range?"

"How about last night, the time I used the access code."

He showed her how to pull up one second-floor camera and three downstairs cameras. The screen split into four parts and Andy saw herself come into the house, look askance at the Art, and go upstairs.

"Can you speed it up?"

"You can. Drag the cursor over the bar at the bottom of the screen."

She did so and, after what was indicated as 40 minutes, Karyn Asgard came in, followed by Alex Elgin. Karyn was carrying a small purse, but appeared to be wearing little but her T-shirt, shorts and exercise shoes. Elgin was in a pair of expensive work-out clothing.

In an upstairs camera, Andy saw herself get up from her bedroom and come down to the edge of the steps. She evidently did not call out to Elgin, or come down the stairs, because the two did not seem to notice her.

Karyn and Elgin spent a lot of time looking at the Art. Andy sped the tape up further.

It was like watching an old silent movie: Andy couldn't tell who touched whom first, but they were embracing, in front of the painting. Then they were on the floor. Curiously, both kept their clothing on. Andy vaguely remembered hearing the sounds of their lovemaking.

Then Elgin got up, whizzed away, and came back with two large bags: one, a canvas duffle bag; the other a doctor's bag. He opened the duffle and gave Karyn a peculiar-looking horned mask and what appeared to be a leather whip. He took his jersey off, put a mask on his face, then opened the doctor's bag. He gave something to Karyn—Andy couldn't see what it was because the images were too small, but she saw her swallow something. He went down on his knees, reached under her T-shirt. She hit him across his back with the whip while he rubbed his crotch.

She kept hitting him, and evidently was drawing blood, when Elgin stopped and seemed to instruct her exactly how he wanted to be struck. They seemed to argue and, again, Andy had a memory of voices raised. She also remembered feeling, at the time, an odd voyeuristic thrill. What they were doing was, in her opinion, pathetic, but it was fun to listen in.

The argument continued and Karyn appeared to be telling Elgin she didn't like him telling her what to do. She pulled back on the whip and struck him across the chest. He wobbled about, shook his head, as if that was something like what he wanted, but not quite. She hit him harder and then began to clutch at herself, as if she was in pain. He seemed to get angrier and then she dropped the whip, and doubled over on the carpet.

A dark stain had appeared at the bottom of her T-shirt. Elgin exhorted her with his hands to get up, but she didn't move. Elgin leaned over her, touched her throat, threw down his mask, and appeared to have a temper tantrum.

Andy saw herself on the tape beginning to go down the stairs. Elgin went to his bag and removed a cell phone. As he called, Andy saw herself go down to the first floor, where she would have been visible if Elgin turned.

Elgin didn't turn. He seemed to be laughing. He put the phone back and removed Karyn's mask. Then he kicked Karyn in her stomach and again in her face.

Andy saw herself go up to Karyn. Elgin was at first surprised, he appeared to be reasoning with her, then he reached back and pulled Andy off Karyn. Andy sprang away, argued with Elgin. Elgin went for the whip and she punched him in the face. He touched his face and tried to grab her but she kicked him in his groin and he went down.

Andy saw lights flash in the windows and saw herself move back. She remembered the siren. She saw the tall man with the inhaler and the Elvis pompadour limp in. He pulled out his knife and Andy backed up. Then Elgin got up and struck her in the side of the face with the whip handle. She saw herself turn and the Elvis guy stick the inhaler in her face and give her a shot from it. She doubled over and the Elvis guy kicked her in the side as Dr. Elgin came around and pulled her hands behind her back and shoved her face down on the carpet next to Karyn. The Elvis guy put both hands flat on Andy's back as Elgin went into his black bag and came out with a syringe that he filled and jammed into the side of Andy's neck.

Andy watched herself become still.

"Are you seeing any of this, Tom?" she asked.

"I'm not seeing the images. I get indications any time you touch a key or move the cursor, but I can't get to the content because I don't have your access code. I should tell you that someone else is trying to access the system right now. What is it you're looking at, a robbery?"

"Not quite."

The Elvis guy went to kick Andy again, but Elgin pointed toward the back door. The Elvis guy went out while Elgin packed up the masks and the whip. He went upstairs and then came down as Elvis returned with a body bag. He and Elgin put Karyn in the bag and carried her out.

They came back and carried Andy upstairs and left her on the mattress in her room. Elgin made a gesture with his finger against his head—Andy interpreted that to mean that whatever he had given her would affect her brain.

They tried to get Karyn's blood off the carpet, then decided to take the carpet out.

Andy heard a signal on her cell phone that someone else was calling her.

"How do I record this?" Andy asked.

"You want all four cameras or just one?"

The camera that included the view of the painting had most of the activity. "Just one."

"Look for the 'A' slot or drawer—that would be a DVD recorder. It probably has a disk in it."

Andy found it.

"Pull up the menu. Select the camera. Enter the range—start time, stop time. Then click on record to disk."

She did. "Thanks, Tom."

"Uh, Andy? Are you going to go to the cops with this?"

She pulled the disk out of the drawer. "Absolutely."

"Then, please, don't let them know that I told you how to do this. Every time there's a case involving one of our systems, the defense attorneys hit me with all kinds of documents asking questions like, is it my fault that my system made their client steal the silverware? You can ask my sister. She's the lawyer."

"I might talk to her."

"You do that. One more thing: just because you have an image of somebody doing something on your property that you think is illegal, doesn't mean they can be arrested for committing a crime."

"You mean if I have a picture of somebody—"

"Don't tell me what it is; I don't want to know. What I'm telling you is, people see what they want in these things. The most dangerous thing, is if the person who did this finds out you have a disk of him in the act."

"How is that dangerous?"

"That person doesn't know what's on the disk. He doesn't know if it's incriminating or not. If he's got any kind of criminal background, or if he's done violent things in the past, or he's in a situation where he's got a lot to lose, or if he's got nothing to lose, he is not going to ask a lawyer about how the courts treat home surveillance images. He's going to try to get at that disk."

"So you're telling me I should make a copy?"

"I'm telling you to be careful. As for me, we've never spoken, okay? I just know you from that article, which was terrific, by the way. You did a lot to clear up misconceptions about the home security business."

"Sounds like I didn't do enough about those misconceptions," Andy said. "I thought these things are supposed to make you safe."

"They are, but what did Mr. Action say in the column last week? Things don't always work like they're supposed to."

The truck stood, blocking traffic on Locust Street in front of Ladderback's apartment building. In addition to the angry horns, Ladderback heard drivers cursing at Gina because they thought she worked for the Parking Authority.

Gina told the drivers to go fuck themselves.

"You haven't learned to ignore them?" Ladderback asked.

"I perform a service. A tow truck is like a lawyer of the road," Gina said. "You don't like to see 'em, you don't like to hear about 'em, you get mad when you hear about the money they bring in, and you really don't like it when they come after you. But you'll roll over and beg when you need 'em. . . ."

Ladderback grinned.

"I'm not going to walk you to the door."

The fear overwhelmed him then. He fought it back and . . . it subsided. He put his hand on the door, then hesitated. "Did you ever find out how Carol died?"

"I told you—"

"I'm asking you what you didn't tell me."

"No," she said as the drivers screamed around them.

"You didn't view her body before she was cremated."

"I couldn't bring myself to do that."

"I did," Ladderback said.

He felt her stiffen.

"I am known in the mortuary business. They permitted me the opportunity."

"I don't want to know. . . ."

"As much as I could tell, she died of exactly the symptoms on the coroner's report: Heart failure brought on by anaphylactic shock. But there were no residues on her mouth that would indicate—"

"Shep . . ."

"She did not die of what killed your brother, or Marandola. The area on her face where she had been getting the plastic surgery had been opened, and was infected by a foreign substance, or some kind of residue that set off a toxic reaction. It could have happened during the scenarios she enacted with Elgin, because there was a light bruising around her face and neck, as if she had been wearing a mask. In the picture that you stole from Elgin's car, was she wearing a mask?"

"It was a wicker and leather thing that came down over her eyes, with red horns sticking out. It looked like something out of an opera."

"She was not playing a Wagnerian Valkyrie. It was most probably a headress for a mambo of the Sect Rouge, a crude voodoo sect based in Haiti that uses some of the plant sources that are refined into the drugs that Elgin was testing at the time. Because the pills killed Marandola and your brother, it is likely that Carol had a genetic sensitivity to them. She may not even have had to take any of the pills. The residue in the headress alone might have been enough to kill her."

"Why didn't they say she died while having sex with him?"

"Because their kind of sado-masochism was consistent with the kind she practiced on clients. There is no penetration, no consummation in the traditional sense. She died a virgin."

He heard her sigh.

"Your daughter obeyed your wishes, in her own way. Or, perhaps, she believed what you did: that your relationship with Marandola was a mistake."

"It was the worst thing I could ever do."

"But you agreed to bear her and raise her and give her the best life you could. There can be a great deal of pain and misunderstanding as a result of the love people have for each other, but our ability to love, nurture and give another the best of ourselves, no matter what it brings, is never a mistake."

She put her arm around him and hugged him so tightly that, for a second, he couldn't breathe. He felt the tears on her face on his face. Her mouth found his, and he wanted never to breathe again, to be this way forever with her: in love, and not caring, not needing, not feeling anything but her.

Then Ladderback made a mistake. He wanted to return to the way things were when he was first in love with her, so he opened his eyes to look at her, and the terrible anxiety engulfed him. He panicked. He shut his eyes and put his hand on the door handle and it opened and he was down on the side of the truck as she was screaming his name, telling him she had nothing now, nothing at all.

He wanted to tell her that she was wrong, but he heard the truck move and he staggered back against a parked car. He groped for a space between the car, felt the filth of the street on his hands, smelled the stench of a sewer grate and finally found the curb.

Then he crawled, on his hand and knees, onto the sidewalk. A pedestrian asked him if he was okay. Ladderback would have answered that he was agoraphobic, and that being agoraphobic was NOT okay, but, as phobias go, it was familiar, and when miracles happen, when you get a wonderful, disruptive, subversive, heart-pounding, world-turned-upside-down moment in your life when something you've been wishing for all these years actually comes true, the familiar can be comforting, it can bring you back to your senses, it can remind you that you're still the same person you were before.

But, rather than talk, he used the effort to propel himself toward the stone facade of his apartment building, where he pulled himself up, groped along the wall, and was through the door by the time the pedestrian grumbled, "Some people," and walked on.

# 19 road test

Andy's cell phone was ringing when she backed the Focus out of the garage. She let it ring as the garage doors obediently closed, and she tried to make a K-turn on Albemarle Way without ramming the sport utility vehicles that were parked like a wall of metal on the opposite side of the street.

She was aware that she shouldn't be driving, that whatever Elgin had shoved into her neck had blunted her reflexes. Her brain moved just as fast as ever, but to accomplish feats she normally did without thinking, such as shifting the car from reverse into forward, and turning the wheel to straighten the car out, required that she concentrate.

So she only heard the phone when she stopped at a light, or a stop sign, or waited to merge into the flow of rush hour traffic.

Fortunately, the majority of cars were heading west—out of the city—so that Andy could drive relatively quickly heading east. She wasn't sure exactly why she was driving into the city: should she go to the newspaper and try to play the disk for someone there? Should she arrange to meet Lieutenant Everson somewhere? Should she just go home and try to sleep and pretend nothing happened?

As she merged into the flood of cars on City Avenue, she thought she may have seen a big, red, boxy emergency services vehicle heading in the opposite direction. In the past, she'd see those EMTs zoom by with sirens roaring and lights flashing, and she'd just pull over.

But with some of her memories returning, she felt tinges of fear, and anger, that a symbol of safety and concern had been used for something worse, by Elgin and that freak with the Elvis haircut.

She stopped at a light and saw her car's overheat gauge go up. And her cell phone kept ringing. She thought about turning the phone off. She pulled the phone out of her shoulder bag and, with her eyes on the road, tried to remember how to turn it off.

Though her reflexes had been blunted, her mind still functioned, and a tiny voice somewhere inside said, "It could be important!"

Andy knew from the ring that it just had to be her mother. She told herself that her mother had trusted her enough to give her access code, the ability to enter the system and copy the images. Her mother could also tell, from a distance, if someone had entered the system, and had been operating it.

Her mother would certainly be concerned.

Andy headed east, past St. Joseph's University, into West Philadelphia and again, she stopped at a light and the engine heat gauge went up, and the phone rang, and this time she answered it.

"Andrea, I'm so happy you picked up," Charlotte said breathlessly. "Where are you?"

"In my car." Andy began driving again.

"Was that you at the house?"

"You know my access code."

"Were you alone?"

"I guess so."

"What's that mean—you *guess* so? Never mind. I was trying to access the system and I knew it was your code but one can't be one hundred percent sure about anything."

"You can be sure enough about some things. He killed her, Mom."

"I was afraid you'd jump to that conclusion. The truth is that Karyn had a medical condition."

"I never saw anybody in better shape than her, Mom. Physically, I mean. Mentally, I don't know."

"Just because people are dedicated and achieve a level of physical conditioning, doesn't mean that their internal organs—"

"Mom, you have to replay it. She walked into the house with him. He got her to hit him with a whip. She became sick. She fell on the carpet. He did nothing to help her. He called an ambulance and he and this wierdo took her out in a body bag. A body bag, Mom. You know what they use body bags for, Mom?"

"I did see the images and you should be aware that Karyn was taking medication"

"She told me they were appetite suppressors."

"A person need not reveal the nature of medication to a perfect stranger. I happen to know that Karyn had kidney problems. She has been a borderline diabetic all her life. She was also taking anti-depressants. Dr. Elgin has studied medicine. He would know if he could have possibly saved her."

"I guess that's why he kicked her when she was down, right Mom? And how is it that she ended up hacked into pieces in a garbage dumpster?"

"Andrea, you are again jumping to conclusions. I don't need to tell you how important Dr. Elgin is to the gallery."

"Especially since he hasn't paid for some of those paintings. Did he give you a down payment on the house, or are you waiting for that, too?"

"You're speaking of a very complicated financial arrangement that I really can't go into at this time. As you're no doubt aware, it is forbidden to discuss matters leading up to an initial public offering with members of the press, even those members who are personal relations."

"What I'm aware of, Mom, is that this guy beat me up and gave me some kind of injection that made me sick and wiped out my memory."

"I believe it was you who attacked him, Andrea. We can't fault the man for defending himself."

"Mom, I'm your daughter. He's a client. He's using your art and our house, and you only have his word that he's going to pay for them. You didn't tell him about the cameras, did you?"

"Andrea, there are things a woman does not, or should not, reveal until her wedding night. Dr. Elgin would have been given a thorough tour during his pre-settlement inspection."

"Mom, you didn't put in that system because you were so messed up when Dad died. You knew Elgin would go for a kind like Karyn. You wanted to get him into that house with her and make a little home movie that you might tell him about if his check got lost in the mail, right? But Karyn died and, I tell you Mom, I don't care what two consenting adults do to get themselves off, but I went for him because . . . because . . ." Andy paused. She couldn't say exactly why she had attacked Elgin. She could guess—he had kicked Karyn, he had done nothing to help her. But she couldn't remember, and her brain was already working hard enough driving the car. She was on Biltmore Avenue, nearing the part of University City where she lived.

And the overheat gauge was in the red.

Andy said, "You told him."

"Of course I did. Who knows what confusion that tape will cause if it is seen by the wrong people."

"What if it's seen by the *right* people?"

"Andrea, I think we can be honest with ourselves: in this situation, there are no right people. Your reputation is more a matter of my concern than his."

"That's just great, Mom," Andy said flatly. "I feel so much better now."

"You'll feel even better when you get rid of that thing. I can arrange for someone to pick the disk up at your apartment."

The overheat gauge was higher than it ever had been. Andy saw a gas station up ahead.

"I have a problem with the car," Andy said. "Let's put arrangements on hold while I get this looked into."

"Andrea, at least tell me where you are. I don't want you stranded with that car in some god-forsaken corner of that city."

"I won't be stranded," Andy said, forcing herself to put her left turn signal on and come to a stop. "I'm going to leave it at this gas station. It's close enough to where I live so I can walk home."

"A single woman shouldn't be alone on the streets at any time of night. I'm going to worry."

"Don't," Andy said, and turned off her cell phone.

Andy parked the Focus on the side of the garage between the tow truck and the rusting hulk of the Fem Fat. She went out and saw that the garage doors were closed. She found only one person, the woman she'd spoken to before, sitting in a dark blue work blouse and work pants, at a desk in the office, whose walls were adorned with packets of potato chips, racks of candy bars, cartons of cigarettes, and multi-colored butane lighters hanging from pegs.

Andy came in and caught an odor of oil and metal. "Are you open?" she asked.

"I'm not closed," replied the woman. Andy saw the name on her shirt was *Gina*.

"I have a problem with my car. It's a Ford Focus and the gauge on the dash says the engine's overheating. Can you fix that kind of thing?"

"If it's a car, I just might fix it," Gina said.

Andy noticed Gina had been crying. "I can come back later. I just don't know how far I should drive it."

Gina turned to her. "Did you hear anything when you were driving? Any pings or pops? Get any steam or liquid coming out from around the front?"

"Just the gauge telling me it was overheating."

"Could be you need more fluid. Might have a leak somewhere. Could also be the temperature gauge. They get balky sometimes." Gina had a tissue in her hand. She threw it into a garbage can that was filled with tissues.

Andy asked if she should leave the keys.

"You can. Or you can wait. I'd take a look at it now, but I won't be able to tell you much until it's cooled down."

Andy saw a battered orange metal folding chair by the desk. She unfolded it and sat down. The woman took out a form from the desk and started filling it out. "Ford Focus, you say?"

Andy saw the station's name on the form. She opened her shoulder bag and found the pad on which Ladderback had written down the name of a mechanic she should interview.

THIS woman knew Ladderback?

Andy saw Gina put down her pen, reach into another drawer, and pull out a tissue. She balled the tissue in her fist, then she threw it out.

"Are you all right?" Andy asked.

Gina shook her head. "Haven't been all right since I was sixteen." She picked up the pen. "How long since you noticed that it was overheating?"

"A few days," Andy said. She glanced into the darkened garage. "Are you alone here?"

Gina kept writing as she said, "Why? You want to rob me?"

Andy almost jumped out of the chair, and probably would have, if the drug that Elgin had given her hadn't made her so sluggish.

"Sorry," Gina said. "I don't mean to be smart with you. Fact is, I am by myself, here. I sent my help home. I wanted to think about things. The man that used to own this place, he used to send the help home when he wanted to think."

"What happened to him?"

"He got killed in a robbery."

Andy looked around. Through the front window she saw a Speed Care Emergency Services vehicle pull up across Biltmore Avenue.

"You have an alarm system here?" Andy asked, her eyes on the vehicle.

"I don't keep guns around either. The owner got shot with his own gun."

"They catch the guy?"

"They tried. Then I told a fellow I know in South Philly. Or used to know. This fellow caught up with him, cut out a piece a him. Sometimes, it's okay to know people in the business. Sometimes it isn't. Fellow wanted to give me the gun back but I didn't want it. I can deal with trouble without a gun."

She noticed where Andy was looking. "Don't worry about him. He does that sometimes. He just sits there and watches a while. Then he goes away. He's a real loser."

"I don't think he's going away," Andy said as the EMT vehicle cut across the street and pulled into the station, stopping in front of Andy's car.

"I guess he wants me for something," Gina said, standing. Andy followed her outside as the thin man with the Elvis haircut stepped out of the truck.

"You know him?" Andy asked.

"Unfortunately." Gina stopped in front of him. "Why you bothering me now, Larry?"

Larry put the inhaler in his mouth, gave himself a shot, and pointed the mouthpiece toward Andy. "Bitch has something for me," Larry said.

"You ain't calling nobody a bitch around my place a business," Gina said.

Larry smirked. "You sound like Orley."

"Get yourself outa here," Gina said.

Larry took out his folding knife. "Not until she gives me that disk."

"Whatever it is you want," Gina said to him, "you're not getting it from anybody on my property with that knife."

Larry acted hurt. "Oh, I was just showin' it to her, Gina. Thought she'd like the size."

"Get your ass out of here, Larry," Gina said. "Before I tow it off."

"You?" Larry grinned, "Gonna tow *me*?" He limped around to the back of the EMT, opened a hatch on the side, and came back with his inhaler clipped to his belt, both hands carrying a fireman's axe. "How you gonna do it, Geeeenah?" he said, swaggering up to her wrecker. "How you gonna do it without lights?"

He took a swing and smashed the right headlight.

"Larry, you crazy fuck!" she shouted at him, ignoring the black Porsche that zoomed in off the street. "I'm sending Dr. Alex a bill for that."

"Send him one, then," Larry said. "He's just come in to pay it. And while you're at it, send him another for this." He smashed the left front headlight.

"Larry, get back from the truck!"

He shook his head and planted the axe's blade in the grill. Then he hauled back and smashed the broad edge against the windshield, shattering it.

"Larry, you just caused upwards of eight hundred dollars worth of damage. Dr. Alex is not going to want to pay for it."

"He'll pay for it," Larry said, hefting the axe as he searched for more damage he could cause. "Now he's got me chopping his girlfriends up, he'll pay for anything I want—"

Andy covered her mouth. The thought of Larry using that axe on Karyn gave Andy a deep and horrible sickness far different than the kind that Elgin had induced with that injection. It was a combination of fear and horror that made her want to flee, and she would have run, but her legs weren't going anywhere quickly and so, another instinct took hold, the one that strikes when you see something dark, loathsome and slimey that is scuttling on the ground, and you're either going to jump away from it or—

Step on it. Step on it as hard as you can and squash it out of existence.

But Andy couldn't quite step on a man who was as tall as she was, maybe taller with what she was close enough to see was a greased wave of dyed, fake hair. So she lifted up her right foot, lifted it up high, and brought her ordinary, flat-soled pump right down on his knee—his bad knee, the knee that she had kicked yesterday—and made it much, much worse.

Larry's knee made a wet, popping sound as his leg caved in sideways and Larry went down, bringing the axe around toward Andy in an arc that should have missed her.

But didn't. The blunt edge of the blade just nicked her left arm above the elbow. It hit her just hard enough to rip her blouse and dig into her skin and cause the kind of paralyzing pain that, even if a bone wasn't broken, it hurt bad enough to think it was.

Andy yelled, and yelled again. Larry was writhing around on the

324

stained concrete paving and Andy was about to stomp BOTH feet on his knee when she heard a low, smooth, calm, thoroughly respectable TV-doctor-type voice say, "Get away from him."

She saw Dr. Elgin, in a smartly tailored leather jacket, a bandage on his face. A chrome semi-automatic pistol in his hand was pointed at her.

"You have something for me, Andrea?" he said.

With the pain shooting up her arm, she found she could think, clearly.

"Don't play dumb, Andrea," Elgin said. "Your brain should be functioning perfectly. The injection I gave you was supposed to inhibit aggression by causing symptoms of nausea when the fight-or-flight reflex was aroused. It was inspired by the *Clockwork Orange* film, but never given FDA approval because it caused severe short- and medium-term memory loss."

He grinned. "Perhaps one day, when this is over, you can do an article on what happens to drugs that cost billions to develop, that aren't approved. They just don't sit on the shelves, you know."

Andy looked for Gina but couldn't see her. She saw she had dropped her shoulder bag.

"I want the disk, Andrea," Elgin insisted. "Is it in your car or that bag?"

She grabed her bag.

"So it's in the bag, then?" Elgin came up to her.

Larry began to moan and Elgin said, "Shut up. I'll get you to a hospital soon enough."

"Gimme for pain," Larry moaned. "I want . . . for pain."

"You do?" Elgin asked merrily. He brought his heel down on one of Larry's fingers.

Larry yelled and Andy turned and looked, past Elgin's shoe, through the wheels of the EMT vehicle, at cars whizzing by on the street. It was the end of September and the sun had not yet set. There was plenty of light, enough for someone in a car, or walking along the street, to notice what was going on.

Then she reminded herself, this was Philadelphia, a city where people *would* notice a man in a smartly tailored leather jacket holding a gun on a defenseless woman, and, upon noticing, they would walk and drive away just a little bit faster.

"Where's the disk, Andrea?"

The drug must have been wearing off, because Andy got a memory of the column she'd done yesterday, about the reader complaining of the edges of CDs and DVDs being so sharp that they could cut skin.

Andy was not defenseless. She put her hand into the bag and felt for the disk.

"I have it," Andy said, moving into a crouch.

Then Gina called from the front of the garage. "Alex! Your car! You better get over here!"

He extended his left hand to Andy. "I'll take it now."

Yes, Andy said to herself, you *will* take it now. She clutched the disk in her hand, gave her legs as much power as she could, while whipping the disk out of the bag in a broad, back-handed arc that went over Elgin's left arm and hit his face, where, Andy's perfectly functioning brain was astonished (even as the nausea began to build in her stomach) that human skin would yield, pucker, and then divide so easily, just like those resealable plastic freezer bags that are supposed to open at the touch of finger, but never quite do.

The disk slashed effortlessly up the left side of Alex Elgin's face. It missed his eye but split his eyebrow, leaving a red thread, that widened to a line, that widened into a stripe that was widening into a torrential gush of blood, but Andy's legs gave out and she fell down again, and with the disk still in her hand, crawled past Larry under the tow truck.

She heard Elgin repeat the word "shit" in rapid succession. She looked back and saw a shiny spattering of blood on the tops of his loafers. She then forced herself to crawl away from him. She banged her head on something under the truck, but kept going until she was at the other side.

She emerged, her right hand awkwardly clutching the disk and her injured left arm, to see Elgin aiming the gun at her.

"You disgusting *thing*," Elgin said, his left eye blinking as one side of his face became a glistening sheet of red. "If not for your mother, I would use this. But because of my regard—"

"Alex!" Gina called. "You come out here or you don't have a car."

He reached down and pried the disk from Andy's fingers. He wiped his face and shuddered at the sight of his own blood. Then he went around to the front of the garage.

Andy grabbed the rusting, dented bumper of the Fem Fat with her right hand and pulled herself to her feet. She wanted to vomit but told herself that she wasn't sick, it was only a drug, that all she had to do was put one foot in front of another and she would be at the front of the garage.

And she was, in time to see Elgin standing about fifty feet away from Gina, who stood very close to his black Porsche, with what looked like a metal watering can in one hand, a flickering cigarette lighter in her other hand.

"You're going to give that lady back whatever you took," Gina said. "Then you're going to put Larry in that EMT," Gina said, "and drive your ass out of here, and you are not going to come back. Not again. Not ever. I am no longer servicing your vehicle or any vehicle you may acquire."

"You work on his car?" Andy blurted out.

Elgin whirled around and pointed the gun at her.

"I overcharge him," Gina said. "He pays. He don't complain because he thinks I made a copy of a picture I got ahold of, of him getting kinky with my daughter."

"*Did* you make that copy, Goddammit!" Elgin demanded.

"You'll never know," Gina said. "Now, give her back what you took."

"I have a gun, Gina," he said.

"And I know, from working on your car, that you ain't cleaned it, fired it, or changed the rounds from the day you got it and put it in your car," Gina said. "I pay attention to little things like that when I work on a car. Gives me insight into the operator. From what insight I got about guns, chances are pretty strong that that gun's going to jam up on you, while what I have here, ain't going to jam. What you're looking at is a pressure nozzle I use to flush radiators. It hooks up to the compressed air. I have it rigged here, to shoot out a vapor spray of regular gasoline, through this cigarette lighter. So if you and Larry don't get out of here, I'm going to burn your car, and then I'm going to burn you."

Elgin wiped the blood out of his face with his arm, put the disk in his jacket pocket, then held the gun with both hands. "I can buy another car."

Gina squeezed the air gun and a wide cone of searing yellow fire pounced on the Porsche like an angry dog leaping for the kill. The car's black paint flew off its metal skin. Andy felt the heat on her face as the car's front lights and chrome pieces popped and exploded. Gina aimed the hose lower and gave it another blast and the front tires buckled and blew.

"Terrible thing to do to a fine automobile," Gina said.

Andy heard a series of tiny clicks as Elgin impotently squeezed the trigger.

"Alex," Gina said, pointing the improvised flame thrower at him. "It's time for you to go."

Elgin threw the gun at her. It missed. Elgin said, "shit, shit, shit," until Gina took a step forward. He wiped his face, turned around.

"Get Larry, now," Gina said.

Andy could think of other things Elgin could do. He could grab Larry's axe. He could run away. He could go to the EMT vehicle and find something he might use to fight Gina.

But there was no fight in him. He had a tiny smile on his face, like he almost enjoyed Gina pushing him around.

Gina, on the other hand, was grim. She clearly hated what she was doing. Hated every second of it, up until Elgin started the EMT vehicle, wiped his face for the last time and backed it out of the lot.

Gina let the lighter go out, dropped the spray gun, and went toward Andy. "How bad did he hurt you?"

"He's got the disk," Andy said.

"Damn!" Gina swore. "I was so into getting rid of him, I totally forgot." She gazed after the EMT vehicle's dwindling tail lights. "Is what's on that disk have something to do with him being kinky with some girl?"

"Worse," Andy said. "The girl died."

"So I let him go, and he's going to do it again." She looked at that shattered windshield of the tow truck. Then she saw Andy's Ford Focus.

"You mind if I take this for a road test?" Gina said.

Andy found her shoulder bag, tossed Gina the keys and said, "As long as you take me with you."

They caught up with EMT at the long light where Biltmore flows into 38th Street.

"He's not taking Larry to no hospital. Bet you he's making for the Schyulkill, so he can head out to that drug factory of his."

Andy noticed the overheat gauge was almost in the red.

"I see it," Gina said, as if reading Andy's mind. "I wouldn't worry about it much. You got a cell phone on you?"

Andy said she did.

"You might as well call the cops and report this vehicle stolen. That way you might get something back from insurance. I don't think you're going to want it back after I'm done with it."

"They're three times the size of us," Andy said. "That EMT is as big as an SUV."

"Bigger and heavier," Gina said as the light changed and the line of cars slowly moved forward. "I used to work on 'em. What he's driving is on the order of the GMC Suburban, but wider and higher. It's a Goliath."

"We're David?"

"Not even," Gina said, peering forward. "I'd feel a whole lot safer if we were in helmets. You don't happen to travel with crash helmets do you? The fireproof kind?"

"Left them at home," Andy said. "I have a basketball in the back."

"You want it back?"

"Yes," Andy said.

"Then it stays in the back. You sure your air bags don't work?"

"The compressor died in them a while ago. I was supposed to get them fixed," Andy said. "Aren't you going to tell me to fasten my safety belt?"

"You get old," Gina said. "You get forgetful."

The light was turning yellow and the EMT vehicle had crossed the intersection. Gina said, "Hold on, but stay loose."

She drove the car up and over the earth divider, went into the oncoming traffic lane, ducked past two cars, and shot through the intersection as the light turned red.

"Peppy little thing," Gina said. "It whines a lot, but it goes where you ask it."

She looked ahead. "Told you. He's heading down to the Expressway. Is it going to be east or west? Bet you it's west, to that factory and . . . it is!"

She hugged the bumper of a lumbering SUV, and cut hard into the westbound Schuylkill Expressway entrance ramp. A few horns honked.

"I don't think he's seen us yet."

"What are you going to do?"

"Not a clue," Gina said. "When a derby starts, you're sitting in your car in a dirt square with all the other vehicles. You don't know what they got. They don't know what you got. You can't make a plan. You have to improvise. Only thing's for sure is that they're all out to get you. So you pick your target and go."

She hit the horn. "Damn, the cars get thick around here, this time of day."

"It's rush hour," Andy said.

"Tail end of it," Gina agreed. "Of course, the challenge we have before us, is to be mindful of the safety of other motorists. Don't want to upset no mothers with children."

"We have to be considerate?"

"We act like we're certifiably insane, so they'll stay away." She started honking the horn. Others honked back. "This time of day, Expressway could be moving fast or slow by the time we get on. If they're fast, we could lose him. If they're slow, it might take us a while to get to him."

The ramp dipped below the highway, then snuck up to merge with the westbound right lane. Gina rolled her window down and told Andy to roll hers down. "You don't want nothing breaking on your side if we get broadsided."

The ramp had a white side line that was supposed to mark a shoulder. The shoulder didn't seem wide enough to let a car pass, but Gina knew from driving the tow truck that it was much wider than it looked.

"The deal with the Expressway," Gina said, "is the shoulders. Some places, you have shoulders on the right side, but not the left. Other places, you have them on the left but not the right. Some places, the shoulders are so wide, you can drive a tow truck anywhere you want. Other places, the shoulders are like those beds they have in a cheap motel. Whatever it is you want to do on it, it ain't big enough."

Gina listened to the whine of truck tires and Diesel motors in high gear. "Hear that? It's going to be fast. Which means there's going to be some asshole down front in some four cylinder piece a shit too scared to floor it and merge."

"This is a four cylinder car," Andy said.

"But it's no piece a shit. Damn! Alex just got on and there's the jerk, holding us back. Grab on, here we go!"

She cut hard, to the right, into the shoulder, coming up so close to the concrete barrier on the right that Andy breathed in. Gina floored the gas pedal and the car shuddered.

"MOVE!" Gina yelled. "When was the last time this had a tune-up?"

The engine started buzzing like a dentist's drill and the car almost hopped off the ground. Gina swerved beside the hesitant Cadillac Cimarron and shot out into traffic.

Horns honked around them. The wind whipped through the car, stirring the papers in the back. Andy saw the Speed Care EMT vehicle three cars ahead. Gina kept the gas pedal flat and threw the car fast into the left lane. "Now," she said as the speed increased, "We let Alex know we don't like him."

The towers of Center City formed a distant wall on right bank of Schuylkill River as Gina hit the horn, blinked the brights, and forced drivers ahead to speed up or drop to the right.

"Can you make yourself small?" she said to Andy as they neared the EMT vehicle.

"It won't be easy," Andy said.

"Just stay away from your door."

Then she sent the car slamming into the back left wheel of the EMT vehicle. The impact made a shattering, smashing sound. Andy banged her injured arm.

"Howdy, Alex," Gina said. "We've come to play."

The EMT wobbled. Its emergency lights came on. Then Andy saw Elgin's blood-soaked face in the side mirror.

He saw her but it was only when he saw Gina that his expression became amused. Elgin sent the EMT vehicle slamming right back at them.

"See how long it takes him to get back at us?"

Andy tried to look but the EMT vehicle came up to her like a wall of red metal that squashed her side of the car.

"We're just playing patty-cake," Gina said. "He didn't hit our tires. We didn't hit his tires. At these speeds, it's all over when a tire goes."

Elgin hit the siren and it was so loud it hurt Andy's ears. She could only lift one arm to close one ear, and by the time she had the ear in place, the EMT vehicle had swung into her side so powerfully that it knocked her teeth.

"He's hitting us. This is good," Gina said.

"It doesn't feel good," Andy said.

"He's playing with us. He's trying to hit us. Anybody else with any sense would just avoid us. But we've got his blood up. He wants to hit us."

As the Expressway dipped under the Chestnut and Market Street bridges, Gina floored the car again and pulled up even with the EMT vehicle's front wheel. They cleared the bridges and the highway soared upward as ramps peeled off toward the 676 Vine Street connector, throwing them forward into a view of the Art Museum on the right, and the tangle of railroad tracks of 30th Street station on the left, and the row of cutsey Victorian boathouses across that deep blue swath of the Schuylkill River.

Gina was almost in front of the EMT vehicle when Elgin, his face contorted in a glistening leer, aimed the EMT vehicle at the Focus's right rear tire.

One of the many endearingly perverse design features of the Schuylkill Expressway are the sudden, inexplicable appearances of left hand entrance ramps.

In trying to hit the Focus, Elgin either forgot about the left hand entrance ramp coming up, or imagined he could pull the vehicle back before going into it.

He hadn't anticipated Gina tapping her brakes and slowing the Focus so the EMT vehicle shot past her, went through Gina's lane and into the left hand entrance lane that, unlike the right hand entrance lanes, did not have a wide shoulder. The EMT vehicle didn't hit any cars—fortunately none were in the lane—but it did smash and scrape its left front fender hard against the lane's barrier wall, slowing the vehicle until Gina, in the center lane, zipped ahead.

"We just did that thing that bullfighters do with a cape," Gina said. "We pissed off the bull."

Andy looked back and saw the EMT swerve recklessly back across the Expressway to follow them three car lengths behind. It had its lights and siren on, so the cars between them edged onto the right hand shoulder.

"Where are the cops?" Andy said.

"Wherever they are, we'll be gone from here before they can find us." She winked at Andy. "I got a plan."

"But we're supposed to improvise."

"That's when you win a derby. This isn't a derby. I just figured it out. We gotta survive this thing, you and me. He's got to go down, not us."

Andy felt her jaw drop. "I thought that was the plan."

"It wasn't. I was figuring we'd just crash cars and see who wins. But I don't want to win now. Now I just don't want to lose."

The EMT was gaining on them as Gina shook the wheel so the Focus shimmied. She aimed for, then, at the last second, did not take the Girard Avenue exit ramp.

"I can't quite see him in the rearview," Gina said. "Tell me if Alex is out for bear."

Andy saw Elgin glaring at them. Larry, in the seat beside him, appeared to be trying to reason with him. Elgin smacked Larry across the face.

"He's in for the kill," Andy said.

"Perfect. I want you to take some of that junk you have in the back seat, and when he's right on top of us, throw it out the window."

"That won't do anything."

"It'll slow him down. Gather up as much as you can. Here, let me grab some. Now, stay lose. Grab hold of the belt. We're about to get rear-ended."

Andy could feel the siren rattling her teeth. Gina tapped the brakes and the EMT vehicle roared up and the rear seat of the hatchback crumpled like the shiny white paper in a candy bar.

"You're lucky this isn't a Pinto," Gina said. "The Pinto put the gas tank almost up against the rear bumper. We'd be barbecue right now, if this was a Pinto."

The car might have fallen under the EMT vehicle's front end if Gina hadn't tapped the gas, and swerved farther to the right.

"Throw out the shit," Gina said.

Andy let go of her seat belt, grabbed some junk and threw it out. Gina did the same from her side. Gina floored the gas and the car shot forward.

"We still have our tires," Gina said.

Andy looked back and saw that the EMT vehicle had slowed. Paper had adhered to its windshield.

"It'll blow off soon enough," Gina said as she moved the Focus into the right shoulder. The shoulder merged with a right exit ramp dropping downward below the highway, onto Montgomery Drive. As Gina entered the ramp she slowed the car. Ahead was a line of cars, waiting for a traffic light to change "You look back and tell me when you see him coming."

For a few seconds Andy saw nothing but empty asphalt. The EMT vehicle seemed to leap out of the road itself and aim for them like a speeding train.

"Remember what I told you about the Expressway shoulders, the way some of them are like motel beds?" Gina said, slowing the Focus until it was almost stopped behind the line of cars.

Andy saw the EMT vehicle gaining.

"I said they were too small to do anything you want on them? Well I happen to be on the short side, so they never bothered me. Alex, though. That thing he's in, he needs king size, you know?"

Just as the EMT's siren set Andy's teeth on edge, Gina turned the Focus into the ramp's very narrow shoulder. It was almost like passing a line of people on the stairs by sliding down the bannister. Andy saw from outside the window on her side that the shoulder ended in a ditch.

And that ditch was just too close for the EMT vehicle.

"You don't know how long I sat at the top of that ramp in a tow truck, wishing I was in a car like this," Gina said. She reached Montgomery Drive and turned right at the light, under the railroad bridge, and crossed West River Drive, a narrow, four lane roadway, and entered a small parking lot and picnic area that jutted out onto the very edge of the Schuylkill River. She turned the car around so that it faced the Montgomery Drive and backed it up so that it was just a few feet from the river's edge.

"That is the longest traffic light in the city, I think," she said.

Andy looked around. "What happens now?"

"We wait for that light to change and the cars to come out."

"That's it?"

"In a couple minutes, either we are going to be in the river. Or him."

"You said you had a plan," Andy said hesitantly.

"I do. But, the problem with plans is, you can never be completely sure how they'll come out."

She pointed to Andy's safety belt. "You want to be sensible, you can undo the belt, because if we go in, you're going to have to get out of the car any way you can. It's fifty feet of water off that bank. I know because I pulled some cars out with my truck. They had to get a diving team to hook my winch up to the car. It was a mess, believe me. You can swim?"

Andy nodded.

"You might want to take off your shoes. Make it easier in the water. Or you can just get out of the car. There's no reason you have to risk anything."

Andy saw that Gina hadn't unfastened her belt. "How come you're not taking off your belt?"

"Because if I end up in the water, I'm not sure I'm going to like it. It'll be losing and I never liked to lose."

"You're not staying in the car . . ."

Gina looked back at Montgomery Drive. "My brother was put to rest today. He was the last person in my life. The very last. I spent the day with somebody. If things had been different, if only . . . if only I'd been somebody different and he'd been somebody different . . . we might've had something."

"I know what you mean," Andy said.

"Oh, come on. You're young. You gotta go through dozens of disappointments. You got a job, right? A career?"

"I'm . . . in the media."

"That makes two in a single day," Gina said. "You sure you don't want to go in the water with me?"

"Positive," Andy said. "And I don't want you going in, either."

"You going to tell me that, with everyone that ever mattered dead, gone, or too old to make a difference, I have so much to live for?"

Andy shook her head.

"What are you going to tell me?"

"That I know what they saw in you," Andy said.

"Who?"

"The people who mattered."

"What about it?"

"What they saw, is worth seeing again," Andy said.

Gina closed her eyes and the tears came out. "Ah, shit," she said. "I forgot to bring tissues."

Andy opened the glove box and took out a small package.

"If I make it through this," Gina said, "I don't want to deal with any more guys that can't control themselves." She dabbed her eyes and then she heard the whoop of the EMT vehicle's siren. Gina and Andy saw it emerge from under the railroad bridge and pause at the intersection of Montgomery and West River Drive.

Then it roared forward.

"Once again," Gina said. "Hold on to something, but stay loose. This one's going to hurt."

Elgin didn't bother to drive the EMT vehicle through the entrance to the parking area. He took it over the curb, running over bushes, smashing aside a picnic table, hoping to shove the battered little car backward into the river.

Gina revved the engine, aimed the car directly at the EMT vehicle. It was like a game of chicken—both vehicles were speeding toward a front end collision that only the wider, higher, stronger EMT vehicle, with its powerful engine, big high tires and steel bumper, would survive.

But the left side of that bumper had been bent up, like half a handlebar moustache, from scraping against the Expressway's left entrance ramp barrier. The impact had also twisted back the fender protecting the EMT vehicle's left front tire.

And so, at the point where she thought the EMT vehicle was committed, when it was going so fast that Elgin could not react fast enough to alter its direction, Gina swerved to the right, then came in hard left and hit that tire a glancing blow on its leading edge. This was a common disabling manuever in demolition derbies, where a hit on the front wheel could knock a tire off a wheel rim and force a car to stop dead in its tracks.

But the larger truck tire on the EMT vehicle did not just fall off the wheel rim. The impact from the Focus's bumper blew the tire's inner frame so that it didn't fall off the wheel as much as disintegrate entirely.

The naked wheel rim dropped hard into the asphalt parking surface, and dug in. The Focus grazed the EMT vehicle's side panels and was thrown aside, while the EMT vehicle spun violently around, tumbled over on its side, and rolled over three times before it flipped into the river.

Gina turned off the engine and ran to the river's edge, which was scattered with red and white remnants of the EMT vehicle's light bar.

Elgin hadn't locked the back doors of the vehicle, so water rushed in and it sank with a rapidity so sudden that only an angry swirl of bubbles indicated where the vehicle had been.

Andy stood beside Gina. The bubbles reminded her of a painting she had seen somewhere.

# 20 just deserts

After watching—again—the full two hour pilot of "The Bassos," Ladderback shook his head. In filming what was supposed to be the "truth" about Chickie Marandola, his Hollywood relatives had got an important detail wrong: there is no way imaginable that Curley Osbert, the fictional stand-in for Orley Roberts, would grind up Chickie's shoes and put them in a cheesesteak.

Or so Ladderback hoped . . .

When she heard the sirens, Andy told Gina they'd better leave.

"There's a guy named Ladderback at the *Philadelphia Press*," Gina said. "You should call him and tell him that Elgin is dead. You don't have to worry about telling him everything. He has a way of finding it out. But whether they print it, is anybody's guess." She started walking toward West River Drive, and the long jogging path that would take her back to West Philadelphia.

Andy looked at her car. It was battered, banged up, leaking in who knows how many places. And the overheat gauge was stuck firmly in the red.

But it had served her well.

She remembered what her mother had said: that it wasn't safe for a single woman to be alone on the street.

She got into the car, turned the key, heard the engine grind and flutter to life. She spun the car around, caught up to Gina.

"Hey," Andy said.

Gina looked at her.

"You know how to fix this?"

"I just might," Gina said, and got in.